CHRISTMAS WITH FAMILY

"How are you, Grandma?" Becca asked, though if there were something wrong with Nora, her grandmother would be the last to talk about it.

"Just fine," she said. "And you, Becca?"

"Fine. Great." Becca knew that Nora hadn't believed her response, which was, even to her own ears, meaningless.

Then, a girl of sixteen came loping into the living room from the direction of the kitchen at the back of the house. She was tall and lanky, with long chestnut hair and the Rowan eyes.

Becca wondered if she had been as pretty at sixteen as Rain was, so fresh and unspoiled. The answer was that yes, she had been. And then, she had not.

"Hi, Aunt Becca!" the girl called.

Aunt. The word tugged painfully at Becca's heart. She was flooded by the all too familiar feelings of loss and regret—and worst of all, guilt. Rain's eyes, so like her own, so not like her sister-in-law's . . . *Yes*, she thought. *My resolve is firm.*

"Hi, Rain," she said, stepping forward to greet the girl.

Then Becca took her daughter in her arms and hugged her . . .

Books by Holly Chamberlin

LIVING SINGLE

THE SUMMER OF US

BABYLAND

BACK IN THE GAME

THE FRIENDS WE KEEP

TUSCAN HOLIDAY

ONE WEEK IN DECEMBER

THE FAMILY BEACH HOUSE

Published by Kensington Publishing Corporation

One Week In December

Holly Chamberlin

KENSINGTON PUBLISHING CORP.
http://www.kensingtonbooks.com

KENSINGTON BOOKS are published by

Kensington Publishing Corp.
119 West 40th Street
New York, NY 10018

ISBN-13: 978-0-7582-1404-1
ISBN-10: 0-7582-1404-9

First Trade Paperback Printing: October 2009
First Mass Market Printing: October 2010

10 9 8 7 6 5 4 3 2 1

Printed in the United States of America

As always, for Stephen
And this time, also for Joey

Acknowledgments

My sincere thanks to John Scognamiglio for his encouragement, patience, and support.

Thanks to Dr. Marc Ouellette for his fine care of Jack and Betty, my assistant typists and constant companions.

This book is in memory of George Lohsen, and in memory of Kevin Brown. It is also in memory of Hank Simmons-Moody.

1

Wednesday, December 20

It was just after five in the evening, the worst possible time to be leaving Boston—no, trying to leave Boston—for destinations north. Add to that the fact that it was only days until Christmas and the weather channels were predicting a fierce snowstorm, and the results were—not good.

Becca Rowan hadn't been able to get out of the office early, as she had planned; as she was walking toward the elevator, her assistant had come charging into the public hallway from the offices of Saville and Co., a mid-size and rapidly growing advertising firm, with a plea for crisis management.

"Can't Ralph handle this?" Becca had asked, knowing, of course, what answer she would get from Mary.

"Well, he could but . . ."

"Fine. Let's go." Better that she solve a problem now than leave it to someone else and be called on to fix what further mess would, inevitably, have been made. Becca had been called that annoying term, a "workaholic," but she preferred to regard herself simply as a professional. And she had a high and accurate opinion of her professional worth. After all, she was Saville's presiding vice president and if things continued the way Becca thought they would, she would be president before her thirty-fifth birthday, less than three years in the future. It was a goal she was pretty confident she had the discipline to achieve.

Later, crisis managed, Mary had wished her boss a happy holiday and asked if she was going anyplace special. It was unlike Becca to take almost an entire week off; Mary's curiosity was justified.

"I'm going to Maine to see my family," Becca had replied tersely.

"Oh, how nice. That should be fun."

What could one say to that kind of standard remark, and still be considered a socially acceptable person? "Like hell it will" would probably not cut it.

"Yeah," she'd said, and then, "Merry Christmas."

As she walked once again toward the elevators, her assistant had called out her thanks for the generous gift Becca had given her that morning. If Becca required dedication from her staff, she also rewarded it well. Becca had raised her hand in acknowledgment, but she hadn't turned around. She was uncomfortable with expressions of gratitude.

Now she had been on the road for half an hour and had only just reached the outer city limits. Under normal conditions the drive from downtown Boston to her parents' house in Kently, Maine, took about two and a half hours. But these were not normal conditions. Snow was falling and drivers were getting tense. And they were getting stupid.

"Merry freakin' Christmas to you, jackass!" Becca leaned on the car's horn. Not that the idiot driver who'd just cut her off would realize the horn was meant for him, but it felt good to make the noise.

Becca drove on, concerned with being hyper-aware of the messy road conditions. She wondered if she'd beat the worst part of the storm. The Boston weather reports varied wildly in their predictions about when the storm would slam the part of Maine to which Becca was headed, an inland area about fifty miles north of Portland, almost as if the meteorologists, or at least the superbly styled models reporting the weather news, didn't quite care. This didn't surprise Becca. To many people in Massachusetts, though certainly not all, anything north of Portland was a hinterland better left to its own devices.

And in Becca's grumpy opinion, those devices were not at all sufficient. "The roads probably won't even be plowed," she muttered. "I'll probably crash into a snow bank and freeze to death before morning. Because of course there won't be cell phone service. Or maybe I'll be trampled to death by a rabid moose as I'm trekking along an abandoned road vainly hoping to come across a house with a light in a window. A house that doesn't contain a gun-toting survivalist and his seventeen wives."

As if in response to her nasty thoughts—but in reality due to her inattention—the car slid a bit. Deftly, Becca got it back on the straight and narrow. She had spent a fair amount for the Volvo S80 T6 and its all-wheel drive, but in situations like this one, with snow falling, roads wet and slippery, and drivers in a hurry, she felt the investment had paid off.

Still, the incident had disturbed her. If it had been any other holiday at any other time, Becca would have unhesitatingly gotten off at the next exit and driven straight home. But this Christmas was different. This time, Becca had to be with the Rowan clan.

The Family Rowan. Currently members ranged in age from Nora at eighty-six to the twins, Michael and Malcolm, aged eight. Four generations of the Rowan family were planning to meet under one roof to celebrate the Christmas holiday. Becca reviewed a mental picture of them all.

She didn't care much one way or the other about seeing her younger sister, Lily. Lily was a nice girl, a young woman now, a senior in college, but she and Becca were virtual strangers. Though Lily shared an apartment in Allston with two schoolmates, and Becca had a condo in the South End, only a few T-stops away, they never saw each other except at family gatherings like the one Becca was journeying to now. In fact, it hadn't even occurred to Becca to offer her sister a ride north. Such an offer would have saved Lily bus fare and offered Becca companionship, if indeed she'd wanted any. But Becca rarely wanted companionship. At least, that's what she'd come to believe. Self-reliance had become a deeply ingrained habit.

As for Becca's parents, Steve and Julie, it had been a full year since she had seen them. Not that they hadn't issued invitations to visit them in Maine. They had, and each time, Becca had made an excuse as to why she couldn't get away from the office. The one time in the past year they'd come down to Boston for a weekend and stayed at the Copley Plaza—her father, she vaguely remembered, had said something about seeing a photography show at the Museum of Fine Arts—Becca had lied to them about being out of town on business. In fact, she'd spent the weekend on her own in Provincetown, trying to relax on a crowded beach and paying inordinate tourist prices for decidedly average meals. All rather than have lunch or dinner with her parents and confront her growing anger toward them. All rather than face her mounting discontent.

Becca registered the fact that she was finally entering New Hampshire. Maybe she would get to her destination before midnight, after all. She wondered if her older sister, Olivia, who lived in Framingham, Massachusetts, would be driving north that night as well, her husband, James, in tow. Poor James. You couldn't help but like him, he was such a—well, such a likeable guy. Not that he exactly suffered being married to Olivia, but Olivia could at times be tiresome. She was a know-it-all and could be bossy and though she was smart—she had earned a masters degree in marketing—she could be oddly rigid and narrow-minded. But hey, Becca thought, James, who seemed to be eminently reasonable and good-natured, saw something in Olivia, so she couldn't be all that bad. Together they owned and managed a payroll service company that employed about six people in all. From what Becca could tell, they did well; she knew that a few years earlier James and Olivia had taken a two-week trip to Paris. And all those ultimately fruitless fertility treatments couldn't have been inexpensive.

And then there was Nora. Becca hadn't seen her grandmother, her father's mother, since the previous Christmas, either. She and Becca's grandfather, Thomas, had originally owned the farmhouse in Kently. When Thomas died, Nora nominally sold the house to her only child, Steve, and when he retired, he and his wife, Becca's mother, had sold their house in Winchester, Massachusetts, and moved to Maine full-time. Becca was looking forward, in a way, to seeing Nora, but at the same time she knew full well that her grandmother might just be her greatest opponent in what was sure to be a full-scale family battle.

Finally, and most importantly, David and his wife, Naomi, would be there, with Rain, and the twins in tow. David, Becca's older brother, was the only Rowan boy of his generation and, in Becca's opinion, was appropriately spoiled and bursting with self-importance. It was David she was most worried about, even afraid of, but the time had come to act. The time had come to take back what was rightfully hers, and no amount of intimidation or bluster was going to stop her from achieving her goal. She wasn't respected in the advertising world for her lack of determination or drive, that was for sure.

Still, Becca yawned, as if just thinking about the upcoming struggle had exhausted her. The truth was, she had been up almost all night working on a report she'd promised herself to complete before heading out for the Rowan house. It would be one less thing nagging at her conscience, one less thing to interfere with her focus and concentration this last full week in December. Becca realized she would need her wits about her if she were to present her case and convince the family of her rights.

Becca shivered and turned up the heat in the car. She hadn't bothered to change out of her work clothes before starting out. The only concession she had made to the trek north was to change her three-inch heels for a pair of expensive, tan leather driving moccasins. She'd bought them a few weeks before at Neiman Marcus and justified their cost by considering them a much-deserved Christmas present.

Becca's clothes probably—no, definitely—weren't suited to life in rural Maine, but she had done the best she could with preparing a wardrobe for the week. Not that an actual "wardrobe" was necessary. A pair of sturdy, waterproof boots; a pair of flannel-lined jeans; a few pairs of SmartWool socks; a heavy wool sweater; a parka of some sort; and fleece hat, mittens, and scarf would do the trick. Oh, and maybe an ice pick, shovel, and blowtorch for getting out of the front door.

No, the clothing that Becca had brought with her was more suited for life in Boston. Two pairs of wool dress slacks; three cashmere sweaters, one beige, one black, the other gray; a gorgeous, soft-as-butter leather coat in a chocolaty brown; a fashionable faux-fur hat. Her only acknowledgment of the northern landscape she was visiting was a pair of sturdy, waterproof boots she'd dutifully bought at L.L. Bean. Even Becca had to admit that "The Bean" knew what it was doing when it came to footwear for the great outdoors. The great, wet, cold, and sloppy outdoors.

Becca loathed and despised the winter and everything about it. She planned to spend as little time as possible out of doors once in Kently. Assuming, of course, the atmosphere in her parents' home didn't grow to be too antagonistic. If it did, she might be forced to bundle up and get away for a while. Besides, knowing the way her mother and grandmother cooked, it would do her good to get in some exercise this week. Fat was their friend; even vegetables were served with a pat of butter melting on top.

Luckily, at thirty-two, Becca could still be called lanky. She suspected that, like her father, at some point in her forties or fifties she would begin to put on some weight, but right now, it was easy to keep fit, given her high metabolism. And the twice-weekly sessions with a trainer at a local gym didn't hurt. But those sessions were more about maintaining health than watching weight. Becca didn't want osteoporosis sneaking up on her. No amount of designer clothes could make you look good when you were doomed to spend your days staring at your feet.

Becca's hair was a classic chestnut brown, of medium thickness. She wore it in a chin-length bob, which required a reshaping every three weeks. It was an expense that Becca had long ago built into her budget. What fashion guru had said that a good haircut made a woman's look? Whoever it was, Becca believed him, or her.

Although not a particularly popular style with women her age, Becca wore her nails long and carefully polished, and she had been doing so since she was about fourteen. Neither her mother nor her grandmother wore their nails long; in fact, only one other woman in the Rowan family—sixteen-year-old Rain—shared Becca's interest in nails not bluntly cut or bitten off at the quick.

Rain also had what were considered the "Rowan eyes," as did Becca and her father, Steve. They were large, slanted slightly upward at the outer corner, and were a peculiar shade, something like moss on a stone, an arresting combination of green and brown.

A familiar sound brought Becca fully back to the moment. Her iPhone, which was clipped to the wide patent leather belt of her fitted suit jacket, was ringing. It was Mary. Becca checked the time on the dashboard. She wondered what her assistant was doing staying so late at the office when the boss was on vacation. Didn't she have anywhere better to be, or anyone special to meet?

Suddenly, it occurred to Becca that she hadn't asked her trusted assistant where she was spending the Christmas holiday. In fact, she realized in a flash that she knew very little about Mary's personal life, or about the personal lives of anyone at Saville and Co. She wasn't sure if this bothered her or not. She did know for sure that she had absolutely no desire to let any of her colleagues into her own personal life—what there was of it.

She took the call. "Hey. What's up?"

What was up was that one of their oldest—and most demanding—clients wanted a major change made to the new print ad before the end of the following day. Becca listened, and then told Mary exactly what the account supervisor should say to the client. It involved the word "no."

"Won't they be angry?" Mary questioned. Becca pictured her mild-mannered assistant with hunched shoulders, as if flinching in anticipation of a blow.

"Yes," Becca said, "they'll be angry. But they're not going anywhere. We've made them more money than they know what to do with. The changes can wait until I get back."

The call ended, Becca glanced in the rearview mirror to assure herself for the tenth time that she hadn't forgotten to bring anything vital. Her laptop rested on the backseat, along with a soft leather briefcase that contained several paper files. Her mother would frown on Becca's bringing work along to what was supposed to be a warm and cozy family vacation, but Julie had never understood the attraction of a career. Her primary goal and function in life had been the raising of her children, and she'd seemed to find great satisfaction in that. Becca had vague memories of her mother dabbling in a pyramid scheme business; she recalled boxes of makeup samples piled up on the kitchen table, and neighborhood women coming over for "parties" that involved homemade coffee cakes, bottles of inexpensive wine, and the sampling of pink lotions and floral-smelling potions.

Finally, Becca spotted up ahead the bridge that crossed over into Maine. The journey to the bridge

from Boston was only fifty-five miles, but tonight it
had seemed interminable. As a matter of habit Becca
read aloud the sign on the bridge, welcoming travel-
ers. " 'Maine,' " she muttered. " 'The Way Life
Should Be.' Yeah, right. A bunch of shaggy moose,
smelly fish, and people whose idea of culture is the
annual lobster-gorging contest."

On some level Becca knew she was being unfair
and prejudicial—Maine was a gorgeous state; nobody could deny that, and its people were strong, re-
sourceful, and independent—but on another level
she just didn't care. If her parents hadn't retired to
the freakin' sticks, then she wouldn't have been
caught in that god-awful traffic and facing a treacherous slog through snow that had been falling heavy
and wet for the past ten miles.

A monstrous SUV roared past in the left lane. Becca
glanced at it with a frown that turned into open-
mouthed astonishment as the perky blond kid in
the backseat gave her the finger.

She was dying to flip the bird right back at him but
wasn't stupid enough to get herself forced to the side
of the road by the no doubt perfectly coiffed,
painfully worked-out soccer mommy behind the
wheel of her insanely large gas-guzzling vehicle, who
no doubt would defend her pampered little brat of a
son from any and all accusations of wrongdoing. And
then threaten to sue Becca (her husband would be a
celebrity lawyer, of course, or a Wall Street CEO rev-
eling in a recent outrageous bailout) for child abuse.

Becca gritted her teeth—her dentist had been
warning her for the past year to stop gritting and
grinding; Dr. Olds had said something about TMJ
and subsequent surgery—and drove on.

If that kid were her kid, there was no way he'd
even think about flipping someone the bird, ever,

not a classmate and certainly not a stranger, a female stranger at that. She wasn't a fan of corporal punishment, but there were plenty of other ways to teach a kid right from wrong and to make him aware of the consequences of acting like a deviant.

Aware of her accelerating heart rate, Becca took a deep and she hoped a calming breath—after her last blood pressure reading her doctor had strongly advised she learn and use several calming techniques—and turned on the radio. Some cool jazz would be helpful, she thought, maybe a song by Madeleine Peyroux or Jane Monheit, but all she could find in this unfortunate zone were cheesy Christmas songs. She tried another station. More cheesy Christmas songs, these fuzzy but unmistakably chipper. Again she changed the channel. Again she was disappointed. Damn it for having forgotten to bring her iPod.

What the hell was a reindeer doing with a red nose, anyway? Did it have a drinking problem? And if any kid really did see his mama kissing Santa Claus under the mistletoe, Becca was sure he'd be in therapy for the next twenty or thirty years of his life, not singing about it like it was all a big joke.

Peace on Earth and Goodwill to All. Yeah, like that was ever going to happen. Becca turned off the radio and glanced at her watch. She still had at least another two hours to go before reaching the dear old family homestead. Just great. Just freakin' great. And now she had to pee.

It could safely be said that Becca Rowan was not in a holiday mood.

2

Lily Rowan supposed she should feel peaceful and grateful and all those good warm and fuzzy things you're supposed to feel at Christmastime, but she didn't feel any of those things. All she felt was sad.

Lily stood at one of the living room windows, watching the snow that had been falling for about an hour and thinking of how Cliff, had he been there with her, would have had his arm around her waist and his head tilted next to hers, his adorably shaggy hair shining in the candlelight.

At this time of the year, Julie Rowan, Lily's mother, liked to place a single white candle in each window of the house in the traditional way. The candles were not electric; Julie Rowan was conservation minded in certain ways, and seemingly unafraid of several open flames in each room in spite of the fact that her dog, a Chinook named Hank, had on more than one occasion nearly swiped a candle to the ground with his tail. But, as Julie pointed out, almost only counts in horseshoes and hand grenades (Lily had no idea what that meant, exactly), so the candles remained on the windowsills and each night, before Julie retired for bed, the candles were carefully snuffed out with an old-fashioned, long-handled pewter candle snuffer. This prevented hot wax from splattering on the windows.

Lily sighed and hugged herself. The reality was that Cliff wasn't here in Maine with her this Christmas. He was back in Lexington, Massachusetts, at his parents' house because he'd done the unthinkable and Lily had found out his crime. Cliff Jones, Lily's boyfriend of more than three years, had cheated on her with a mutual friend, a girl they knew from economics class and someone they'd chatted with at a few parties.

It was horrible. It was unforgivable. Lily felt—no, she knew—that she would never get over Cliff's betrayal and that, quite probably, she would never love again, certainly not like she'd loved Cliff. Like she still loved Cliff, and that was the real problem. Because as much as she hated Cliff, she also still loved him and wanted him back, though she couldn't imagine any circumstance under which she would take him back—assuming he wanted to come back—because once a cheater, always a cheater. That's what she'd always believed. You got one shot with someone and if you ruined it by sleeping with someone else—like your girlfriend's classmate!—well, that was it.

Still. Cliff. Lily missed him, his broad shoulders (in truth they were kind of bony) and his fantastic smile (albeit a fairly crooked one), and his ability to make her laugh (Lily was the only one on whom this magic seemed to work; Cliff's buddies found him somewhat dull but tolerated his company for the way he threw around his cash; no one knew where he got the cash because he didn't have a job, but no one hesitated to take it).

Cliff was supposed to have joined the Rowan family for Christmas but, given the circumstances, Lily had come alone, taking the bus from Boston to Portland, where her father, Steve, had picked her up just the day before. They'd had lunch at Becky's Diner on Commercial Street before heading north, and the tuna melt and hot chocolate Lily had ordered made her feel just a little bit better about being without the love of her life for Christmas.

Lily sighed again and turned away from the window. Her grandmother was giving the swags of pine draped along the mantelpiece a final adjustment. Nora might be eighty-six years old but to Lily she would always be—well, ageless. Just—Grandma. It was she who'd decorated most of the first floor, with fresh pine branches and small sprigs of mistletoe and folk-art-inspired wooden Santa Claus statues. She had a knack for making an already cozy space even cozier, a pleasant moment somehow truly happy. Lily appreciated that quality in her grandmother and hoped that she would become half the woman Nora was. And that meant being caring and sympathetic and, when required, tough enough to stop a self-indulgent flood of tears.

Lily remembered the night she had learned of Cliff's perfidy. She'd called her grandmother in hysterics. She hadn't even thought about the possibility that she might have gotten Nora out of bed, or that Nora might have been busy at some important task. No. When Lily needed Nora she simply reached out. She'd always been closer to her grandmother than to her mother, at least for as long as she could remember, which was back to the time when her older sister

Becca went to live for a year with their brother, David, and his wife. Anyway, that night Nora had managed to calm Lily's grief with a few well-considered words of advice and a few genuine endearments. Lily had even managed to sleep through the rest of the night without disturbing dreams of violent revenge against her errant boyfriend.

If some people found it odd or unusual that two people, two women of the same family but so far apart in age, could be so close, that was not Lily's concern. Besides, she wasn't looking for a hip older companion; she wasn't in need of a cool, Botoxed grandma in low-rise jeans and a page on MySpace. Instead, in Nora, Lily found just what she did need—the maternal warmth her mother didn't quite provide, the wisdom of someone who'd learned from the experiences she'd lived, and the common sense that comes only from having survived the making of plenty of mistakes.

Nora retreated into the kitchen just as Steve Rowan came down the front stairs and reached for a navy blue parka on the coatrack.

"Where are you going, Dad?" Lily asked.

"Just out to my studio for a bit. I had a brainstorm about my project." He smiled. "Well, I think it was a brainstorm. I want to go and find out."

Lily assured him of his brilliance as a photographer, and he was gone. Lily thought that her father looked very tired and worn. She worried about him a little; sometimes he seemed so much older than her mother though they were only months apart. Lily knew her father had worked very hard for his family, spending long hours at the firm and often working all weekend. In fact, it was his dedication to the law that had inspired her to apply to law school. She hadn't made a final decision on which area of law she wanted to specialize in, but she thought that elder law sounded interesting. Or maybe probate, though she knew that some estate settlements could be angrily contested. She didn't think she had the stomach to be a criminal defense attorney or, for that matter, a divorce attorney. The idea of counseling a person on how to make the life of another person miserable—even if he or she deserved it—didn't appeal to her in the least.

Julie Rowan came into the living room, put her hands on her hips, and sighed.

"Now where in the world did I put my glasses?"

Lily smiled. Her mother was far from scatterbrained, but for some reason Lily couldn't fathom, she liked to pretend that she was. Lily thought it was kind of an endearing quirk.

"They're on your head, Mom."

Julie patted the top of her head and laughed. "Of course! I knew that all along."

Julie was a warm person overall, if not sentimental, and she'd always been a devoted mother. But the truth was that by the time Lily came along—and quite a surprise she'd been—Julie's energy for the little girl was limited. Then, a few years later, when everything had happened with Becca, well, Lily might have been little more than an afterthought in the course of Julie's days. But there'd been Nora to fill any emotional gap left by Julie's preoccupations, and Lily had thrived. If she hadn't exactly been spoiled, she had been pampered, but it seemed to have done her no great harm. If a little naïve, Lily was also kindhearted; if a little sheltered, she was also eager to learn.

Nora joined them and together the three women conducted a last-minute check of the house to be sure it was ready to receive its guests. Lily had

learned that the house had been constructed in a
very traditional New England style that some called a
"telescope house." The original part of the building
had contained the two rooms now used as the living
room and dining room, as well as the kitchen. The
center stairs, still in existence, had led to the second
floor; originally that had consisted of four small,
equal-sized bedrooms. Above that was the attic that
had once been used as the children's bedrooms and,
if there were any, the servants' quarters.

Over the years, and long before the Rowans had
bought the place, an addition had been put on that
was a smaller version of the original. This had contained the bathrooms and additional bedrooms; one
of those rooms now served as the den, and another,
as Nora's bedroom. Lily didn't know exactly what
other work had been done over the years to result in
the house her family occupied now, but she thought
the overall affect was very pleasing.

The exterior of the house was just as pleasing in its
overall simplicity—white clapboard with no decoration; four-over-four windows; a fairly steeply sloped
shingle roof. Unlike other, extreme versions of the
telescope house, the barn sat about an eighth of a
mile from the house. In the few years before retirement, Steve had begun a renovation that trans-
formed the barn into a photography studio and
workshop. It was now a clean, well-lighted space (Lily
couldn't place the phrase but knew she'd heard it
somewhere) to which her father enjoyed retreating.

When it had been determined that fires were roaring in every fireplace (originally, the house had had
one in every room) and that food was warming in the
oven, the women turned to a review of the sleeping
arrangements.

"Nora, of course, will be in her own room," Julie said.

"Of course," her mother-in-law said. "There's no point in even trying to dislodge an old woman from her domain."

"Or an old married couple from theirs, so Steve and I will be in our room. Rain will bunk with you, Lily, all right?"

Lily nodded. "Sure. It'll be nice to get some girl time with her."

"David and Naomi are in the Lupine Room, and Olivia and James will be in the Queen Anne's Lace Room." Julie had stenciled flowers on the doors of these rooms and enjoyed referring to them by their flowery names. She and her husband slept in the Peony Room. Steve did not share his wife's enthusiasm for this pretension, but he said nothing. He believed that everyone had a right to her quirks and hobbies. "And I'm putting the twins in the Foxglove Room."

"The old sewing room?" Lily said. "But what about Becca? That's where she usually sleeps."

"Oh, I thought I'd ask her if she'd mind sleeping on the couch in the den. Naomi called the other day. It seems the boys have been clamoring to sleep in their own room and not on the floor of their parents' room. They grow up so quickly, kids these days. Anyway, I'm sure Becca won't mind sleeping in the den. There's just not enough room in there for two air mattresses!"

Lily wasn't at all sure that Becca would be happy about the new arrangement. She guessed that her sister would agree with good grace but knew that underneath she'd be seething. The last few times Becca had been with the family, Lily had sensed something she could barely articulate, some notion that Becca didn't feel like one of them, like a Rowan, that in some way she felt alienated. But maybe Lily had misread her older sister. That wouldn't be surprising. Becca was kind of distant with everybody, kind of hard to figure out. Lily hadn't once heard Becca mention a friend, and now the thought occurred to her that maybe Becca didn't have any friends.

"It's hard to believe," Nora was saying, "that the family hasn't seen Becca since last Christmas."

"But, Grandma, she's visited David and Naomi."

"Well, of course," Julie said. "That's to be expected. But the rest of us haven't seen her. She's always had some excuse or other not to show up for a gathering."

"She does work very hard," Lily said, though in fact she didn't know much about her sister's work or how much Becca claimed about her hectic schedule was true. Not that she suspected her sister of lying about it—why would she lie?—but the fact was that Lily and Becca weren't close and never really had been. At least, not that Lily could recall.

The phone rang and Julie hurried off to the kitchen to answer it. When she returned a few moments later it was to announce that Olivia and James had decided to drive up from their home in Framingham, Massachusetts, the next day. They hadn't been able to close up the office early enough and didn't want to risk driving in a storm.

"That would be James's decision," Nora said. "I suspect Olivia would be willing to move Heaven and Earth to get here tonight."

"Did you see that e-mail Olivia sent last week?" Lily asked. "The one about wanting us all to sign up with some ancestor research Web site?"

"Your grandmother and I aren't online, my dear. The only computer around here is the one in your father's studio."

"Oh. Right. Anyway, I was wondering where Olivia got her fascination with the family's history. With genealogy and the family tree and all that."

Nora shook her head. "It's more like an obsession, it seems to me. Mark my words, she'll spend most of the time this holiday rummaging up in the attic, looking for whatever it is she's looking for."

"Ghosts?" Lily wondered aloud. "The real kind, not something from a horror movie."

Nora smiled. "I'm not sure there's a difference, is there? Anyway, mark my words, she's looking for something."

"Treasure," Lily suggested, only half joking. "I bet she thinks there's treasure buried somewhere in the attic walls."

Julie removed the place settings she'd put out for her oldest daughter and her husband. "I think she's looking for answers. But I'm not sure to which questions."

"Skeletons! Every family supposedly has skeletons in their closets. Maybe Olivia's looking for scandalous secrets."

"Well, she won't find any evidence of scandalous secrets in a pile of old junk," Julie said.

The three women quietly finished setting the table for dinner. The tablecloth was a cheerful affair Julie had picked up at Marshalls on her last visit to Boston; it was decorated with images of massive red poinsettias and bordered with lacy, intertwining pine branches. The napkins, large white squares, were embroidered around the edges with depictions of holly clusters. The fact that they were still brilliantly white amazed Lily. Laundry wasn't one of her strong suits. And the thought of ironing made her squirm. She had heard that in "the old days," some women actually ironed their husbands' underwear and their babies' cloth diapers. Well, disposable diapers had solved one problem, but there was no way the ironing of underwear was going to happen in her household!

"Whatever happened to the idea of James and Olivia adopting a baby?" Lily asked suddenly, prompted by the thought of diapers. "Wasn't there some talk about that a year or two ago? Or am I imagining it?"

"You're not imagining it," Lily's mother replied. "James spoke to me about the possibility once or twice, after it was clear that Olivia wasn't going to be able to sustain a pregnancy. But then, I heard nothing more. And it's not a topic I feel comfortable bringing up, especially with someone as—tense—as Olivia."

"Of course not. I was just wondering."

"That woman can be prickly," Nora said, as if to herself. Then: "Well, I'd better tend to the cinnamon rolls if they're going to be ready for dinner. You know how David likes my cinnamon rolls."

Yes, thought Lily with yet another sigh. And Cliff, the love of her life, had liked Nora's cinnamon rolls, too.

3

"Are we there yet?"

"Are we there yet?"

David didn't reply. Why the boys thought it so hysterically funny to drive their father to the brink of insanity by chanting that question—in unison—over and over and over again, David just didn't know. He knew the reference. Michael and Malcolm had picked it up from *The Simpsons*. He just didn't know why they should find it so funny. David, it had been pointed out to him, didn't have a great sense of humor.

"Okay, guys," he said wearily. "I get it."

"There's nothing to get, Dad!"

The boys laughed and were on to another pastime, this one less annoying to their father. David peered in the rearview mirror to see their brown and blond heads bent over some sort of comic book. Or something. David hoped it had been printed on recycled paper.

David Rowan, thirty-eight years old, was the second child and only son of Steve and Julie Rowan. He

worked for the state of New Hampshire as a geologi-
cal engineer; his primary concern was preservation
of the environment, and he could preach about the
joys of greening for as long as someone would let
him. And few people had the energy to stand up to
or resist David Rowan once he got going. His personality was forceful and dynamic. And as the only boy of
the Rowan family, he was also a bit spoiled (though
he would deny that) and used to being "special."
Still, David was a good guy, someone people natu-
rally turned to in a crisis.

David glanced quickly at his wife of seventeen
years, seated in the passenger seat beside him. Naomi
Henley-Rowan was also thirty-eight. They'd met while
still in college and had married just before David
started graduate school. After all the years together,
David still found Naomi to be beautiful, inside and
out. He knew he was very lucky to have found her
and he tried very hard to let her know how deeply he
appreciated her loving him back. At least, he hoped
he did. David knew that he could—on rare occasions—be a bit of a stubborn jerk.

Naomi, sensing her husband's glance, smiled at
him. She noted for what was likely the millionth time
his long, dark eyelashes. Though she would never
admit to being bowled over by so frivolous a thing as
eyelashes, she had been bowled over from the moment she first saw David in their sophomore year in
college. After a while, of course, she'd been attracted
to the strength and goodness of his character, but
those long dark eyelashes still could work their magic.

Naomi was a busy, productive woman. She had a
potter's wheel on which she made planters and bowls
and mugs that she sold on consignment at a small
local store specializing in local handmade goods. She
tended a thriving vegetable garden that provided a

good portion of the family's produce, and she had recently learned how to put up preserves. One afternoon a week she was the library's Storytime reader, a project she enjoyed more so as her own children were past the point of wanting to be read to by their mother. On Tuesdays and Thursdays she worked as a salesperson at a family-owned and -operated hardware store in town.

Naomi dressed to fit her lifestyle, in jeans or chinos or cords, topped off by loose-fitting blouses or T-shirts. She tended to wear sturdy sandals well into the autumn, with socks when the temperature dipped below 45 degrees; in winter she replaced them with standard L.L. Bean boots. Still, she wasn't averse to the very occasional evening out in Portsmouth at a decent restaurant that served the kind of wine she would never dream of buying at home—expensive—and delicacies such as duck liver pâte, even if it meant shunning the usual footwear for one of her two pairs of high heels. On these rare occasions, Rain took pleasure in teasing her mother about her usual ultracasual wear; she also helped Naomi with her makeup, which Naomi appreciated since she had virtually no skill in that department.

Naomi looked over her shoulder. Rain sat slouched against the door of the seat just behind her father, listening to her iPod, mouthing words Naomi was glad she couldn't make out. Rain had the Rowan family eyes—large, slanted slightly upward—and they were a very distinctive shade, a mix of green and brown, a color shared by Steve and Becca. In fact, from her chestnut brown hair to her lanky frame, Rain looked all Rowan, almost as if there had been no other set of DNA involved in her making. Sometimes, this unsettled Naomi.

It was hard to believe Rain had been their daugh-

ter now for sixteen years. Naomi could remember
with great clarity the moment she had carried the little bundle of pink baby and blanket over the thresh-
old of their small, clapboard farmhouse—a mini
version of the one David's parents now lived in—and
officially welcomed her home.

Naomi had always wanted a family, and Rain's arrival, though quite unexpected, was for her a joy. For
David, too. He'd risen to the occasion as he always
did—David was nothing if not responsible and proud
of it— and taken on the role of adoring father.

Rain hadn't yet begun to date in any serious way,
for which Naomi was glad and David even gladder.
Naomi pitied the first boy who would come to their
door to pick up Rain for a movie or party. David
would intimidate him; there was no doubt about
that. If her husband was a bit of a throwback to the
age of manly men whose primary job it was to protect
the women in his life, then so be it. He could be a lot
of worse things, like an alcoholic or a criminal, someone like that guy Becca had gotten involved with all
those years ago. . . .

"Mom! Michael poked me!"

"I did not! Anyway, you looked at me."

"I'm allowed to look at you. Right, Mom?"

"Looking is allowed, Malcolm."

"See? I told you so."

Naomi rolled her eyes into the darkened sky. The
boys were a proverbial handful, but Naomi got a real
kick out of their antics. Most of their antics, anyway.
They were high-spirited rather than unpleasantly
willful, with Michael more the ringleader and Malcolm more his willing follower. Twins ran in Naomi's
family—two of her cousins had had twins and her
mother had been one of two girls—so neither she
nor David had been surprised when the doctor had

first detected two heartbeats. Sure, the family budget
had to be reimagined a bit, but so far, Naomi felt that
they'd been very lucky, blessed even.

She had three wonderful children. She lived in a
lovely little town in a sweet little house. She did work
she enjoyed. And best of all, she had a husband who
loved her as much as she loved him. In Naomi's ad-
mittedly prejudiced opinion, she and David were
quite a team.

Naomi knew she was a good foil to David's somewhat domineering style; she could subtly reign him
in when they were with company and David began to
pontificate or control the conversation. He didn't
mean to offend or alienate people; he just had a firm
belief in the sense and truth of what he had to say. To
be honest, most of what David stated was reasonable
and intelligent; it was just that his manner could turn
off his listeners and, on occasion, even his wife.

A memory came to Naomi's mind just then. Early
on in their relationship David had taken her home to
meet his parents. Naomi had been nervous, of
course, but Julie and Steve were casual and welcoming and before long, she'd felt right at home with the
older Rowans. Still, during dinner, when David had
launched into a rant against his parents' ignorance
on matters concerning the environment—a rant,
Naomi came to learn, that was largely unjustified—
and Julie had castigated her son, calling him "an ar-
rogant jerk," Naomi had been shocked. After dinner,
while the women were cleaning up (that was Naomi's
first indication that the division of labor in the
Rowan house ran along pretty traditional lines), Julie
had given her future daughter-in-law some advice. "If
you don't talk back to him and point out his inap-
propriate behavior," she'd explained, "he'll simply
become unbearable. Besides, once you let him know

he's out of line, he always tries to step back in. He really is a good boy." Naomi supposed that was true; after his mother's scolding at dinner, David had been almost docile, even sweet. That mood had lasted all the way home.

Naomi's parents had died long before she met David, leaving her not only an orphan, but also one without siblings. She was grateful for the Rowans, glad to be part of the family that had embraced her warmly from the beginning. In truth, the Rowans were pretty easy to like. Most of them were, anyway.

Everyone got along well with Steve; he was as inoffensive a person as Naomi had ever met. What he had been like in his law practice she had trouble imagining. Given his financial success and his stellar reputation, no doubt he had been tough, smart, and dogged.

And Julie. Naomi got along very well with her mother-in-law; she and Julie were quite similar in several ways. They were both devoted to their family, both practical women, hardworking and generally easygoing. And, of course, the secret they shared served as a further bond between them.

Her relationship with her sister-in-law Olivia wasn't quite so close or so smooth, but honestly, Naomi couldn't think of one person other than Olivia's husband, James, who really got along well with her. Even Olivia's parents seemed at times to tiptoe around their oldest daughter. Olivia had definitely changed since Naomi had first met her, when she and David were dating in college. Now she seemed rarely to smile; she seemed to have lost what little sense of humor she'd had back then. But Naomi didn't spend inordinate amounts of time worrying about her sister-in-law's disposition. For all she knew, Olivia was a ball of fire when alone with her husband or out with her girlfriends. Well, she doubted it, but anything was possible.

From the sudden and unusual quiet of the backseat came Michael's voice.

"Are we there yet?"

A half second later, Malcolm said, "Are we there yet?"

"Yeah, Dad." It was Rain, unplugged. "Are we?"

Naomi grinned at her husband. "Well, David? Are we?"

4

Becca made only clinical note of the surroundings—dark, velvety sky strewn with bright pinpoints of cold, clear light; fresh, crispy air; the encouraging smell of a wood fire—as she hauled her luggage from the trunk of her car and then, laptop slung across her chest and briefcase on her shoulder, she stumbled through falling snow to the front door of the house she hadn't visited in over a year.

As she drew nearer to the house, L.L. Bean boots now replacing her driving moccasins, she heard sounds of laughter from within, laughter and a familiar booming voice. She hadn't noticed David's SUV—he must have parked in back—but there was no mistaking that voice. David was announcing his presence to the world, as was his very annoying habit.

Through one of the living room windows she could see her sister-in-law, Naomi, still in her coat. The family must have just arrived.

Preoccupied, Becca jumped when the front door swung open and her mother came dashing out—

wearing no coat, only a sweater—to greet her. Julie loved the cold weather.

"Becca! Come in, come in! It's so good to see you. Here, let me help you with those bags." Julie reached for her daughter and Becca backed away.

"No, Mom," she said, "it's okay, I've got them."

"Don't be silly." Julie grabbed the briefcase from Becca's shoulder. "Give me that. Lord, what's in here, bricks?"

"Just some stuff for work."

"Now, don't tell me you're going to be working all week. It's Christmas!"

There was no point in arguing; it was the same old refrain. Becca, you work too hard. Mom, it's my job and I like it. But you know what they say about all work and no play. But I like it. But. But. But.

Julie turned and led the way into the house. Becca rolled her eyes behind her mother's back. Wasn't Julie too old—or something—to be wearing her hair in a braid down her back? Couldn't she at least wind it on top of her head? Why a swinging braid of thick, graying hair should so infuriate her, Becca didn't care to examine.

Once inside, she was met with the usual chaos of arrival. Greetings were shared; coats were removed and passed along to the coatrack in the front hall; bags were tumbled at the foot of the stairs. It was all as usual. It made Becca feel very uncomfortable and she stood for a moment, silent and stiff, until her younger sister approached her.

"Hi, Becca." Lily gave her sister a weak and awkward hug.

"So, how's school?" Becca said by way of greeting.

"Fine." Lily shrugged. "You know."

"When do you graduate?"

"Next June."

"Huh," she said. "Time flies." What now? "And what are you planning to do after graduation?"

"Going to law school," Lily replied. "If I get into one."

"I'm sure your grades are fine," Becca said, though she had no knowledge whatsoever of her younger sister's academic track record. In fact, Becca realized that she had no knowledge of just about anything having to do with Lily. In fact, if she turned away from her sister at that very moment, she doubted she could tell you the color of her eyes. Becca looked—really looked—and noted that Lily's eyes were cow brown, like their mother's. Those eyes must have come from her mother's side of the family, from the Dobbs family. She would try to remember that. If she remembered to remember.

Lily turned to answer a question posed by her mother, and Becca found herself receiving a quick, one-armed hug from her brother. And then he was off, lifting an enormous duffel bag and heading for the stairs.

"Hey to you, too, David," she mumbled to his back.

Naomi came close and smiled her familiar, genuine smile. "It's so good to see you, Becca," she said.

Naomi meant it. She was happy to see her sister in-law. She was incapable of guile. Her sincerity upset Becca. It was much more difficult to confront a nice person than a nasty one.

Michael and Malcolm tore out of the kitchen, each clutching a cookie, raced through the living room, and made for the stairs to the second floor.

"Boys!" Naomi called. "Say hello to your aunt!"

Something was shouted over their shoulders. It sufficed for Becca. If the truth were to be told, the twins meant virtually nothing to her. She certainly didn't hate them, but neither did she love them. When they were out of sight, they were out of mind. Even now, greeting the boys, she felt surprise at their existence. She felt vaguely bad about this but not bad enough to attempt a closer relationship. Besides, she got the distinct feeling that Michael and Malcolm weren't all that interested in her, either.

Becca turned to her grandmother now, and gave her a slightly awkward hug. Nora felt frailer than Becca remembered. It had been only a year since she'd last seen her grandmother. Could so much have changed in a year? Of course. Why not? Time was not a friend.

"How are you, Grandma?" Becca asked, though if there were something wrong with Nora, her grandmother would be the last to talk about it. Nora was as close to stoic as anyone Becca had ever known.

"Just fine," she said. "And you, Becca?"

"Fine. Great." Becca knew that Nora hadn't believed her response, which was, even to her own ears, meaningless.

Then, a girl of sixteen came loping into the living room from the direction of the kitchen at the back of the house. She was tall and lanky, with long chestnut brown hair and the Rowan eyes. She was dressed fashionably but appropriately for her age—Naomi would have seen to that; no bared midriff—in medium-rise jeans and a striped wool hoodie.

Becca wondered if she had been as pretty at sixteen as Rain was, so fresh and unspoiled. The answer was that yes, she had been. And then, she had not.

"Hi, Aunt Becca!" the girl called.

Aunt. The word tugged painfully at Becca's heart. She was flooded by the all too familiar feelings of loss and regret—and worst of all, guilt. Rain's eyes, so like her own, so not like Naomi's . . . *Yes*, she thought. *My resolve is firm.*

"Hi, Rain," she said, stepping forward to greet the girl. Then Becca took her daughter in her arms and hugged her.

5

Her mother was babbling on. "I told the others I was sure you wouldn't mind sleeping in the den. I mean, really, what's the big deal, and this way, you're closer to the kitchen."

Was her mother implying that she had a problem with overeating? That she raided the fridge while sleepwalking? Becca was furious. She wanted to forget the whole plan, grab her bags, and drive right back to Boston that night, storm or no storm.

It was always this way with the Rowans. They would always see her as the troublemaker, the one not worthy of consideration, the one who could be ousted from her own bed for the convenience of others, even for a couple of sticky eight-year-old boys!

"You aren't upset, are you, honey?" her mother was saying, her face a mask of confusion. "You do understand how it is with kids."

How the hell would I know how it is with kids? Becca answered silently. *You took my child away from me before I could know anything about her.*

Becca fought for and won a modicum of control.

She had to remain outwardly calm. She was a responsible adult. She was a parent. "No," she said, "I'm not upset. I understand. It's no problem. Really."

Steve had been listening to the exchange between his wife and daughter. "If it is a problem, Becca," he said now, "I'm sure we could—"

"No," she snapped. "I said it was all right."

Julie shot a look at her husband. She hadn't cared for Becca's tone; maybe Steve hadn't noticed. But the tightness of his mouth told her that he had, indeed, noticed.

Without another word, Becca retrieved her bags from the hallway and carried them off to the den. Becca hadn't met her father's eye since she'd arrived. She didn't want to. Besides, she wasn't sure she could. And when he had pretended to care about her feelings regarding the sleeping arrangements . . . well, that had been too much. Was there no end to his hypocrisy?

Becca had just finished unpacking her clothes when Rain called out from the hall that dinner was on the table. Becca had no appetite, but the idea of a big glass of wine held great appeal.

A few minutes later, she joined the other Rowans in the dining room. As was usual when the entire (or almost entire; James and Olivia were missing, Beccca noted) family was gathered, Steve and Julie sat at the heads of the dining table. Nora sat to Julie's right and the others were left to choose their own seats. Becca, one of the last at the table, found herself sitting across from her daughter.

Rain. Becca had chosen the name because she liked the sound of it. And she liked the fact that rain brought flowers in the spring. Rain brought renewal. It brought relief on a dry and bitter day. And Becca liked the other meaning of the word, with its different spelling but same sound. She liked the idea of one person reigning over the heart of another. Like her daughter had come to reign over Becca's heart.

There was only one problem. Rain hated her name. She thought it was stupid and she'd confided to Becca that she suspected her parents must have been on drugs when she was born, though the image of a stoned mom and dad was pretty hard to conjure. Of course, Rain had no idea that Becca had chosen her name and that every time she complained about it in her aunt's hearing—and every time she announced her desire to legally change her name as soon as she was eighteen—Becca cringed. If she could do it over again, rename her daughter at birth, she would, and she would give her a more traditional name, Elizabeth or Katherine, or maybe even Virginia or Alexandra. But what had a sixteen-year-old known about the importance or the reverberations of names? Besides, none of the older Rowans had suggested she reconsider her choice. No one had offered a word of advice.

Other than complaining about her silly name, Rain was a joy to be with, smart, funny without being sly, and friendly without being false. Of course, some credit was due to David and Naomi, Becca could grudgingly admit that, but she also believed that Rain was inherently good. She was enormously proud to be her mother, even if she couldn't shout that pride to the world.

Suddenly, between the salad and the serving of the pork roast with apples, and in spite of her great resolve, Becca experienced a decidedly unpleasant twinge of doubt. She wondered if she should, after all, break the family's agreement not to reveal the truth about Rain's birth mother until her twenty-first birthday. For an awful moment, Becca wondered if

she was really and truly prepared for the consequences of such an act, consequences which, and it
didn't take a creative genius to figure this out, might
very well be disastrous. Becca reached for her wineglass. In vino veritas. Maybe the merlot had something to say about the matter.

"Mom." Rain had turned to Naomi, who was
seated to her left. "Tell everyone about that cool bag
you made for me. It's purple velvet. All my friends
want one. You should see it, Aunt Becca," she said,
looking her way now. "It's awesome. Maybe Mom
could make you one, too."

Becca managed a smile. At least she thought she
did. "Yes," she said, lifting her wineglass again. "Maybe."

Conversations continued around her. How to get
squirrels out of an attic, humanely, of course. What
the twins' friends were getting for Christmas and why
the twins thought they should be getting it, too. The
neighbor, some artist guy, would be stopping by the
next day, per his usual habit. Nora's annual checkup
had gone well; her cholesterol had even gone down.
Becca heard words, but they had no meaning. Her
mind was focused on one thing only and that was her
decision to lay claim to her daughter. She was resolved.

She should be the one Rain called Mom. She
should be the one making awesome purple velvet
bags for her daughter, not Naomi. (She couldn't sew
but she could learn, couldn't she?)

The meal was a trial for Becca. She was hardly
aware of what she had eaten. Cinnamon rolls might
have been involved; they usually were, being one of
David's favorites. Everyone always wanted to please
David.

Finally, dinner was over. David and Naomi were
eager to get to bed. It had been a long day for both,

and the boys were showing signs of grumpiness. Rain and Lily took off to listen to some new music Rain had brought along, and Nora retired to the living room to read. Becca had no intention of being alone with her parents, who had begun to clean up after the meal, any more than was strictly necessary and made her own excuses. Besides, tonight was not the night for her revelation. She wanted the whole family to be present, not that Olivia and James were likely to contribute much of use to what would no doubt be a—lively—discussion.

Becca closed the door of the den behind her. She wondered why her mother hadn't given this room a name, too, something like the Stinkweed Room.

It was crammed full of miscellaneous furniture, or so it seemed to Becca, who was not prepared to look charitably on her new sleeping quarters. An old bookcase stood about six feet high against one wall and looked dangerously close to exploding, so many books in all sorts of conditions were stuffed onto its shelves. The couch had seen better days, but to her mother's credit, she had provided plenty of ultra-clean sheets and blankets, which would cover the cracked leather. A small desk was shoved against another wall and on it were stacks of yellowing magazines, an ancient typewriter with no ribbon, and a jumble of framed photographs, including one of Becca's grandparents on their wedding day. The floor was made of pine boards, painted a farmhouse gray; in the center of the room was a small braided rug in maroon and gold.

Becca sighed and sank onto the couch. The room would have to do. She had brought with her several days' mail and now shuffled through it. Bills; what else was new? An announcement from a local discount furniture warehouse. How had that not gotten tossed in the garbage immediately? And finally, what seemed from the colorful Santa Claus sticker on its front to be a holiday card from a name and address that Becca, at first glance, didn't recognize.

Becca tore open the envelope and found inside a garish greeting card printed on cheap, glossy card stock, the kind of card you bought in bulk at the dollar store.

Who did she know who would have chosen such a thing? Becca opened the card. Molly Hansen, that's who would and had sent such a greeting.

Molly Hansen. Becca frowned at the round, childlike signature. She hadn't seen Molly since junior year of high school. And apart from one or two birthday cards during Becca's college years (Molly's family hadn't been able to send their daughter to college at that time; Becca now wondered if Molly had ever managed to get a degree), there had been nothing, no communication between the girls.

It was odd, then, hearing from her old neighbor now. Odd, coming on this Christmas in particular, when Becca was determined to claim her child, the child who, inadvertently, had been the cause of Becca's break from Molly and from all her former friends. Because when Becca had gone to live with David and Naomi and await Rain's birth, she'd never answered any of her friends' calls or letters, and when she was finally ready to go back to school, she'd begged her parents to let her graduate from a private high school in a neighboring town, instead of having to return to the local public school. Steve and Julie had agreed and at some expense had enrolled Becca among a senior class of strangers, none of whom seemed to care much about Becca or where she had come from, which was just as she'd hoped things would be.

Anonymity. That was what Becca had sought and it was what she had achieved ever since, so that her personal life was largely devoid of intimate connections. Becca feared prying eyes and wagging tongues the way some people feared snakes or mice.

And now, here was Molly Hansen, innocently, perhaps, asking questions in her rounded script, like what Becca was "up to" and how she'd been and even, daringly, suggesting that they get together sometime soon to "catch up."

Becca closed the card. There was nothing she would like to do less than "catch up," especially with someone who was witness to her exodus from town all those years ago, someone who might have suspicions about the reason for Becca's absence and who, in spite of her seemingly pleasant nature—Becca did remember Molly as a very sweet and natural girl—might really be in search of dirt. Gossip. "So, Becca. Tell me the truth. You were pregnant, weren't you? Who was it? Who knocked you up? What happened to the baby?"

Becca slid the card into her briefcase. She might have torn it up and thrown it in the little trash bin under the desk but she didn't, and she didn't ask herself why. Instead, she began to prepare for bed. Over a flannel nightgown she zipped a sweat jacket; on her feet she wore thick woolen socks. The den certainly wasn't warm enough for Becca, who increasingly felt the cold weather and hated it thoroughly.

It was interesting. Vague memories, old photographs, and amateur video proved that as a child she had loved the snow and icy weather. She'd even owned a pair of white ice skates with faux-fur pompoms on the end of the laces. When had things begun to change?

Somewhere along the line, Becca thought as she turned off the small lamp on the end table by her head, she had lost her old self. Somewhere along the line, she'd changed so much, it was almost as if her old self had been killed and she'd been reborn as . . .

As who? That was the question.

Her thoughts, as she tried to fall asleep, were troubled.

6

As their children and grandchildren were settling down for the night, Steve and Julie were in the kitchen cleaning up after dinner. Neither minded the chore; it gave them time to be alone together, which when all the other Rowans were at the house became a precious commodity.

Now, in the brightly lit kitchen, Julie stood at the sink washing dishes, pots, and pans, and Steve stood next to her, drying them. Hank nibbled contentedly at his bowl of kibble. Henry Le Mew, reigning feline, was nowhere to be seen.

Julie, now in her mid-sixties, had been married to Steve Rowan for almost forty-five years. Her primary focus during that time had been the raising of their children, a job she had thoroughly enjoyed. That, of course, and keeping a clean and well-ordered home, one to which her husband could look forward to returning each evening after a long and arduous day at work.

She'd never been much interested in a career outside the home. And honestly, Steve's salary and all the perks that attempted to compensate for his spending inordinate hours at the office were in fact sufficient for the family's needs. Still, for a while Julie had tried her hand at being an Avon representative; she remembered how Olivia had loved to play with her makeup samples and how David once had—accidentally, he claimed—dumped an entire bottle of body lotion on the living room carpet. But sales hadn't captured her mind or her imagination the way parenting had, and after two years she'd given up the job with no regrets.

And then there had come another child. Though Lily was a surprise, and the notion of yet another child had made Steve more than a bit nervous, Julie had embraced the pregnancy with joy. In spite of her "advanced" maternal age, the birth was an easy one, as those things go, and Julie got down to the business of breast-feeding and child rearing with her usual gusto. It was really only when Becca got pregnant at sixteen that Julie, for the very first time, began to feel tired and not entirely up to every task that presented itself.

She was vaguely aware that she'd passed the primary emotional care of her youngest child to her mother-in-law. But Julie was not one for guilt and worry; she rarely dwelt on a subject or a problem for more than an hour before devising a solution or a plan and acting on it as soon as possible. So she didn't feel as if she'd abandoned Lily; she simply felt that she had identified a problem—a lack of emotional energy available for the girl—and solved that problem—a transfer of the girl's emotional care to someone who did have the energy at hand. And everything had worked out just fine. Lily was a good person, an excellent student, and a generally happy young woman. The sadness she felt over this Cliff character would, Julie was sure, pass before long. And in the meantime, there was always Nora to help Lily through the rough times.

The sound of lapping water made Julie glance down at Hank, her New England–bred Chinook, with a smile. Julie was a dog person. Each morning, come rain or shine—or snow—she and Hank walked two or three miles together. Now three years old, Hank was the sweetest dog Julie had ever lived with, and she'd lived with dogs since she was a small girl. Big ones, small ones, short-haired and long-haired canines, it didn't matter to her what the dog looked like or even how he behaved—as long as a dog wasn't rabid, Julie loved him.

Maybe because of all the fresh air and exercise being with her dogs required, Julie looked younger than her years, or so she'd been told. Not that she cared much about her appearance. In fact, there was only one thing about which she was vain and that was her hair. Once a lustrous brown, it was still thick and only slightly gray. She liked to wear it in a long braid down her back or, on occasion, wound around her head. Steve had once told her that she looked like a Swiss milkmaid—but only once.

Julie pretty much liked most people and was slow to voice a negative opinion when she met someone she didn't care for. Like the obnoxious boy Lily had been dating for some time, Cliff something-or-other. Yes, Cliff Jones. Julie was glad that relationship was over! And then there'd been that former partner of Steve's, an overly ambitious and definitely suspicious type named Bob Yarrow, who'd sold his practice when only fifty to retire on what, in Julie's opinion, were ill-gotten gains. Good riddance to him, too! How her husband had put up with that man was a mystery.

But then again, maybe it wasn't so much of a mystery. One of the qualities that most impressed Julie about Steve was his patience and his tolerance for all but the most openly bad behavior.

Steve, now also in his mid-sixties, was the only child of Thomas and Nora Rowan. Almost two years earlier he'd retired from law after many, many years as a partner in an influential Boston firm. Nowadays, instead of bringing in clients, supervising his staff of junior lawyers, and hiring litigators, he spent the majority of his time taking photographs of just about anything that caught his eye—the deer that regularly paid a visit to the herb and vegetable garden; the hedgehogs that lumped themselves on the remains of an old stone wall behind the house; the bright orange of the autumnal oak leaves on the tree just behind his studio; the way the late afternoon sun hit the living room windows; his wife as she rolled dough for a pie. And even Julie had to admit that some of his best, most artful photographs were of his beloved cat. Steve Rowan was a cat person and proud of it.

As if summoned by Julie's thoughts, a distinctive howl came from the kitchen doorway.

"I wondered where he'd been hiding all evening," Julie said, without turning from the sink.

A massive Maine coon cat lumbered over to where Steve stood by the drainboard and glared up at him. At his last weighing in, Henry had been recorded as twenty-four pounds.

"Not hiding," Steve corrected. "Avoiding. You know he doesn't care for crowds."

"Family is not a crowd."

"Tell that to Henry."

While his wife was rarely without her canine sidekick, Steve was rarely without Henry Le Mew, his fur-child of the past eight years.

"I'd better sit down," Steve said, a note of apology in his voice. He put aside the dish towel he'd been using and sank into a chair at the table. Henry Le Mew heaved himself onto Steve's lap, circled several times, and collapsed in a heap of shaggy black and white fur.

"I suppose there's no point in telling you that you've dreadfully spoiled that animal."

"No point whatsoever," Steve agreed. "Besides, I didn't do anything. Henry makes all the decisions around here."

Henry Le Mew was, in fact, a bit of a dictator. He tolerated Julie's canine companion, but barely. If he could get in a swipe of his massive paw, he would; though in deference to the family peace he rarely drew blood. Henry was one of those particularly intelligent cats; he knew how to get what he wanted, even if it meant learning—yes, learning—how to wrap his giant paw around a cabinet knob and pull. Witnessing this one afternoon, Steve had decided to put a lock on the cabinet in which Henry's food was kept. This had not gone over well with Henry; he'd refused to meet Steve's eye for a week.

Anyone observing Steve sitting in his kitchen that night would have noted that he looked like a man who had paid a price. He had a thin, careworn face and his shoulders were slightly stooped. Both physical traits were proof of years of slavish devotion to his law practice; unlike his wife, he looked older than his years, though according to his doctor, he was in robust health.

As was true of many men of his generation, he was not as obviously close to his children as his wife was; most of his days and many of his nights had been spent at the office while Julie had been at home with their brood. But Steve loved his family dearly and considered his children his greatest achievement. Well, his and Julie's greatest achievement.

An important part of his job as father was the dispensing of advice, a job he took very seriously. He considered it a responsibility as well as an honor. It might have been a habit formed from years of practicing law; people paid for his advice and had a right to expect it to be valuable. So both at the office and at home, Steve's words were considered and kind. This habit had no doubt helped build decent relationships with each of his four children.

In fact, the only familial relationship that troubled him was the one he had with his third child, Rebecca, or Becca, as she'd asked to be called after her twelfth birthday. In the past few years she had become increasingly distant and, at times, combative or cold. And earlier that evening, before retiring to her room, she'd been barely civil to him, refusing to meet his eye even once. Steve suspected he knew the reason behind her behavior and it worried him that Becca might be regretting the decision he and other members of the family had made for her when she was a shattered, pregnant sixteen-year-old.

Nora came into the kitchen for a cup of tea, interrupting Steve's troubled thoughts. She raised her eyebrow at her son and the feline on his lap.

"I see you're helping Julie with the dishes," she said.

Steve shrugged. "What can I say? He demanded I sit."

Steve's relationship with his mother had always been good, uncorrupted by dark resentments or Freudian jealousies. The fact that his wife and mother got along so famously was, in his mind, nothing short of a miracle. It certainly made their current living situation more than tolerable, even pleasant, for which he was very, very thankful. Over the years he'd heard horror stories from colleagues who lived with a spouse and parent or parent-in-law; at times he felt almost guilty in admitting his own happy situation.

As an only child, born when his mother was about twenty, Steve might have been overly pampered, but he hadn't been. It wasn't Nora's style to send a child out into the world ill prepared for some cold hard facts of life, like failure and competition and injustice. She hadn't been unnecessarily harsh with her only child, just fair, thus preventing Steve from becoming an insufferably spoiled man-child, unfit for career, marriage, and fatherhood.

"If only all men were so easily commanded," Nora remarked now, giving Henry an amused look. Unbidden, an image of her late husband came to mind. Oddly, she saw him in his fishing gear, waders and all. Now, there was a man who was not easily swayed by anyone, man or beast. Or, in Thomas's case, fish. He'd never been one for pets, especially the kind that shed. He'd claimed he had allergies, but Nora had always suspected he simply didn't care for animals underfoot. Steve's pleas for a puppy or kitten had met with disapproval; the moment he had gone off to college, Steve adopted his first shelter cat.

Nora and Thomas had been high school sweethearts; they married the summer after graduation. With virtually no money but a lot of love—and, of course, the natural energy and optimism of youth— they scratched together enough money so that within three years of the wedding, Thomas was able to enroll in the local community college. After earning a degree in accounting, Thomas found a job with a small local accounting firm. As it had grown, so had

Thomas's position there and by the time he retired, he owned a decent share in the company's future.

Nora had been a homemaker primarily, though around the time of her son's fifth birthday, when he began to need her less exclusively, she began to take secretarial jobs, most notably at the local parish house and later at the family-run pharmacy in town. She was smart and good with numbers. More importantly, she was good with people, which made her invaluable to her more difficult employers. Nora would never forget Father Roger and his eccentric demands for Peeps with his morning coffee and pens with green ink. Every other secretary the parish house had hired quit within weeks. But Nora, amused rather than annoyed by the old priest's habits, had lasted in the job for seven years.

The years of the Rowans' long marriage had passed largely without misfortune—at least, without unusual misfortune. And then, in his early sixties, Thomas had been diagnosed with pancreatic cancer. He died of the disease just months before the birth of his youngest grandchild, Lily.

The struggle had been short but intense; he'd spent his final days in hospice, with Nora by his side, relieved by Steve or Julie only when the need for sleep overcame her desire to keep vigil.

The older grandchildren remembered their grandfather with fondness. He'd taken them fishing and for ice cream; he'd taught them how to annoy their parents by sticking their fingers in the pudding bowl and making silly noises with their armpits. And he always had a pocket of loose change ready to dole out. In short, he'd been the perfect grandfather, offering guidance in the form of fun and companionship. Everyone missed him, but mostly, of course, his wife.

Those first years as a widow had been terribly difficult for Nora. She was still relatively young, in her sixties, and Thomas had been her one and only love. She had never lived alone and though she'd been involved along with her husband in making the important decisions for their family, she was used to working as part of a team. Thankfully, due to the couple's careful spending and even more careful savings, Nora was in fine financial shape; that was one less worry in a life that suddenly seemed fraught and, even, at times, terrifying.

Grief was something that, until her husband's untimely death, Nora had never known. At least, the kind of grief that came with the mourning of something or somebody lost forever. Nora had survived drastic change before, but not change of this magnitude. Her friends were as supportive as they could be; her son and his wife did whatever they could to help Nora meet the challenges of widowhood. But in the end only time, and a personal journey through all the stages of mourning, helped. Nora grew through the pain and into acceptance. She felt lucky to have done so. She knew that not everyone survived the loss of a beloved spouse or partner.

Now, twenty years after Thomas's death, Nora found herself in relatively good health, aside from a few of the typical complaints of old age, like achy, creaky joints and a diminished ability to eat the spicy foods she'd once loved. She'd had cataract surgery in her early seventies, the only surgery she'd ever needed, though in her fifties a podiatrist had tried to persuade her to have bunion surgery. Nora had stood firm—if a bit painfully—and put aside her heels in favor of more comfortable shoes. No one, she declared, was taking a knife to her unless it was a matter of life and death. Or eyesight. Vanity, she could sacrifice, though truth be told, taking her beloved three-inch heels to the local thrift shop had hurt worse than the bunions.

All in all, Nora was enjoying her life—her "twilight years," as some called them, though the term made Nora think of people stumbling through life in a zombielike fashion and she preferred to be bright-eyed and decidedly awake—in the house she and Thomas had bought so many years before. When Steve and Julie had retired there, Nora relinquished the largest bedroom, the one she and Thomas had used, in favor of a smaller room on the first floor. She rarely ventured to the second floor, there being no real reason to since Julie took care of the bulk of the housekeeping, but had easy access to the living room, dining room, den, and kitchen. As with many people her age, Nora was in the habit of waking early. She had always hated to feel useless—being not-needed was something akin to a sin in her mind—so she'd taken it upon herself to make the morning coffee for Julie and Steve. Nora preferred tea, English or Irish Breakfast, without milk or sugar. She was almost boasting when she swore she'd never tasted a sip of coffee in her entire life.

Nora had no desire to be "in the way" and with one notable exception had consistently refrained from voicing her opinions about matters not directly related to her. In this way, according to Julie, she'd been the perfect mother-in-law. And as a grandmother, she'd been wonderful to all four children, though she had a special fondness for Lily, a fondness that she had never bothered to hide.

Julie turned from the sink with a sigh. "Well," she said, folding a dish towel, "that's all done. I think I'll head on up to bed." Discerning her intention, Hank came to her side.

"I'll be up early tomorrow to start the coffee and breakfast," Nora assured her.

"And as soon as Henry gets bored with sitting on my lap, I'll be up to bed," Steve promised.

Julie met her mother-in-law's eyes and the two women laughed. "I'll see you in the morning, then," Julie said.

The women, accompanied by Hank, left the kitchen, leaving their favorite man sitting contentedly with his best and furriest friend.

7

Thursday, December 21

Becca sat on the edge of the couch, fully dressed in wool slacks, a Thinsulate T-shirt, a silk blouse, and a cashmere cardigan. She was hungry, and in desperate need of coffee, but not yet ready to join the other Rowans.

One was told by mawkish television commercials and sappy greeting cards—and Becca would know all about mawkish and sappy, being in advertising—that being in the bosom of one's family, especially at Christmastime, should be comforting, but Becca was feeling anything but comforted. So far, every moment she had spent under the roof of her family's house had been tainted by the secret she held from them. Everything was—wrong.

Absolutely everything her parents had done or said since her arrival the night before had gotten on her nerves, even completely innocuous things like her father using his pocket handkerchief to wipe his glasses—really, who used a pocket handkerchief anymore!—and her mother pretending to be the sweet, absentminded old lady. And that stupid braid!

Becca checked her watch. Time was passing, but she wasn't quite ready to emerge. So she imagined what was going on in other parts of the house while she hid in the den. Her mother would already have taken a long walk with her dog, a big hairy beast she'd adopted about three years ago. Becca experienced a dim and only vaguely acknowledged sense of jealousy whenever she saw her mother catering to Hank. He was the youngest child and, with everyone else all grown and gone, the focus of much love and attention.

Her father, she knew, would have fed his monstrously hairy cat, Henry Le Mew, first thing that morning, before coffee or toothbrushing or toast. Steve explained—unabashedly—that Henry would have it no other way, and besides, the cat needed to have something in his stomach before his twice-daily insulin injections.

Becca herself couldn't be called an animal person. She thought it slightly crazy that whenever it was time for a checkup, her father loaded his protesting cat into his carrier and drove all the way down to a vet in Portland. Steve loved living the rural life, he said, as long as he had access to big-city medical people for Henry. What he wouldn't do for that cat . . .

Becca's mother, who was a far more relaxed person than her husband about pretty much everything, found the local vet, who dealt routinely with everything from horses to pigs to chickens, perfectly acceptable for her Hank. Plus, he was far less expensive than Henry Le Mew's doctor. Julie wanted everyone to know that she loved to save money wherever she could.

At the same time that Becca admired this trait of her mother's, she also found it incredibly annoying. Come on! How expensive could a box of plastic storage bags possibly be! To Becca's mind, reusing plastic bags that had once contained food was way beyond reason. Had her mother never heard of food poisoning?

Becca sighed and checked her watch. It was almost eight-thirty. She hoped her father had already gone to his studio, cat by his side. She got the feeling that Henry Le Mew—really, what a ridiculous name!—didn't much care for her. More than once she'd caught him giving her what could only be termed a malevolent yellow-eyed stare. And she didn't think she was being in the least bit paranoid.

Becca lingered another few minutes in the den until the desire for coffee became too strong to resist. Besides, she couldn't very well avoid the Rowan clan all day. She had come to this house with a purpose. She left the den, shutting the door behind her.

On her way to the kitchen, she encountered one of the twins. He was poking at the pasted-on fuzzy beard of one of the many wooden Santa Claus statues that filled the house. *Think,* she told herself. *You should know the difference between them by now. This one is—*

"Hi, Malcolm," she said.

"I'm Michael." He continued to poke at the Santa.

Becca cringed. She was glad David hadn't witnessed her slip. It wasn't the first time she'd confused her nephews and she was pretty sure it wouldn't be the last. Becca was aware that she was the only one in the family who regularly confounded the boys' identities, and she did try to differentiate them, really. For God's sake, they weren't even identical; it shouldn't have been hard to keep them straight. But she just didn't seem able to do it. Something about not paying close enough attention, she supposed.

"Oh. Right," she said, walking on. "Sorry, Michael."

Becca came into the kitchen. David, Naomi, Lily, and Nora were seated at the table. Her father had indeed already gone to his studio. Perfect. Now she wouldn't have to work to avoid him before coffee. She walked directly to the counter on which the coffee-maker sat, hoping the brew wasn't the usual weak blend her parents favored and knowing that it probably was. Some things never changed, and they always seemed to be the ones you really wished would.

Julie came from the sink, where she had been rinsing a plate, and launched what Becca thought of as her first assault of the holiday.

"You've been almost like a stranger this past year," she said, pouring coffee into a mug for her daughter. Naomi had made the mug for Julie's birthday the year before; it was decorated with the profile of a Chinook dog like Hank. Becca thought it was ridiculous. "Your father and I haven't seen you since . . . well, since last Christmas! Is everything all right, Becca? I mean, aside from . . ."

"Aside from what?" Becca was further annoyed by the meaningfully lowered voice, the trailing off of words. She held her mother's gaze steadily.

"Oh, I don't know, stress at work?"

Becca wasn't at all sure her mother understood the nature of her job as vice president of a business-to-business advertising firm. "Work is fine," she said. "And of course everything is all right. Why shouldn't it be? I've just been very busy. Did I tell you I almost single-handedly landed the Loring account? You know that's a biotech company, the fastest-growing in the business. They've got beautiful offices in Cambridge. The Loring account is the biggest account our firm has ever had."

"Really?" Julie said. "That's wonderful, dear."

In spite of her words to the contrary, Becca didn't think that her mother sounded very impressed. "Yes," she said with emphasis, "it is wonderful. I worked very hard to land the account. I don't think I was in bed before midnight for over three months. But it was worth it in the end. This is going to be excellent for the company."

"That's nice." Julie toyed with the tip of her braid; Becca wanted to rip the braid out of her mother's head. "Tell me, Becca. Do you have any time for fun? When was the last time you had a vacation, a real vacation, not a weekend visiting your brother and Naomi?"

"And Rain."

"Of course. But a woman your age must want something more out of life than spending time with her family."

And there it was, the old theme. When are you going to meet a nice man and get married? Have another child? Start working part-time and being a soccer mom in your off hours? All work and no play serves only to make Becca a dull daughter. "I'm fine, Mom," Becca said, her voice tight. "Leave it alone."

"Some adventure," she went on, ignoring her daughter's command, "maybe a trip to Europe, or a romance. Have you tried any of those dating services I see advertised on television? Those couples seem awfully happy. It's all about compatibility, you know. I read an article the other day about the success rate of—"

"Mom!" Becca shot a glance at the family members at the table. No one seemed to be paying her any attention. She turned back to her mother and in a lower voice said, "Enough. If you're going to grill me on my personal life every time we're within ten feet of each other I—"

"Yes, dear?" Julie said with eyes wide and maddeningly calm. "You what?"

Becca hesitated. She could threaten never again

to visit, but after what she had to say to the family this holiday, she might never again be invited to visit.

"I need my coffee," she said and took a seat at the kitchen table.

Becca couldn't help but feel like a wolf in sheep's clothing. Everyone around her was ignorant of what was about to befall the Rowan family. Not one of them could possibly guess that the holiday would not be an ordinary one. No doubt they were expecting, even looking forward to, decorating the large evergreen in the corner of the living room, and going to church on Christmas Eve, and the revelations of the Secret Santa exchange on Christmas morning.

Though still resolved in her intentions, Becca again felt nervous, as she had the previous night at dinner. It was one thing to make a resolution in the safety of her own home back in Boston, in her neat and orderly South End condo, but when faced with the very people whose lives she was about to interrupt . . . Well, that was quite another thing.

Becca reached deep down for the store of courage she believed she possessed—and didn't find much there. Maybe the weak coffee was to blame. Next time, if there were a next time, she would remember to bring a bag of the strong blend she usually consumed by the potful.

"Where's Rain?" she asked, aiming for a casual tone and afraid she'd betrayed some of her anxiety.

"Sleeping late." Naomi laughed. "It's no surprise. When I was sixteen I slept late any chance I could get."

Becca bristled. What did Naomi's childhood habits have to do with Rain's? They weren't even related, by blood anyway. Becca might have been having trouble finding the courage to forge ahead with her decision to tell Rain the truth about her parentage, but she was having no trouble at all finding a huge store of resentment. Resentment would give her the guts to see things through. Resentment was underrated as a motivator.

Lily was toying with a piece of toast. Becca restrained herself from snapping at her sister. She wanted to tell her to eat the stupid piece of toast or throw it in the garbage. It really wasn't like Becca to be so short-tempered with someone who'd never done her harm. She blamed her bad mood on the earlier confrontation with her mother. And on the lousy coffee. Why not?

Clearly, her younger sister was bothered by something, but even if Becca had wanted to ask her what was wrong and to offer help, she really didn't know how. Only once had the sisters come anywhere near intimacy and that was when at eighteen, Lily had learned the truth of Rain's birth. Lily had approached Becca, wanting to offer sympathy and needing to talk through such shocking news, but Becca had rejected Lily's attempts at communication. Lily hadn't tried again.

"Do you want some jam for that toast?" Becca blurted.

Lily startled at her sister's voice. "Uh, no," she said. "Thanks."

Well, at least she had tried. Becca turned her attention to more important matters, like wondering if she had even one ally in the family, one person who would support her decision to reveal herself now as Rain's biological mother. She doubted that she had.

She took another look around the table. David was engrossed in the local paper. David, she knew without a doubt, would be hostile to the idea. Naomi would, as well. She might look like a warm and fuzzy pushover with her pale hair and big blue eyes and cozily rounded figure, but her looks were deceiving. Becca had seen her face down her husband when others had backed away, intimidated by David's occasional arrogance.

What about Olivia, who presumably was arriving later that day? Becca certainly couldn't expect support from her. They'd never been close, and increasingly, Becca sensed from Olivia a feeling of envy, though what she might envy about her younger sister, Becca didn't know. Could Olivia be jealous of her sister's successful career? Maybe, but she and James had a pretty good business of their own. It was a puzzle, and one Becca didn't really care to solve.

"Hey, everyone, listen to this."

David began to read aloud an inspiring bit from the paper about local siblings, a brother and sister, who together had raised one thousand dollars for the care of one of their schoolmates who'd been stricken with cancer. Suddenly, the story brought to Becca's mind a memory of a time when she was probably about seven and David a young teen. She remembered that she'd entered a Halloween poster contest at school. She didn't quite remember why she'd entered the contest; she'd never been artistic. Probably she'd wanted the recognition of winning; that seemed a likely motive. Anyway, the night before the contest deadline, she'd sat facing an empty square of poster board, completely stumped, not one idea of what to do with the tubes of orange and silver glitter and black construction paper her mother had bought her at the craft store. And David had come to the rescue. She hadn't won a prize, but at least she'd shown up with an entry, thanks to her brother's skill with scissors, paste, and glitter.

How close she and David had once been, in spite of the six-year age difference!

Becca frowned down at her silly dog-cup of weak coffee. She knew she had to close her mind to the past, lest sentimentality weaken her resolve. Sentimentality wasn't for people like her, people who had known fear and sacrifice so young. Sentimentality was as dangerous as its troublemaking cohort, nostalgia.

There was a knock on the kitchen door, and a moment later a large man appeared by the table.

"Good morning, Julie, Nora. Everyone."

Becca looked at the visitor without much interest. It was . . . She struggled for a moment to recall the man's name. Yes. Alex. Alex . . . Mason. Becca realized she'd almost entirely forgotten about her parents' nearest neighbor out here in the wilds.

"Becca," Julie was saying, "how long has it been since you've seen Alex?"

She looked back to the bowl of cereal her mother had placed before her, unasked. It was probably some almost inedible "health" stuff that was actually packed with unnecessary calories. "I imagine it's been since my last visit," she said.

"Yes. Of course."

"Alex stacked all of our wood this year," Nora informed the family. "We have enough for fires all winter. Wasn't that nice of him?"

"Well, I don't how nice it was of me," the man replied. "I did have a motivation other than kindness. I stack the Rowans' wood, and Nora and Julie feed me whenever I forget to cook for myself, which is just about every other day."

David laughed. "I'd say you got the better end of the deal."

"Oh, yeah. And speaking of which . . ." Alex turned to Nora. "There wouldn't happen to be any of your famous cinnamon rolls left over from dinner, would there?"

"Nope!" David crowed. "I'm proud to say I ate the last one."

"That's what you think, David." Nora walked to the cabinet over the toaster, reached deep inside, and pulled out a plastic bag containing two cinnamon rolls.

"Grandma, you were holding out on me!"

Becca thought her brother looked genuinely upset. If losing out on a few balls of sugary dough upset him, how was he going to feel about her announcement? Not good, that's how.

Alex kissed Nora's cheek and accepted the bag. "Sorry, David. And thanks again, Nora. I'll eat these on my way to Steve's studio. See you all later. Becca, it was nice seeing you again."

Becca had heard her name. "Excuse me?" she said, looking up.

Alex smiled. She noted that his eyes were very blue and piercing. "I just said good-bye."

"Oh," she said, turning away from those eyes. " 'Bye."

8

"Did I tell you I'd already bought Cliff's Christmas gift? It was a week before I found out—what he had done."

Nora didn't look up from the dough she was mixing in a blue ceramic bowl that had belonged to her mother. "No," she said. "You didn't. I hope it was returnable."

Lily and Nora were alone in the kitchen, baking the second of what would no doubt be many, many batches of holiday cookies. Lily set down a measured amount of flour for her grandmother to add slowly to the mixture.

"I got him a RiskRunner. It's a handheld gambling machine, basically. You can play poker or the slot machines, pretty much everything they have in casinos. Roulette, too, I think. Cliff's into gambling now." Lily paused. "At least, he was when I last talked to him."

"This—contraption—sounds expensive." And, Nora thought, the young man clearly hadn't been worth the time, effort, or expenditure. He was into gambling? Did her granddaughter not find something problematic about that?

"I know," Lily admitted. "It was expensive, at least for me. I probably shouldn't have spent so much money. But I thought he would really like it, so . . ."

"I hope you've returned this thing."

"Well, not yet."

Had she taught her favorite grandchild nothing? Nora stopped stirring—her fingers were cramping a bit anyway—and put her free hand on her hip. "Lily, if I learn that you gave that boy the Lose Your Shirt on the Ponies or whatever it's called in some ill-advised attempt to win him back, I'll give you a talking-to the likes of which you've never heard from my mouth."

Lily smiled, but the thought of such a major reprimand scared her. Nora could be formidable. "I'll return it first thing when I get back to Boston. I promise."

"And if you two do get back together, it's that young man who will be buying you expensive presents for some time to come."

"Yes, Grandma."

Nora turned back to her work, but Lily's thoughts were still fixed on her former boyfriend and how he was supposed to have spent the holiday with the Rowan family. From there her mind latched on to the fact—she thought it was a fact—that Becca had never brought anyone home for Christmas or for any other special occasion. Not even a girlfriend.

Lily asked her grandmother to confirm this. She did.

"In fact," Nora said, "I don't think I've ever heard Becca mention a close friend. Which, of course, doesn't mean that she doesn't have any friends. Becca's been somewhat—private—since . . ." Nora glanced toward the door, then lowered her voice. "Since she was six-teen."

Lily watched Nora deftly, and with one hand, crack an egg into the blue ceramic bowl. Lily liked to eat baked goods, but she didn't have her grand-mother's skill at making them. Maybe if she watched closely, her own skills would develop in time. Then again, maybe they wouldn't. As long as there was someone around to bake cakes and cookies for her, Lily thought she'd be just fine. Cliff, she noted, was not a baker. Come to think of it, she wasn't sure he had any culinary taste or talent whatsoever. His diet consisted mostly of soda and processed foods. He liked Sno Balls, those pink and white things that came two in a package. And, when visiting the Rowans' house, Nora's cinnamon rolls.

"Will you hand me that wooden spoon?"

Shaken out of her reverie, Lily handed Nora the spoon and asked, "Grandma, do you think Becca seems kind of weird this holiday?"

The dough ready, Nora began to shape small balls of it and drop them onto a greased cookie sheet. "I'd prefer to use the term 'troubled,' " she said. "But yes, something is going on with her. When she was a child she was never good at hiding anything, feelings, little lies. She was the proverbial open book. I haven't seen that part of her—the transparency—in a very long time."

Michael and Malcolm charged into the kitchen, interrupting the women's conversation. Lily won-dered if they ever did anything at normal speed.

"Are the cookies ready yet?" they chorused.

Lily looked at the fraternal twins, Malcolm so like Naomi, blond and of medium height and build, Michael brown-haired and lanky like his father.

"The first batch is over there. They're still hot so don't—"

"Ow!"

Lily smiled and wondered what part of "don't" little boys didn't understand. Well, big boys, too. Cliff hadn't understood the meaning of "don't cheat on your girlfriend."

"I told you they were hot," Nora said mildly. "Patience pays off, Michael."

"What?"

"Never mind." Nora used the spatula to slide a few cookies onto a plate and handed it to Malcolm. "Here, take these but wait a few minutes before you try to eat them."

With shouts of thanks the boys were off.

"Grandma," Lily asked then, watching her nephews go, "did you ever want more children? Maybe a daughter?"

"Oh, yes. Your grandfather and I would have welcomed a large family, but it just wasn't to be. Anyway, I've got all these grandchildren and great-grandchildren to care for. And to spoil, when I'm in the mood. My life certainly isn't lacking in family."

"You know, Cliff and I talked about having children someday."

"Yes," Nora said with feigned patience. "You mentioned that."

Lily sighed. "Everything reminds me of him, Grandma. I can't listen to the radio because I might hear one of 'our' songs. I can't walk past his dorm without imagining him in his room, with all the posters of those eighties bands he loves. I can't even eat peanut butter anymore because Cliff loved it so much. Some days I don't think I'll ever get over him."

Nora felt slight annoyance with her granddaughter's

dramatic statements, but the annoyance was tempered with pity. Poor Lily really did believe that her romantic life was over forever. And Nora knew that it would do little if any good to tell Lily otherwise, to assure her that, yes, she would get over this heartbreak and probably a lot sooner than later. In Nora's experience, the miserable didn't like to be assured that their misery would come to an end. Misery was real and of the moment; what would come after that was intangible and of no immediate comfort.

Nora turned at the sound of nails clacking on wood. It was Hank, coming for a nibble at his bowl.

Lily sighed. "Cliff loves dogs. Did I tell you we talked about getting a dog after graduation? He's never had a dog and he wasn't thrilled about having to pick up the poop, but he really wanted one, anyway."

Nora rolled her eyes behind her granddaughter's back and then remonstrated with herself. She had been young once, too. It was essential to remember that. It was essential to be kind. Too many people forgot that.

There was a knock at the kitchen door. Hank, not much interested in guard duty, turned and clicked out of the room.

It was Mr. Pollen. Nora thought he could be anywhere from sixty to eighty years old. He lived in what amounted to little more than a rude cabin off a minor back road and what he did for a living—or what he had done in his younger years—she didn't know. Nobody did. Some in town said he survived entirely on the land and by his own wits, with a little help from a shotgun. Others said that back in the fifties, during the Cold War, he'd stockpiled enough canned goods to last him until the middle of the twenty-first century. Whatever the truth, Mr. Pollen was a bit of a local legend, the source of all kinds of rumors and strange stories. And whenever he was seen, which wasn't often and always at random times, some new tale would emerge, full-blown from the head of a local with a creative brainstorm.

"I've brought you a Christmas present," Mr. Pollen said, handing Nora a brown—thing.

His ill-fitting false teeth smacked loudly against his shriveled gums. Lily unconsciously took a step back, as if she were afraid the teeth would come flying out of his mouth and clamp on to her face.

"How—nice," Nora replied. "What is it, exactly? I'm afraid I don't have my glasses handy. . . ."

"It's a nut bowl." The man beamed. He was obviously proud of his creation.

"A bowl for nuts," Nora repeated. "And it's made of pinecones. Well. How—original."

"Oh, you can do just about anything with pinecones!" Mr. Pollen said with great enthusiasm. "In fact, I'm building myself a whole chest of drawers made of pinecones!"

"You don't say? Did you hear that, Lily? A chest of drawers."

Lily could only nod. If she dared to open her mouth, she just knew she'd collapse with laughter.

"Well," Nora said, easing Mr. Pollen toward the kitchen door, "thank you for the lovely gift. And good luck with your project."

Mr. Pollen was almost out into the cold when he turned back. "I could make you a chest of drawers, too. Really, it would be no problem."

"Well, that's a very kind offer, but I'm afraid we're all set with our chests. Of drawers. Thank you, anyway."

Nora began to close the door on their guest, slowly but firmly.

"All right, then," he said, "I'll be on my way. Merry Christmas to you all!"

When he was gone, Nora sat the pinecone nut bowl on the table. She thought it looked like some massive growth, like something a doctor might remove from a diseased body and then send on to a top-secret lab for further intensive study. She couldn't help but shudder and wipe her hands down her apron.

Lily stood next to her grandmother.

"Oh. My. God. What are we going to do with that thing? It's disgusting!"

"Yes, it is, isn't it?"

"I half expected him to pull out an axe and chop us both to bits!"

Nora reached for a dishcloth and draped it over Mr. Pollen's gift. "Oh, Mr. Pollen is harmless," she said. "Crazy, but harmless. Now his wife, may she rest in peace, she was the one you had to watch out for."

Lily laughed. "Oh, tell me what she was like!"

Nora, too, began to laugh. "Well, locals called her Flying Hammer Hattie. That should tell you all you need to know. When her temper was up, you'd do best to duck."

"What's so funny?"

Becca stood in the doorway to the kitchen, frowning.

Lily wiped tears of laughter from her eyes and turned toward her sister. "Oh, hey, Becca."

"Hey."

Becca's awkwardness was palpable. Nora had the feeling that Becca thought they had been laughing at her.

"How about a cup of coffee?" she offered briskly. "Or one of these oatmeal raisin cookies. They're fresh out of the oven. The twins seemed to like them.

Then again, eight-year-old boys aren't particularly fussy about cookies, are they?"

Becca took a small step back. "No, thanks, Grandma. I've got to check in with my office."

How, Nora wondered, did drinking a cup of coffee or eating a cookie interfere with checking in with one's office? Didn't everyone these days multitask? Or had she missed some recent change in the social order?

"But I thought nobody really does any work in the days before Christmas." Lily took one of the cookies from the plate her grandmother offered.

"I'm not nobody," Becca snapped.

There was a decidedly awkward silence, which Nora took it upon herself to break.

"Of course not, dear. Nobody meant to imply any such thing."

"Yes. Well, I'd better go."

And she did.

"Oh, yeah," Lily said, reaching for another cookie. "Definitely something weird."

9

Olivia and James arrived at the Rowan house at about four that afternoon. It was already quite dark and, being December in Maine, quite cold. Becca, in the front hall with the others, shivered when Julie opened the door, and stepped back farther into the house.

Immediately, and in spite of being absorbed with her own emotionally fraught situation, Becca noted an air of tension between her sister and brother-in-law. And she figured if she could sense it, then pretty much everyone else could, too. Well, maybe not David. David was always all about David. You could fall down in front of him and he'd walk right over your body, his attention caught by something more important to him, like a cinnamon roll or someone dropping garbage in the recycling bin.

James Moody was of middling height and build. While he'd put on a few pounds over the years, and while his hair had gone prematurely silver, he was, most people thought, still a handsome man. Part of his attractiveness, Becca thought now, watching him greet his in-laws, was his seemingly complete lack of pretension or guile.

Becca shifted her attention to her older sister, Olivia Rowan-Moody. At the moment, she was giving her mother a hug while simultaneously ordering James to do something with her bag. Olivia didn't have the long and lean frame shared by Steve, Becca, Rain, and to a lesser extent, David. Like her mother and youngest sister, Olivia was of medium height and middling weight. Her hair was a light shade of brown; Becca couldn't help but note that it was now streaked quite liberally with gray. Where Olivia had gotten her dark blue eyes was anyone's guess. They weren't the "Rowan eyes," but neither were they the cow brown Julie and Lily shared. Becca tried to remember if her grandfather had had blue eyes, but she couldn't summon a clear enough picture in her mind. That, she realized, was something she wouldn't like to admit to her family. They already thought her self-centered enough.

James came over to Becca now and they shared a brief hug. "You're looking well, Becca," he said.

Becca smiled at him. "You, too, James," she lied. In fact, she'd never seen him look so unhappy.

Somehow, Olivia managed to avoid an official greeting with her younger sister. Becca wasn't sure how she pulled it off but she had, and Becca didn't feel in the least slighted.

Julie ushered Olivia and James off to the Queen Anne's Lace Room while Nora, with Lily's and Naomi's help, finished preparing dinner. Aware that she, too, should be helping in the kitchen, but not feeling overly guilty about her dereliction of duty, Becca chose instead to join Rain in the living room, where she was entertaining her brothers by gustily singing the theme song from SpongeBob Square-

Pants. Becca had caught the show once, by accident. She'd liked it but would never admit that to her family.

Dinner was at seven that evening. The Rowans gathered at the big table, complete now since the arrival of Olivia and James. Becca had little appetite, but to excuse herself from dinner would be disastrous for her plan. She wanted to catch her family off guard. She wanted them to feel as bad as she felt. So she sat at the table and pretended that all was well.

Julie came to the table, carrying a massive platter on which sat a large roast surrounded by sliced potatoes, carrots, and parsnips.

"Ah, the perfect roast beef!" David rubbed his hands in a gesture of appreciation and anticipation.

Nora brought in a large bowl of mashed potatoes; Becca spied several large squares of butter melting on top. Red meat, slabs of butter. She was sure she'd have cholesterol poisoning, if there were such a thing, by the time she got back to Boston. She'd call her trainer first thing in the morning and schedule a few additional sessions with him. And she'd go on a strict diet of low-fat foods for a few weeks. The last thing she wanted was to have to rely on medication to manage a situation a little self-control and willpower could handle.

"May I have the gravy?" Olivia asked.

Julie passed a large, silver-plated gravy boat to her daughter. Olivia stared at the object, then looked at her mother, puzzled. "I don't remember this gravy boat. Whose was it? Where did it come from?"

"You know, I don't quite remember," Julie said. "I haven't used it in ages. It might have belonged to my mother's sister, Agnes. Or maybe it was her aunt Clara's. No—"

"How can you not know for sure?" Olivia demanded. "Didn't you make a note when it came to you? Mom, I've told you it's irresponsible not to keep records of the family heirlooms. Do you even remember when you got it?"

"Well," Julie said, unruffled, "I'm not sure I'd call it an heirloom, Liv. I certainly don't think it's worth any money."

Rain shrugged. "I wouldn't buy it. I think it's kind of ugly."

"God, Mom," Olivia went on, "it's not about the money, it's about the sentimental value. It's about honoring all the people who've used that gravy boat down through the years. It's about family and the meals they've shared."

Under his breath David said, "*The Chronicles of the Gravy Boat,* coming soon to a theatre near you." Becca forced herself not to smile.

"Well, I'm sorry, dear, but I just don't remember where it came from."

Olivia flushed. Becca hoped her sister wasn't going to have a stroke at the dinner table. Her rabid interest in a tarnished piece of junk didn't seem like a sign of good health and well-being. Becca could understand getting riled up about politics or religion. But to have a heart attack over antiques seemed a complete waste of time.

"It's only a gravy boat, Liv," David said aloud. "Not the crown jewels."

James put his hand gently on Olivia's arm, as if to calm or comfort her, but she shook it off.

Steve had been silent during this heated exchange. Well, heated on Olivia's side. His wife had remained unperturbed. It was Steve's policy not to get involved in disputes between his wife and their children. Julie knew how to handle herself. He felt he'd only be in the way.

Nora now changed the subject. She was talking about an ordinance that had passed in the summer, something having to do with the garbage dump. And about a new restaurant that had opened in the next town over, a classic diner type of place. Her friend Emily had gone there with her daughter and had told Nora they served the best chicken salad sandwich in the state. Or maybe it was tuna salad. Nora laughed and admitted that her short-term memory wasn't what it used to be.

Becca only half listened. She was trying to "act normal," but the enormity of what she needed to discuss with her family weighed heavily on her. She picked at her food, strangely repulsed by the sight of it, and realized she had already drunk a bit too much wine. Casually, she slid her wineglass out of easy reach.

Finally, the interminable dinner was over. Naomi went off to coax the twins to bed; she was back within half an hour with the news that a day playing in the snow had knocked the boys right out.

Becca listened with relief as Rain announced that she and Lily were going upstairs to watch a DVD. She didn't care if Lily missed the family meeting she was about to call, but she had been concerned about getting—and keeping—Rain safely away.

"What are you going to watch?" Naomi asked.

"*Juno*," Rain replied.

And if that wasn't a coincidence, Becca thought, then what was?

David raised his eyebrows. "Again? How many times have you seen that movie?"

"Three. This will be the fourth. Come on, Lily."

The two young women went upstairs to Lily's room. When she was sure they were out of earshot— she heard a bedroom door slam—Becca seized her moment.

"I'd like to talk to everyone," she blurted.

Julie added a final dirty plate to the stack at the end of the table. "Is anything the matter, honey?" she asked.

Yes. Everything. "No, nothing's the matter. I just need to talk to everyone about something very important."

Becca saw her father blanch. Good, she thought. He should be afraid. He should be made to acknowledge the pain that he caused.

"Can it wait until I clean up a bit?" Julie asked, lifting the empty bowl that had once been full of mashed potatoes.

"No, I'd prefer to do it now. In the living room."

Julie put the bowl back on the dining room table.

"Well, then," Nora said briskly, "let's get to it."

10

"So," Becca concluded, "the sooner I tell her that I'm her birth mother, the better things will be." Becca sat with her back straight, hands firmly planted on her knees. There. She had said it. She had announced her intentions.

The Rowans were in the living room, Nora in her favorite armchair and the others ranged around on the couch and in various chairs. Becca had moved hers a bit apart from the others in an unconscious gesture of avoidance, or maybe even of fear.

Her brother, predictably, was the first to speak. "Excuse me," he said, loudly and with a rough laugh, "but I don't see it that way at all!"

Becca was ready for her opponent, which was how she viewed every member of the family in that room. "I'm sorry," she said, "that you don't agree with me. But I've given this a lot of thought, David."

"I don't think you have," he retorted. "This is crazy."

Olivia's expression was cold and hard. "You're out of your mind, Becca."

Julie frowned at her oldest child, then she turned to Becca. "Becca, dear, we agreed that when Rain turns twenty-one we'd discuss whether or not to tell her the truth about her birth. We agreed to talk about her level of emotional and mental maturity. We agreed to assess the risks. But not before then. Certainly, not when she's only sixteen. She's still so young."

"Sixteen is not so young, Mom," Becca argued. "Not these days. The popular culture in which kids are raised today—"

David cut her off. "Why are you doing this?" he demanded. "Are you sick or something? No, seriously, are you dying? Is this your crazy dying wish? Because if it is, I need the name of your shrink right away."

"Of course I'm not dying. I'm perfectly fine. I'm in excellent health, physical and mental. I'm in perfect condition to take care of my child."

Finally, her father spoke. "But as your mother said, we had an agreement." To Becca, he sounded utterly bewildered. Well, she would attempt to make things perfectly clear.

"Not a legally binding agreement," she pointed out. "And we all know that even insignificant things like rules and regulations and promises can always be ignored when necessary." Becca looked pointedly at her father. "Right, Dad? You were the chief architect of the plan to pass off Rain as David and Naomi's daughter. You know all about breaking things. And you know all about lying."

Steve didn't answer. Maybe he couldn't. His wife took his hand.

"Becca," Nora murmured, "that's unfair."

"Is it? Look, I want to be more to Rain than her aunt. I deserve to be more to her."

David shot to his feet. Becca couldn't help but

flinch. "I'm not sure you deserve anything other than a good thrashing. I'm totally shocked that you would even consider disrupting Rain's life in such a—in such a brutal way. Your own daughter."

"David," Naomi murmured.

He sat down again heavily, reluctantly.

"The only reason you're all so upset is that you just want to maintain the status quo," Becca argued, somewhat lamely, even to her ears. "You don't want things to change. You want the world to continue to see us as a perfectly happy family."

"A perfectly screwed-up family." Olivia's words were almost inaudible, but the bitterness in her voice was loud and clear.

Becca looked to James. His expression was pained. "James, you haven't said anything. What do you think about my telling Rain now the truth about her birth?"

Olivia shot him a warning look—nobody could miss it—and James dutifully responded.

"Becca," he said, "to be fair, I wasn't involved in the decision all those years ago. I've no right to get involved now. I hadn't even met Olivia when—when Rain was born."

"But you were brought into the conspiracy—"

"Conspiracy?" David barked.

"Still," James argued, "I don't feel that I have a right to voice an opinion."

Well, Becca thought, *so much for my brother-in-law's support.* Not that she had expected much independent thinking from James. Olivia had him pretty well in hand.

"Look," she said, "I told you all, I've thought this through very carefully and—"

"Again, I don't think that you have," David interrupted. "I don't know what brought on this—this insanity—but it stops right here. Right now. You are not going to tell my daughter—"

"She's *my* daughter."

"You are not going to tell Rain anything."

"You're not the boss of this family, David." Becca looked at each of her family in turn. It took some effort to do so. She was painfully aware that her cheeks were flushed. "The truth is," she said, "that I'd like everyone's consent to tell Rain the truth soon, but I don't need it."

"I was afraid this would happen someday." Naomi's voice was thin. Becca was alarmed. Her sister-in-law looked terribly pale. Becca hoped that she wouldn't faint. Naomi lying on the floor in a heap would not help her cause. "Things have been too good," Naomi said. "Life has been too kind. I knew it would never last. I've been scared of some—some disaster like this ever since . . ."

"Ever since you took my daughter away from me." Becca hadn't meant to sound so rough, but the words were out. If Naomi fainted, well, then so be it.

There was a plea for understanding in her sister-in-law's eyes—a plea for real communication. "Becca, you know that's not what really happened! Why are you distorting the truth like this? What have we done to you to deserve this now?"

"What did I do to deserve my family ganging up against me?" Becca retorted.

"Ganging . . ." Again, David shot to his feet. "What the hell does that mean!"

Julie stood now as well. "Enough," she commanded. "We'll resume this conversation tomorrow, when we've all had some time to calm down and to think clearly."

As far as Becca was concerned, no further discussion was necessary, but she nodded her agreement.

Emotions were riding too high at the moment for any hope of success.

"Becca." Julie looked closely at her daughter. "Promise me, promise us all that you won't say anything to Rain until the family has talked again. Promise."

"Of course. I promise."

"How can we trust her promise? She's already decided to break one vow. Her word means nothing!"

"David!" Steve's tone was unusual enough to command the attention he intended it to. "Enough, now. You're not making this any easier."

Chastened for the moment, David took Naomi's arm and they left the room without another word. Olivia and James followed; James offered a quiet "good night" to those remaining.

Becca suddenly felt horribly exposed, alone with her parents and grandmother, the authority figures of the Rowan family. Annoyed by her own lack of courage, she mumbled something that she thought was "thanks" and fled.

Well, Becca thought as she left the living room, aware of the accusing eyes behind her, *this is certainly not turning out to be a Hallmark Channel Christmas.*

11

"I think she's crazy. She should be on medication."
Olivia snapped shut her vanity case—which contained little other than a jar of Pond's cold cream, moisturizer, and lip balm—with more force than was strictly necessary.

James sighed. Olivia was in one of her less charitable moods. Again. "I think," he said, "that she's very lonely."

"She should see a psychiatrist. She's unstable. I always knew it."

"Let's try to be fair about this. Let's try not to judge."

"Are you taking her side?" Olivia stood with her fists on her hips, a caricature of the stern wife.

"Of course not. No. I just—" James reached for a bottle of aspirin. He felt a headache coming on. Lately, he had been getting headaches almost every day. His doctor had told him to address the stress factors in his life. But James didn't quite know how to go about addressing the stress caused by his marriage.

"She's always wanted to be the focus of everybody's attention. When she was a kid, she was always performing, she was always the dramatic one. And then getting pregnant at sixteen by some, some bum. If that isn't the ultimate 'look at me!' I don't know what is."

"I'm sure she didn't get pregnant on purpose," James said carefully, thinking that the ultimate "look at me!" would have been a bid for suicide.

"Of course she says it wasn't on purpose, but I never really believed her. Besides, you weren't there. How would you know what she was like?"

James didn't answer. There wasn't much he said these days that Olivia actually seemed to hear.

Still, he was an optimistic man at heart. After a few minutes, during which Olivia had seemed to calm down, he said, "I couldn't help but think that all the talk tonight about motherhood and parental rights and all . . . Well, I hope it didn't upset you too much."

Olivia turned from the dresser, holding a cotton nightgown, and looked at him blankly. "Of course it didn't upset me. Why should it?"

"Well—" he began, but she cut him off.

"Oh, I forgot to mention earlier that before we left the office, I got a call from that pain in the ass Toby Stapleton. I swear he's the most annoying client we've ever had. Can't you do something about him, James? I've really had enough of the man."

"I'll call him first thing when we're home."

James had wanted to put aside work concerns at least for a few days. He badly felt the need for some peace of mind and had hoped—maybe vainly—that a few days away from the business might, just might, be good for him. For Olivia. For their marriage. He was beginning to feel at his wit's end.

"I thought," he said, trying to ignore a flash of pain between his eyes, "that tomorrow afternoon we could go to the annual Quilt Show at the Baptist church. I saw the brochure in the kitchen."

Olivia looked at him without expression. And then she said, "No, I don't think so."

"I thought you liked the show. We had a good time there last year."

"I did like it. But I don't want to go this year. You know, you can go on your own."

There was no nastiness in Olivia's tone. There was no emotion or affect at all. She was simply making a suggestion. Yes, James could go to the Quilt Show on his own. Being on his own was becoming more and more familiar to him. In fact, he was becoming an expert on being on his own. He was becoming an expert at being alone.

When the lights were out and both had settled in bed, James leaned over to kiss his wife's cheek, something he did every night and every morning upon waking.

"I love you, Liv," he whispered.

"I've got so much to do tomorrow. Do you know there's an entire wardrobe in the attic I haven't inventoried yet?"

It was too dark for James to see that Olivia was looking intently at the ceiling, as if seeing through it and into the attic, the repository of her dreams.

12

Down the hall in the Lupine Room, David and Naomi were preparing for bed.

David tossed his flannel shirt onto the floor by the painted wood dresser. The women in his life had always picked up after him. "Mom told me that Becca's been avoiding the rest of the family for a year now. I should have known something was up."

"But you didn't, and neither did I, I'm afraid." Naomi retrieved the shirt and hung it in the room's tiny closet. "I mean, she has seemed pretty tightly wound lately, but I just assumed work was weighing on her. And I thought that she hadn't seen the others because her schedule was so crazy. You know how dedicated she is to her job."

David hadn't really heard his wife. He was thinking back to when Becca was a little girl. He saw her at the age of about eight, showing up at school wearing full makeup and a pair of their mother's clip-on earrings. How she'd made it out of the house in that condition David never knew. And instead of sending her to the principal's office, Becca's teacher had just laughed. He remembered the time when she'd climbed up onto the roof of the garage on a dare, and then how she'd made it down unharmed, and was puzzled by her parents' anger and concern. She'd always been lucky. Until she had made that one big mistake.

"She was a wild kid," he said. "I shouldn't be surprised she's pulling this stunt."

"What she was like as a child has nothing to do with who she is now and you know that," Naomi argued reasonably. "Ever since she graduated from high school, she's done nothing wrong or wild. In fact, it seems to me her life has been pretty dull. She's done everything the right way, exactly by the book. Which is why this decision of hers puzzles me so much. It's so out of character."

"Well, whatever's behind this, we can't let her tell Rain the truth. Not now, not yet. Anyway, it's not her decision to make. This is a family affair."

Naomi sighed. "I wonder if anyone can actually prevent Becca from doing what she wants to do. She's not planning on committing a crime, after all. We can't punish her for wanting to tell the truth."

"We can threaten to cut her off from us all if she says a word to Rain without everyone's approval."

"Oh, David, what good would that do once she's told Rain that she's her birth mother? Becca won't care if she's lost the rest of us because she'll have her daughter back. . . ."

"If," David said, sounding downright glum, "if Rain will speak to her—or to any of us ever again. You know, there have been cases where kids divorce their parents."

Naomi slipped her nightgown over her head and sighed. "David," she said. "Don't be so dramatic."

"It's hard not to be dramatic. It's hard not to scream and yell and—and DO something."

"Yes," she said. "I know. I feel terribly frustrated, too. But we might just have to accept this, David. Not everything in life is within our control."

"Now you're being fatalistic. You can't be so negative about this, Naomi. There's a solution to every problem," he said forcefully. "A good solution."

Naomi shook her head. "No, David, not always. Sometimes there's only another problem in place of the first one. A bigger, nastier problem."

"I don't believe that. I'm a scientist, Naomi. The things that we don't have answers to or explanations for aren't unanswerable or inexplicable. We just haven't found the solutions to the problems yet. But they can and will be found."

"Science has nothing to do with human emotion, David," Naomi said. "You know that. You can't will everything in this world to go your way. I know that might be hard for you to understand, to accept. You're a powerful person. You're persuasive. It's one of the qualities about you I most admire. But the problem is that you don't know when will is not the right tool. Not the right weapon. Now is one of those times. Now we need—finesse. We need to act with calm and sympathy."

"Women's tools. I'm not sure I can, Naomi."

Naomi frowned. "Women's tools? Please, David. Don't be archaic. Anyway, you have no choice. Don't antagonize your sister. It won't help our cause."

"The whole thing is so damn complicated!" David balled his socks together and threw them into a corner. He wished he had something heavier to throw; he wanted to hear a satisfying thud or smash, but flinging one of his mother's bedside lamps into the corner was probably not a good idea.

"We knew that going in," Naomi agreed. "But now . . . that knowledge doesn't make things any easier, does it? David, I'm scared."

David was, too, but it wasn't in him to admit it. Not yet. "I just wish I knew what brought this on. What possible motive can she have? And why now?"

"I have no idea. I wonder what's going on in her personal life."

David laughed. "Like I would know? She doesn't talk to me any more than she talks to you, to any one of us. Not about anything personal anyway."

"I suspect she doesn't have much of a personal life. Maybe that's why she's suddenly so keen on—re-claiming—her daughter. Maybe she's lonely. I just don't know."

Naomi finished her bedtime routine by rubbing a thick lotion into her hands. It was awful how dry her skin could get in the cold weather. She was glad she'd never been vain about her hands. To her, they were tools rather than ornaments. But from some-where, Rain had gotten the taste for wearing her nails long and carefully polished. Naomi cringed. That's how Aunt Becca wore her nails.

"Well, in that case," David was saying, "someone had better find her a boyfriend and fast. That or a dog."

The couple got into bed, David on the left, Naomi on the right, as always. Daily routine was good. It was something you could count on in an unpredictable world where financial markets could crash seemingly without warning—and where out of the blue a family member could threaten to disturb the long-established peace.

"Speaking of dogs," Naomi said, "the boys have been asking me about when we're getting one."

"Oh."

"Yes, oh. We did promise them we'd visit the pound come spring."

"Okay, okay. In the spring. Let's get through this crisis before we take on puppy training."

David turned off the lamp on the bedside table. The room was very dark. The bed was comfortable. The night was quiet. But neither Rowan slept for some time.

13

The light in the Peony Room was low. Julie had chosen the small, old-fashioned bedside lamps with care. Their rose-colored shades gave a sense of calm and security to the room.

Too bad Steve couldn't feel either calm or secure. Though he had spent over forty years as a high-powered, sharklike attorney, he was a sentimental man at heart. In spite of the fact that he'd suspected that something was troubling his daughter, he hadn't been properly prepared for her announcement and felt terribly stricken. He felt physically ill.

As was her habit, Julie tried to reassure and to comfort him, but this time it was to no real avail.

"Things will appear brighter in the morning, honey," she said, stroking his cheek with her work-worn hand. "I promise you. They always do."

Steve squeezed his wife's other hand and said good night. Within minutes he heard the slow and deep breathing that told him she was asleep.

He envied Julie's ability to compartmentalize, to put aside a problem until morning, to be generally imperturbable. He envied her because he was so different. Steve was a brooder, and though he knew the futility of worry, he was a worrier. It wasn't the first night he'd lain awake for hours, futilely reviewing the past.

First, there had been the stunning news of Becca's pregnancy, and her refusal to have an abortion. She'd known she couldn't raise the child on her own—the idea was incomprehensible, terrifying—but she simply couldn't bear the idea of aborting the pregnancy. Of course, the family had respected her decision. Then, there had been the family meetings to discuss David and Naomi's offer to raise the child as their own. Nora had been the strongest supporter of the plan. Then, there had been the phone calls. The delicate way Steve had tried to put the family's requests. The promises he'd made of future support and the assurances of the most sincere thanks. The lectures he'd listened to patiently from those reluctant to get involved in a scheme not entirely legal. Finally, there had been the financial arrangements. And it had all gone off without a hitch. It was a miracle, really. It was an incredible stroke of luck. It was an example of almost unbelievable good fortune.

But now the universe was seeking its payment. The universe in the form of the person he had most wanted to protect. Becca had become her own avenging angel.

Steve had truly thought he was acting on his daughter's behalf, arranging the adoption that was not a legal adoption but, in reality, a subterfuge. He'd thought he was acting unselfishly. But not for the first time he wondered if all along, there had been an element of self-preservation in his actions. Had he wanted to avoid the embarrassment of having a pregnant teenaged daughter in his home? Had he worried about his professional reputation, what his colleagues might think of him, what the other fathers he knew might say behind his back? Had he been ashamed of Becca? And had what he'd convinced himself to be a kind and humane act really only been the whitewashing of an unpleasant truth?

Steve sighed. Sometimes, he thought, even a well-meaning father just didn't know what was best for his family.

It wasn't until Henry Le Mew leapt up on the bed and curled at his feet that Steve finally slept.

14

The hardest part was over. At least, Becca hoped it was. Her intentions had been announced. If they hadn't been met with enthusiasm, well, it was only what she had expected. Maybe not quite as much anger, but shock, yes, surprise, and initial resistance. That was normal. No one really enjoyed sudden, dramatic change, no matter what they might claim.

While she undressed for bed, Becca reviewed details of the meeting. She saw her father's look of disbelief. She recalled Olivia's hostility, a hostility that seemed general, not entirely directed at her sister. At one point David had looked apoplectic. James, her one hope, however dim, had been useless. And Naomi . . . Naomi's evident sorrow had shaken Becca's confidence, though it had not weakened her resolve.

Becca lay down on the couch and pulled the blankets up to her neck. *Maybe,* she thought, *someday Rain and I can move to a warm climate, or maybe take a second home in someplace exotic like Anguilla or Belize.* True, Rain liked the snow—she had been skiing with the family since she was seven; she was like the childhood Becca that way—but Becca was sure her daughter would also get to love waterskiing, or maybe windsurfing.

Olivia had said that Becca was out of her mind. David had threatened a thrashing. Her grandmother had told her she was being unfair. Becca squirmed under the blankets. It wouldn't be easy getting to sleep that night, so she decided to indulge in a few of her favorite fantasies about life with her daughter by her side. The fantasies always soothed her.

On Saturday mornings they would make a big breakfast together. Becca would forgo her usual breakfast of black coffee and a small yogurt and happily indulge in one of Rain's favorite foods, French toast with lots of syrup. In the afternoons, Becca would take her daughter to a museum or a movie. Once a year they might take a plane down to New York for a shopping spree that would set Becca back in the thousands. But it would be worth it. Rain was too old for mother-daughter outfits, and the notion slightly sickened Becca, but maybe they could wear matching silver bracelets, something elegant and discreet but engraved with each other's birthday.

Becca reached to the end of the couch for another blanket and burrowed as deep as she could. One thing was for sure. She'd never make her daughter sleep on so uncomfortable a surface. When she and Rain traveled to Paris, and from there, on to Venice or Rome, you could be sure they would have first-class accommodations all the way. Becca had a lot of time to make up for and she would do it in style.

And someday, far in the future, Becca would proudly walk down a church aisle arm in arm with her daughter, in the time-honored—if paternalistic—gesture of deliverance. After, of course, Becca had vetted the husband to be, had him thoroughly investigated, and had personally grilled him about his intentions.

If Becca were any other thirty-two-year-old woman, single, successful, and attractive, she might have been dreaming of travel and cultural expeditions and walking down the aisle of a church as activities she might pursue with a boyfriend or a fiancé or a husband. But Becca had long ago stopped dreaming about—even thinking about—romantic relationships.

Long ago she had convinced herself that she didn't need a romantic relationship, that intimacy could only bring trouble. How could she ever know someone well enough to trust him with the secret of Rain's birth? What if she made another horrible mistake? What if she so badly misjudged a man's character that she shared her secret with someone who was incapable of keeping it safe?

Becca shifted under the weight of blankets. The couch was a nightmare of lumps and bumps. But at least it was horizontal. At least her mother hadn't asked her to sleep in a chair.

A romantic relationship. Well, even if a man proved to be capable of keeping a secret, even if she trusted him enough to tell him the truth about her daughter, there was always the chance that he might react with shock and disappointment. There was always the chance that he might consider her duplicitous; he might even think her an uncaring mother, and Becca felt that such a wrong judgment would destroy her.

There was, of course, the option of continued secrecy. But the thought of living with or marrying someone from whom she was keeping such a huge secret—well, the thought made her physically nauseated. She was tired of deception. It had made her isolated and afraid. It had alienated her from friends and, eventually, from her family. And if Becca had chosen the path of alienation rather than having it thrust upon her, well, she'd done so because she had seen no other way.

Once it was known to the world that Rain was her daughter, that obstacle—that lie—would, of course, be removed. But then Becca would have Rain and there would be no room for a romance. There would be too much time to make up for with her daughter—her rightful dearest friend forever.

15

"But why wasn't I involved?" Lily asked her grandmother. The two women were in the kitchen preparing breakfast for the family. "Why didn't she ask me to be there, too? After all, I know the truth about Rain. Gosh, doesn't that sound horrible? 'The Truth About Rain.' It sounds like the title of a book or movie where you learn that 'the truth' is something bad and dirty."

Nora turned on the coffeemaker, noting that it needed a good cleaning. Of course she'd told Lily about the family meeting the night before. She believed that Lily had a right to know.

"I don't know why Becca didn't want you to be there," she said now. "Maybe she wanted only those people involved in the original decision to be involved."

"But that doesn't explain why James was invited, or allowed to stay." Lily brought a small pitcher of milk to the kitchen table. The breakfast stampede would start soon.

"True," Nora acknowledged. "But I think Becca

was hoping for an ally, and the only one she thought she might be able to count on was someone who wasn't a Rowan. And we know how mild-mannered James is, how reasonable a man."

"And did he come to Becca's aide?"

Nora handed her granddaughter a newly filled sugar bowl. "No. Not only is he reasonable, he's wise. He declined to offer an opinion."

"I bet Olivia gave him one of her looks and that kept him quiet."

Nora couldn't help but smile. "Yes, I believe there was a look. But on occasion James still does act on his own."

The twins burst into the kitchen, their father just behind.

"It's snowing! It's snowing!"

"Can we go outside, Dad?"

"Not until you have some breakfast. Sit."

"I want a Pop-Tart," Michael announced.

"You're having oatmeal."

"Can't I have a Pop-Tart, too?"

"Grandma doesn't keep Pop-Tarts in the house. And neither do we. Where are you getting Pop-Tarts, anyway? Good morning Grandma, Lily."

Naomi followed her husband and children. "I think it's that boy Christian at school. His mother feeds him all sorts of garbage. And I've heard from another mother that he's got quite a little business going, trading garbage for lunch money."

"That's not trading," David pointed out. "That's selling."

"He only charges twenty-five cents for a Pop-Tart," Michael said.

"And only twenty cents for a Twinkie." Malcolm eyed his bowl of hot oatmeal warily. "Can I have some sugar?"

"No. Have a banana."

Becca came into the kitchen as her brother was handing his son a peeled banana. She felt the atmosphere change from one of tension to one of manic tension.

It took a lot of effort to say "good morning" in a voice that didn't betray the sudden nausea she felt upon facing the Rowans in the light of day.

Her grandmother put a plate of toast on the table and said, "Good morning, Becca," firmly, neutrally. David and Naomi each mumbled something that might have been a greeting or a curse. Lily, by now, Becca assumed, in the know, gave her a brief, awkward smile. The twins didn't seem to notice anything but the food they were rapidly consuming, sugar or no sugar.

Becca poured herself a cup of the useless coffee her parents served and took a seat at the table. The thought of eating anything made the feeling of general nausea worse.

Moments later, Olivia and James joined the others in the kitchen.

"Good morning," James said. His wife said nothing; she went straight to the coffeemaker and poured a cup for herself. Her husband, it seemed, was on his own.

The kitchen door opened, letting in a blast of cold, clear air. Julie appeared, with Hank at her side. He shook himself dry—further dampening his unconcerned mother—and clicked out of the room.

"Where's Dad?" David asked.

"Up at dawn and off to his studio. Your father hardly slept last night. Or so he tells me."

Becca felt everyone's eyes on her, accusing. She was responsible for her father's sleeping badly. She was always the one who caused trouble. She glanced up from her coffee; she felt, rather than saw, the eyes slip away.

Fine. Let them not meet her eyes. She was glad. She knew all about alienation.

Rain's distinctive step was heard in the hallway. Becca's fingers tightened on the cup's handle.

"Good morning, everyone," she called brightly as she came into the kitchen. Immediately, she went over to where her mother sat next to the boys.

Rain kissed the top of Naomi's head and took a seat next to her. "You look kind of tired, Mom," she said. "Are you okay?"

Naomi managed an anemic smile. "Oh, I'm fine, honey. I guess I was just up too late."

"And she's always telling me about the importance of sleep! Mom, you're such a hypocrite."

Rain reached for the pitcher of juice, oblivious to the tension Becca felt was choking her.

"I'm going for a walk." Becca rose abruptly from the table, banging her thighs into it, causing it to shake. She hurried from the kitchen, grabbed her coat from the rack in the front hall, and let herself out into the frosty morning. Icy air and the snow that drifted through it were far less hostile than the atmosphere in the Rowan house.

Becca hadn't gone ten feet before movement off to the left caught her eye. It was her father and the neighbor, Alex. The two men were coming out of Steve's studio in the old, renovated barn. In this wide, open, and very white space, there was no way to avoid them, no way to pretend she hadn't seen them.

Becca swore under her breath. She'd wanted, needed isolation and the protection that provided, but it seemed she wasn't going to get it even in the relatively vast wilderness of her parents' land. She stopped walking. In a few moments, the men were close enough to speak with. But Steve only nodded at his daughter, and walked rapidly toward the house. Alex stopped and watched him go.

"Your father doesn't seem himself this morning," he said when the older man was out of earshot.

"He didn't sleep well."

"Ah, that will put anyone off his game."

Becca wondered if that been a sarcastic retort. She looked closely at Alex Mason, as if seeing him for the first time. He was a tall man, an inch or two over six feet, she thought, and powerfully built. His clothes were nondescript; his style, nonchalant—jeans, winter boots unlaced, a well-worn leather three-quarter coat over a turtleneck and brown flannel shirt. His hair was brown, clean but raggedy, as if he'd neglected or forgotten to have it cut since summer. His eyes, a very bright blue, could be described as intense; his gaze was penetrating. Becca didn't like a penetrating gaze; it meant a person might be snooping for secrets.

For a dreadful moment she wondered if her father had told Alex about the family meeting, and she was flooded with anger. It was nobody's business, really, but hers, she thought. Her business, and Rain's.

"What were you doing in there?" she demanded. "With my father?"

"Planning to take over the world."

Becca stared. Did Alex think he was being funny?

"Uh, actually," he said, "we were talking about one of his photographs. I'm giving him some help, though photography isn't my strong suit. I'm a sculptor by trade. But you might know that already."

All right. If Alex knew what had gone on in the Rowan living room the night before, he wasn't giving anything away.

"Isn't it beautiful?" he was saying now, gesturing to

what most people would consider a winter wonderland. "I love a cold, clear winter morning. Look at the way the snow rests on the branches of that pine. It's more beautiful than anything we humans can create."

"I hate the cold," Becca said bluntly. "I hate everything about winter."

Alex looked at her. He seemed a bit taken aback by her vehemence.

"If you hate the cold weather so much," he asked, "why haven't you moved to a warmer climate? North Carolina is supposed to be nice. Maybe California. I hear that in Arizona it's a dry heat."

It would be so easy simply to blurt out the truth: "I can't leave New England because I can't leave my daughter." It would be too easy. Becca caught herself and muttered something about her career being centered in Boston.

Alex shrugged. Maybe he'd bought her excuse, maybe not. It didn't matter to Becca. This guy was a stranger, and as far as she was concerned, he could stay a stranger.

"Then I suppose you have a very good reason for being out on this winter morning. Without gloves."

Becca shoved her hands into the pockets of her leather coat, a coat that was not meant to be worn in wet weather. It would cost a lot to get it properly cleaned once back in Boston. "I forgot them," she said.

"Mind if I walk a bit with you?"

Becca shrugged. "Suit yourself."

Alex was not a man easily deterred. He kept pace with what he considered Becca's angry or impatient stride.

"You know," he said when they had gone several

yards, "I feel as if I've gotten to know you a bit since I became your parents' neighbor. Your father speaks so highly of you."

Becca laughed and kept her eyes focused straight ahead. She was pissed she'd forgotten her sunglasses, too. Winter sunlight, even during a snowfall, seemed far more intense than summer sunlight. She felt as if her eyes were being stabbed. "Yeah, right," she said. "Of me?"

"Yes, of you. Why shouldn't he? Is there some deep dark dirty secret you're not telling me?"

If he only knew! Becca walked on in silence. After a moment she said, "It's just that my father and I haven't been close for—for a long time."

"Oh. That's too bad."

Becca stopped. Alex walked on a step and then looked back. He couldn't quite read the expression on Becca's face. It seemed to contain hostility, embarrassment, even . . . hope? He was puzzled.

"Is it?" she said.

"Is it what?"

"Is it really too bad? That we're not close?"

Alex didn't know how to answer. He'd said what he'd said unthinkingly. Finally, he shrugged. "Sure. I mean, how bad can a guy so devoted to his cat possibly be?"

Becca didn't know what she had wanted to hear from Alex, but it wasn't that. She walked on and Alex fell back into step with her. She wished he'd go on home. She had nothing to say to this man. Maybe he'd read her mind—or, more likely, he'd read her obviously uncommunicative mood—because after a few yards he gestured off to the right.

"My house—and my studio—is in that direction. Just over that rise. It's the first house you come to, about half a mile off. An old farmhouse and barn. It's a lot like your parents' place but not in half as good shape, and it's a lot smaller."

Why, Becca wondered, was he telling her this information? It wasn't as if she had any intention of paying him a visit.

"Oh," she said.

"I'd better get back to work. I suppose I'll be seeing you later."

Becca shrugged. "Okay," she said. " 'Bye."

She kept on walking, aware now that she was alone, and glad of it. But she couldn't help herself from squinting in the direction that Alex had gone. For a moment she watched his dark form tromping into the snowy distance. For a moment she had the strangest urge to follow him. But just for a moment.

Becca walked on, no particular destination in mind—not that there was any place in particular to go here in Kently, Maine. That is, unless you had an interest in picking up the local paper in the tiny general store five miles off, and Becca did not. Besides, the encounter with Alex had left her feeling—unsettled, but she couldn't say exactly why. She acknowledged, dimly, that he was attractive, in a sort of gruff, outdoorsy, arty way, but what did that matter? The truth was that she had pretty much ceased to consider herself a sexual, available woman some time ago. A long time ago. Her momentary attraction to this Alex person—if indeed it could even be called that—was insignificant.

Insignificant because Becca had gotten in the habit of telling herself that it didn't matter if she lived the rest of her life celibate. There were far more important things in life on which to focus than sex. And sex brought trouble. Look what trouble it had wrought in her own life. Trouble. Isolation. Pain.

And as for romance and love . . . Well, Becca had pushed aside those possibilities, too, but for more murky reasons. If she were honest with herself, if she could be honest with herself, she would acknowledge that she felt undeserving of love and romantic happiness; she would acknowledge that she felt she should be doing penance always for her "mistake." But what was that mistake? Getting pregnant or giving up her child?

Becca shook her head as if that would help clear away troublesome thoughts. Of course, it did not help. Fingers near frozen and eyes near blinded, she turned around, defeated by the elements, and headed for home. Such as it was.

16

The Rowan family was gathered in the living room. David was standing, his hands on his hips, the self-appointed commander in chief. His parents sat next to each other on the couch. Hank sat on the floor at Julie's feet, his face and attitude alert, as if he sensed that she might need support.

"Dad," David said, with more than a touch of impatience, "it's the results that count. Look at Rain. She's happy and she's healthy. What we all did was the right thing. You know that."

Steve sighed quietly. "I thought I did," he said. "But what about Becca? She's obviously very unhappy."

David snorted. Naomi had talked to him about that annoying habit, but David seemed incapable of giving it up. "Dad," he said, "Becca needs to get over her misery and move on. It's not like she never sees Rain. For God's sake, Rain adores her. They talk on the phone, they e-mail all the time, and they see each other at least once a month. And let's keep in mind that Becca is an adult."

"Yes," he admitted. "Becca is an adult, now. But when we made the decision to take her baby from her, she was just a child herself."

"That's right, David," his mother said. "I tried to talk to her about the adoption, once Becca was back at school. But she always shied away from a conversation. All she would ever say was that she was 'fine.' Maybe all that time, all those first few years, maybe she was really suffering inside. And we just didn't know it. What if we failed our daughter, after all?"

David gripped the sides of his head. Naomi had rarely seen him act so dramatically. "Look," he said, "there's no point in rehashing the past. What's done is done, and from what I can see, the results of our actions are overwhelmingly positive. Rain is happy and healthy. She does well in school and has good friends. What more could we ask for?"

Julie gave a long sigh. "Well, I suppose David is right." Then she looked around at the others as if to command their attention. "And I suppose now's as good a time as any to tell you all that I've been keeping tails on the boy who got Becca pregnant."

David looked at his wife. "Did she say 'keeping tails'?"

"Yes, David, I did. And don't look so surprised, Steve," Julie said in response to her husband's look of wonder. "You're not the only one with connections. And I was perfectly discreet. There's not a way in the world any word of my surveillance—"

"Oh, Lord," Olivia mumbled.

David rolled his eyes. "Suddenly she's Jessica Fletcher."

"Of my surveillance," Julie went on, giving emphasis to the offending term, "could have reached him. And my connections—my sources—are un-impeachable."

"Why, Mom?" Lily asked. "Why did you keep track of him?"

"To be prepared for just such an emergency. If this turns out to be a real emergency . . . and I refuse to believe that it will."

"I still don't understand."

"It's simple, Lily. If Becca were to learn just what a loser this boy—this man—now is, there's no way she'd want her daughter to have anything to do with him."

"I'm not sure what Becca would want, but Naomi and I sure as hell wouldn't want any contact," David muttered.

Nora nodded. "None of us would."

"And," Julie went on, "I'm afraid that if Rain learns the truth before she's mature enough to handle it without doing something rash, well, she might set out to find her father, and that would be disastrous."

"I feel as if I'm in some two-bit soap opera." The words seemed to shoot from Olivia's mouth. "This is getting disgusting. We should just send Becca packing. Ostracize her from the family. Cut off all of her access to Rain. Get a restraining order. Dad, you must know someone who can help with that."

James put a hand on his wife's arm. As she'd done the night before at dinner, she shook it off.

"Enough, Olivia." Nora turned to her daughter-in-law. "Julie, where is this man living? Becca's biological father."

David's lips set in a grim line. He hated to be reminded of the fact that he was not entirely responsible for Rain's existence.

"My latest report indicates—I saw you roll your eyes, Olivia—my latest report indicates that he's living in a trailer in a little town in Vermont. He's generally unemployed, though there have been stints as a bouncer. He has two prior convictions, one involving possession of drugs. Jail time served. I believe the charge involved a meth lab in his garage. No other children that anyone's cared to acknowledge. One domestic abuse complaint, but that didn't stick. When the police showed up, it turned out the woman was the one with the baseball bat. Oh, yes, and his medical records—"

"You got his medical records!" Steve looked aghast.

"Well, no, dear," Julie answered calmly, "not exactly."

"Not exactly?" he repeated.

"What I mean is that I'm not in actual possession of them. I simply have access to them when I need them."

"Oh, my God." David rubbed his forehead. "My mother the private investigator. Go on, Mom. We might as well hear the worst of it."

"Well, it seems he's a heavy smoker well on his way to a full-blown case of emphysema. Oh, and he has genital herpes."

David sank into a chair. "Of course he does. So we're looking at a downright pillar of society here, aren't we?"

"What a creep!" Lily cried. "There's no way Rain or Becca—or any of us—should have anything to do with him. He makes Cliff sound perfect! He's only gotten two tickets for moving violations and neither of them was really his fault."

Nora frowned at her youngest granddaughter. Cliff-the-dangerous-driver-and-gambling-fiend had no part in this family saga.

"Genetics," Olivia mumbled, shaking her head. "You can't argue with genetics because that's an argument you just can't win. That's why I would never adopt. Ever. You just don't know what you're getting. You've got to watch Rain closely, David. What we know about the father isn't promising. Naomi, maybe you'd better have her screened for incipient mental illness."

"Jesus, Olivia, shut up, will you!" No one told David to shut up.

"Nature isn't the only factor in a person's life, Liv." Naomi knew she sounded almost desperately hopeful, as if trying to convince herself as well as her sister-in-law. "Nurture plays a part, too. A big part."

Olivia opened her mouth to reply but was silenced by the distinct sound of the front door opening, then closing. Becca was back from her walk. Without a word, the family dispersed.

17

Becca turned from the coatrack just in time to avoid being run over by Olivia, stomping her way toward the stairs and then, probably, to the attic.

"You're excused," Becca mumbled as her sister charged on.

"Becca." David stood in the hall. "We need to talk."

"I'm going to my room." She knew he would follow her there. She knew that once she had spoken her mind, she would be pursued until the battle was over. So be it.

The encounter with Alex had upset and confused her. Her blood was up. She was primed for conflict. David, too, seemed itching for a fight. Barely had the door closed behind him than he blurted:

"Look, Becca, what the hell is going on? Will you please just tell me so we can get past this whole ridiculous notion you have of disrupting everyone's life?"

"Ridiculous?" she cried. So she was escalating the anger, not trying to defuse it. She had the right to her anger. "Why is it so ridiculous that I should want my daughter to know her real mother?"

"Ssssh! Keep your voice down! I don't want Rain to hear us."

"*You* don't want? It's always about you, David, isn't it? It's always about what David wants. And it's always been that way. Well, news flash, David. Rain is my daughter, not yours."

David took a step closer, finger jabbing the air for emphasis. Becca stood where she was, arms crossed.

"I'm not the selfish one here, Becca. You are. You're the one being totally selfish. You're like . . . You're like that woman in the Bible who comes to Solomon claiming a baby is hers, and just so she can get what she wants, she agrees the baby should be cut in half. She's not thinking of the welfare of the child. She's thinking only about herself."

"Oh, please," she laughed, "don't start quoting the Bible at me!"

"I wasn't quoting. I was referring."

"You're such an ass, David, you know that? A self-centered, pretentious ass."

David looked absolutely disgusted with her. Becca didn't care.

"We seem to be getting nowhere," he said coldly.

Becca didn't reply. Where was there to go? She couldn't deny that she was standing firm in her decision to tell Rain the truth of her birth before another year passed away.

"We'll resume this conversation later." David stalked out of the den.

Becca slammed the door behind him. So what if everyone felt the reverberations? She was tired of hiding in plain sight. She was ready to be seen, and to be heard.

18

David had been gone only minutes when there was a knock on the door. Before Becca could ask who wanted another piece of her, the door opened and her mother was inside.

Becca sighed. "Mom, I'm busy. We'll talk later, with everyone. Like we planned."

"Yes," Julie said, "we'll talk as a family. Later. But I need to talk to you about something important. Now."

Becca leaned against the desk and folded her arms across her chest. She was getting used to this half aggressive, half self-protective stance. "Fine."

"I want to talk to you about Rain's father."

"What?" Becca almost laughed. "I don't understand. What does he have to do with anything?"

Julie didn't answer immediately. Instead, she moved farther into the room and stood with her hands folded in front of her. It struck Becca as an odd pose for a woman who would never be described as demure.

"Maybe quite a lot," she said finally. "I think you

need to know about him. I think you need to know about what he's been doing all these years. Because if you tell Rain now about her birth, there's every chance she's going to be very upset and want to rush off and find her father, and let me tell you, Becca, that would be a very big mistake."

Becca shook her head. Frankly, Rain's biological father hadn't at all figured into her thinking. "What makes you think she'd want to rush off to find her father? Anyway, maybe he can't be found."

"I've found him."

"You what?" Becca felt flooded with anger. She felt betrayed. No one trusted her to live her own life. No one would let her get past her one big mistake.

"Well, as a matter of fact," her mother was saying, "he was never lost. I've kept track of him." And Julie told Becca what she'd told the others earlier.

Becca fought for control of her emotions. It was hard. Shame warred with fear. Shame over her foolish action all those years ago. Fear that the horrible man who had fathered her daughter might one day come to claim her. Finally, she answered with false bravado.

"All right," she said. "So he's a bum. No big surprise there. I just won't tell Rain his name. None of us will."

"Becca, be reasonable. You sound like a stubborn child, standing in a puddle of orange juice, holding an empty carton, and refusing to admit you're the one who spilled it."

"Orange juice?" Was her mother losing her mind? "What are you talking about?"

"Think about it," Julie said. "First you shock Rain with the revelation about her biological parents and then you refuse to tell her the identity of her father. Consider how absurd that would be. Becca, I really don't think you've thought things through completely."

"I wish everybody would stop saying that!"

"And I wish you would let me help you. Tell me what's going on. Tell me why this is so important to you right now."

"I don't need help, Mom," Becca said firmly. "I need my daughter."

Julie sighed deeply, walked the few feet to the old leather couch, and sunk onto it. She hadn't wanted to lose her temper or to make Becca angry or, worse, to further alienate her daughter. But she didn't seem to be making a very good job of this conversation.

"Becca, please, sit with me for a moment."

"I'd prefer to stand."

Julie paused. It felt as if her daughter were a million miles away, rather than just across the room. "Please," she said, "for Rain's sake, please try to be reasonable."

"Reasonable?" Becca glared at her mother. "Excuse me, but is it reasonable to expect a pregnant sixteen-year-old to make such a monumental decision about her future? About the future of her child?"

"No, it isn't reasonable. Which is why the adults who loved you stepped in and helped make those decisions for you. You should be grateful, Becca."

"Grateful!" Becca cried. "Why? Because you didn't toss me out onto the street? Because you allowed your embarrassment of a daughter to remain part of the Rowan family? How noble of you, Mom. How generous. Wow."

Becca snatched up her laptop and stormed out of the den. Julie slowly got to her feet. Suddenly, she felt old. She didn't like the feeling. She made her way to her bedroom, the notion of a little nap leading her on. She couldn't remember the last time she felt a situation might just be out of her hands. She felt almost helpless. Almost. Julie Rowan didn't give up hope easily. It was one of her best and, according to her husband, one of her most annoying traits.

By the time she reached the upstairs hall, she'd changed her mind about a nap. Calling to Hank, she headed out for a good, brisk walk.

19

Becca strode into the kitchen, head down, unaware that she was muttering, and was pulled up short by the sound of a voice.

"Hello, Becca," it said. "Come join us."

As if to protect herself against another assault, Becca hugged her laptop to her chest. Naomi and Rain were sitting at the kitchen table, each flipping through a glossy magazine.

Retreat now—escape, really—would look ridiculous, so Becca came all the way into the kitchen. Keeping the laptop close, she leaned against the sink.

"Hey, guys," Rain said, her eyes fixed to a page. "Listen to this. It says in this article that after fifteen or so years of decline, last year teenage birth rates in the U.S. rose three percent. It says that's about four hundred thousand teen births a year!" She looked up at Becca and made a face. "What's wrong with those girls? Who would want to have a baby at fifteen or sixteen? It's insane. I am going to be so careful when I start to have sex."

Becca felt faint. She thought she was going to have a heart attack before the week was over. Maybe her mother—and David—had been right. Maybe she hadn't thought this all through.

"What—what are you reading?" Becca squeaked.

"*Krazee Girl.* It's a new magazine. It's okay, but I'm not sure I'll get a subscription. The horoscope page is really lame."

"About having sex," Naomi said, looking up from her home decorating magazine. "That will be some time from now, right?"

Rain assumed the classic teenage I-am-so-put-upon look. "Mom, we've been through this, like, a million times. I'm not stupid. I'm not going to ruin my life because of some boy."

Becca flinched. That's what so many girls and women said and then . . . And then. And then, by their very existence, their children shamed their mothers into admitting their frailty.

Becca unwittingly caught Naomi's eye. Her sister-in-law looked as uncomfortable as Becca felt. Uncomfortable and—was it possible?—sympathetic. Becca looked away.

"Remember a few years ago," Rain was saying, oblivious to the impact her words were having on the two older women, "when those high school girls in some town in Massachusetts all made a pact to get pregnant at the same time? Talk about bizarre!"

"More than bizarre," Naomi said. "It was horribly irresponsible. Who did those girls think was going to take care of the babies? There are too many children in foster homes and too many young families on welfare already. And too often the burden of raising the children of children falls on the grandparents or—"

Naomi put a hand to her mouth. Becca was pleased to see that her sister-in-law looked mortified.

Of course Naomi wasn't sympathetic to Becca's plight. That earlier look had been an act. Naomi had been trying to trick her into letting down her guard, into backing away from her plan. And Naomi had also been trying to shame her by emphasizing the carelessness of her long ago misdeed.

"Yeah, and if you have to drop out of high school," Rain went on, "good luck getting a job that pays enough for day care or a decent apartment. And how could you possibly stay in school? I can't imagine going to my parents and saying, 'Hey, Mom and Dad, could you take care of my baby while I hang out at photography club and go shopping for a prom dress?' Yeah, right!"

Naomi had found her voice again. "I'm sure," she said carefully, "that in the case of those Massachusetts girls, there were a lot of things going on, a lot of problems we just don't know about."

"Maybe. Or maybe they were just stupid." Rain noisily pushed back her chair, got up, and went to the fridge. "Aunt Becca, do you ever think about having children?" she asked on her way back to the table with a glass of juice.

Unconsciously, Becca tightened her grip on the laptop still pressed to her chest. "Yeah," she said, mustering every ounce of studied nonchalance she could, "and then I think about you and your brothers and I change my mind."

"Ha-ha. No, seriously."

Becca shifted her weight to the other leg. The conversation was nerve-wracking. She was going to have a heart attack and a stroke on top of it. Maybe she'd have an aneurism, too, just for good measure. "Seriously, Rain, now's not the time for me to bore everyone with my life plan."

"But you'd make a great mom—"

"Rain." Naomi put her hand on the girl's arm. "This is a very personal subject. Stop quizzing your aunt. Now, let's have some hot chocolate. Becca, would you like a cup?"

No, she thought, *but if you're offering a double shot of bourbon, I'll take two.* She supposed she should feel some gratitude toward Naomi for having diverted Rain's questioning. But it was hard to feel anything for the enemy other than anger; it was imperative she not let her defenses down for one moment or all might be lost.

Becca stood away from the sink. "No, thanks," she said. "I've got some work to do. I'll be in my room." *My cramped little study of a room, where no doubt someone else will track me down to cruelly harass me in an organized attempt to weaken my resolve.*

Naomi didn't press the invitation. On slightly wobbly legs, Becca left the Rowan family kitchen.

20

Lily flinched. "Did you hear that?"

It had come not from the floor above but from the attic above that, a series of sounds resembling a small plane taking off from the roof.

"I'm not deaf," Nora said, eyes toward the ceiling. "Yet."

"What is she doing up there? She's like a rodent, always rooting around in piles of rags. Or, I don't know, a stray dog digging through an overturned garbage can."

James came into the kitchen then, trailing Michael and Malcolm. Lily hoped he hadn't heard her unpleasant comments about his wife. Lily liked Olivia, mostly. She just didn't understand her.

"I'm going to take the boys to the Christmas fair in Cornwall," James said.

"How nice," Nora replied. "If Mrs. March is selling any of her jams, will you pick us up a jar?"

"Sure."

"And can we get hot chocolate after?" the boys chorused.

James smiled at his charges. "I don't see why not. A little more sugar won't make that much of a difference. I hope."

Nora was glad the three would be spending time together. It would certainly do James good to be needed for a while, and to be with children who had no cause to be unhappy. "Be good for your uncle James," she said to their retreating backs.

They promised they would.

There was another rumble from the attic.

Lily sighed. "Poor James. He seems so down, doesn't he? So sad. Not like his usual self."

"Yes. And I don't think it has anything to do with Becca's—threat."

"Well, living with Olivia is probably pretty difficult," Lily said. "And maybe there's some trouble with the business. The economy is a mess. It must be hard to shoulder all that responsibility."

Nora doubted the payroll business was at the heart of what was troubling James, but she didn't feel inclined to continue the discussion. Already, she felt it was verging on gossip, which always happened when there was a paucity of real information and a glut of speculation.

Gossip and rumor, assumption and speculation. As long as people engaged with each other in romantic relationships, there would always be talk. No relationship, Nora reflected now, was entirely private. Even her own marriage had no doubt been a subject of curiosity. . . .

Ever since her granddaughter had told her about Cliff's betrayal a month earlier, Nora had been considering sharing with Lily her own tale of romantic woe. There were several reasons for wanting—for needing?—to break the silence after many long years. Nora wasn't perfectly sure all of them were valid.

Lily broke the silence that had settled on the kitchen. "Oh, Grandma," she said, "I really miss Cliff. I'm—well, I'm thinking of calling him. Or at least I'm thinking of taking one of his calls. I mean, the poor guy seems to miss me so much. Why else would he be calling every hour? And his voice mails sound so—so sad."

Nora didn't much believe in mind reading or signs and omens, but her granddaughter's words, coming right upon her own particular thoughts, decided her.

"Come to my room and sit with me a while," she said. "I want to make some progress on that sweater for my friend Cassie."

As the women left the kitchen, Lily asked, "The woman you knew back in Massachusetts? Doesn't she live in some sort of nursing home now?"

"It's one sort of nursing home, yes," Nora said with a frown. "And she could use some attention as those children of hers—" Nora stopped. There was no good to be gained by speaking badly of others. Besides, Nora knew that she was luckier than most women her age; not every grandmother could have a granddaughter who considered her a best friend, or a daughter-in-law who happily shared her home.

Nora opened the door to her room. It was Lily's favorite room in the house. She couldn't imagine her grandmother not occupying it forever.

The walls were painted a warm, creamy white. The floor was made of wide pine boards; some years ago Nora had had them painted a deep, dark brown. On the windows (one faced out back, the other, the side yard) hung filmy white curtains that let in enough daylight to make the room cheery even on a gray and dismal day. The bed's stained pine frame had once been Steve's, though, of course, the mattress and box spring had been replaced several times over the years. The comforter was a creamy white; on top of it sat several pillows, a few of them chosen by Julie. Lily had to admit that her mother was a bit pillow crazy.

The room was the distillation of almost ninety years of a life and yet to Lily it felt uncluttered and clean, not fussy or crammed. She wondered what a stranger might think of it, and suddenly remembered that on Cliff's last visit to the Rowans' Kently home, when shown Nora's room, he'd merely shrugged. "So?" he'd said. "It's an old lady's room." Only now did Lily realize the disdain with which he'd spoken. The complete lack of interest in someone his girlfriend dearly loved. Had she been so stupidly besotted that she'd failed to defend her beloved grandmother?

And this was the guy she was considering calling? Lily shook away the memory. Anyway, maybe she was misremembering. Maybe her current feelings of hurt were distorting the truth of the past.

"So," she said, when she had settled against the largest pillow on her grandmother's bed, and Nora had settled into her second favorite chair in the house and picked up her most recent knitting project. "What do you think about my calling Cliff?"

Nora paused before speaking. "Why don't you let me think about that for a little while. Right now I want to tell you something I've never told anyone. Not a soul. Not until now."

Lily shot off the bed. "Oh, my gosh, Grandma, what it is? You're not sick, are you?"

"No, no, it's nothing like that."

"Whew." Lily dropped back down on the bed. "You scared me for a minute!"

The young, Nora thought, with some amusement,

could be so dramatic. Or maybe it was just a Rowan trait.

"First," she said, "I want you to know I'm telling you this in the hopes that it will help you. You've been through a painful time and I want you to understand that you're not alone. All right?"

Lily nodded. Nora thought she still looked a little frightened.

After all this time, the words were surprisingly easy to say. "Your grandfather," she began, "had an affair. We were in our thirties. It had gone on for several months before I learned about it."

Lily gasped but could say nothing.

Nora went on. "I found a few letters in his sock drawer. They were from—her. I don't know why he left them in such an obvious place. I did all of our laundry and clothing maintenance. I don't know, maybe he wanted me to find the evidence of his betrayal. Anyway, at first I considered not saying or doing anything about it. I was so scared. That is, after I got over the shock. I thought that maybe I could just pretend that I had never seen the letters."

"But you couldn't pretend?" Lily guessed, her voice almost a whisper.

"No. I couldn't. When I confronted him—and that was the most awful moment of my life; I don't know where I found the courage, knowing what I might hear, that he might want to leave me and our son—when I confronted him, he didn't deny anything. He admitted right away to the relationship. And that, in a strange way, was a relief."

Lily put her hands to her face. "A relief? I can't believe I'm hearing this," she said. "Who was she, Grandma? Did you know her?"

"No," Nora answered, "I didn't know her. She was a woman Thomas knew through work. He said that she was single and lived a few towns away. Thomas swore no one knew of the relationship. Except, now, for me. I never did learn if the woman had told her friends about Thomas. Maybe there were people out there sniggering about me, the poor, stupid wife." Nora paused, as if once again considering that unpleasant possibility. "But I guess it didn't really matter in the end."

"So . . . so what happened then?" Lily asked.

"Well," Nora went on, "Thomas told me that he'd ended the affair a few weeks earlier. But, obviously, he'd kept some of the woman's letters, so I had to wonder if he was still attached to her. I made him promise never to see or to talk to her again. And I asked him to throw out anything she'd ever given him, including those letters."

"And he promised he would?"

"Yes. And I chose to believe that he kept those promises to me."

Nora looked closely at Lily. She wondered if her granddaughter thought her stupid for that decision.

"And you had no idea before you found the letters?" Lily asked then. "All that time and you didn't know that your own husband was having an affair?"

Nora smiled ruefully. "You've never heard the expression 'the wife is always the last to know'? Well, there's a reason for that. Sometimes the husband is awfully good at deception, that's true. But many, many times the wife doesn't know about the affair because she doesn't want to know. She needs the evidence to be put right in her face before she'll believe what she might have suspected. At least, that's how it was in my case. I was quite happy to be ignorant. Until I was forced not to be."

"I don't know why you stayed with him, Grandma." The words seemed to burst out of Lily's mouth. "I would have walked right out the door the minute he admitted that he cheated."

Nora hid a smile. The irony of her own words was lost on her granddaughter. Cliff had cheated on Lily and yet she was pining for his return—while at the same time condemning her grandmother's reunion with her cheating husband. Perspective was an interesting thing.

"Really, Grandma," Lily went on, "how could you have stayed with him once you found out? How could you have trusted him again after he lied to you so badly?"

"Because I loved him and I believed that he loved me. That made our continued life together possible. That, and time."

Lily made a face. "Are you trying to tell me that time heals all wounds?"

"Something like that," Nora conceded. "Time passed and we grew comfortable together again. Our relationship was different, but relationships are always changing, anyway. Especially long-term relationships like marriage."

"But, Grandma, weren't you furious with him?"

There was no point in lying when she'd come this far, Nora thought. "Yes," she admitted, "I was, for a time. But the anger was mixed up with other emotions. And of course I had to face the possibility that I was partly responsible for, well, for having driven him into the arms of another woman, if you'll pardon the expression."

Lily laughed in disbelief. "I don't believe for one minute, Grandma, that you were responsible for Grandpa having an affair. You can't blame yourself for someone else's bad behavior."

"Oh, I'm not blaming anyone," Nora explained. "Not the other woman, and not even your grandfather. Until you're in a marriage, or any long-term relationship for that matter, you just don't know how easily things can fall apart. You just can't imagine how easy it is to drift away from each other. All I'm saying is that along with feeling angry with your grandfather, I also felt conscious of my responsibilities to him and to the marriage. And maybe, just maybe, I'd been negligent, without even realizing it."

Lily didn't want to believe this. More, she simply couldn't believe it. "So you never even thought about getting a divorce?" she asked.

Nora sighed. "There was an awful lot of stigma attached to divorce back then. Not like it is today. Today it's almost too easy to give up on a marriage. But back then—"

Lily abruptly got to her feet. "Don't say 'things were different in those days.' That's not an excuse for—"

"For what?"

Lily felt uncomfortable. "For . . . for forgiving Grandpa."

Nora raised an eyebrow, a little skill of which she was oddly proud. "Didn't you mean to say for being a fool?"

Lily dashed to where her grandmother sat, and hugged her thin shoulders. "Grandma! I would never call you a fool."

"Of course you wouldn't. But you might think I'm one. It's perfectly all right, Lily. I don't expect you to understand my motives—right away. I do hope that someday you'll understand." Nora paused, then sighed dramatically. "Though I suppose there's a good chance I'll be dead by then."

Lily laughed, which was what Nora had hoped

she'd do. "Grandma, really! You're awful. You shouldn't talk about dying."

"Why not? It's inevitable, isn't it? And it can't be that far off."

"Maybe so. But that doesn't mean we have to talk about it."

"All right," Nora said. "I'll try not to mention the subject again."

Lily sat heavily on her grandmother's bed and picked up a length of discarded wool, which she then began to twist around her finger. She seemed to be thinking hard, if her frown was one of concentration and not merely unhappiness.

Nora watched her, and waited. She saw in her granddaughter the rigidity of the young and idealistic. Situations were black or white; shades of gray were ignored or disdained as excuses or prevarications. They were seen as evidence of cowardice. The young thought they were noble, but nobody untested can be noble. To persevere in the face of disaster, that was bravery. To forgive in the wake of betrayal, that was nobility.

Nora knew, of course, that the concept of compromise was one that came to a person only with the accumulation of experience, with the experience of joys as well as of disappointments.

"Do Mom and Dad know that Grandpa had an affair?" Lily asked suddenly.

The question didn't surprise Nora. She guessed that Lily would have a lot more questions as she came to terms with her grandmother's secret. "No," she said, "I'm almost certain they don't. Your father was fifteen years old when it happened. Just starting to date. It was your grandfather's wish that his son not know the truth. He was ashamed, you see. In fact,

I'm not sure how he'd feel about my telling you now. But I guess I just had to. I thought the knowledge might help you in some way, help you to accept the fact of an affair and to move on." Nora paused. "But maybe I was wrong. Maybe the secret was weighing on me too heavily, after all these years. Maybe my telling you was selfish. Maybe I just wanted someone to share the burden I've been carrying alone for so long."

It was true. One did need to tell one's story. And Nora was old, almost ninety.

Maybe it had just come down to this: She had wanted to pass on an important truth of her life so that she could be remembered, at least by one person, as who she really was, not as who she was perceived to be.

But what if it had been a mistake, unburdening herself to her granddaughter? Maybe instead of helping Lily come to terms with her heartache, the knowledge of Nora's secret would only serve to further confuse and pain her.

Nora sighed. Well, what was done was done, what was said was said. Now she'd just have to wait and see what trouble her decision had wrought.

"Lily, dear. Did you hear what I said?"

Lily looked up from the piece of yarn she had now twisted into a knot. "Yes, Grandma," she said. "I heard. I don't mind your telling me. It's—it's weird, but you kind of never think about your parents or your grandparents having gone through stuff like you're going through. You kind of never think of your parents and grandparents as—well, as real people."

And the older we get, the more real we'll become, Nora thought, *with our aches and pains and failing memories.*

So real that we'll make you long for the days when we seemed perfect and untouchable and uncomplicated.

"Yes," she said. "Each and every one of us is a real person, in all our tarnished glory. Now, let's talk about something more pleasant. Would you like me to show you that new stitch I was telling you about?"

Lily said that she would.

21

"Steve?"

The older man turned from his primary worktable (he had several worktables in all; photographers, he had learned, even amateurs, needed an awful lot of equipment) and smiled. "Alex, come in."

"Am I interrupting?" he asked from the doorway.

"Not at all."

Alex came into Steve's studio—which was a hell of a lot neater than his own—and closed the door behind him. Immediately he noted the looming presence of Henry Le Mew. He sat on a high stool next to Steve's worktable, eyes fixed on his friend. Could a cat, Alex wondered, be obsessed with a human? When it came to Henry Le Mew, anything seemed possible.

Family members had been asked to stay away from the studio in the weeks leading up to Christmas. Steve had told them that he was working on a special gift he wanted to be a surprise. It was a unique sort of family portrait, a photomontage that included an image of his deceased father. Often while working on it Steve had ruminated on the notion of family; he thought about its inherent strength—and about its inherent fragility.

Alex, not being a member of the family in the strictest sense, was a welcome and frequent visitor to the studio. He enjoyed spending time with his neighbor. He saw in Steve a man he would someday like to be—only not so bowed. Alex had nothing against hard work, but he preferred not to have to spend much time at a desk. Alex wasn't comfortable in offices and he owned only one suit. He wasn't even sure it still fit. He hadn't had occasion to wear it since a function at Barner College of Art, where he taught courses in sculpture and art history. That had been over a year ago, and since then he'd been consuming an awful lot of the Rowan women's warm meals.

He watched Steve for a few minutes, in silence. There was something about his bearing, something—tense—about the set of his shoulders. Alex sensed that his friend was troubled. He didn't like to pry. On the other hand, if there were something Steve wanted to talk about, as a friend Alex owed him the opportunity.

"Everything okay, Steve?" he asked, casually, he hoped.

"Sorry?" Steve looked up at Alex as if startled. "Oh, yes, fine, thanks, Alex. Maybe you could give me some advice on this montage. I'm having trouble with this passage here. . . ."

Alex made a suggestion and looked on as Steve followed it using his Photoshop software.

"Much cleaner," he pronounced when Steve was done. "But there is one more thing. . . ."

Steve looked up. "Out with it. I can handle criticism."

"Good. Because I think you, ah, overdid it a bit

with James's teeth, over here. They glow. It's kind of freaking me out. No offense."

Steve laughed. "None taken. I asked for the professional opinion. Now, what do I do to correct this—thing—I've created?"

The men worked for a while on Steve's project. When Steve had retired and was finally able to indulge in his passion for photography, he'd really gone all out in equipping his studio with gear. At one point, Alex had counted three camera bodies and a box of nine different lenses. In addition to the computer, printer, and scanner, the studio housed a tripod, a slide viewer (from Steve's predigital days), shelves stocked with reference books, stacks of various sorts of papers, a paper cutter, a collection of precut frames, and a table on which framing could easily be done. On one wall Steve's tools hung in precise order, unlike Alex's own hodgepodge system of storage. For comfort, Steve had added a small fridge, a microwave that he'd bought at a garage sale, and a portable CD player Lily had abandoned a few years earlier. And of course, the studio had been insulated, which, however, didn't mean that Steve could work in comfort without a space heater close by. Maine winters, as Alex had noted many times while working in his own rather chilly studio, could not be conquered entirely. They could be only partially tamed.

"Have you ever thought about starting a family, Alex?"

Alex was a bit taken aback by the question. First, it was random, having nothing to do with photography, at least as far as Alex could make out. (Could the montage family portrait have prompted Steve's thoughts?) Second, it was a question usually asked by women, not by men. At least, that's how it had been in Alex's experience. His mother was the worst of-

fender in this regard. His sister, Anna, was the second worst.

"Uh, sure," he said. "My former wife and I talked
about having kids. For a while. But then things began
to fall apart between us, and planning a family
seemed like a pretty stupid thing to be doing."

"Yes," Steve said, "there's no good to be had by
bringing a child into a fraught environment."

"That's true. Unfortunately, not everyone has a
choice about it."

Steve looked around at Alex sharply but said nothing. Again Alex sensed his friend's anxiety or worry
about—something. Better stick to a neutral topic, he
thought. "You know," he said, pointing to the screen,
"you might want to lighten this background a bit,
right here."

The two men continued to work until something
made Alex look at his watch, a well-worn Timex on
an even more worn leather band. "Whoa," he said, "I
should get back to my place. I set myself a schedule
this morning and already I've blown it. Badly."

Steve thanked him for the constructive criticism—
brutal as it had been—and the advice, and then
asked Alex to join the family for cocktails that
evening.

"Say, six o'clock?" he suggested.

Alex agreed. He wasn't keen on intruding into
other people's family business and he'd gotten a
clear sense that the Rowans, at least a few of them,
were not exactly happy with each other at the moment. But he could admit to himself that he was a bit
lonely—it was Christmas, after all, and a commission
was keeping him from traveling to see his own family—and he could also admit, though it troubled him
a little, that he was interested in knowing more about
Becca. Sure, from what he'd seen in the past day or

so, she wasn't the most easily approachable woman he'd ever known. But there was something else there, something interesting, something worth finding out about, even if it meant putting up with a few rude remarks and an obvious lack of interest on her part.

Besides, it was only cocktails, only an hour of his time. And Nora might be making her cheese puffs. He didn't know what she put in those things—besides cheese—but he was addicted.

"Sure," he said gratefully. "And thanks."

22

"Are you insane, Dad? What were you thinking asking a stranger into our home in this time of crisis?"

Julie rolled her eyes. Olivia really had become ridiculously obsessed with the notion of The Family and it's—it's almost sacred nature.

Steve looked embarrassed. Henry, lumped on his lap, glared at Olivia. "I don't know," he said. "I guess I hoped a guest, a friend, might help lighten the mood around here a bit."

"Well, I think it was a big mistake and if I were you,"—and here she pointed her forefinger at her father—"I'd call him and tell him he can't come."

Olivia stormed out of the kitchen, where her parents had been enjoying a cup of tea. Rather, where they'd been trying to enjoy a cup of tea until their oldest child had appeared.

"It probably wasn't a good idea, was it?" Steve asked his wife.

"Maybe not. But it didn't call for finger pointing."

"Maybe I should call him and make some excuse—"

Julie got up from the table and took their cups to the sink. "No, no," she said. "Everything will be fine. After all, no one's mad at Alex. And you're right. Maybe a diversion is what we all need."

Steve certainly hoped so.

An hour later, Alex arrived at the Rowan house. Julie greeted him with her usual warm manner but . . . but something was wrong. He didn't consider himself the most sensitive guy to have ever lived, but he'd have to be a block of stone not to feel the tension in the Rowan household. Olivia, the oldest sister, wore an expression that resembled a thundercloud. Lily, usually as bright and lovely as her name, looked sad. Becca sat in a straight-backed chair, and while she wasn't exactly glowering, she also very clearly wasn't in a holiday frame of mind. Alex wondered what the hell he had walked into.

Rain, he was told, was out with the boys, sledding on a good-sized hill the locals liked to refer to—not very originally—as Dead Man's Hill. For a second he was tempted to bag the cocktail party in favor of a few runs with the youngest Rowans, but politeness got the better of him. After all, he'd promised Steve he'd be his guest that evening.

Plus, true to Rowan hospitality, there was plenty of food and drink, and for a guy who couldn't cook more than pasta and scrambled eggs, this was a big enticement. Nora had, indeed, made her cheese puffs, and Alex spotted a platter of scallops wrapped in bacon on the coffee table. Bowls of mixed nuts were strategically placed around the room. Good, Alex thought. There was sure to be plenty of cashews. He'd think about his weight after the holidays. Maybe.

Playing bartender, Steve was offering alcoholic and nonalcoholic eggnog, Brandy Alexanders, and for those less inclined toward the creamier holiday drinks, scotch. Alex asked for a glass of scotch—he couldn't afford the good stuff and knew that Steve bought only the best—and felt no compunction about accepting his host's generosity.

Alex glanced at Becca and saw her murkily through the bottom of her glass. Neither, it seemed, did she have a problem accepting her host's generosity. If she kept knocking back those Brandy Alexanders she was going to have to be carried off to bed. And something told Alex that Becca Rowan would not take kindly to being carried off anywhere without her full and waking consent.

Alex took a seat next to Lily just as her pocket began to ring. It took Alex a moment to recognize the tune. It was a pop love song that had been briefly popular a few years earlier. He knew this because one of his former students was always humming it in class. It had driven Alex mad.

"Are you going to take that call?" he asked, assuming it was that idiot boyfriend who had been stupid enough to cheat on someone so genuinely nice and trusting.

Lily shook her head. "No. It's nothing important."

A moment later, the phone rang again. Ah, Alex thought, the idiot was cruel as well as persistent.

"I'm sorry," Lily said, aware that she was blushing. "I should probably just turn the ringer off."

Alex refrained from sharing his opinion that the person who was repeatedly calling Lily could be considered guilty of harassment. The phone rang again and Lily got to her feet.

"Excuse me," she said, and hurried off to a far corner of the living room.

"And I'll be right back, too." Nora lifted the empty tray from the side table by Alex and gave him a warm smile. "There are more cheese puffs in the kitchen."

But before going to the kitchen, Nora joined her granddaughter. Lily was staring at the phone in her hand. "It's Cliff," she said, her voice uncertain. "He's texting me now. He says he has to talk with me. He doesn't want to leave another voice message."

Nora spoke quietly, though the others were too involved in conversation to hear. "And you're not sure you want to talk to him."

"No. I'm not. Not anymore. I wish . . . I wish he would just give me some time. I've got a lot of thinking to do."

Good, Nora thought. *That's just what I was hoping to hear.*

"Grandma?" Lily was saying. "You didn't tell me about staying with Grandpa because you think I should stay with Cliff, did you?"

And now Nora was horrified. She took Lily's free hand and squeezed it. "Oh, Lily, no! I didn't mean . . . Each relationship is different. Thomas and I—we were married, we had a family, we owned a house. We—"

Lily squeezed back and smiled. "That's okay, Grandma. I didn't really think you were telling me to take Cliff back. I just wanted to be sure."

"Lily, I want to apologize."

"What for?" Lily asked. She clicked shut her phone and put it in the pocket of her woolly cardigan.

"For telling you about your grandfather's affair. I don't know why it mattered, not to let the secret die with me. I became lonely in the silence, I suppose. I acted selfishly. I hope I haven't bothered you unduly."

"No, Grandma," Lily said, "you haven't. I mean, I am confused but . . . But it's okay. I'm glad you trusted me enough to tell me. Really."

Nora thought of pressing another apology on the girl, but then thought better of it. Like Lily had just said, she needed some time to think things through. "All right," she said. "We'll let it go at that. Well, I'll be right back. Alex seems to like these cheese puffs of mine." Nora went into the kitchen with the empty tray.

Lily returned to the others in the living room. She took her seat next to Alex again and offered what even she knew was a wan smile.

"It's tough being in demand," he said, with a reassuring smile. He would not mention the idiot ex-boyfriend. They would discuss a neutral topic, like telecommunications.

Lily rolled her eyes. "Yeah. It really can be annoying. If you don't pick up the phone or return an e-mail, you're accused of being out of touch. What if I want to be out of touch? What if I want to be unreachable? What's wrong with wanting to be alone sometimes?"

"Nothing," Alex agreed. "But good luck with trying to be alone in this world. Short of escaping into the wilderness and going entirely off grid, which I can't see you enjoying, I think you're stuck with the ever-increasing intrusiveness of technology."

"I know. I mean, if I was off grid I couldn't check the *Daily Mail UK* celebrity gossip pages! I am so addicted to that site."

"Is British celebrity gossip any different than American celebrity gossip?" Alex asked, amused by the girl's candor.

Lily shrugged. "Mostly it's the same. A total waste of time but fun, even if I don't know the person they're talking about. Or if I don't understand the jargon."

Becca, until then silent, spoke. "If you care at all about your professional standing, it's important to be entirely plugged in. I have no patience with people who can't be tracked. It's just stupid."

Alex cleared his throat; he hadn't been aware that Becca was listening to his silly chat with Lily. Lily checked her wristwatch for no good reason. Becca, seemingly unaware of the discomfort her words had produced, took another long swallow of her drink.

"Who wants more cheese puffs?" Nora had returned from the kitchen with a full tray. Before she had put the tray on the coffee table, Alex had snatched two of the savories.

"I think it's irresponsible not to carry at least a cell phone." Becca uttered her latest statement just as Nora sank into her chair. "I keep telling Mom she should have one when she goes out on those long walks every morning with Hank. What if something happened to her? How could she call 9-1-1? It could be hours before anyone missed her, and by then she could be dead. Bear have been spotted around here, you know. And a frightened moose protecting her young could be deadly."

Nora tried not to smile. There was a glimpse of the old, dramatic Becca, imagining her mother mauled by a hungry bear or squashed under the hooves of an overprotective mother moose. "People lived for many years without cell phones, Becca," she said. "And we got along quite nicely without them."

"That might be true, but now that they're available, what possible good excuse can you have for not carrying one?" she argued. "Look, surgeons operated without anesthetic for years, but now a surgeon deciding to do a liver transplant without it would be called criminal."

Alex laughed. "I'm not sure we can equate anesthetic with cell phones, Becca. But I see your point. Now, if you'll excuse me, I should spend some time with Steve."

Becca watched as Alex joined her father across the room. Immediately, they were deep in conversation. Probably talking about some minute detail of photography. Or maybe they were talking about the Maine weather. Snow, snow, and more snow. Or local politics, if people in this uncivilized place even had a political system. Whatever the topic of their conversation, Becca thought that if Alex knew the real Steve Rowan, the manipulative man behind the friendly exterior, he wouldn't be so chummy with him.

Julie, Olivia, and James joined the circle around Nora. For the past few minutes, they'd been in the kitchen. Naomi, who had been talking with Steve, joined them as well.

"You know, Olivia," Julie said when she'd taken her seat, "I was thinking about your notion of giving this house an official name and—"

"Mom!" Olivia shot a wide-eyed look in the direction of Alex and her father. Neither man seemed in the least interested in the others' conversation. Alex was sketching on a paper cocktail napkin; Steve was watching closely.

"What, dear?" Julie asked.

"Not while there's an outsider present!"

Julie looked puzzled. "An outsider?"

"What's this about naming the house?" David asked. He'd just come from Nora's room, where he'd been sent to retrieve a heavier sweater for his grandmother.

Olivia scowled; when she spoke, it was in a tone far lower than her usual one.

James stared down at his cup of eggnog. Becca thought he looked a bit embarrassed.

"I think this house should have a proper name," Olivia was saying. "It's been in the family now for two generations and we know that one of us will inherit it when Dad and Mom die, so—"

"Excuse me." Julie laughed. "Your father and I are a very long way from dying and I'd prefer that nobody make assumptions about our estate. That's a very private matter between your father and me."

Olivia wasn't at all chastened. "All I'm saying is that the house is an important part of the Rowan family heritage and we should treat it with the respect it deserves."

David laughed. "For God's sake, Liv, we're not royalty! We're not aristocracy. This is just an old farmhouse, not a grand estate built in the sixteenth century and full of priceless paintings and tapestries and antiques. We have no topiary maze. No butler and maid on staff. We don't change clothes for dinner. And we certainly don't ride to the hunt."

"We get your point, David," Julie said, with a frown. Her son really could belabor a topic.

"I don't see anything wrong with Olivia's idea." Naomi shrugged. "We could choose a nice name and have a little sign made for beside the front door. Maybe Alex could help us make the sign. Or maybe I could paint one."

Becca shared David's disdain; she thought the idea was ridiculous but wasn't about to voice her alliance with her brother.

"Grandma." Olivia turned to Nora, who sat in her favorite armchair, one she'd had since the early days of her marriage. Nobody could remember exactly how many times it had been reupholstered. The current fabric pattern was one of dark pink cabbage roses. "What do you think?"

"I think," she said, "that the decision should be your mother's and your father's. After all, the house is theirs."

Julie smiled. "Well, I think it's a fine idea and I was thinking that in keeping with the flower theme I began with the bedrooms, we might call the house Rose Cottage. Oh, I know this isn't a cottage, but doesn't that have a nice ring to it?"

"I had," Olivia said, "something a little more—sophisticated—in mind. Something like, for example, Kently Manor."

Becca couldn't help it. She let out a laugh—and was disconcerted to hear her brother's bark of laughter at the same time.

Lily, who hadn't spoken since her mother had introduced the topic, now said, "Don't be mean, you two. If you don't like the name, you don't have to use it."

"It's just that it sounds so pretentious." David laughed again. "Manor? Come on!"

The discussion came to an end when Alex appeared to offer his farewells. Olivia ignored him, but the others were gracious. Even Becca. Alex smiled to himself. He hoped she could hold her liquor. If not, she was going to have one major headache the next morning.

23

The Brandy Alexanders had softened Becca's mood; maybe the cream had absorbed some of the alcohol (could it do that?) because she didn't feel at all drunk, just—mellow. Even the site of Olivia leaning across the table toward their grandmother, armed with a notebook like a rabid journalist, didn't bother her. Her sister was harmless. Strange, but harmless.

"So you're okay with the idea of my interviewing you on tape? I don't want to make all the preparations if you're going to change your mind, Grandma."

Nora seemed to be controlling a smile. "I told you, Liv, I have no inordinate fear of tape recorders or microphones. I may be old, but I am familiar with basic electronic recording devices."

"Good." Olivia sat back, relieved. "I'll take some preliminary notes this week and when I come back next month, we'll sit down and start recording."

"You're coming again next month?" Julie asked.

"Why, is that a problem? I thought I'd take a week off to do some research and take an oral history from

Grandma. James can handle the business on his own."

From the look of surprise on her brother-in-law's face, Becca would have put money on the fact that he'd known nothing of his wife's plan.

Olivia, oblivious to her husband, was chattering on, pen poised. "For example, I'm hoping you can describe for me what it was like before your family had a dial phone. From what I've read, automatic telephone exchanges were phased in through the early 1950s, but until then, most people didn't have dial phones."

"What's a dial phone?" Michael asked. He was ignored.

Nora laughed. "Well, on the topic of phones I'm going to have to disappoint you, Liv."

"What do you mean? You don't remember anything about using an operator to place a call?"

"Not really. It has been quite a few years."

"Try, Grandma," Olivia urged. "Just think really hard. Did it feel like you had no privacy on the phone? How did you pay for calls? Did you get a bill in the mail?"

"Olivia, dear." Nora sounded exasperated. Becca couldn't blame her. If she were the one being badgered, she'd have popped Olivia in the nose by now. "I just don't remember! Really, one of the pleasures of growing old is that so much just escapes your memory. Life is a lot less complicated than it used to be and, trust me, that's a relief."

"Grandma, how can you say that? Without our memories we're nothing."

James dropped his knife. It clattered against his plate and he murmured an apology Olivia didn't seem to notice the interruption.

"That may be so, Olivia," Nora said, in what Becca thought was a placating tone of voice. "I'll try to jog my memory and see what comes up, all right?"

"Now that that's settled," Julie said brightly, "did I mention I got a call today from my friend Marion—you remember, the woman I met at that preservation society I belonged to back in Massachusetts?"

There were a few murmurs on the order of "No, you didn't" and "Sure, I remember."

"Well, she told me the funniest story about her grandson. It seems he's always wanted to be a marine biologist. Well—"

The mention of marine biology had jump-started Becca's memory. Years ago, when she must have been only six or seven, her parents had taken the family to a marine show in Cape Cod. At least, she thought it was Cape Cod. Anyway, the memory was really about how excited David had been about getting to pet the tame dolphin. Right then he'd announced he was going to work for a cleaner natural environment so the dolphins could swim in a cleaner ocean. Impatiently, Becca waited for her mother to finish relating what seemed to her, who was only half listening, a remarkably boring tale.

"You know what I just remembered?" she said the moment her mother had finished speaking. "I don't know where it was exactly, but, David, you were there, Olivia, too, and Mom and Dad, and it must have been summer and we were all—"

David was staring at his plate, his expression tight. Everyone else, it seemed, was staring at her.

Becca flushed with embarrassment. What was she doing? How could she expect her family to share with her a happy memory when she'd set herself up as their enemy? She knew there was a good chance that if she pursued her decision to tell Rain the truth about her birth, she would alienate her parents and siblings forever. She thought she had known loneliness before now, but to be cut off from her family forever could be far, far worse than anything she'd experienced. Was it, she wondered, a risk worth taking?

Whatever the answer to that question, how could she go on with her anecdote, given the current fraught situation, a situation she had created? The answer was that she couldn't.

"I—I'm sorry," she said. "I suddenly can't remember what I was going to say. I guess Grandma's not the only one with a bad memory. Sorry."

Becca imagined a collective sigh of relief from her family. Someone changed the topic. They had to have because conversation was going on around her, though Becca was entirely unaware of the content.

For the remainder of the meal, Becca was silent. To herself she vowed to avoid the Brandy Alexanders in the future. Alcohol only lured you into a false sense of security and well-being. It only made you weak. It made you vulnerable, not only to the designs of others but maybe worse, to your own demons. It made you vulnerable to the parts of yourself that tormented you. It made you defenseless against the facts of your life that haunted you.

Facts like—like loneliness. And facts like guilt.

24

Nora caught Becca's arm as she attempted to pass out of the dining room after dinner. Becca flinched at the touch.

"We're ready to have that conversation," Nora said. "Everyone is gathering in the living room."

No, Becca thought. *I can't*. She felt beat up by the individual encounters she had barely survived that day, and chastened by her own blunder at dinner. She simply couldn't handle any more conflict. She needed time to recharge her energies. Plus, she felt a headache coming on. A big one.

"Maybe not tonight, Grandma," she said. "I'm exhausted. We can all talk in the morning."

"Everyone is exhausted, Becca," Nora countered. "You can't just drop a bomb on us and then ignore the damage. You've got every one of us scared of the next hit. We don't know when it's coming or how bad it's going to be. You owe us that discussion we talked about last night."

A bomb? Well, she could out-cliché her grandmother. A string of expressions flooded Becca's head.

It was time to cowboy-up. Time to face the music. Time for the fat lady to sing. Well, maybe that last one wasn't quite right. "I'm sorry, Grandma," she said. "You're right, of course."

She followed her grandmother into the living room, where the rest of the family—minus Rain and the boys, of course—were gathered. Becca took the only remaining seat, a straight-backed chair that usually lived in a corner. She moved it slightly so that she wouldn't be directly facing her father.

"Have you thought more about our—conversation—last night, Becca?" Julie said as soon as her daughter was settled.

And about your badgering me today, Becca thought. *And about David's harassing me.* "Yes," she said. "I have."

David leaned forward, his expression tight. "And?"

"And I haven't changed my mind."

Olivia huffed. "As if any of us expected better from her." Becca thought that James looked more embarrassed by his wife's comment than she, Becca, felt.

David went on, as if his older sister hadn't spoken. "You're going to put a huge emotional burden on Rain if you tell her now, and in this—this ridiculous way. She might try to act like an adult, but she's not, Becca. She's still a child."

"I don't see what's so ridiculous—"

But David cut her off. "We'll leave right now if you persist with this nonsense," he threatened. "I will pack up my family and we'll be out of here within the hour."

"Like your leaving this house will stop me from talking to Rain?"

"Now just stop this," Julie snapped. "No one is leaving—don't be silly, David. And Becca, calm down, please. You two sound just like you did when you were kids fighting over what show to watch on TV."

After a moment of silence heavy with tension, Naomi spoke.

"Becca, what do you envision happening after—after you tell Rain that you gave birth to her?"

"Don't indulge her, Naomi," David scolded.

Nora shook her head. "No, David, it's a good question. Becca, do you have an answer to it?"

Becca felt her mouth go dry. The truth was—and how could she admit this, she who was the most organized person in her career and financial life!—the truth was that she hadn't thought through every single detail of the matter. Not entirely.

"Well," she said finally, "I suppose I expect Rain to come to live with me in Boston."

"Of course." The words burst from Olivia. "Because Boston is so much more sophisticated than Framingham!" Her seemingly pointless comment was ignored.

"What if she doesn't want to live with you in Boston?" David asked.

Of course she would. Becca had to believe that her daughter would want to be with her real mother. She had to believe that. Before she could put words to her belief, Naomi pressed on.

"But what about all of the friends Rain has made over the years? What about school? She's been with some of the same kids since first grade. It would be terrible if she had to transfer now. Especially—especially without her family. Without those of us, including the boys, who spend every day and night with her. We've been her daily support system for all these years and she—she's been ours." Naomi pulled a tissue from her sweater pocket and wiped her wet eyes.

"The boys would miss their sister terribly," Julie

said, almost as if to herself. "What would we say to them? How could we explain?"

The mention of the boys, Rain's ostensible brothers, called Becca up short, again. She hadn't thought about them at all when she was planning her new life with Rain. She felt uncomfortable. Was it possible that Rain would miss her little brothers so much that she would choose to return to them? Of course it was possible.

Becca took a deep and steadying breath. "Look," she said, "I'll admit that I haven't ironed out all the details and considered all the logistics yet but—"

"And yet you've been claiming exactly the opposite!" David cried. "You keep telling us you've thought everything through!"

Naomi hushed him with a significant look. The last thing they needed was Rain coming downstairs to see what all the noise was about.

"Becca," her mother said now, leaning forward as if to emphasize her point, "if you want to be a parent, the kind who is responsible for the day-to-day raising of a child, you have to focus on the details. You have to plan every little thing, from what the child's going to eat for breakfast to what vaccines she's going to need at her annual physical. I can't believe you can sit here with us and demand the right to tell your daughter the truth of her birth and say you want her to come to live with you and yet you haven't even thought about, oh, I don't know, which doctor she'll see or what school she'll attend."

Becca was at a momentary loss for words. She didn't want to feel chastened, but she did and it annoyed her.

David was now talking at her, again. "God, Becca, even if you planned on Rain staying in New Hampshire with us—her parents!—what did you expect to have happen? You drop your bombshell, then walk away and leave us to deal with the emotional mess you've created? Is that it? Are you trying to punish us or something? Because if you're angry with me or with Naomi, fine, tell us, but don't drag your child into it."

"All children get dragged into other people's dramas." Olivia's second enigmatic pronouncement of the evening also went unanswered.

Thus far in the conversation, Steve had remained a silent but emotionally involved observer. Now he felt the need to speak; at the same time, he seriously doubted that anything he might say would make much of a difference to his daughter.

"Why are you doing this, Becca?" He knew his voice sounded pleading. "And why now? Please, tell me. Help me to understand."

"Why?" she shot back. "So you can try to change my mind about wanting Rain to know the truth before any more time is wasted in deception?"

"No," he said calmly. "So that I can—so that I can help you."

Becca felt helpless to stop a smirk from appearing on her lips. "I don't need any more help, Dad, thanks. You and Mom and Grandma have already done quite enough for me."

Nora rose to her feet. She was actually trembling. Becca had never seen her grandmother so angry. "Do you really have to be sarcastic?" she said. "Do you really have to talk this way to your mother and father? It's unworthy of you, Becca."

Again, Becca felt chastened. Things were getting out of hand. She was losing control. She had spoken disrespectfully and had made her eighty-six-year-old grandmother scold her. But really, a small voice inside Becca challenged, what did you expect? You are threatening to destroy the peace in which this family has existed for close to twenty years. You are threatening to undermine the structure of the family. You have announced yourself as the enemy of a system that works without a hitch, a system that has served everyone well for many, many years.

Everyone, the voice said, even you. *Everyone*, Becca said back, *except me*.

"We agreed," her grandmother was now saying, repeating the same old argument they all had been using. "We made a deal. We all promised, each one of us. Doesn't that mean anything to you? You gave your word, Becca, that you would keep the truth of Rain's birth a secret until—if—we all agreed it was best for her to know."

"My word was given under pressure," she replied. "You can't hold someone responsible for a promise she made when she's under duress."

And there was that voice again. But isn't that selective morality, Becca? the voice asked. By that reasoning, any promise could be broken with a claim—true or false—of duress at the time the promise was given.

"Oh, please," David spat, "you were fine! Maybe a little scared, but come on, Becca, you were perfectly lucid, even eager for us to do something with—to take care of Rain."

"I never wanted to abandon my child." Becca hated the note of desperation she detected in her voice.

"No one is saying you abandoned your child," Naomi pointed out. "You placed her into the care of your brother and sister-in-law. That's quite a different thing from abandoning."

Becca wasn't quite sure it was, and opened her mouth to say something—she wasn't sure what, exactly—when David cut her off.

"This is insanity," he said. "We're making no progress here at all. Becca, you haven't even tried to see things our way. How can we come to a compromise if—"

"I don't want a compromise. I want my daughter."

"Speaking of whom." Nora turned to Lily. Thus far, Lily had said nothing. "Lily, do you know if Rain suspects anything—odd—going on?"

Lily seemed uncomfortable being the center of her family's attention. "Um, no," she said, fidgeting with a button on her wool sweater. "She hasn't said anything to me."

"You'll let us know if she does?"

Lily agreed that she would. She hoped, though, that her niece could be spared a too early knowledge of the common practice of duplicity, even the kind meant to protect someone from harm. Lily was still processing—and would be for some time, she thought—the news of her grandfather's affair, and the knowledge that at the heart of the Rowan family lay not one but two big secrets.

No one, not even David, seemed to have anything to say, until Julie cleared her throat and spoke.

"Becca," she said, "I am asking for your promise not to approach Rain until the family can meet again after the holiday. This is absolutely not the time for such a conversation with her."

"It wouldn't be a conversation," Nora corrected. "It would be an ambush. You must see that, Becca. It would be grossly unfair of you."

"Please, Becca," Naomi pleaded, "if things are going to—change—at least let her enjoy one final Christmas as . . ." Again, her words were cut off by tears.

Becca shifted in her seat.

"You're demanding something enormous from us,

Becca," her grandmother went on. "The least you can do is meet this simple request for time and more family consideration. If Rain is to be told the truth of her birth, then there must be preparation."

David opened his mouth—no doubt to argue that there would be no telling of the truth except on a family consensus—but Naomi's hand on his arm stopped him.

Becca felt the eyes of her family upon her, anguished, angry, and confused.

"All right," she said after a moment, her reluctance obvious. Vaguely, she wondered if she would lose resolve over time. It worried her but at the same time, she knew the wisest strategy was to go along with the others. This one last time. "I agree."

25

Becca went to bed that night—rather, to the old leather couch—feeling very unhappy and not at all triumphant, as she thought she would feel once her decision had been announced.

Why was it that in her professional life she was strong and confident, unafraid of criticism or argument, but that in her personal life, while with her family and the few acquaintances she could count, she was defensive and suspicious, and yes, let it be said, afraid?

She wondered. Had this been the dynamic only since her pregnancy? Yes. She thought that it had. She had been a rebellious kid, a good kid overall but never one to slink around or feel put-upon. She had been happy.

A strange thought suddenly occurred to her. Had her family really been the cause of this change in attitude and behavior—or had she?

Troubled, Becca pushed the thought aside. Earlier she had brought a decanter of scotch to the den and now she got up from the couch and shot a glass, in spite of the headache that still loomed. Her trainer would not be happy if he knew how many empty calories she was consuming this holiday season, but for once, Becca just didn't care. Again, she tried to fall asleep. She relaxed her body, part by part, from feet to stomach, from shoulders to head. It was no good. She turned on her side and curled into the fetal position. Still, consciousness prevailed. Another shot of scotch was out of the question. She didn't need to face the morning with a Brandy Alexander/scotch hangover. After over an hour, she succumbed to her mind's refusal to let go.

Becca reached for the lamp on the end table, and pulled its frayed cord. She crawled out of her makeshift bed, drew one of the heavier blankets around her, and walked over to the room's only window. It faced the rear of the house; though Becca couldn't see much outside with the light on behind her, she knew that she was looking in the direction of a thick stand of pine trees, like sentinels on guard, or like an army amassed before an attack. Neither image made her feel good.

Nor did the fact that the wind was gaining in velocity and power. The dark pines, the howling wind, and the relative isolation of the house all compounded Becca's already melancholy, lonely mood.

Appropriately enough, her memory conjured a line from a poem by Anne Sexton entitled "Unknown Girl in the Maternity Ward." She had first come upon the poem in a college course on American women poets. It had touched a nerve in her then, with its exploration of the relationship between the maternal bond and the sometimes very different maternal role. It had upset her by coming too close to her own truth, with which she was struggling. Now, in a soft whisper she recited the line that had stayed with her all these years: "Yours is the only face I recognize." Yes. In a way, Rain was the only face—the only person—she recognized in her life.

But unlike the experience of the poem's speaker, it hadn't been that way at first, not until about Rain's fifth birthday. She had fallen in love with her child, but it had taken time. First, she'd had to get past all of the negative and confused emotions swirling around the arrival of her child—guilt, shame, self-reproach, and anger—at herself, at Rain's father, and at her own family. Well, if she hadn't exactly gotten past those debilitating emotions, at least she had learned to keep them in check. Mostly.

In fact, during those first few years, her daughter had been largely a stranger to her. No one had given Becca a set of rules to follow; no one had counseled her or explained to her what rights she might have or what duties she should shoulder. Yes, David and Naomi were to be Rain's parents. That much was clear. But how was the sixteen-year-old "aunt" supposed to behave? What was she supposed to feel?

Becca had a vague memory—more a sense, really—of her mother having approached her a few times, wanting to talk about "the situation," but Becca hadn't wanted to, or maybe she simply hadn't been able to articulate feelings and questions. Becca did remember that she had very much wanted to move on. And more than that, she had wanted to make a success of her life so that never again would she be thought of as a problem for her family to solve.

Initially, Becca hadn't felt guilty about her—distance—from Rain, but over the years, as Becca matured and her maternal feelings blossomed, she grew to be horrified at her original lack of strong feeling for her daughter. What was wrong with her that she hadn't felt an immediate bond? Was she some kind of an emotional cripple?

Maybe. Because in her harsher moments Becca couldn't help but wonder what sort of normal, healthy person would have done what she had done—have unprotected, spur-of-the-moment sex.

Becca shivered as the memories came back, as they too often did. She had been frightened yet anxious for the experience. It wasn't what she'd thought it would be—but what had she thought it would be? The truth was that she didn't remember much about that night, but memory didn't matter. All that mattered was the end result. All that mattered was the product.

God, she thought, holding the blanket tighter around herself, *I've made my daughter, a human being, sound like something on a belt in a factory, a widget, whatever that is, or a cupcake packed in plastic. The end product of my thoughtless action.*

She supposed people, most of her family, assumed that she'd been drinking that night, that fateful night, but she hadn't been. The guy—she refused anymore to name him, even to herself—had had a few beers, but there'd been no coercion, no bullying, not even any pleading or pathetic attempts at evoking pity in her tender female breast for an adolescent boy's desires, his needs.

No. She'd gone with him willingly, like a lamb to the slaughter.

Becca laughed out loud at herself. There was that old, long-repressed flair for the dramatic. A lamb to the slaughter, indeed!

Anyway, that wasn't quite right. Becca was pretty sure a lamb had no idea what was in store for it at the end of the evening, while at least she'd had the clinical facts down and some brief, incomplete experi-

ence to guide her. Tales from her friends were of no
use; the girls she knew who had "gone all the way,"
who had "hooked up," were of two types—those who
obviously exaggerated the experience and those who
spoke with an annoyingly romantic vagueness. Both
sorts of tales were useless.

And Becca's having sex with that guy hadn't been
premeditated, not like what a few girls she'd known
had planned down to the last plan-able detail.
They'd set out to lose their virginity as if they were
setting out on a mission for NASA. How, when,
where, with whom—it all was organized and arranged
and there was no room for the slightest bit of emotion in it all. There was even an escape plan in place,
in case something went wrong, like the unexpected
arrival home of a parent.

For Becca, had it been passion or perversity that
led her to spend those minutes with the guy, Rain's
father? No, it definitely had not been passion. And if
it had been perversity, it was of the curious kind, on
the order of "I know that if I put my finger in this
candle's flame, my skin will burn. And yet, I can't resist."

Well, Becca reflected, burns heal and sometimes
don't even leave a scar, so that the memory of the
burn eventually fades away, too, but a baby conceived
because a girl was too perverse to do what she knew
was right and use birth control, well, that baby isn't
going to become a faded memory. That baby is going
to be a living, breathing reality for as long as Fate
would allow.

She thought about Rain's father. About how there
was a good chance he didn't even know a baby had
ever been born. She hadn't even told him that she was
pregnant. It was news she could barely bring herself to
articulate to her parents, so deep was her shame and

terror. And the father—he was, after all, a stranger to her. Besides his first and last name, Becca had known virtually nothing about him. Still, the idea of ending the pregnancy was something she couldn't face. She couldn't say why, exactly, but every feeling rebelled against the idea. So, nine months later, Rain had been born.

Suddenly, standing at the window of her parents' house, Becca remembered an incident that had taken place a long time ago. She had been out of college two, maybe three years, and was living in a small apartment in Somerville. She'd gone home to spend the weekend at her parents' house; Saturday afternoon her mother realized she was out of milk, and Becca had offered to go to the supermarket. Once there, she was waylaid in front of the display of one percent milk by a man about her parents' age, a man she vaguely remembered as having been to a party at the Rowan house many years before, when she was still in middle school. Had he been a neighbor? Whatever he'd been then, at that moment in the supermarket he was a nosy, insinuating man who stood too close to Becca as he introduced himself and then, to her horror, had said: "Wasn't there some—difficulty—with you a few years ago?" Briefly, she'd been paralyzed with fear, and then anger had gotten the better of her. She felt violated. "The only difficulty with me," she spat, taking a large step away from the man, "is having to endure another second of your presence." She'd left the supermarket in a hurry, without the milk; she could pick up a half gailon at the gas station's convenience store.

Becca sighed. Yes, anonymity. Silence. These had been her only and her constant companions; one certainly couldn't call them friends.

She felt terribly, overwhelmingly alone. And she

felt scared. But when she tried to identify just what it was that scared her, she couldn't. Not really.

Becca turned from the window, crawled back into her makeshift bed, and switched off the lamp. The wind was still growing in intensity, roaring now, and rattling the windowpanes. It was a mournful sound to match her mournful mood.

Sleep was a very long time in coming.

26

Julie was dusting the furniture in the living room
when her oldest child confronted her. That's how it
felt when Olivia approached you, Julie had decided.
Like you were being confronted. And it had gotten
far worse in the past few years. Julie wondered if the
sight of Olivia first thing each morning made her
employees cringe. It was an uncharitable thought
but there it was.

"Mom," she said, "I was looking for that old salt
cellar, you know, the silver one with all the chasing. I
can't seem to find it. I could have sworn I last saw it
in this breakfront. But that was more than a year ago.
What did you do with it? Did you move it somewhere
without telling anyone?"

This time, Julie didn't have to feign absentminded-
ness. For a moment she really couldn't remember
what had become of the silver salt cellar her grandmother had bought in a flea market—so the story
went—when, as an eighteen-year-old, she had traveled to France for a month with a wealthy aunt.

"Now, let me think for a minute," she said, squinting as if that action might aid recall. "Oh, yes, I remember now. I sold it."

Julie wasn't a sentimental person. To her, expediency and practicality mattered far more than tokens or things and the arbitrary meanings people attached to them. To sell an object almost never used—and one she didn't think very pretty—meant nothing more to her than what it was, a sale. It was a business transaction, and emotions had nothing to do with business transactions.

To her oldest daughter, however, it meant something quite other. The look on Olivia's face startled Julie.

"Liv, dear, what's wrong?" she asked.

"I cannot believe that you sold your grandmother's most precious possession."

Julie shrugged. "Actually, she didn't much care for it, which is why she gave it to me."

"That's not the point," Olivia retorted. "Your grandmother touched that salt cellar. For all we know, her fingerprints were still on it!"

The thought struck Julie as slightly macabre. Her daughter wanted to collect the fingerprints of a dead woman, who, from all Julie could remember, wasn't a very nice woman to begin with. She thought of the old habit of putting a bit of a dead loved one's hair in a locket and shuddered. "Oh, Liv," she said, "aren't the living more important than the dead and their artifacts?"

"No, they're not! How can you say that? If everyone took the position that history didn't matter, then—"

Olivia stopped abruptly. Julie watched her daughter carefully. She seemed overwhelmed by her own emotions.

"Then what?" she prompted. "Oh, honey, I'm not

saying we can't treasure and cherish memories and stories and traditions. And I certainly believe that we should learn from mistakes made in the past. All I'm saying is that—"

Olivia interrupted her. "I'm going to get that salt cellar back. When exactly did you sell it? Who did you sell it to? Maybe I can still track it down. Was it to a dealer in Boston? Do you have the receipt? If I leave early tomorrow morning, and if the snow slows down, I can make it to Boston in time to—"

Julie reached for her daughter's arm, but Olivia stepped away. "Olivia," she said. "Don't be absurd! That troublesome old salt cellar is probably long gone. Besides, your proper place is right here with your family. And with your husband. Not chasing down some dusty old—artifact."

Olivia stalked off a few feet, then abruptly turned to face her mother. "Why did you sell it anyway?" she demanded. "On a whim?"

"No, not on a whim. The boiler needed to be replaced and I didn't want to dip into our savings. That old salt cellar was just sitting there, doing nothing but taking up space and collecting dust, so I thought I'd see if it was worth something. Well, it turned out it was worth something, just about the cost of a new boiler."

"A boiler!" Olivia cried, her face a mask of horror and incomprehension. "God, Mom, why didn't you ask me for the money?"

"Oh, Liv, don't be absurd," Julie said with a laugh. "I'm not asking my children to pay for repairs to my home. Besides, I didn't say your father and I didn't have the money. I just didn't want to spend it."

"So you sold a precious family heirloom instead."

Julie was beginning to lose patience with her oldest child. "Liv, it was only a salt cellar! It wasn't, oh, I don't know, a functioning body part! I'm not dealing in the illegal selling of human organs!"

Olivia suddenly stalked off to the other end of the room, and then back, as if her body contained negative energy it just had to burn. "Mom, don't you understand that objects have meaning beyond their physical presence or their usefulness or their monetary value? The objects we own are—they're talismans. They bespeak memory. They're treasures."

Julie sighed. How had her daughter become so . . . What was the word? Fixated. Obsessed. It didn't seem normal.

"Well," she said, "in my opinion, these objects we say we own far too often own us."

"That makes no sense, Mom. And anyway, that salt cellar wasn't yours to sell!"

Julie raised her eyebrows. "Oh? Then whose was it? Yours?"

"It was no one's to sell. We are the custodians, our family, we are the keepers of our past."

"Custodians!" Julie couldn't help but laugh. "That's ridiculous, Liv. This is a family, a living, breathing organism, not a museum."

"Yeah, well, next time don't do me—don't do this family—any favors."

Julie felt hurt, and annoyed. But she tried to retain an even temper. Shouting wasn't going to get her point across; maybe reason would, and maybe it wouldn't. It was still worth a try. "I truly don't know why you're so upset, Olivia," she said. "We have plenty of family heirlooms. I'd be more than glad to give you a few special pieces. James likes to cook, doesn't he? Well, we still have all of Great-Grandma Rowan's recipes."

"This is not about James. This is about the family."

If James wasn't Olivia's family, then her daughter's

marriage was likely in worse shape than she'd imagined. Julie sighed. She felt defeated and, more annoyingly, puzzled. "Well, it's too late to do anything about the salt cellar now. What's done is done, what's gone is gone."

Olivia rubbed her eyes and it suddenly struck Julie that her daughter looked older than her forty-two years. There were lines around her mouth that hadn't been there six months ago, and deep shadows ringed her eyes. Could sadness—emptiness—really wreak such havoc? Apparently it could.

"I've got some sorting to do," Olivia said, dropping her hands and turning toward the stairs.

"Liv? Before you go . . ."

"What?" she said, turning back with obvious reluctance.

Julie wasn't a coward. She would risk an explosion on the chance that her daughter would open up about any trouble she and her husband might be having. "Is everything okay between you and James?"

Olivia looked stunned. "Of course it is," she said. "Why would you even ask?"

"Well, I don't know, you both seem a little—well, not yourselves. I couldn't help wondering if maybe the subject of adoption had come up again."

"No," she said flatly. Firmly. "It hasn't."

"Oh. Well, and then this news about Becca wanting to tell everything to Rain . . . I thought it might—upset you. After all you and James went through trying to start a—"

Julie stopped mid-sentence. A look had come across her daughter's face that frightened her. It was a look of—fury. Olivia stalked back toward her mother.

"You want the truth, Mom?" she said. "I'll tell you what upsets me. I'll tell you what's upset me for the past sixteen years. The fact that you and Dad and Grandma decided to give Rain to David and Naomi and not to me."

Julie was alarmed by her daughter's anger. She wasn't afraid, at least, not for her own sake, but for her daughter, she was. She'd had no idea Olivia had been harboring such terrible resentment toward her family, a resentment that easily might have been fueled by the trouble she'd had conceiving—and by the ultimate acceptance of the fact that she would never be a biological mother.

"But, Liv," she said, hoping her sympathy was obvious, "you were single, on your own, working your way through grad school. David was married, settled. And he and Naomi planned on starting a family soon, anyway."

Olivia poked her forefinger at her own chest. Julie flinched at the force of the gesture. "I'd planned on having a family, too, Mom," Olivia said. "And my being single was no reason for you to deny me custody of Rain. Plenty of single people are parents, and damn good ones at that. I've always been responsible. For God's sake, Mom, I babysat for David, Becca, and Lily. It's not as if I had no experience being around children. And you remember I took that child psychology class in college."

One college course didn't make you an expert on anything, but Julie let that comment slide. "I'm sorry, Liv," she said. "But . . . why didn't you say anything to us back then? At least your father and I would have known your feelings on the matter."

Olivia let out a brief and nasty laugh. "Because I was a fool. I thought you or Dad or Grandma would know how I might feel. But you probably never even considered my feelings, did you?"

"We're not mind readers, Olivia. I'm sorry, but as

far as I recall, you never indicated to any of us that you wanted to be Rain's adoptive mother."

"Yeah, well, what good would it have done, anyway? You still would have chosen David. David is the favorite. He always has been and he always will be."

"Oh, stop that, Olivia," Julie said, with rising anger. "You sound like a child. David and Naomi came to us with an offer to be Rain's parents. And their willingness convinced us that giving Rain to them was the right thing to do. I refuse to be made to feel guilty about this situation. By you or Becca or by anybody."

Olivia shook her head. "Fine. Wash your hands of all responsibility. Sell off the family's property. Deny any guilt in passing over your oldest child in favor of the favorite child. Life must be really easy for people like you. People without a trace of sentiment or family feeling. People who don't give a damn about anyone but themselves."

Before Julie could open her mouth to reply—and she had no idea what to say to that horrible and unfair accusation—Olivia stormed from the living room and clomped up the stairs, leaving her mother feeling, for the first time in years, truly wounded.

27

Lily leaned against the doorjamb and watched her mother, her perfect mother, as she stood at the kitchen sink, washing dishes. Lily had always thought of her mother as one of the most straightforward, honest, and dependable people she had ever met.

Until now. Until Cliff's cruel betrayal and Nora's shocking revelation and Becca's strange demand. Until Lily's mind and her heart had begun to accept the incredible complexity of people and their motives.

There had to be more to Julie than Lily saw before her. There had to be more than she had ever seen and maybe more than she ever would see. There had to be some event that Julie kept all to herself, like a youthful engagement to another man, or a miscarriage, or—impossible thought!—an affair of her own. Secret desires, maybe never acted upon but cherished. Hidden resentments. There had to be.

Or did there have to be? Maybe Julie Rowan was keeping nothing to herself. Maybe some people were, indeed, "open books," showing their one and only face to the world. Maybe some people simply had nothing to hide from the world. They lived one hundred percent honestly and behaved one hundred percent ethically. If guilt was possible, then why couldn't innocence be possible, too?

Maybe. But Lily was beginning to doubt that a truly innocent life was a possible one.

Her mother squatted to retrieve a new sponge from the cabinet under the sink. Really, Lily thought, her mother had the energy of a person half her age. Most people she knew, even some people Lily's own age, would have needed to grab on to the sink for help in rising, but not her mother.

Lily's thoughts drifted back to Cliff. Cliff had kept his affair a secret from Lily. For weeks it had been going on with Lily none the wiser, until a well-meaning girl in her dorm, who'd heard a rumor from a friend of the girl Cliff was cheating with, alerted her. At first, of course, Lily couldn't believe that Cliff—her Cliff!—would ever have betrayed her. But then, suspicion crept in as it is wont to do and, screwing up her courage, Lily confronted the guy she had considered the man of her dreams.

It had taken Lily's persistent questioning over several hours before Cliff finally broke down and admitted that yes, he'd slept with Ashley Griggs from economics class, and that yes, it had happened more than once. Maybe more than twice; he couldn't exactly remember. He thought he might have been drunk the last time.

How did you not know if you were drunk, Lily—who hardly ever drank—had wondered.

"Why did you lie to me?" Lily had asked then, bewildered. "When I first asked you if you'd cheated on me with Ashley, why did you swear that nothing had happened?"

Cliff claimed that he hadn't wanted to hurt her, that's why he hadn't confessed before and that's why, when confronted, he'd lied about his innocence. He was sorry for the affair. It had been wrong of him. He'd hoped that if Lily never found out about it, they could go on just like before. He'd wanted to spare her the ugly truth.

But Lily had wondered if she could believe him. Maybe he hadn't told her about the affair because he was afraid of getting into trouble, of losing his attractive, intelligent, warmhearted girlfriend. And as long as he could pull off a sordid relationship behind her back, well, why not keep his mouth shut? He could, as the saying goes, have his cake and eat it, too.

Lily simply didn't know. Maybe secrets were essential to life, at least to human life, to society, whether "society" meant a neighborhood, an extended family, a husband and wife, or a small group of friends. Maybe secrets weren't what were so bad. Maybe it was intent that really mattered. If you kept a secret to protect someone from being hurt—assuming of course your decision wasn't entirely selfish, assuming you weren't keeping quiet because if the truth got out you'd be in big trouble—maybe then you weren't doing anything wrong. Maybe, instead, you were being kind. Maybe you were being good and unselfish.

It was complicated, this thing called life. People wore masks. One person might harbor various personalities within herself, and might comprise several layers of characters. And because of this, a person might never, ever know for sure if or when she was doing the right thing or the best thing or the smartest thing. And if a person couldn't be sure about the quality of her own words and actions, how then could she ever judge the words and actions of anyone else?

Sureties, Lily was coming to realize, were not a part of human interaction. Maybe that old saying about death and taxes being the only inevitable, definite things was true.

Take her grandmother, for example. Lily had always seen her grandmother as—well, as perfect, as a person without doubt or cause for regret. How naïve she had been! Nora had known deception and secrecy, too, just like everyone else. She had known heartache.

Lily's cell phone rang. It was the tone she'd chosen to indicate a call from Cliff, a passage from a pop song he loved. Once she'd thought his having a special tone was—special. Lily put the phone on Silence. He could leave a message if he had anything important to say.

"I didn't know anyone was there!" Julie had turned from the sink at the sound of the phone.

"Sorry, Mom." Lily came all the way into the kitchen and flopped into a chair at the table. "I didn't mean to scare you."

"Oh, I don't scare easily. I was just startled. Who was that on the phone?"

"Cliff."

"Why didn't you take his call?" Julie asked, folding a dish towel over an old-fashioned drying rack by the sink.

"Because I didn't want to talk to him."

Julie joined her daughter at the table. "Has he been calling a lot? Or, what is it, sending typed messages?"

"Text messages. Texting. Yeah," she said. "He's been pretty relentless."

"Well, I hope you're not thinking of getting back with that boy."

"Not really," Lily said, surprised by her own reply. Not very long ago she'd been considering that very possibility. "Why?"

Julie shuddered for effect. "I never liked him. He gave me a bit of the creeps."

Lily was stunned. "The creeps! I can't believe this! Why didn't you ever say anything to me?"

Julie reached over to pat her daughter's arm.

"As if you would have listened to your mother! No, Lily, every woman has to find out certain things on her own. Besides, you know I don't like to talk badly about a person. Especially one I don't know very well. Remember, I only met the boy two or three times. Evidence, or the lack of it, Lily, that's what you need to be careful of when forming an opinion about someone."

"Well," Lily argued, "if you even suspected he was going to cheat on me, I think you should have said something. You should have warned me."

Julie waved her hand as if dismissing an annoying fly. "Oh, it was nothing as specific as that. I just didn't care for the boy. It was something about his face, something I thought I saw lurking there. Anyway, he's in the past, so let's let him stay there."

Lily was stunned. What other secrets was her family keeping? She felt disoriented, as if everything she'd thought she could rely on was being revealed as an illusion.

"Well," she said finally, "I still think that if everyone thought Cliff was a jerk, someone should have given me an honest opinion!"

"First of all," her mother was saying, justifying her silence on the matter of Cliff, "I have no idea what the other family members thought about Cliff. And second, it's very hard to advise someone about a matter of the heart. And it can be very dangerous. People tend not to want to hear that their significant other is a—jerk, as you put it. Especially if it's true. If I had protested your relationship with Cliff, you might very well have run off and married him by now."

"Oh, I would not have run off and married him!" But even as she protested, Lily wondered if her mother was right about relationship advice, that people really didn't want it. She thought of Nora and wondered if any of her friends had offered their opinions on what Nora should do about her cheating husband. Assuming Nora had told anyone about Thomas's affair, and now Lily remembered that Nora had claimed she hadn't. Maybe she'd been too ashamed to tell anyone. Or maybe—and Lily didn't much like this idea—maybe Nora had wanted to protect Thomas's reputation among their friends.

"Well, I'm sorry," Julie was saying. "I seem to have made an awful lot of mistakes with my children and I'm just finding out about all of them today!"

Lily squeezed her mother's hand. "Oh, Mom, I'm sorry. It's just that, I don't know, I have a lot on my mind right now. Suddenly it feels like everything I thought I knew to be one way is really the other way, or both ways at the same time. Which makes no sense, but maybe nothing makes any sense. Maybe that's the point."

Julie sighed, got up from the table, and gave her daughter a brief but strong hug. "Welcome to the gooey mess we call life. Every time you think you've got something in your grasp, it seems to slip away or change beyond recognition."

It was not what Lily wanted to hear. "I think I'm going to lie down," she said.

Lily retreated to the bedroom she always used when visiting her parents. It was the same room in which she had slept as a child when visiting her grandmother. There was comfort in the familiar surroundings. Lily was not a person who relished constant change and newness.

Julie had sewn the curtains by hand when Lily was only four; for Lily's twelfth birthday, Nora had made the quilt that covered the bed in sections of vibrant yellow, deep green, and multicolored calico. Though the curtains could use replacing and the quilt was threadbare in parts, Lily refused to let them go.

Over the low, painted wood dresser hung a mirror that was original to the house. At least, it had been part of the sale when her grandparents had bought the house back in the 1960s. Or maybe it had been in the 1970s. Anyway, the glass wasn't very clear, but Lily loved the rather ornate, heavy oak frame and was glad the old mirror hadn't been moved to another location in the house.

A small bookcase against one wall held a variety of old schoolbooks, as well as several often-read copies of Nancy Drew mysteries; a paperback copy of *Jane Eyre* that Lily had bought at a garage sale for fifty cents; and an oversize illustrated book about horses, from the time when Lily had been obsessed with the idea of owning a horse of her own. That phase passed after her first horseback riding lesson had ended in disaster. She'd been too frightened of the size of the animal in actuality to enjoy one moment of the experience. In books, horses looked so noble and romantic. In reality, they were terrifying and had very big teeth.

On a shelf over the bookcase sat a row of dolls: a Barbie with impossibly matted blond hair; a small rubber baby doll, naked; a threadbare Raggedy Ann.

Lily had always found it hard to part with things she'd once loved. Maybe in that way she was a bit like her grandmother.

Lily curled up on the old single bed—Rain was using an air mattress during her visit—but was unable to drift off to sleep. Instead, she found herself thinking more about secrets and silence. She found herself thinking about how deceptions both large and small were so much a part of human interaction. About how easy it was to find yourself alone or apart. About how suddenly you could feel lonely.

Lily remembered when Nora had asked her what her friends had said about Cliff and his cheating. Nora had asked if her friends had been supportive, if they'd offered advice good or bad, if they'd sworn their loyalty to her as fellow women, warriors in the battle with men.

But the truth was that Lily had no real friends, and hadn't fully realized that until the break with Cliff. The person she'd turned to first had been Nora, her grandmother. The only place she'd wanted to run off to for sanctuary had been her parents' house in Maine. Aside from informing her roommate and a few other women in her social circle that she and Cliff were through, she hadn't opened up to anyone but her family.

Why? Lily turned on the bed so that she could get a glimpse out the window. The sky—at least the part of it she could see—was that weird winter white. It seemed foreboding and Lily turned her back on it. She wondered if other large families were like hers, a self-sufficient unit, a self-sustaining environment. As far as she knew, none of her siblings had close friendships. In the Rowans's case, the Rowans were enough.

But that couldn't have been entirely true, not always true. Because Lily had learned that lots of people had cared enough about Steve and Julie and their children to come to Becca's rescue, to help the Rowans execute their scheme to pass off Rain as David's child.

She wondered. Had the family dynamic changed after that? Had Lily, only five at the time, absorbed a new modus operandi, one that taught it was best to turn inward in times of trouble, as well as in times of joy?

Lily sighed. Secrets. Was she the only person over eighteen who didn't have any secrets? Try as she might, she just couldn't think of one piece of information she was deliberately holding back from the people she loved. She wondered if it was inevitable that one day she would, like most everyone else, have something she could reveal to no one, or to only a select few. A word she regretted having spoken. An act of betrayal, perhaps. Maybe even a crime.

No. Lily knew that she was in many ways inexperienced, but she was one hundred percent certain she'd never commit a punishable crime. But there was a lot of life ahead of her—she hoped. And it seemed entirely possible that some day in the distant future, she, too, might be sharing a deeply held secret with her own daughter or granddaughter.

Lily sat up. That was the future. For now, she was going to live and enjoy as simple and honest a life as she could.

28

"Uh, Liv? Could you try to keep the noise level to a dull roar? I'm trying to get some work done and I can hear you all the way down in the den."

Olivia hadn't heard her sister enter the attic. She got up from the dusty wooden floor and turned, wiping her hands on her jeans.

"Maybe you shouldn't bring work home," she said.

Becca let that remark slide. She had no doubt that her older sister brought work home all the time. When you owned your own business, your work was your life; the public invariably leaked over into the private. It was much the same for the vice president of an ambitious business-to-business advertising firm.

An old, porcelain-faced doll in a long, dusty white dress was propped on a painted bureau. It caught Becca's eye now and she reached for it. "I remember this from—"

"Don't touch it!" Olivia cried.

Becca jumped and withdrew her hand. "Take it easy, Liv. I wasn't going to throw it at the wall. I just wanted to see it."

"See with your eyes, not with your hands."

Before she could stop herself, the words were coming out. Stupid, hurtful words, spoken unthinkingly as most stupid and hurtful words are spoken. "It's a good thing you didn't have kids after all," she said. "They'd be petrified to breathe around you."

Olivia's face became a mask of fury. "How dare you say such a cruel thing to me!" she cried. "You have no idea of what you have. You have more than I ever will, and yet you're so selfish you're grasping for more! My children would suffer? What makes you think your child won't suffer with you as her mother? What makes you think you deserve your daughter?"

Becca knew she should apologize, but she simply didn't want to. Not now, not after her sister's last challenge. "Uh, I deserve my daughter because I gave birth to her," she said. "Anyway, what business is it of yours? My relationship with Rain has nothing to do with you."

"Yes, it does," Olivia shot back. "This is a family issue, Becca, and like it or not, you're part of this family. We all are. What one of us does affects every other person."

Becca laughed. Really, her sister was unbelievable. Her obsession with the unit called The Family was ludicrous. "Oh, please, Liv," she said, "get a life!"

"What does that mean?"

"It means that you're obsessed with this idea of The Family and it's driving everybody crazy. I'm an individual, Liv. It was an accident that I was born into this group of people who call themselves the Rowans. We're all alone in this world. We all have to act independently, each one of us. We all have to live and die by ourselves. We all have to be self-sufficient."

"If you really believe that," Olivia said with a sneer, "it's probably why you're so miserable. Everyone can tell, you know. You've become like a—like a pod. When was the last time you went on a date? When was the last time a man even looked at you with interest?"

The questions were like barbs in Becca's side. "My personal life is not open for discussion," she replied lamely.

Olivia laughed a mean-sounding laugh. "You know, Becca, this whole thing is entirely unfair. I'm the one who wanted a baby and I'm the one who tried and tried to get pregnant. Do you know how much time and money I spent at fertility clinic after fertility clinic? Only to find out that even if I did manage to get pregnant, my body wouldn't be able to maintain the pregnancy? Do you know how much that hurt me? Of course you don't. You don't care about anyone but yourself."

"That's not true!" Becca protested. "I—"

But her sister wasn't listening. "It's just so goddamn unfair. You're the one who got pregnant just like that, first time around, and you didn't even want a baby. You didn't even care enough about your child to fight to keep her. And now you're demanding her back? You have no right to that girl. I should have been the one to have her. Mom and Dad should have given her to me!"

Becca was stunned. And a little bit scared. She'd had no idea her sister had wanted to raise Rain as her own. She had no idea her sister had been harboring such rabid resentment. For a mad moment she wondered if Olivia was capable of harming her—or of harming Rain. But no. She didn't think her sister was that far gone into sadness. Still . . .

Olivia stood with her shoulders thrust back, arms held straight at her side, a completely unnatural, terribly rigid pose. Becca hardly recognized the woman who stood before her.

"I'd like you to leave," Olivia said.

Becca was only too happy to oblige.

29

The two women sat in companionable silence. Nora was knitting, her workbag at her feet, neatly organized. Her granddaughter sat cross-legged on her grandmother's bed, idly twisting a length of yarn.

Lily looked now at the tall pine dresser against the wall. A white lacy cloth was laid across the top. On it, next to a photo of Nora and Thomas on their fortieth wedding anniversary, sat a small square object. It was a daisy, first pressed in a book and then glued to a piece of wood and coated with shellac. It was a keepsake from Nora's first date with Thomas. She had been fifteen and Thomas, just turned sixteen.

Lily had always thought it terribly romantic of her grandmother to keep such a token of remembrance. She herself had saved a ticket stub from the first movie she and Cliff had seen together. But when just a few months later Cliff professed to not remembering ever having seen the movie, let alone with Lily, she'd tucked the stub into an old book, figuring she'd find a more meaningful token of their relationship someday, something that mattered to both of them.

And now, looking around her grandmother's room, Lily realized that she never had found such a token and she wondered why.

Nora had kept other things, too, each one representing a member of her family. A cat's eye made of purple and lilac wool that Olivia had made in grammar school hung over the bed. In a case on a shelf sat David's various medals for excellence in high school science. A framed photograph of Becca as an oak tree in a first-grade play stood on the dresser, alongside a terribly juvenile poem Lily had written and framed for her grandmother's birthday many years before.

All these things were evidence of love. They were gifts given because the givers had wanted to give them, not because they were forced. They were items Nora had chosen to keep because they held a special meaning or evoked a special memory. Unlike the "gift" that Mr. Pollen had brought to the house . . .

"By the way, Grandma," Lily asked, breaking the long silence between them, "what did you do with that—thing—Mr. Pollen gave us? I've got nothing against pinecones on a tree or in a wreath but . . . as tableware?"

Nora looked up from her knitting and grimaced. "I put it in a plastic bag and asked your father to keep it somewhere in his studio. Preferably out of sight. I didn't have the heart to throw it out after poor Mr. Pollen went through so much trouble to make it for us."

"Maybe he made it for you, Grandma. Maybe he has a crush on you."

Her grandmother gave her a look. "Are you trying to give me a heart attack? Because the thought of living under the same roof as Mr. Pollen—which, quite possibly, is made of pinecones—just might kill me. And what about the ghost of Flying Hammer Hattie?"

Lily laughed. "I'm sorry. I was only kidding."

The women lapsed back into silence. Lily's attention was caught by another photo of her grandparents, this one on the bedside table. The couple was arm in arm and smiling broadly. They were dressed as if for church or an important event. As far as Lily could tell, both of her grandparents looked as if they were about thirty-three or thirty-four. Was the photograph taken during the time that her grandfather was having the affair with the other woman? Would he have had the nerve to smile into the camera while holding the arm of the woman to whom he had vowed to be faithful, knowing full well that he was being unfaithful to her?

Lily looked away. She was beginning to feel as if she were a character in a creepy Victorian sensation novel, like Wilkie Collins's *The Moonstone* or one of the other novels she'd had to read in a course she'd taken her sophomore year. On the outside, the family looked completely normal, even dull, but on the inside, every single member of the family was either insane or evil. Sometimes they were both. Everyone was embroiled in lies; everyone held dark and dirty secrets.

Well, maybe the Rowan family wasn't exactly as bad as all that, but still, Lily had caught another glimpse beneath the veil of respectability, and it depressed her. Was everybody doomed to dissemble? If that were the case, she thought with a wry note, then she would make a fortune as a lawyer.

"Grandma," she asked suddenly, "are you going to tell Olivia the truth about Grandpa Thomas? About the affair, I mean. I was thinking that because she's so obsessed with the past, she might want to know the full truth about her grandparents' marriage."

Again, Nora looked up from her knitting. She was astonished at the idea. "Lord, no," she said. "What does Thomas's affair have to do with whatever it is Olivia is experiencing? No. Olivia is a very unhappy woman. I don't know for certain what it is she's looking for up in that attic, but I don't think 'truth' has anything to do with it."

Lily sighed. "Well, whatever it is, I wish she'd stay out of the attic at night. Rain slept through the noise, but I was awake until almost two in the morning with her rummaging around up there."

"Are you sure it wasn't squirrels?" Nora asked with a smile. "We did have a bit of an infestation last spring."

"How can you have a bit of an infestation? Aren't infestations by nature overwhelming? Anyway, if it was squirrels, they were on steroids. No, only a human being could clomp around like that. I swear she dropped a trunk right over my head."

"I'm afraid asking her not to make so much noise probably won't get you anywhere. At any rate, it will only be a few more days. James told me they're leaving on the twenty-seventh."

"I guess they can't leave the business for too long. And they probably have New Year's Eve plans."

"Yes. Maybe." Nora simply couldn't imagine her oldest grandchild and her husband enjoying a romantic dinner for two. Not this year. Not given the all too obvious tensions between them. Nora would have liked to help—if there was a way to help save another person's marriage, and she doubted that there was.

Lily got up from the bed and walked over to a

framed photo of her grandfather. She looked at it closely. It had been taken at a lake, probably somewhere in Massachusetts. Her grandparents hadn't had much money to travel often or far; what money they had they'd invested in the Kently house. In the photo, Thomas stood on the grassy shore, just by a wooden dock. He wore a floppy hat and was holding a fishing rod in one hand and in the other, a huge fish, obviously his catch. He was grinning and looked happy and proud.

"Everyone always says what a great guy Grandpa was," Lily said, returning the photo to the dresser. "Everyone says he was so nice and funny. The way David talks about him, it was like Grandpa was his hero. How could everyone have been so wrong?"

Had Lily not learned anything from their talks? "They weren't wrong," Nora said with emphasis. "Your grandfather was a good man. He was loving, and smart, and hardworking. But nobody is perfect, Lily. Even good men—and good women—make mistakes."

"An affair is a pretty big mistake!" Lily protested. "It's not like it happens without you knowing it. Ooops, I seem to be having an affair! How did that happen? I mean, you have to want to do it and decide to do it. How can a good person consciously decide to break his wedding vow and still be a good person?"

"Oh, Lily," Nora sighed. "You are so young! And, at the risk of angering you, I must say that you are also quite naïve. How did you manage to remain so—untouched—for so long?"

Lily didn't seem to be offended by her grandmother's question. "I'm not naïve, Grandma," she replied. "I know affairs happen. I just don't think they should."

"Of course affairs shouldn't happen. But they do and, really, it doesn't help to condemn the one who strayed without at least trying to understand why. And without then trying to forgive. And, in certain circumstances, without trying to give the relationship another chance. That's what mature adults do, Lily. They try to understand, to forgive, and to put broken relationships back together."

Lily didn't say anything for a long moment. Finally, she admitted to her confusion. "I don't know if I'll ever see things the way you do, Grandma," she said.

"Well, only time will tell." Nora rose from her chair. "Right now, why don't we go to the kitchen and have a cup of tea?"

30

"May I come in?"

Naomi looked up from the book she was reading. "Oh. Becca. Sure." She was sitting on the bed in the Lupine Room, propped against two of the many pillows Julie provided for each of her guests. Becca thought that her mother was one of those women who put a little too much importance into sacks of synthetic down. The living room alone was strewn with no fewer than twelve pillows of various sizes, shapes, and comfort. A few of them had had tassels before Henry Le Mew had gotten to them.

"Thanks," Becca said. She gestured toward the door behind her. "Do you mind if I—"

"No, go ahead."

Becca shut the door and perched on a low bench, close to the bed, that had once been part of a vanity set. There was a pillow on the bench, too. Becca pushed it aside.

Naomi shut her book. "I guess you want to talk about—the situation," she said.

Becca nodded. But oddly, she didn't know quite

where to begin. So much had already been said, some of it wrong. So much more was still to be said, none of it easy.

Maybe Naomi sensed her sister-in-law's sudden confusion because she began the conversation. "You know," she said, "I have to admit that there are times when I completely forget that I'm not Rain's biological mother. There are times when I completely forget that I didn't actually give birth to her. We've been— together—for so long. . . ."

Becca nodded. Naomi and Rain had been together since moments after Becca had delivered Rain into the world. Right from the start. Someone—who was it?—had suggested that it might be easier for Becca not to hold the baby, but to have her given directly to Naomi, who was waiting just yards away from the birthing room. Something about the prevention of bonding . . .

Becca hadn't argued. At least, she didn't remember protesting this suggestion. So much of that time was lost to memory—if it had been registered at all.

She did, though, sometimes wonder if not being the first to hold her baby was the cause of the delayed onset of love. No matter. In the end it certainly hadn't prevented a bond from developing between Becca and Rain, a bond that had brought her to this place in her life where she felt the urgent need to reclaim what was rightfully hers.

"I do sympathize with you, Becca," Naomi said now, her tone begging belief. "I do. I know what it's like to give birth to a child. I know the bond that forms—it's visceral and immediate. It can't be replaced or imitated or ignored."

Becca believed her sister-in-law, though she was surprised that Naomi, of all people, seemed to be the only one sympathetic to her cause. Or, at least, to some of what she was feeling. But why should she be surprised? Hadn't Naomi always shown sympathy, as well as empathy, toward those around her? Yes, Becca had to admit. She had.

"But you think that what I want to do is wrong?" Becca asked now, sure that Naomi had more to say and, strangely, wanting to hear it.

Naomi moved to sit on the edge of the bed, her legs crossed at the knee. "Did you talk to anyone about this?" she asked, ignoring Becca's question. "A friend, maybe, or a therapist?"

"No," Becca said promptly. "No one." There was no need to lie about it. No one but family knew the truth. She had no close friends, no friends at all really, if friends meant people you opened up to, people with whom you shared your secrets and dreams, your heartbreaks and your triumphs.

"Oh." Naomi nodded. Her tone was gentle when she went on. "I was wondering what a friend might have advised. You know, talking through an important decision before acting on it can give you perspective you just didn't have before."

I don't want perspective, Becca thought. *I want my daughter.* "No," she repeated. "I haven't spoken to anyone."

Naomi seemed to be considering her next words carefully. Finally, she said, "I wonder if maybe you might want to talk to a professional. Maybe you could find a therapist or a counselor of some sort. What you're suggesting seems so—disruptive—that I can't help but wonder—"

"Are you saying I'm mentally ill?" Becca was aware of her defensive tone. "That if I get some medication in me, all this 'nonsense' about wanting Rain to know her real mother will just go away?"

Naomi moved closer to Becca; the two women were now sitting almost knee to knee. "Please don't be angry with me, Becca. Please believe that I only want what's right for you and for Rain. I'm not your enemy. I never was your enemy."

Becca looked down at her hands. As much as she might have wanted to, she couldn't deny the truth of that statement. And she couldn't help but recall all that Naomi had done for her during the pregnancy. They had been close during those long months. With her brother's wife, Becca had felt little of the embarrassment she had felt with her parents and grandmother. She'd never been close with Olivia, so with Naomi at her side she finally felt the comforting presence of an older sister, someone who could advise her as well as someone who could laugh with her.

And more than any other family member Naomi had admired Becca's decision not to have an abortion. Not that an abortion would have been an "easy way out"; it would have carried emotional ramifications and it wouldn't have erased the fact that Becca had been pregnant. It wouldn't erase the fact that she had acted carelessly.

But the point was that Naomi had been there for Becca. She had even wanted to be with Becca for the birth, though at the last minute Becca had felt too shy. She'd asked to be alone, with only the medical team. Even her mother waited outside the birthing room. Not once had Becca cried out for her family. Later, the doctor had told Julie she'd never seen such a young woman handle the trials of childbirth with such courage.

And then . . . It had taken some time for Becca to feel comfortable with the baby. After all, she was desperate to go back to school and to graduate. . . . It confused her, to feel so awkward with someone she had carried in her own body for nine months. Again, as Becca sat with her sister-in-law in the Lupine Room, the haunting line from the poem by Anne Sexton came to mind. "Yours is the only face I recognize."

On the contrary, Naomi had slipped easily into the role of new mother. The primary bonding between mother and child had occurred between Naomi and Rain. It had to be that way if the "plan" was going to work and Rain was going to be a happy child and eventually a well-adjusted adult.

Quickly, and perhaps inevitably, the women's relationship changed from one of friends and co-conspirators to one less companionable, to a relationship—in Becca's mind—of inequality. One was powerful and the other was powerless; one was an insider and the other was an outsider; one was entitled and the other, not entitled. Naomi had the responsibility of ensuring another person's well-being. Becca had only the responsibility of not screwing up again.

After what seemed like many long moments, Becca spoke. "I know you're not my enemy," she said, looking back up at her sister-in-law. "But please, Naomi. Please consider my feelings in this."

And what exactly are those feelings? It was that small, annoying inner voice again. Loneliness? Guilt and the need to make atonement? And do those feelings really have anything to do with Rain? Or are they all about fixing your wretched life?

Naomi reached out and gave Becca's hand a brief squeeze. "I'm trying to, Becca. I really am."

"I just want to claim my daughter."

Naomi sighed with impatience or frustration; Becca couldn't tell which. "Oh, Becca," she said, "a person isn't something you can claim! She's not a coat at a coat check. She's an autonomous, independent, free being."

"You know what I mean, Naomi. I want to—I want to acknowledge her as who she really is. My daughter."

"She's a lot more than that, Becca. She's also my daughter. And David's daughter. And Michael and Malcolm's big sister. And a granddaughter and a friend and a student and . . . and her own person." Tears began to stream from Naomi's eyes. She got up and went to the bedside table for a tissue.

Just then the door to the Lupine Room opened roughly and David came stalking in.

"What the hell are you saying to my wife?" he demanded.

Becca looked up at him and wondered if he had been eavesdropping. "We're just talking, David."

"Then why is Naomi crying? Naomi, what the hell did she say to you?"

"This is not about you, David," she answered calmly. "This is a private conversation."

"But I want to know—"

"David!" Naomi pushed past him and ran out of the room.

"You're a bully, David." The words were out before Becca could consider the wisdom of speaking them.

David slammed the door shut and turned on his sister. "And you're a troublemaker."

"Lower your voice, David. Talking at the top of your lungs doesn't make your argument any stronger. And it doesn't intimidate me."

David stood with his hands clenched at his sides. Becca wondered if her brother had ever thrown a punch, in anger or in self-defense. She suspected he had.

"Can't you try to spare your daughter your own

pain?" he said now, in a voice marginally softer than the one he'd used before. "She'll stumble across her own traumas someday. She'll create her own sadness. She doesn't need to carry the burden of your sadness as well. Don't make a victim of your daughter."

"A victim! Don't you think she's a victim already? A victim of deception?"

"If she is a victim—and I'm not saying that she is— then you're one of the victimizers. Don't try to pass all the blame onto us. You were a part of the decision."

"I was coerced."

"You were counseled," he corrected. "You're revising history, Becca. You're remaking the story so that it conveniently supports your current needs."

Her brother's words came very close to hitting their intended mark. Becca felt her insides squirm. She couldn't help but think that there was a bit of truth in David's accusation.

"You can't cast off pain altogether," he was saying now. "Some of it will always stick to you."

Becca's insides stopped squirming. "What are you talking about?" she said. "I'm not looking to cast off pain, whatever that means. I'm just trying—"

But David cut her off. "I swear I'll never forgive you if you ruin my daughter's life. And yes, I know what I just said. For all intents and purposes, Rain is my daughter and she always will be. And Naomi. You'll destroy her, too. I'm sorry, Becca. I won't let you do that. After all Naomi's done for you—"

And there it was again. The old argument: Becca should be grateful. She should keep her mouth shut and her head down and just be glad the Rowan family hadn't thrown her out into the big, bad world to fend for herself and her bastard baby.

"Oh, don't start with that 'my wife is a saint'

garbage, David," Becca cried. "She only did what she promised to 〔 〕. no more and no less."

"A lot mo.., Becca. You don't know what it's like to raise a child day in and day out. The challenges that spring up, the unexpected crises, the times when you feel entirely depleted of energy but you just have to keep going no matter—"

"You're right," she interrupted. "I don't know what it's like to be a day-by-day parent. But it's through no fault of my own."

"No one's been stopping you from getting married and having another baby."

"That's not the point and you know it, David."

Even as she uttered those last words, Becca was dimly aware that she was continuing to fight with David for the sake of fighting itself. And she wondered how much she even believed in what she was saying, the arguments she was making, the accusations she was flinging. What had happened to her compassion for Naomi, the woman who had befriended her so thoroughly?

But she couldn't seem to stop the flow of feelings and words. She didn't know how to back down, to cry for help, to say, "I am so terribly lonely."

Why was it so much easier to fight than to negotiate, to demand than to request?

Was she the bully, after all? Was she the one acting like a brute?

She became aware that David was ranting on. "If you tell Rain the truth, it'll open a whole can of worms about her father. Do you really want that for her? You don't even know where the guy is, though if Mom's sources are right, it's probably behind bars or dead drunk in some alley."

"Oh, don't be so self-righteous, David!"

David glared. "I'm not being self-righteous. I'm trying to prevent a young girl from coming into contact with a man even you have to admit she's better off not knowing."

"I promise I won't let Rain go anywhere near her biological father," Becca said. "And I won't let him come anywhere near her."

"That's not a promise you can keep."

"Maybe not," she conceded after a moment. "But the fact remains that I have a lot more to offer Rain than you and Naomi."

"Like what, money? Things? Designer clothes and whatever else it is those spoiled Hollywood kids can't seem to live without?"

Really, Becca thought. He makes himself out to be a pillar of self-sacrifice and moral rectitude. Like he didn't have a flat-screen television? "Yes, David," she said, "money. And things. Things like vacations in Europe and the best colleges and . . ."

David laughed that bark of a laugh. "Oh, I get it now! You want to buy your daughter's love! What makes you so sure she won't throw the money in your face? What makes you so sure she won't hate you for giving her up and for lying to her all these years?"

"What makes you so sure she won't hate you and Naomi for lying to her?"

David couldn't answer. The truth was that nothing made him feel sure that Rain wouldn't hate him and Naomi and the whole Rowan clan for what they'd done sixteen years earlier.

"This conversation is going nowhere," he said. His tone was clipped. "When you can talk calmly and dispassionately about your daughter's welfare, let me know. Until then . . ."

As soon as David had left the room, Becca sank onto her brother and sister-in-law's bed, head in her hands. She felt suddenly and utterly deflated. Nothing was going as she'd hoped. Everything, everything was going horribly wrong.

31

Later that afternoon, David lay on the bed in the Lupine Room. He was fully dressed and his shoes were on. He knew that he shouldn't put his shoes on the clean bedspread; Naomi was always telling him that, just like his mother had told him until he'd left home for college. But he always seemed to forget their admonishments until it was too late and the damage had already been done.

The house was quiet, except for an occasional thump from the attic. Of course it was Olivia, on her never-ending, obsessive expedition into the past. Well, David thought, good luck to her. For himself, he could do without the past. In fact, there were great big chunks of the past he wished he could forget or, better yet, erase.

Like the adoption. Not that he wanted Rain to go away; he adored the girl and couldn't imagine a life without her. It was just . . . Just the way in which she had come into the life of the family that was bothersome.

There was something else that was bothersome.

David was beginning to suspect that his protectiveness involved more than a little self-interest. He didn't want the girl he thought of as his daughter to think badly of him, to lose respect for him. He didn't want her to stop loving him and if she learned the truth of her birth now, in Becca's abrupt way, there seemed a pretty good chance that she would stop loving the man she'd always considered her father. There seemed a pretty good chance that she might even hate him. And David didn't believe he could handle that. He was strong, even tough, but that was one thing he was dead sure would knock him down for good. He needed to be seen as a good man, an honest person, and the idea of being shown for who he seemed after all to be, a deceiver though one with the best of intentions, was abhorent to him.

David kicked his legs against the mattress, aware that it was a childish way to show frustration. But yes, damn it, he did harbor feelings of guilt about his own role in the secret that had so largely defined the life of the family. Not terrible, debilitating guilt, but guilt all the same. Not that he was going to admit to those feelings publicly, not while Becca was on her insane campaign to destroy his life. David winced. He meant, on her insane campaign to destroy the life of his daughter.

There was a knock on the door. Before David could speak, it opened and Naomi slipped into the room.

"Hey."

"Hey," he replied.

"Am I interrupting?"

"Of course not."

Naomi stretched out next to her husband on the bed and kissed his cheek. "I'm sorry I yelled at you, David," she said.

"I'm sorry I was such a bully. That's what Becca called me, anyway."

"You were just concerned about me. I know that."

"Yeah. I'm pretty concerned about us all, right now. I feel so powerless, like I'm a victim. Like we're all victims." David gave a wry laugh. "You know, if this were a movie or a novel, we'd all plot to silence Becca once and for all."

"David!"

"What?" he said, his eyes wide in a look of feigned innocence. "It's true. Here's this person threatening to destroy our family by revealing a long-kept secret. She won't listen to reason. She refuses to change her mind. And we're all sitting here trembling, waiting for her to strike. If we were fictional characters and not decent human beings, we'd join forces like we did sixteen years ago and—make something happen."

"But we're not fictional characters," Naomi pointed out. "So stop entertaining such crazy notions."

David turned his head to look at his wife, the person he loved more than anyone else in the world. "You're my best friend, you know," he said. "Whom else could I talk to so honestly?"

"No one."

"Come to think about it, you're my only friend."

Naomi lightly slapped his arm. "Oh, come on, David. Don't sound so self-pitying. What about Johnny, at work?"

"Sure, he's a good guy to go bowling with. But . . . I wouldn't call him a friend. It's not like we talk about anything but work."

"And bowling."

"Yeah," he conceded, "and bowling. I don't know, Naomi. I guess I've never been very good at keeping friends. Do you realize I don't keep in touch with one buddy from high school or college? Not one."

"What about your father? Wouldn't you call him a friend?"

David thought about that. "Yes," he said after a moment. "Dad became my friend over time. When I was growing up, he was only my father. That was good. I didn't need another buddy to hang out with. I needed a parent to guide me, to teach me right from wrong. But now . . . Yeah, it looks like you and Dad are my best friends. Now that Grandpa is gone."

"You're a pretty lucky guy, you know."

David lifted Naomi's hand and kissed it. Yeah, he was pretty lucky. He got to spend every day of his life with the woman he adored. "I do know, Naomi," he said.

"So no more talk about rubbing out your sister."

"I didn't say we'd have to kill her," he argued. "We could, I don't know, inject her with a drug that would erase her memory and then pack her off to start a new life in—in the Siberian arctic."

"You know how Becca hates the cold weather."

"Maybe she wouldn't be able to remember that she hates it."

"David."

"All right," he said, with exaggerated reluctance. "No more fantasies of Becca disappearing from our lives."

"Good." Naomi kissed her husband's cheek again and got up from the bed.

"But maybe she could just go away for a little while, like a couple of months."

Naomi turned back to her husband, her hand on the doorknob. "You always have to have the last word, don't you?"

David grinned. "Yes."

32

Rain was sitting cross-legged on the living room couch, flipping through yet another of the seemingly endless supply of glossy fashion magazines she'd brought with her. Becca, coming into the room from the direction of the kitchen, opened her mouth to say hello, or maybe to comment on the magazine—and suddenly found that she couldn't speak.

Because for the very first time in sixteen years, Becca had caught a glimpse of Rain's father in the girl on the couch. The recognition had been fleeting but all too real. The tilt of her daughter's head as she read—it had been nothing more than that, but that was everything.

Becca felt as if she had been issued an emotional slap so brutal it had sent her flying to the hardwood floor of the living room, where she lay prone, unable to summon the energy to rise.

It was crazy, she knew, but over the years she had almost come to believe that Rain was the product of her body alone, just another version of her own self, uncontaminated by the genetic contributions of anyone else.

But she was not. Rain was unique. She could not be incorporated or consumed or even claimed. She was not a copy, not a clone. And she was not entirely a Rowan.

Becca walked to the closest chair and sank into it.

"What's wrong, Aunt Becca?" Rain said, finally looking up. "You look like you just saw a ghost. Hey, you know what? I don't think I've ever actually used that expression before."

With supreme effort, Becca managed to reply. "Everything's fine," she lied. "I just—I just remembered something I'd forgotten. Something I was supposed to have remembered."

"Getting old, huh?" Rain teased. "Having a senior moment? Don't worry. I'll come visit you in the nursing home."

Becca smiled weakly in response. Rain went back to her reading and Becca watched her. And as she watched she wondered what exactly she had given Rain in terms of genetics, biology. Her lanky build certainly. The Rowan eyes. An interest in fashion maybe, if such a thing could be passed along via DNA. Her high spirits? Maybe. But Rain's father also had been full of high spirits. . . . Was there nothing else?

Not for the first time, Becca wondered how much more Rain would be like her, her biological mother, if they had lived together from the start, if Becca's presence had served as a primary example of being and conduct, and not Naomi's. And would Rain's being more like Becca be a good thing or a bad thing or something in between? It was impossible to say, and almost as impossible to imagine.

"Hey, Grandpa."

Becca jumped. She hadn't heard her father come into the living room. Abruptly, she got up from her chair.

"Hi, Rain," he said. "Becca."

Rain unfolded her legs and got up from the couch. "Well, I'm out of here," she said. "I promised to let Lily hear this new CD I got last week."

"She's growing into a lovely young woman," Steve said when she had left the room.

"Yes."

The silence that followed this brief exchange was awkward but not hostile. Becca waited.

Finally, her father spoke. "I'd like us to talk. Please."

It was a moment before Becca could reply. "I can't, Dad," she said, her voice unexpectedly wavering. "Not now."

Steve nodded. "All right. I can't force you to talk to me. I wouldn't force you even if I could."

"I'm sorry," she said, though she wasn't quite sure what she was sorry about. At that moment it could have been nothing, or everything.

Becca stood perfectly still until her father had disappeared upstairs. Then, she escaped into the den—and that was how it felt, like an escape—and shut the door behind her. Her breath was coming rapidly now and she wondered if she was having a panic or an anxiety attack. She'd never had either sort of experience; she'd never allowed herself to feel enough of an emotion that might upset her so.

Becca sank onto the couch and concentrated on getting her breathing under control. But it was not so easy. The fact was that she was as scared now of a confrontation with her father as she had been eager for it only a few days earlier. Her confusion troubled her. What had happened to her steely resolve?

And her father's latest request coming hard upon the heels of Becca having seen evidence of Rain's biological father in her daughter . . . well, it had thrown her.

She felt very unhappy about having made Naomi cry, and so often. Until this week she'd never made anyone cry, not that she knew of. And really, Naomi had always been so generous with Becca, offering her access to Rain and, though she didn't strictly have to, even asking for Becca's opinion on certain matters of Rain's upbringing.

And then there was the latest argument with David. There had been moments when she had felt unable to control the words coming out of her mouth. There had been moments when those words—her own words—had befuddled her. It was almost as if she was losing hold of her original desire, her primary goal, and fighting blindly, for the sake of the fight alone.

Something concrete and clear and without passion. Something she could fix or solve without emotion. That's what Becca badly needed right then. That's what would bring everything back into hard, clear focus.

So she checked her e-mail. There were no messages from anyone at the office, or from clients. She checked her phone. There was one message, from her dentist's receptionist, confirming an appointment for a cleaning on January 2. For a moment she considered calling Mary, her assistant—she had Mary's home number—just to be sure she wasn't needed, but she abandoned the notion. Mary didn't need her few days off interrupted by her boss. Becca had never considered it before, but now she wondered what Mary and the other staff thought about her. She knew she was a fair leader; she knew she had never been and would never be an abusive boss. There could be no, or very few, complaints there. But did her staff, her colleagues, find her to be . . . odd? One of those slightly strange single women who didn't seem to be quite—complete—as a person? Did they think of her as a character, rather than as a woman, a human being?

Becca slumped back onto the old leather couch. She felt vaguely disappointed that there was no crisis to be solved or critical decision to be made. She wondered: Of what did her life really consist?

Becca searched for a word that could describe what she was experiencing right then. It came after a few moments. She felt—desperate. She felt as if she could jump out of her skin and through the window. She felt as if she might start screaming and not stop for a very long time. She had never felt this way before, so unmoored, so untethered, and it scared her. Maybe, she thought miserably, Olivia wasn't the only Rowan woman with a serious emotional problem. Working out at the gym and eating right was all well and good, but the body wasn't of much use if the mind and the heart were ailing.

Beccca lay back on the couch. Take deep breaths, she told herself. Just take deep, slow breaths. And you might want to call your doctor when you get back to Boston.

33

"This is nice, just the two of us. It can get a little—close—with everyone at the house."

James waited for a response from his wife, seated next to him in the passenger seat of their car. "Liv?" he said.

Olivia started, as if she had been a million miles away in her thoughts. "What?"

"Nothing. Just . . . Nothing."

He had persuaded her to take a drive with him this afternoon. It had taken a good degree of coaxing, too. Olivia had been reluctant to leave the house and her hunting and cataloguing—or, was it that she'd been reluctant to spend time alone with her husband? James couldn't dismiss the thought, not entirely. True, they spent much of every day together at the office, but there, talk was of business. Evenings were invariably spent at home, but for a long time now, there had been little real communication. Most nights Olivia bolted her dinner and headed off to her computer, where she spent hours reading through Web sites that focused on ancestor searches and family trees. Olivia had made it perfectly clear that she'd rather spend time e-mailing the strangers she met on those sites than watching television—or doing anything else—with her husband.

"Oh!" she said now. James was glad to hear her so animated. "Guess what Hilary told me the other day! I can't believe I forgot to mention this."

"Who's Hilary?" he asked.

Olivia shot him a look of supreme annoyance. "I've only told you about twenty times. She's one of the coordinators of the FamilyTime chat room."

"Oh, yes. Sorry." James tried but he couldn't remember the names and obsessions of his wife's new online friends. When, he wondered now, was the last time Olivia had met with one of her flesh-and-blood friends in town? Not that she had many friends, but James knew of a few nice women with whom his wife used to socialize.

"Anyway," Olivia was saying, "she told me that someone stole her list of members' e-mail addresses. She thinks it was probably someone from a rival site. Can you believe that?"

James really didn't know what to say in response to his wife's question. It didn't seem like such an unusual crime to him. "Huh," would have to suffice.

He waited a few moments before speaking again. "We could probably still catch the Quilt Show if you'd like."

Olivia frowned. "No, thanks."

James took a chance. "Quilts play an important part in folk history, don't they?"

"Yes."

"And they're often made by several generations of women within a family, aren't they? Women working as a sort of team."

"Sometimes."

"I just thought that since—"

"The Rowans have no really old quilts. It's too bad. I've been through every trunk in the attic and there's simply nothing. Grandma says she has a vague memory of her mother having an old quilt, but she has no idea where it went. Can you believe that?"

Again, James just said, "Huh."

So this was the nature and extent of their communication. And it had been months—almost half a year—since they'd had sex. James didn't like to think of himself as one of those selfish, sex-obsessed men, but he did have a normal appetite, and the prospect of adopting a celibate life while still in his forties didn't excite him. He wouldn't cheat on his wife; he didn't have the stomach for such crude behavior.

Besides, it wasn't just about the sexual act. What bothered James about the distance that had grown between Olivia and him was that it was not only physical but also emotional. Olivia's lack of interest in making love was, to James's perception, a lack of interest in maintaining his friendship and his affection.

He was certain there was no other man in Olivia's life. If he were a dramatic sort, he supposed he could feel jealous of her preoccupation with the Rowan family's past. But James didn't think anyone could feel jealousy over a rival that didn't seem able to bring any real joy. In fact, Olivia seemed to grow increasingly unhappy the longer she spent poring over census reports, chatting online, and digging through her parents' attic.

Still, James did feel a bit like the proverbial third wheel in his marriage these days, that or an afterthought in his wife's frantic schedule. But he hadn't given up trying to assert and maintain his position as partner.

"I thought," he said now, "that on the way home on the twenty-seventh we could stop in Portland. We could go to the museum, or maybe visit the Victoria Mansion. I've heard they decorate really beautifully for Christmas. Then we could get lunch somewhere. We could go to that funky old bar on the water, what is it called, J's Oyster? Remember, they have those raw scallops you love."

"I can't," she said quickly. James thought he heard a hint of panic in his wife's tone. "I can't miss my Wednesday night chat group. We're meeting at five and we've got a renowned social anthropologist joining in. It should be fascinating."

"Oh," he said. "Okay." He was disappointed but not surprised by Olivia's answer. For close to a year now, Olivia had seemed entirely uninterested in all their old routines; she'd showed absolutely no interest in doing the things they used to enjoy doing together, like taking walks and hunting out funky little restaurants and watching old movies. James had wondered if maybe Olivia was clinically depressed, but he had resisted talking to her about this, scared off by her continual rebuffs, some of which could be angry and cold.

Still, James continued to tempt Olivia with suggestions of her usual favorites. And yet in return she never offered a kind word or a compliment; she never made a gesture toward him, to let him know that yes, he still mattered to her. James wasn't looking for any special favors, just some recognition that she was still aware of him as a person—and as her husband. James didn't think he was asking for too much. . . .

But maybe this was just the way his marriage was going to be from now on. Maybe he would just have to learn to accept conditions the way they were. Lots of couples simply existed side by side without any particular warmth or real companionship. Lots of couples survived if it seemed they couldn't actually thrive. He'd just never thought he would be part of one of those couples.

James sighed. He hadn't meant to. He glanced over at his wife, but she didn't seem to have noticed. Her head was turned to the passenger's window and to the snowy landscape outside. James wondered what it was she actually saw as they drove through the Maine landscape.

34

She'd seen Alex from the window of the den. He was doing some work out back, by a small toolshed her grandfather had built many years ago. At least, Becca assumed he was working. Alex was wielding a hammer. That's what people did with hammers. They built things or destroyed them.

On impulse, she bundled into her coat and boots and joined him. Maybe, she thought, fresh air, no matter that it was cold, might make her feel better. Calmer. More normal. Maybe. When you felt as desperate as Becca felt then, anything was worth a try.

"What are you doing out here?" Alex asked when he looked up to find her standing a few feet away. His nose was red-tipped with cold and he wore a suede and shearling hat with earflaps. Becca thought it made him look slightly goofy but not in a bad way.

Becca shrugged. She hadn't thought of what excuse she would use for being out behind the house, where there was absolutely no reason for her to be unless she wanted to build a snowman or go cross-country skiing, nether of which she wanted to do. Ever.

Before she could make up a hopefully plausible lie, Alex went on. "Not that you need a reason to be out here. It is your parents' property. I just meant, what are you doing out here in the cold? It's only just above freezing, you know."

"Thanks for the reminder. What are you doing out here? Well, I mean . . ."

She gestured to a pile of tools laid out in a large, rough suede pouch.

"Those heavy winds we had the other night just about finished this old shed. Your father was going to repair it himself, but I didn't think it was a good idea. He's not as young as he used to be. . . ."

"Is he sick?" The question was out before Becca could grasp the genuine concern she felt for her father.

"Not that I know of, no."

"Isn't it an odd time of the year to be repairing a shed?" she asked. "I mean . . . there's snow all over the place."

Alex grinned sheepishly. "You caught me. I'm avoiding work at the moment. One of the projects I'm supposed to be finishing in the next weeks is . . . Well, it's giving me some trouble. So I'm hoping that some physical exercise will, I don't know, renew my energies."

"You're a procrastinator."

"Guilty as charged. But at least I'm doing something positive for someone else while I'm procrastinating. Steve's really such a good guy that—"

"Why are you always defending my father?" Becca asked, cutting him off.

Alex looked at her, puzzled. "I wasn't aware I was

defending him. Why? Should I have been? Has he done something he needs defending for?"

"He . . ." Becca paused. Suddenly, she didn't know how to answer that question. "No," she said. "Never mind."

"It bothers you that I'm friendly with him."

"That didn't sound like a question."

"It wasn't," Alex said. "It's pretty obvious you're not thrilled about my spending time with your father."

"I know it's none of my business who you spend time with but—"

"You're right," he said, yanking an old, bent nail out of a piece of the rotted wood. "It is none of your business."

Becca was taken back. Alex's tone had been matter-of-fact, not at all nasty, but still, his response had startled her. It was so—honest and blunt. And in spite of her determined aloneness, in spite of her dependence on isolation, she could no longer deny that she found him interesting. She had sought him out this afternoon, hadn't she?

"So," Alex said, his voice loud in the cold, still air, "what did you want to be when you grew up?"

"What?" Becca laughed a little, taken aback. "What a bizarre thing to ask."

Alex shrugged and tossed aside another length of rotted wood. "Why is it bizarre?"

"I don't know," she said after a moment.

"So, what's your answer?"

"I don't know," she repeated. "When I was a kid I never thought much about the future. I guess I was kind of—shallow. I was a bit wild. What was right in front of me seemed interesting enough. I can't really explain it."

What she could explain—but couldn't voice—was

that the wild, shallow girl had gotten pulled up pretty short at the age of sixteen, and that ever since, life had been all about focusing on school and career in order to provide for her daughter. Life had been all about proving to her family that she wasn't entirely a screwup.

"Well," Alex said, "if you could start all over again, what would you like to be when you grow up? Pie in the sky. In a perfect world. Just say whatever's in your heart."

"I can't answer that," Becca said finally.

"Why?"

"Because I have absolutely no idea what to say."

"I can't believe there's nothing in your heart. . . ."

"It's not that," she said quickly. "I just don't know what I—what I like. I just don't know what, if anything, interests me. Other than work, of course."

It pained her to realize this, and it surprised her to be admitting it, especially to someone she hardly knew. Such admissions could lead to exposure of her secret—and of herself—and that was what she had feared most for the past sixteen years. And yet here she was telling her parents' neighbor an awkward truth. She felt uncomfortable, but not uncomfortable enough to run. Why was that?

"I have no hobbies," she went on. "I have no passions. I go to work. I go to the gym. I read but . . . But not what I want to read, whatever that is. I mean, I read work-related stuff. I listen to the news."

Alex wiped his sweaty forehead with the back of his gloved hand. Yes, it was cold, but the sun was strong and he'd been working hard.

"So," he said, "it's safe to say that you find little pleasure in life. I mean, in your life, in the way you're living it."

"God, Alex," Becca said with a laugh that was not

one of pleasure, "I might not be the happiest or most fulfilled person around, but I'm not suicidal!"

"I'm sorry," he said. "That wasn't at all what I meant to imply. It just sounds as if . . . well, as if you don't have a lot of fun."

"Is fun so important?" she asked, very much wanting to hear his answer.

"I think it is. Look, I'm not talking about amusement park fun, though I've got nothing against a good roller coaster ride. I mean—fun as in simple pleasures. Laughter with friends. Picnics. Chocolate cake if that's your thing. Museums. Movies. The stuff of daily life. Do you have a pet?"

"I work too many hours. I'd have to hire someone to walk a dog."

Alex smiled. "Have you considered fish?"

"No."

"Do I dare to ask about plants?"

"You just did. No plants."

"Just an idea."

Becca was silent for a moment. She lived in a neighborhood replete with galleries and she hardly ever glanced in a window, let alone attended an opening. When was the last time she'd been to the Museum of Fine Arts? It was within walking distance of her apartment; what good excuse could she have for not seeing a show or attending a film there? And then there was Fenway Park, and the aquarium, and the science museum, and the Isabella Stewart Gardner Museum. . . . She hadn't been to any of these places in years. As for entertaining at home, she never did any; who was there to invite for dinner or cocktails or Sunday brunch? And in spite of the fact that Becca had a fully furnished guest bedroom, the only person who had ever spent the night at the condo was Rain.

Becca felt slightly sick.

"So," she said finally, "here I am, a person with no pleasures in her life. What does that say about me?"

"I don't know." Alex eyed her curiously. "Do you really want an answer from me?"

"Does it say that I'm boring?"

Now he laughed heartily. "Oh, I wouldn't say that!"

"So, what would you say?" she pressed.

"It's not what I'd say that matters, Becca. It's what you would say about yourself."

"Humor me."

"All right." Alex paused. "How about: Becca Rowan is a person who hasn't yet discovered her bliss."

Becca grimaced. It wasn't a good look for her, but she couldn't help herself. "My bliss? I've never much cared for that word."

"Okay. How about this: Becca Rowan is a glass half empty."

"A what?"

Alex gave a sigh of feigned irritation. "Fine. How about: Becca Rowan is a person who hasn't yet discovered—love."

"You mean that I should get married?" she blurted. "Because a man will solve all of my problems? Because a man will give me a life I don't seem capable of making on my own?"

Alex put up his hands as if defending himself physically. "Hell, no. I'm the last person to claim a man is the answer to anything! Besides, I don't mean romantic love, necessarily. I mean love as in a passion for something. Love as in a motive for getting up in the morning and looking forward to doing whatever it is you're going to be doing. Love as in—love as in having a real purpose in your life."

But I do know love, Becca argued silently. I know

the love for my daughter. And I have a purpose. I'm a mother and an aunt. Isn't that enough?

No, that pesky other voice replied. It's not enough. And I think you know that by now. Becca shut her ears to the voice's message.

When Becca didn't say anything more, Alex went back to the job of repairing the old toolshed. And while he worked, she thought.

Since Rain's birth, she had come to think of herself as a person living post-trauma, as a person living post–defining incident. She saw everything in her life, every word and incident, to be in some relation—even if it was a strained one—to the fact of Rain's birth. Part of her suspected that this was an unhealthy way to live. But she simply couldn't imagine her life being otherwise.

Suddenly, she found herself wondering about the nature of Alex's emotional life. He had gone through a divorce, and though Becca knew no details of the situation, it couldn't have been pleasant. No divorce was free of pain. Did Alex, too, consider himself as living in a state of "after," forever suffering the effects of one traumatic moment in time?

"So," she blurted, almost surprising herself, because she hadn't been sure she would speak, "what is it like to be divorced?"

Alex looked up from his work and laughed. "Excuse me? Talk about a bizarre question."

"Oh." Becca felt her cheeks flush. "I guess that didn't come out the way I meant it to come out. Sorry. It's just that my mother told me that you had been married. I just . . ."

Alex smiled kindly; he didn't seem to be at all angry with her. "You just wanted to know if I'm an emotional wreck?"

"Well, that's not it, exactly. I suppose I'm just wondering what it feels like to go through something so traumatic and then, you know, have to live on. I mean, people get married thinking—hoping—they're going to be together forever and then if they get divorced, well, it's got to be a pretty big shock. I would think you, anyone, might feel—lost. And very alone," she added. *Like the way I feel.* "And angry. Even hopeless sometimes."

Alex nodded. "Yes to all of those feelings. But I try not to let my divorce define my life. Yes, it was painful but . . . But I guess I'm just not the type of person to dwell on the past. It happened, it's part of me, but there are lots of other parts, too. Lots of other experiences have defined me, many of them good, so I try to acknowledge the whole of my life."

"Yes. I mean, that must be hard, though. To remember the good along with the bad." Very hard, she thought. Sometimes, it seemed impossible.

"At times it's hard," Alex admitted. "But as I said, I'm not the type to dwell on or wallow in my misery. In my experience I've found that the type of person who dwells on his pain tends to make other, innocent people part of that pain. It's not pleasant to be around someone who's let something sad infect every aspect of his life. People who dwell in their misery seem to show a lack of imagination. But hey," he said, throwing up his hands, "that's just my opinion."

A lack of imagination. Becca thought about that. Was that what unhappiness came down to, a lack of imagination? A failure to imagine other futures than the one you'd convinced yourself was your lot in life?

"Do you have a family?" she asked abruptly. "I mean, are they living? Do you see them?"

"Yes, I have a family. Some are living, some aren't. My father died a few years ago. Heart disease, and yes, I go to the doctor once a year. My mother lives in Riverview, New Jersey, and my sister and her husband and their two kids live in the next town over. I see them when I can, which isn't enough, or so they tell me. I'm the baby of the family, you see. Mom and Anna want me living right under their watchful eyes, but I just can't do that. They love me to death and that's the problem."

Becca smiled. "To death?"

"Well," Alex said, "to smotheration, if that's a word. They mean well and I appreciate them. I just need to live out of easy visiting distance or I'd have no personal life whatsoever."

"They must have been very upset when you got divorced."

"Of course. According to my mother and sister, the divorce was all the fault of my former wife. But then again, she—her name is Bridget—never really cared for Mom and Anna, so I suppose for the women it all worked out nicely."

"And for you?" Becca could barely believe the boldness of her question.

Alex grinned. "I'm doing pretty good. I could be better, but maybe I will be before long."

Becca wondered if he meant something—pointed—by that remark but decided that he couldn't have. "When was the last time you saw your family?" she asked.

"Oh, this past summer. Late July, I think it was."

"That's a long time ago."

Alex smiled. "You should talk. You haven't been here since last December."

Becca looked off at a large crow perched in the naked branches of the ancient oak that in summer held a tire swing. Crows, she'd always thought, were frightening birds, too black and sleek to be friendly. The bird shifted on the branch and seemed now to be staring at her. She turned away.

"Any particular reason for the long absence?" Alex was asking.

Though Alex's tone betrayed no prurient motive, his question made Becca feel threatened. There it was, that old, powerful fear of exposure.

"I've got to go," she said, already heading for the house. "I have to check in with my office."

"I'm sorry."

Becca stopped and turned to look back at Alex.

"For what?" she asked, struggling to meet those intense blue eyes without flinching.

"That the office can't be left at the office."

Again, his tone was neutral, but Becca didn't know if she could trust that neutrality. What, exactly, had Alex meant? Was he criticizing her devotion to career? "Yeah, well," she said, "that's just the way it is."

Becca again turned toward the house. "Just the way it is." The words and the attitude behind them were more evidence of her failure of imagination. Why did anything in her life have to be " just the way it is"? Besides, the truth in this case was that the office could very well be left to fend for itself. The empty e-mail box and the silent phone attested to that.

Behind her the crow in the ancient oak tree cawed loudly.

"Besides," she said, turning back once more to find Alex watching her with those penetrating blue eyes, "I'm cold."

35

Later that afternoon, Rain came upon her aunt Becca alone in the kitchen. She was making a pot of tea the old-fashioned way. At least, water was boiling in the kettle. Julie didn't care much for microwaves; she thought food tasted "funny" after being nuked. She did, however, concede to the convenience of tea bags.

Rain held out her long, well-manicured hands for inspection. "Aunt Becca, you haven't mentioned my nails once since we got here. Do you like the color?"

Like mother, like daughter, Becca thought. Rain had inherited Becca's strong, natural nails and her penchant for wearing them long, no matter what the current fashion. "I think the color is fantastic. What's it called?"

"Blue Moon. When it first came out a few years ago I bought a couple of bottles, even though it's pretty expensive. I just love it, but I save it for special occasions."

"Like Christmas with your family," she suggested,

pouring steaming water into another of the cups that Naomi had crafted. This one Becca actually liked. Naomi had used a striking teal glaze and done away with further decoration, like doggies and kitties and smiling pumpkins.

"Sure. It's always special when we all get together."

The obvious honesty of that reply touched Becca. "Come, sit with me," she said.

"Dad, of course, hates this color," Rain said as she plopped into one of the chairs at the table. "He says he doesn't know why I can't wear pink. He says if I want blue nails I should just spill a bottle of ink on my hands."

Becca laughed. "Well, no one ever said my brother had much of a fashion sense. He spent all four years of college in what I'm pretty sure were the same pair of gray sweatpants."

"That's gross," Rain said, making a face. "Well, Alex has a fashion sense, even if he does need a haircut. He told me that he likes my nails."

"He did?" Becca was startled.

"Yeah. He told me he doesn't know many women with nice nails. He probably likes yours, too."

"Was he flirting with you?" Becca demanded. Because if he had been flirting with her teenaged daughter, she would destroy him. End of story. They could put her in jail, but they'd have to find her first. They could—

"Ugh, no!" Rain cried, interrupting Becca's silent fury. "He's so old! Anyway, he's not like that. He's nice. I know because Dad likes him."

It was true. David had always had a good instinct about other men. *Too bad he hadn't met Rain's father,* she thought. *Maybe he could have warned me to stay far away from him.* Yeah, right. Becca knew that if her brother had warned her to stay away from the guy, it only would have made her run to him even faster than she had under her own impetus. She'd been a heedless girl. She'd become a cautious woman.

"Wait, let me show you something in here." Rain grabbed one of the fashion magazines she'd left strewn across the table and flipped it open. "There's an incredible pair of jeans in here you've just got to see."

Julie appeared just then. She came into the kitchen and stood with her arms folded, giving Becca a look that could only be interpreted as a warning. Becca couldn't help but wonder if she was being followed, watched. Had someone alerted her mother to the fact that she was alone with Rain? It seemed entirely possible.

"What do you want, Mom?" she asked, meeting Julie's eye.

Julie laughed, though there was nothing funny about Becca's question or tone. "Can't a woman come into her own kitchen for no reason at all?"

"Of course. I certainly didn't mean to imply—"

"So, what have you girls been talking about?"

"Nothing," Becca said.

"Rain?"

She looked up from her magazine. "Yes, Grandma?"

"What were you two talking about?"

Rain looked at Becca. "Uh, like Aunt Becca said, nothing." She shrugged. "A pair of jeans I want that Dad won't let me get."

Julie shot another warning look at her daughter. "I'm sure your father has a good reason for not wanting you to have them."

"Yeah. They're too expensive."

"Well, I hope you're not asking your aunt for the money to buy them."

Rain looked embarrassed.

"Mom." Becca's tone was firm. "She didn't ask me for anything. We were just talking."

Julie hesitated a moment. "Fine," she said then. "Well, I'll leave you two to talk about—jeans."

Her mother left the kitchen. Becca wondered if anyone in the Rowan family would trust her ever again. She doubted they would. She doubted that any of her relationships with the family would ever be the same.

Even her relationship with Rain? Becca watched her daughter flipping through the magazine. Suddenly, she felt—uncomfortable. And she wondered if she'd already, irrevocably destroyed something good between them, between her and her daughter, simply by considering breaking the family's agreement. God, she hoped that she hadn't.

Rain looked up from the magazine. "Are you okay, Aunt Becca?" she asked, frowning.

"Fine," she said quickly. "Why?"

Rain shrugged. "You seem a little, I don't know, distracted. Everyone seems a bit strange this week. I mean, what was up with Grandma just now? She was quizzing us like we'd done something wrong. Is there something going on I don't know about?"

"Of course not," Becca lied. "I mean, if there is something going on, I don't know about it, either. No." Careful, she warned herself. It's stupid to protest too much.

"Whatever. Just that Aunt Olivia seems angry all the time and Uncle James looks so sad and my parents are all tense. Even Grandpa and Grandma seem—different. I mean, I know Lily has a reason to be upset because of that Cliff guy, who, by the way, I met once. What a jerk."

"Sometimes people get emotional during the holidays," Becca said, desperately hoping that her daughter would believe her and not continue to pry. When had she become so curious about her relatives? "Adults, I mean. They feel—pressures. That's all."

"Well, I think it's pretty sad. If you can't be happy during Christmastime, then when can you be happy?"

Yes, Becca thought, taking a sip of her lukewarm tea, then when? "Adults are often stupid," she said. "We know we shouldn't be, but we are. We're always doing things we know we shouldn't do. Things that hurt us."

"Like smoking?"

"That wasn't exactly what I was thinking about," Becca admitted, "but yes, I suppose."

Rain rolled her eyes. "Well, I just don't understand why people do things they know are bad for them. I mean, it makes no sense! There's this guy in my school, he's a senior, he's kind of cute, but he gets drunk every Saturday night and then brags about how bad he was hung over on Sunday. That's just so lame!"

"Yes," Becca said, "it is." At least she didn't have to worry about her daughter developing a smoking or drinking habit.

"And this girl in my history class," Rain went on. "Amanda. She's really overweight and she knows she is, her doctor told her she has to lose, like, thirty pounds, but she can't stick to a diet. Every day at lunch she eats four Hostess cupcakes. She could get diabetes or have a heart attack or something! I don't understand why she doesn't just do what her doctor tells her to do."

No, Becca thought, Rain doesn't at all understand how hard life can be for some people. And Becca was struck now by how young her daughter really was, how simply she saw the world, how she didn't seem able to grasp human complications. How would Rain react to the truth of her birth? Maybe David and Naomi were right. Rain was still very young, level-headed but naïve, ill equipped to handle such a startling truth.

Becca wondered. Had she been that innocent, that unknowing when she was Rain's age? It didn't seem possible. But if she had been, no wonder her parents had acted so forcefully to remove Rain from her care. And no wonder Becca had wanted them to help—and though she didn't remember that time very clearly, she had been told that she'd been eager for David and Naomi to take the child. And—she could admit this now, at least to herself—thank God that they had.

Sixteen was far too young to be a parent, at least a good one. Sure, at sixteen you could drive your mother's car to school, but did that mean you should be allowed to commandeer the controls of a jumbo jet? At sixteen you might be pretty good at feeding and brushing your dog, but did that mean you should be allowed to operate on his liver? At sixteen you could have sex, but did that mean you really knew anything about sexuality? No. It did not.

"Aunt Becca? You're staring off into space again. And your tea is probably ice-cold."

"Oh," she said. "Sorry. I was thinking about work stuff."

Rain groaned dramatically. "That's another weird thing about adults. They go on and on about how they hate their jobs—well, some of them do—and then they can't stop thinking about them when they're away from the office."

Becca smiled. Yes. A sixteen-year-old might have a part-time job, but that didn't mean she understood anything about bills and mortgages and insurance payments and severance packages and shrinking retirement accounts and ... "Yes," she said, "it's another one of our more annoying habits."

36

"I thought we might exchange our Christmas letters today, Liv. What do you think?"

James and Olivia were in their room, the one Julie had designated the Queen Anne's Lace Room. James was fond of his mother-in-law and of her little fancies. She was formidable at the same time that she was lovable; she was strong at the same time that she was whimsical.

Olivia, sitting in the room's only chair, hadn't answered his question. She continued to study a report she had brought with her from the office. James had tried to get her to agree to leave work behind just this once, but she'd refused.

"Liv?" he said again.

Now she raised her head. "What?" she asked.

James repressed a hint of irritation. "Our letters. I thought we might exchange them now."

It had been Olivia's idea originally. Every Christmas of their marriage, each wrote a letter to the other, and then they exchanged the letters with some ceremony. In the letters they took the time to assess the health of their relationship—and to celebrate the firm fact of their love.

This year, it had taken James several months to write his letter. It had been difficult to write, difficult to find words to express both his love for his wife as well as his concern for the state of their relationship. The last thing James wanted to do was to put Olivia on the defensive by implying that his unhappiness was her fault exclusively. He knew it wasn't—but he also knew that something was wrong with Olivia. And as long as she was troubled by whatever demons were troubling her, he, too, would suffer. And their marriage, which had once been so strong and the source of so much contentment . . .

Well, James didn't like to think about what might eventually happen to the marriage if things continued in the way they were heading. For the first time, he was both eager and afraid to read what his wife had written to him about the state of her feelings

When Olivia didn't reply, just continued to stare up at him blankly, James took action. He handed her a folded piece of thick, creamy-white paper on which he had written, in his own hand, his thoughts for his wife.

Olivia immediately put the letter on the old pine dresser beside her and sighed dramatically, as if she'd been terribly put-upon. "I've been so busy. I meant to write your letter, but I just didn't get around to it. Don't worry, James. I'll get to it after the holiday."

James felt as if he'd been struck across the cheek with the back of her hand. "I'm not worried about the letter, Liv," he managed to say after a moment. "I'm worried about what it means that you chose not to write it."

"I told you," she repeated. "I've been busy."

"And I haven't been?" James felt the anger rising in him. He was unused to anger and struggled to keep it under control.

Olivia shrugged. "Well, it's not like I forgot about the letter."

"Frankly, I think it would have been better if it had slipped your mind. Everybody forgets things on occasion. But to deliberately ignore a cherished ritual . . ." James laughed bitterly. "And you say you care so much about family and tradition. I guess in your mind that leaves me out."

Olivia felt slightly shaken by her husband's anger, but only slightly. She sighed again, exasperated. "I really don't understand why you're making such a big deal about a silly little letter, James. I told you I'll get around to writing it in a week or so."

There was a sound from the hallway. Olivia turned toward the door, but she didn't seem at all concerned that someone might have overheard the argument. James, on the other hand, was concerned.

"Lord," he whispered, "someone's out there and probably heard everything. I'm sorry, Liv. I didn't mean to raise my voice."

Olivia looked back at her husband. She didn't read the pain and embarrassment on his face. She did, however, see that he'd shaved badly that morning. His carelessness annoyed her. "It's fine, James," she said, rising from the chair. "I'm going to go downstairs for a while."

Olivia opened the door. Naomi was only a few feet down the hall.

"Naomi," Olivia called. "What do you want?"

Naomi turned back. Her cheeks were a bit flushed. Olivia wondered why.

"Nothing," she said. "I was . . . I was just passing by and I knocked into the hall table and . . ."

"Do you know where Nora put that old family Bible, the one that belonged to her mother? She told me it was in the den, but I couldn't find it. It's a mess in there to begin with and now Becca's got her stuff all over the place."

"What? The old . . ." Naomi shrugged. "I'm sorry, Olivia. I have no idea."

Of course not, Olivia thought. *You're not really a Rowan. It was stupid of me to ask.* "That's all right," she said, heading for the stairs. "I'll ask Mom if she's seen it."

37

That evening the twins were allowed to eat dinner in front of the TV in the living room. One of their favorite holiday shows was playing, the old animated *Rudolph the Red-Nosed Reindeer* with Burl Ives as the chubby, umbrella-wielding Snowman. Naomi was only too glad to relax the "no TV at dinner" rule on this occasion. The show was harmless—the boys had long ceased to be afraid of the Bumble—and given the gloomy atmosphere of the house, the more times the boys could be on their own, the better for them. Lots of people seemed not to realize how perceptive children were, but Naomi wasn't one of them.

Everyone else was gathered at the dining room table. Julie had made her Bolognese sauce and served it over fettucine. The sauce had been one of Becca's favorites since she was a little girl. She wondered now if her mother had remembered that when she'd planned the night's menu. Was the choice of Bolognese sauce a gesture of love or merely a coincidence?

Since Becca's bombshell of an announcement,

conversation in the presence of Rain had been general and careful. That evening was no exception. Steve commented on the current price of gas. Julie wondered what Rain and her friends were doing for New Year's Eve. The answer was attending a supervised party at a friend's house. James mentioned a book he'd just read, the latest in a long line of biographies of Abraham Lincoln. In her usual suave way, Naomi mercifully cut short David's latest lecture on the greening cause. Not that Becca wasn't all for recycling and reducing her carbon footprint, but she could do without listening to a lecture, especially over dinner.

And then, Olivia spoke.

"Listen to this," she said. "One of our clients, a woman named June Larsen, told us last week that she's in the process of adopting a child from Russia. A girl, I think she said, about a year old."

James's fork stopped halfway to his lips; he looked horrified. Becca felt for him; she, too, was wary. What was Olivia doing bringing up the volatile subject of adoption?

"Liv—" James said, but his wife cut him off.

"Personally, I think she's crazy. I mean, she's forty-eight, she's single, she's got no family close by to help out, and I know she's not wealthy. I'm not even sure she can afford a part-time nanny, let alone a babysitter for a Saturday night! I really don't know what she's thinking. It's like she's deliberately setting out to ruin her life."

Becca couldn't help but wonder if her sister's comments were partly meant for her. Wasn't she also a single woman wanting to take on the responsibility of parenthood? True, the situations weren't exactly the same but . . .

"I don't think adopting a child is 'ruining' your life,"

Naomi was saying. "Actually, I think it's pretty impressive."

Naomi, too? Becca shot a look at her mother. She wondered why someone wasn't putting an end to this potentially volatile subject. She certainly wasn't the one to do it.

"What's impressive about it?" Rain said. "I mean, it's nice that she's adopting, but it's only a baby. Practically everyone has babies. There's nothing so special about that. I mean, maybe if she was, like, forty-eight years old and competing in the Olympics, that would be impressive."

Becca took a fortifying sip of merlot. Yes, Rain was indeed a very young sixteen. Her comment had demonstrated that she couldn't quite imagine the enormity of the task the woman had undertaken. Her comment also had betrayed a failure of sympathetic imagination; it had betrayed the unthinking cruelty of the young, a cruelty that Becca felt sure her daughter would someday outgrow. But what if she didn't? Would Rain ever be capable of accepting and understanding what her mother had done for her sake? Would she ever be capable of forgiveness? Only time would tell.

"I don't mean to interrupt," Nora was saying, clearly in an effort to change the subject, "but before I forget, I wanted to ask—"

But Olivia talked right over her grandmother, who, Becca thought, looked both tired and angry. "I've said it once and I'll say it again. Adoption is just riddled with problems. And adopting from a foreign country is just asking for trouble. It's likely the child might not come with a detailed medical history, and what then? What happens if she gets sick with some disease that requires a history in order to be properly diagnosed and treated? My God, what if there's madness in her family?"

David meaningfully cleared his throat. "I don't think anyone uses the term 'madness' anymore, Olivia. Mental illness is preferable. Psychological difficulties, maybe."

"Call it what you like," Olivia said with a dismissive flick of her hand. "And then there's resentment. What if the child grows to hate the adoptive parents for having taken her from her native land? What if she's an ungrateful child, after all the pains her so-called parents have endured, after all the sacrifices they've made?"

Nora spoke, and this time she was heard. "How sharper than a serpent's tooth . . . Olivia, any child can be ungrateful. It's not the sole province of the adopted child. Besides, I'm not sure a good parent should be seeking gratitude. If you receive it, fine. If not, well, that's a risk you accept when you decide to have a family. You risk being rejected or ignored by your children. You risk losing them in all sorts of ways."

Why had her grandmother even bothered to answer Olivia's ranting? Becca poured another glass of wine and considered excusing herself before yet another family member indulged Olivia in her plan to drive Becca insane before the dessert was served.

"Maybe so," Olivia conceded. "But I still say the risks of disaster are far greater with an adopted child than with a biological child."

"I'm not sure there's any scientific proof of that, Liv," James said quietly, but with some force. "Anyway, I think it's quite wonderful of June to be doing this. Adopting a child in her circumstances requires enormous sacrifice."

"That's for sure!" Julie shook her head. "I can't imagine being in my forties, without a partner, and taking on a small child. It would require a huge amount of energy, not to mention patience."

"This girl in my political science class," Lily said now, "is pregnant. It's been a really tough pregnancy, but she's determined to finish up the school year. And then she's getting married to the baby's father. They're a really good couple, but I have to admit it's kind of weird seeing a classmate already having children. I mean, I just can't imagine myself having a baby at this age. Honestly, I feel too—young."

"You want to have fun before settling down to raise a child, right?" Rain guessed.

"It's not that so much. It's that I feel I'd make so many mistakes if I had a baby now. I feel I just don't know enough to be responsible for someone else's life."

Instantly, the look of embarrassment that came to Lily's face proved she knew she'd tread on dangerous turf. "Not that all young mothers make terrible mistakes," she said hurriedly, with a quick glance at Becca. "I didn't mean it that way. I just meant—"

But Becca simply could not keep silent any longer. She looked directly at her older sister, and then at the other members of her family, one by one. She looked at everyone except for Rain.

"I don't see why we should talk about this woman's adopting a child as a sacrifice," she said. "I don't see why we should talk about it as being something noble or, as Naomi said, impressive. I'm assuming she's going into the process with her eyes open—and yes, I know how dangerous a thing assuming can be. She's an adult. Presumably she's responsible and has enough money to pay for legal rights to the child and then enough money to support her, nanny or no nanny. Why should this woman be lauded any more than—than a teenaged girl who gets pregnant accidentally and then is forced to—"

Becca stopped short. She saw—she felt—the looks of anger, panic, and pain on the faces of her family. David's face was almost purple, as if he were about to spout blood. Only Rain's expression was neutral.

And Becca herself felt a little sick. She was worse than Olivia. She knew she'd been torturing her family just now. She knew she shouldn't have said a word in response to her sisters' insensitive comments. But something had come over her and once again she had found herself saying things she instantly regretted, saying things she wasn't even sure she meant. Now Becca didn't know if she could erase the further damage to the family—and to her own reputation as part of it—that she had just caused by her careless words.

"And what, Aunt Becca?" Rain prodded, all innocence.

Before Becca could reply—and she still didn't know what she would say to salvage the moment— Nora's knife was tapping against her crystal glass. "I'd like," she said, "to use what authority I have as the eldest Rowan and change this conversation to one less—fraught. It is Christmastime, after all. And there are far more pleasant, less contentious topics to discuss."

Steve unclenched his hand and put his fork gently on the table next to his plate.

"Good idea, Mom," he said. "Any suggestions?"

"As a matter of fact, yes, I do have a suggestion. Why don't we—"

But Becca could hear no more of her grandmother's words over the accusatory din in her head.

38

Nora retired to her room rather early that night. Carefully, she hung up her skirt and blouse and put away the heavy wool cardigan she had been wearing, one Julie had given her for a birthday. Once dressed in a warm flannel nightgown, she eased into bed and sat up against the pillows to read for a bit before sleep.

But her mind would not stick to the story on the page before her, interesting though it was. Instead, she found herself reviewing the far more compelling story of her own family's life.

Nora knew, on an intellectual level, that she was not in a direct way responsible for the happiness of her child—not any longer, not since he was a boy— or of his children. Still, as matriarch of the Rowan family, it was hard not to feel like—it was hard not to feel like the prime cause, the well from which all else had sprung. Maybe if Thomas were still alive, she wouldn't feel this burden quite so acutely. They could share the feeling of responsibility for the personal success of their family members.

Nora smiled to herself. No. If Thomas were still alive, it was more likely he would tell her to stop being so silly. He'd remind her that she had done her job and done it well. If a child or grandchild decided to live his or her life badly, then so be it.

Nora put the book she had intended to read on her bedside table. She still slept on the right side of the bed though her husband had been gone for over twenty years. Thomas. In some ways life had been a lot easier for Thomas than it had for Nora. Maybe, she wondered now, life was in some ways a lot easier for all men than it was for women. Maybe. Her own son seemed to be a person deeply touched by the emotional lives of those he loved. She could see it on his face, in his every movement, how intensely he was feeling his daughter Becca's distress. And she knew that he, like Nora, felt an inordinate amount of responsibility for that distress.

Now, Julie was a different sort of person. Her daughter-in-law wasn't as deeply touched by the emotional burdens of others. At least, it seemed that way to Nora. Unless Julie was a master of concealment, and Nora didn't think that she was, she managed to sustain a balance of caring and—could one call it unconcern? Where Julie could detach from sorrow or fear, many people—including Nora's son—could not.

Well, when she was gone, Julie would be the matriarch of the Rowan family. And Julie might be inheriting that role sooner than she anticipated because Nora felt something inside her slowing down. She felt something coming to an end. It was nothing physical, nothing tangible—not like a building ache or an increasingly violent pain that signaled a breakdown of the body. She just had a sense that she wouldn't be around for another Christmas. Still, she couldn't help but wonder if this sense was "real." Was her mind really in close tune with her aging body? Or was she simply experiencing the common sense of the old, telling her that time was, indeed, running out?

Nora hadn't lied to Steve and Julie about the results of her recent physical examination. She just hadn't told them every little detail. Her doctor, a man in his sixties and close to retirement himself, was, like Nora, a firm believer in the older person's right to retain a degree of independence in all things for as long as was possible.

Inevitably, with the thought of a person retaining independence, her mind turned to Becca, her fiercely independent granddaughter. Nora had resisted forcing a private conversation with Becca as Julie and David had done, and as she knew Steve had been trying to do. She hoped that Becca would come to her grandmother when she was ready. But would she ever be ready?

She didn't blame Becca for what had happened at the dinner table earlier. Olivia had brought up the dangerous topic of adoption, and the others had unwittingly goaded Becca to a point of explosion. And Nora was pretty sure that Becca felt bad about having succumbed to the temptation to fight back. She'd seen the look of remorse on her face, even if the others hadn't.

She wanted to help her granddaughter. No, more than that. She wanted to solve the problem; she wanted to be the architect of a resolution that would satisfy everyone, especially Becca. But she just didn't know how to go about doing that.

And as for Olivia . . . Nora sighed. In her opinion her oldest granddaughter was nearing a nervous breakdown. Professional help sooner rather than later just might stave off the worst of it, but there, too, Nora's hands were tied. If James, Olivia's own husband, couldn't convince his wife to seek help, well, then . . .

Nora was worried a bit about Lily, too. She seemed extraordinarily naïve for a woman her age. Or maybe she wasn't naïve as much as she was romantic. Either way, Nora didn't like the idea of Lily being released into the wider world without a few more years of— guidance. Nora wasn't self-important; she didn't tend to overestimate her worth. No one could ever describe her as "full of herself." But in this case she did believe that she was needed. She did believe that she was an important person for her youngest grandchild.

Well, her time would come when it would come, whether it would be next year or the year after that. There was little if anything she could do about that. The Rowan family would survive without her. It would be changed, but it would survive.

Nora stretched her legs under the covers. She never failed to enjoy that delicious feeling of relaxation. Stretching, Nora thought, had definitely added quality to the quantity of her life. Still, it didn't much help ease the tensions roiling outside her own diminished body, those tensions ebbing and flowing in the other bedrooms of the Rowan house.

Nora turned off the small lamp by her bedside. She loved her family, each and every one of them. But at that moment all she wanted was for each and every one of them to go away, just for a little while. She was tired.

39

Sunday, December 24

James hadn't slept much the night before, and when he had fallen asleep, it had been fitfully. But the outcome of this restless night was positive. He'd woken with the firm conviction that he had to take a stand, a conviction that he had to do something before the marriage—and its two unhappy members—fell entirely into dust.

It was now late morning. James had eaten breakfast and been for a walk in the bracing winter air. Olivia had opted for a quick cup of coffee and a return to their room, where she planned on working.

Now it was time. James knocked softly and, without waiting for an answer, came into the room. Olivia was sitting on the edge of the bed, sorting through a pile of old family photographs. She didn't look up.

James took a deep, steadying breath. He had steeled himself for this moment. He knew that people mistook his mild manner for weakness, but they were wrong. Yes, he was a patient man, more patient than most, but he was not a weak one.

"Where's my letter, Liv?" he said now, his manner calm and, he hoped, nonconfrontational.

Now Olivia looked up at him. She opened her mouth to answer, and closed it again. She suddenly realized she had no idea what she had done with the letter.

"It's . . . it's in the night table," she lied, "by my side of the bed."

James shook his head. "No, it isn't. You left it on the dresser. Unopened. Unread. I took it back."

"I'm sorry," Olivia said quickly. She felt a tiny bit afraid, as if something were different about her husband in this moment. She sensed that she was not in control of whatever it was that was happening. "I meant to read it. I guess I just . . . I just forgot."

"Yes."

Olivia's hands fluttered in the air as if to illustrate her words. "You know how things slip my mind these days."

"Things like your husband."

Olivia laughed, and to James, it sounded nervous. "What are you saying, James?"

James took a step closer to his wife and spoke softly. The last thing he wanted was to be overheard.

"I'm saying that lately, I feel as if I don't exist to you. I don't know, Liv, it's almost as if you're trying to substitute your life—our life—with the lives of other people, people from the past, all these ancestors you're obsessed about. What's missing in the here and now, Liv? Are you still longing for a child of your own, a child of our own?"

Olivia didn't reply, and honestly, James hadn't expected her to. "All right, then," he went on, "let's work on that. Let's revisit the idea of adoption. And if you really can't go through with an adoption, fine, then we have to find a way for you to be happy—even content—in the present. Content with what you have, not miserable about what you don't have. And one of the things you have, Liv, is me. But if you can't see that, can't appreciate it, if you can't love me . . ."

"But I do love you, James!" she burst out.

"It's been very hard to believe that, Liv. Ever since we decided against adoption once and for all last year, things have been—different—between us. You hardly ever look me in the eye anymore. I feel like we've become strangers. Maybe that's partly my fault, and if it is, I'm sorry. I want to fix that." James paused for courage. And then he said: "But I'm not sure I can do that while living under the same roof as you. I think that a separation might be a good idea."

Again, Olivia opened her mouth and then closed it. She wasn't at all sure what she had just heard. She wondered if she had experienced an auditory hallucination. Or was this what it felt like to be in shock? Finally, she said: "What?"

"I'm suggesting a separation, Liv," James replied steadily.

Several emotions warred in Olivia's breast—fear, sorrow, and anger. Anger, the most effective weapon of emotional self-defense, won the battle.

Olivia jumped to her feet, scattering the pile of photographs she had been sorting. "I can't believe you have the nerve to tell me you want a separation while we're at my family's home!" she hissed. "How dare you!"

James sighed. "I'm sorry, Liv," he said honestly. "I wanted to wait until we were back home. I had no intention of spoiling this holiday for us. But—Liv, it's already spoiled. I just had to speak now."

Olivia turned her back to him. "I could just kill

you," she muttered. And then, she whirled around to face this man who suddenly was a stranger. "What about tonight?" she demanded. "Where am I supposed to sleep?"

"Of course you'll sleep in our bed. And if you want me to, so will I. If not, I'll be fine on the floor."

James walked over to the dresser and picked up his car keys. When he was at the door, Olivia asked: "Where are you going?" Her voice was high and verging on frantic.

James turned and looked at his wife. He wondered if she could see the pain he knew was written all over his face. Once she would have seen it. But now, he doubted she saw anything that really mattered.

"I really don't know," he said.

And then he was gone.

40

It seemed to be a universal truth. The kitchen was where people wanted to be. It was where they congregated during parties and where they journeyed in the middle of the night when they couldn't sleep. The kitchen was the scene of the hearth, the symbolic center of the home and of the family. So it was that Lily and Nora found themselves once again at the kitchen table, drinking tea, and talking.

Nora needed the caffeine that the strong English Breakfast blend provided. She'd slept badly the night before, her rest interrupted by thoughts of the family's current concerns. But she had gotten up at her usual early hour, loathe to waste the day. Now she was suffering for her decision.

"Grandma," Lily said, "did you ever consider marrying again after Grandpa died?"

Nora wasn't really in the mood to talk about anything more important than the evening's menu. But she knew she owed her granddaughter the courtesy of a considered answer. After all, it was Nora who had introduced the subject of her marriage.

"Not immediately," she answered. "But after about a year, maybe a little more, an old friend of mine from high school, a man named Tim Coombs, got in touch. I hadn't heard from him—or about him—in years. He and his wife had moved away ages before. Anyway, he was back in the Boston area after his wife's death a few months earlier—his children lived in Framingham, not far from where Olivia and James live now—and he suggested we get together."

"And you did?" Lily prompted.

"Yes," Nora said. "We met for lunch a few times and he was the same as ever, such a nice man, funny and smart. And after a few months he suggested we get married."

Lily's eyes widened. "Wasn't that kind of fast?"

"Maybe," Nora conceded. "But when you're an adult you do know yourself pretty well—at least, you should—and you don't tend to waste time. You hope you finally know what you really want and need to live a satisfying, productive life."

"I guess," Lily said doubtfully. "A proposal after only a few months still seems pretty fast to me. A whirlwind courtship. Isn't that what it used to be called?"

"Yes," Nora said, "though at our age it was more like a gentle-breeze courtship. In any case, Tim's proposal made a lot of sense for us both. We had much in common and the companionship such a union would have afforded each of us was a strong appeal. I did give the matter some serious consideration. But in the end I just couldn't accept his proposal."

"Was he upset?" Lily asked.

Nora smiled. "He wasn't exactly pleased with my decision, but it didn't break his heart, either. He married another old friend of ours the following year. Actually, I heard that he died about a year ago. . . . It was cancer, I think."

"So, why did you say no to him?" Lily said. "Were you afraid of being hurt? Frankly, Grandma, I don't know how you could even have considered getting married again after going through all that emotional trauma with Grandpa."

Nora took a sip of her cooling tea before speaking. "Oh, no," she said then, "I wasn't afraid. If there was one thing my marriage taught me, it was that I could take care of myself if I had to. No, it wasn't fear."

"Did you love him?" Lily asked. "Your old friend. Because if you loved him, then I don't understand why you didn't marry him."

Nora smiled. "Oh, no," she said. "Love didn't have anything to do with our relationship. Respect, yes. And friendship. But not love. At least, not in the sense I'd known love with your grandfather. Or, for that matter, in the sense that Tim had known love with his first wife. They had met when they were very young, too. No, with Tim and me things were different."

"Now I'm even more confused," Lily admitted. "If he didn't love you, then why did he propose? How can you ask someone to marry you when you're not really in love with the person? Unless it's one of those awful political marriages where you know it's just a deal between ruling families or business empires. And that just sounds like prostitution to me."

My, Nora thought. Her granddaughter did espouse a strict moral code! "I'll try to explain," she said. "For a lot of people, Lily, marriage—or any longtime union—becomes in and of itself a desirable state. It becomes a habit that's hard to give up, so that sometimes, in a marriage that comes late in life, it's not so much about the individual as it is about the union, the companionship, the need for another human being in the bed, the need for another person at the breakfast table." Nora smiled. "For that matter, it's about the need for someone with whom to share household chores."

Poor Lily. She looked horrified. "That's all?" she said. "Someone to share chores with? Like, you dust and I'll vacuum? You take out the garbage and I'll change the sheets on the bed? I'll cook and you wash the dishes?"

Nora laughed. "That's a lot, Lily. Don't under-estimate the appeal of domestic habit. I know it must sound pretty boring to a young person but—"

"But I'll think differently when I'm older?" Lily sounded doubtful. "Maybe. But from where I am right now I just can't imagine marrying someone I'm not madly in love with."

"And you shouldn't. Not when you're so young and have so much of your life ahead of you. I ap-prove highly of marrying for love, Lily. I married a man I loved dearly."

"And yet, he betrayed you. So love isn't a guaran-tee of anything." Lily reached across the table and gently squeezed Nora's hand. "I'm sorry, Grandma, I'm trying to come to terms with it, but it's really hard. I just feel so bad for you."

Nora squeezed back, with more force. "No, no, Lily, don't feel bad for me," she said. "The last thing I need—or want—is pity. I don't deserve it. Bad things, painful things happen to everyone. There's nothing any of us can do about that."

"Maybe. But I still want to punch Grandpa in the nose!"

Nora laughed. "Oh, and so did I! Only I was rather vain about my hands back then, before they were all gnarled and speckled, and the last thing I wanted was to break one."

"Oh, Grandma, your hands are still beautiful!" Lily said, and in her eyes, they were. "So, you still haven't told me why you said no to your old friend?"

Nora hesitated before speaking. "I don't know if I can properly explain it without sounding like a crazy old lady. Or worse, a romantic fool."

"Try." Lily smiled. "And you could never be a crazy old lady, Grandma, or a romantic fool."

"Well, thank you, dear. I'll try to explain. I suppose I felt that after all Thomas and I had been through, after all we'd survived . . . our success seemed like a sort of monument or shrine to me . . . I didn't want to—to betray us by marrying another man." Nora raised her hand, as if to forestall an argument from her granddaughter. "Yes, yes," she said, "I know, Thomas had betrayed us and there I was not wanting to betray what was only a memory. But the fact was that the marriage still felt alive. Do you understand?"

Lily considered for a moment before answering. "Yes," she said, "I think so."

Nora nodded. "Good. Anyway, I made the right decision in saying no to Tim. I have no regrets about not marrying again."

"Well, that's good. Regrets are—I don't even know what to say about them. Except maybe that they're horrible."

"What do you regret?" Nora asked, and as she did she wondered how early it was in a person's life that she could identify the feeling of regret in herself. Surely, a little child didn't experience regret. A person had to be old enough to realize that she was responsible for actions both taken and not taken. Consciousness had to be developed to a certain point, as did conscience.

"I regret not seeing the truth about Cliff early on," Lily said promptly.

"And do you regret falling for him in the first place?"

Lily thought hard about that. "No," she said after a few moments, "I guess I don't. I mean, we did have some good times. And in the end . . . Well, I certainly learned a lesson, even if it was the hard way!"

"Yes. And more often than not, the hard way is the best way to learn a lesson."

Lily thought about that. It was too bad that people had to learn lessons "the hard way." And she supposed that meant that in general people were reluctant to change old habits, reluctant to listen to the experience of those who'd come before. She supposed it meant that in general people thought they knew best the way to be happy. She supposed it meant that people were simply too stubborn and self-deluded not to bring about their own suffering.

"It seems to me, Grandma," she said after a time, "that this family has been defined by deception."

"No, Lily," Nora corrected. "This family has been defined by love."

"Maybe. But how did love and deception get all mixed up with each other? I know that's a rhetorical question."

"Good." Nora got up from the table. "Because I'm far too tired to attempt a coherent answer."

Lily looked more closely at her grandmother. Was she a bit pale, a bit drawn? "Are you okay, Grandma?" she asked.

"Oh, I'm fine. I think I'll just take a little rest."

"All right," Lily said, hoping that her grandmother wasn't lying. "Well, let me know if you need anything."

Nora patted Lily's shoulder and went off to her room for a nap.

Lily made herself another cup of tea and sat back

at the kitchen table. Ever since that first conversation with her grandmother, the one in which Nora had told Lily of Thomas's affair, Lily had been wondering about something. Nora had said that she'd had to face the possibility that she had been in some way responsible for her husband having strayed. The notion of her grandmother accepting some of the blame for her husband's affair had made Lily angry. But it had also made her think about the dynamics of her own situation.

Had she been at all responsible for Cliff's affair? She felt sure she had not done anything to drive him away. But what if—just what if—she'd unknowingly contributed to Cliff's unhappiness or boredom with the relationship? What then?

Lily shook her head though there was no one present to witness her conviction. No. Lily was one hundred percent certain that the entire responsibility for the affair lay with Cliff Jones. True, maybe she and Cliff were simply not meant to be a couple. Or maybe Cliff was just a jerk. Maybe the whole answer to what had gone wrong in the relationship was as simple as this: Cliff Jones was a bum. It had to be true that in some breakups, only one person was responsible. Didn't it?

Lily's thoughts were interrupted by the sudden and slightly unsteady arrival of Olivia. Lily watched as her oldest sister fumbled for a cup on the drainboard, and then, as she stood staring at an unopened cupboard, as if lost or confused.

Lily got up from her seat and walked over to her sister. "Liv," she said gently, "are you okay?"

Olivia continued to stare at the cupboard. Her expression was unreadable; Lily wondered if she was in some sort of shock.

"Let me make you a cup of tea," she said. When

Olivia nodded, slightly, Lily did just that. When the tea was ready, Lily carefully handed the cup to her sister.

"Liv, where's James?" she asked. "Do you want me to get him?"

Olivia lowered her eyes and left the kitchen without a word.

Lily stared after her sister. She was concerned. She wondered if she should tell her mother that Olivia seemed upset, and then remembered that her mother had gone to pay a visit to a distant neighbor who was recovering from surgery. Besides, would setting her mother to look after Olivia be interfering? Lily wasn't entirely sure, but she strongly suspected her oldest sister wasn't the type to welcome unasked-for assistance.

Lily sighed. Maybe she was being overly concerned. Olivia was tough; she'd proved that time and again. Probably she was just angry about the loss or misplacement of another moth-eaten coat or cracked china pitcher. Or maybe she'd taken a muscle relaxer because she'd hurt her back hauling around boxes and wardrobes up in the attic. Lily supposed that might account for her shaking hands.

Lily put thoughts of her oldest sister aside and went off to find the mystery novel she'd brought with her to read this holiday week, the latest Elizabeth Peters title. That was one of the best things about holidays—the opportunity to read a book that had absolutely nothing to do with curriculum requirements.

41

He would try once more. Just one more time. He'd seen the look of—contrition—on Becca's face at dinner the night before, at the end of that dangerous conversation about adoption. He would bet anything that she regretted her words. Maybe something had changed for her in the past days.

Maybe. But if his daughter still wouldn't—couldn't?—talk to him one to one, well, then, it would have to rest. At least he would know that he had tried. What more could a father do?

He found Becca emerging from the den. Personally, he still felt bad that she had been ousted from her regular room. "Becca," he said, "I was wondering if you were ready—I mean, I was wondering if you would like to talk?"

Becca seized the moment, unaware that she was ready to do so until the words, "Yes, let's talk," were out of her mouth. And when she realized what she had agreed to, she felt a thrill of anticipation. Fear was gone. When had it fled?

Steve smiled, but guardedly. He didn't want to

take too much for granted. Besides, he was as afraid
of this interview with his daughter as he was looking
forward to it. "Okay," he said. "Let's go to my studio.
We'll only be interrupted here."

Without speaking they put on their coats and
other cold-weather gear and left the house. They had
gone only a few yards when they both spotted a car
halfway to the local road.

"Who is that?" her father asked, squinting after it.

Becca recognized the make and color of the car.
She could also see that only one person was inside.
"It's James. I wonder where he's going?" she asked,
though silently she knew the answer: any place Olivia
wasn't.

Henry Le Mew was waiting for them at the studio.
He greeted them with a loud and, what sounded to
Becca, demanding cry.

"Let me just give him some food before we talk,"
Steve said with a note of apology in his voice. "If he
doesn't have something to eat just before his insulin
shot, he could get very sick."

Becca nodded. Her father retrieved a small bag of
specialty dry food from a locked cabinet under his
worktable. (Yes, she remembered hearing something
about Henry's uncanny ability to open doors and
drawers.) He poured a bowl for Henry, who immediately set to his meal with gusto. It made Becca smile.
Henry Le Mew was one lucky kitty. One very spoiled,
very lucky kitty.

Just like she had been one very spoiled and very
lucky little girl. As her father prepared the insulin shot,
Becca thought back to her childhood. There hadn't
been one thing she lacked. Really, it had been as
close to idyllic as she could imagine. She remembered laughter. There had been lots of laughter. And
then, she had grown up.

Becca looked around her father's studio. On a large corkboard were posted photographs of the Rowan family, including, of course, Steve's father, Thomas. There was a photo of Becca riding on her grandfather's shoulders. In another, she, David, and Olivia waved from their campstools around a fire. She was sitting to David's right. Above his head she was making devil's horns. Becca smiled. *Oh, boy,* she thought, *what a spitfire I was!* Another photo showed Nora blowing out a forest of candles on an iced cake. Becca remembered the occasion; it was her grandmother's seventieth birthday. There was a photo of her parents with a newborn Lily. Her father still looked stunned, as if he couldn't quite understand where this latest, unexpected child had come from. Finally, there was a photo of Rain, Michael, and Malcolm, taken last Halloween. Rain and her brothers, a Goth witch holding the hands of two small, green goblins.

Suddenly, a child's voice spoke in her imagination. It was the voice of Michael, or maybe it was the voice of Malcolm. It was saying, with confusion, "So you're not really my sister? You're my cousin? I don't understand."

"There." Her father's voice startled her back to the moment. "Henry's taken care of for the moment. Please, have a seat."

Steve settled in his own chair as Becca perched on a wooden stool close by.

"How many rules did you break, Dad?"

It wasn't how she had wanted to start the conversation. She hadn't meant to sound so aggressive or challenging. But the question had been asked. Before she could retrieve it, her father replied.

"Becca," he said, "please try to understand. It wasn't like that. It wasn't—underhanded. People did us

favors. Everything—everything was done in a spirit
of support for our family. In a spirit of support for
you."

"I believe you," she said honestly. "But you're a
lawyer, Dad. And you participated in a deception that
could have cost you your practice if you'd been
found out. It could have cost other people their jobs,
too, their reputations. So much was at stake."

Steve smiled ruefully. "I know. What else can I say,
Becca? What I did, I did. I can't undo it. I don't know
that I would if I could. A parent will go to great
lengths to protect his or her family." Here, Steve
paused. "But you know that."

Becca didn't take her father's words as an admon-
ishment. A day or two earlier she would have replied
defensively. But not now. "Yes," she said. "I do know
that. And I'm really sorry about what I said at dinner
last night. Believe me, I had no intention of—"

Her father cut her off. "Apology accepted. It was a
conversation that should never have been started.
Olivia had no call to bring up the subject of adoption, for several reasons."

Father and daughter sat quietly for a while. Becca
watched Henry, who was on top of the worktable,
groom himself in rhythmic strokes of his large pink
tongue. The sight was oddly soothing.

"Family closes ranks when there's trouble."

Becca looked back to her father. He'd spoken quietly, almost as if unaware he had spoken at all. She
wasn't sure that he wanted a response, but she said,
"Sometimes it feels more like the family closed ranks
and left me outside."

Steve leaned forward; his expression was earnest.
"I'm sorry for that, Becca. I'm sorry you feel that way.
None of us ever intended for you to feel alienated,
least of all me."

For the first time in a long time, maybe ever, Becca felt the truth of those words.

Steve went on. "No doubt we made mistakes caring for you after Rain was born. Maybe we should have insisted you see a therapist. Maybe we should have insisted you talk to someone about what you were feeling."

"Maybe," Becca said. But the truth was that at first, all Becca had wanted to do was move on. She hadn't wanted to dwell on her feelings about being a sixteen-year-old mother/aunt. She'd wanted to finish high school, go to college, make a career. She'd wanted to prove to everyone in her family that she would no longer be a problem.

"Dad?" she said. "Did you ever, even once, regret what you did for me?" Only days before, Becca would have said "what you did *to* me." She was aware of this change. She wondered if her father had heard it.

"I'm not sure if I'd use the word 'regret,' " he answered. "But I did have second thoughts. I did wonder if what I'd done—what we'd done—had really been the best thing. Of course I wondered. How could I not have doubts? But the adoption was a fait accompli. And for all I could see, things were turning out for the best."

"Yes," she said, almost to herself. "For some." Becca looked back at Henry Le Mew. He was sitting in a lump, staring fixedly at her. It unnerved her.

"I'm sorry, Becca, for your unhappiness. I truly am. I only wanted . . ."

Becca turned back to her father. He looked so terribly sad. Becca felt her heart ache for him. If that was sentimentality, so be it. If it was love . . .

"What, Dad?" she asked. "What did you want?"

"I only wanted what was best for my family."

Becca nodded. "One more thing, Dad."

Her poor father looked justifiably apprehensive.

"What is it, Becca?" he asked.

"Well, I was just wondering why Henry doesn't like me."

Steve's eyes widened with surprise. "What makes you think he doesn't like you?"

"Look at him, Dad. Look at that stare! He hasn't blinked for minutes. He looks like he wants to kill me."

Steve laughed. "Oh, that's nothing. He gives everyone that look. Even me when I give him tuna when he's in the mood for turkey."

"I don't know," she said doubtfully.

"Look, I'll show you. Henry, come on over and say hello to Becca."

Henry stood up on his fistlike paws and stretched to a magnificent arch. When he'd regained his normal, still impressive stature, he yawned, showing, to Becca's unease, many very pointy teeth. And then, to her utter amazement, he walked, with some dignity, to where she now stood by her father.

"Let him smell your hand," Steve directed.

Hesitatingly, Becca put her fingers under Henry's large pink nose. Henry sniffed—and before Becca could panic, he was rubbing his face against her fingers.

"Oh, my God," she whispered. "I can't believe this!"

"I told you he liked you. He just hates crowds. With everyone in the house he prefers to stay on his own." Steve chuckled. "Can't say I blame him."

Abruptly, Henry Le Mew turned and walked back to where he'd been sitting a few moments before.

"He's got some napping to do," Steve explained.

"And I've got some thinking to do," Becca said softly. "I'll see you back at the house later, Dad."

She left her father's studio before she could allow herself to be hugged.

42

Becca had told her father the truth; she did have some thinking to do. But first, she had to deal with something that had been nagging at her for the past hour.

Olivia was one of her least favorite people—and clearly, if their confrontation in the attic had proved anything, it was that Olivia didn't care much for her younger sister, either—but Becca felt compelled to check on her, to see if she was all right. Seeing James drive away earlier had given Becca a bad feeling. She was afraid that the Rowan family was to see yet another dangerous rift in its once sturdy structure.

A quick check of the first floor assured Becca that her sister wasn't to be found there.

"Have you seen Olivia?" she asked Lily, when the younger girl passed her in the hall, a paperback novel in hand.

"Yes," she said. "About ten minutes ago she came into the kitchen for some tea. She was acting strangely. Her hands were shaking. I asked her if she wanted me to get James, but she just went up to her room. I mean, I guess that's where she was going."

"Okay. I'll go see if she's all right. And I know what you're thinking," she added. "That I'm the last person Olivia wants to see."

Lily smiled ruefully. "Anyway, it's nice of you to check on her. Thanks, Becca. I was a little worried, but I wasn't sure what to do."

Becca shrugged. She felt embarrassed by Lily's thanks. "Whatever," she said, and headed for the stairs.

She knocked softly on the door of the Queen Anne's Lace Room. Really, her mother was so silly with these ridiculous names.

"Liv? You in there?"

There was no response.

"Olivia?" she called, knocking again, this time more loudly. "Are you okay?"

Still there was no response. Becca gently tried the doorknob. The door was locked from the inside.

"Olivia," she called, "if you don't answer me I'm going to get Mom."

Finally, a hoarse voice responded to Becca's knocking and threat. "I'm fine," it said. "I'm just—resting."

Becca didn't believe for one moment that her older sister was "fine," but at least she'd proved to be alive. "Okay," she said. "I'll be downstairs if—if you need anything."

Becca walked back down the hallway. It had felt odd to offer help to her older sister. It had felt odd, but also somehow right.

As she approached the room that Rain was sharing with Lily, Becca noticed that the door was now partway open. She stopped and peeked inside. Naomi was sitting on the edge of the bed. Rain lay there with a wet washcloth over her eyes, probably suffering from a migraine. She had inherited that awful genetic trait from her grandmother, who had been hit by the pain and nausea every month just before her period.

Becca didn't mean to spy, but the scene arrested her. She watched surreptitiously as Naomi adjusted the washcloth and murmured what were no doubt consoling words to her daughter.

Her daughter.

And suddenly Becca knew, deep down, knew without a doubt, that it would be a crime to shatter the bond she was witnessing.

It would be a crime against every one of the Rowans.

Time marched on. At the age of sixteen, Becca herself had given birth. Now Rain, at sixteen, was capable of bringing new life into the world. The reality was that time passed; no matter who was Rain's acknowledged mother, Rain would move away from her. Even if she were to come to understand and accept that Becca, not Naomi, was her birth mother, she would still be off on her own path before long. It was inevitable that everyone moved forward and that all ties loosened even as they endured. Love, it could be said, was elastic.

And it had a cost. Sometimes it seemed a cost too high to meet. But you just had to pay it, because a life without love was simply not worth living.

Suddenly, Naomi turned her head and saw Becca at the door. She smiled, her expression questioning but not unkind or suspicious.

"I'm sorry," Becca whispered, already beginning to tiptoe away.

Once back in the den, Becca, suddenly exhausted, stretched out on the lumpy couch and pulled a heavy blanket up to her chin.

She used to think that the stupidest thing she had

ever done was getting pregnant at sixteen, and the smartest, the best thing she had ever done was going through with the pregnancy. Well, she still thought that giving birth to Rain was the best and most beautiful thing she had accomplished. But now she was beginning to think that the stupidest—the most selfish— thing she had ever done was threaten to destroy her family—each and every one of them—with the truth.

The truth. What was the truth in this situation? The truth was that Becca loved her daughter. That was the biggest and the best truth. Becca loved Rain. That should be enough.

And Becca now knew something she hadn't really known only days earlier. She knew that even if Rain were to be told the truth about her parentage, that truth would never erase the fact of the relationship that had existed between Rain and Naomi for sixteen years. Today's truth didn't invalidate yesterday's reality. It might taint it, but it could never erase it entirely.

No. To attempt to consume her daughter, to attempt to assume her daughter in the way she had been planning to would be, as Olivia would say, a form of madness. To attempt to force her into becoming a best friend would be wrong.

And really, Becca thought now, hadn't she been one of the lucky ones? She'd read stories and seen movies about women who had given up a baby for adoption at birth, women who'd never seen or who had only glimpsed their children before they became the children of other mothers. She'd read how years later, so many of those women were filled with regret and longing, how many of them were desperate for contact with those babies, for assurance that they had grown and thrived. She'd read how so many women were never, ever to know the fate of their children.

But Becca had had the opportunity not only to observe the baby she had given up at birth but also to interact with her, to love her face-to-face. If that was sometimes painful because it was done in the guise of an aunt and not a mother, so be it. In the end it was a hell of a lot better situation than it might have been. What if David and Naomi hadn't offered to raise Rain as their own? What then? Becca might never have had the privilege of watching her little girl grow into a young woman.

Becca threw off the blanket and sat up. She had a sudden, burning need to see Alex, and she wasn't at all sure why. She had never been to his house or studio, though he'd given her directions of a sort the morning she'd run into him after breakfast. Was it really only days ago that Becca had sworn she'd never have an intention to pay her parents' neighbor a visit?

Now the thought of just showing up on his doorstep scared her a bit. She wondered what sort of reception she would receive. She considered calling ahead but didn't want to ask her mother for his phone number. God knows what sort of ideas her mother might get, matchmaker that she was. Besides, she hadn't seen her mother for a while; she might be off running an errand or stalking through the snowy woods with Hank.

Becca wanted to act now. She bundled up in her sweaters and coat. In the hall she pulled on the heavy boots that now seemed like the smartest investment she'd made in some time. And once again she ventured out into the Kently winter.

43

Olivia watched from the window of the room she shared with James as Becca, dressed in so many layers of clothing she looked almost unrecognizable as a human, trudged off in the direction of the neighbor's house and studio. Vaguely she wondered why her sister was visiting Alex—if that's what she was doing—but the thought vanished as quickly as it had come.

Olivia turned away from the window. Nothing but her own sorrowful predicament concerned her right then. She had been taken entirely by surprise earlier that day. Never in a million years would she have expected James to confront her the way he had. Never. And yet . . . why hadn't she seen this coming?

The cup of tea her sister Lily had made her sat untouched on the dresser. Olivia felt sick. She felt overwhelmed. She felt confused.

For too long now she had been fighting against the feelings of darkness and despair, burying herself in work and in an obsession with family history, frantically moving, afraid that if she stopped for one moment, she would be consumed by the sadness that was welling deep inside her, just waiting for one moment of inattention on her part to spring forward and drown her.

When had it all begun? Olivia knew when. The sadness had come when she had finally been forced to let go of the hope for a biological child of her own.

Olivia began to pace the small room. She felt that no one understood the depth or the nature of her loss, not even James, though he did try to be empathetic. In spite of her despair, she couldn't deny that James had tried to be of help.

And there was no one else to whom Olivia could turn. Who else could empathize? Her mother's experience was too alien to permit real understanding. She had given birth to four children of her own; she had three grandchildren and quite possibly could be given more. Besides, Olivia thought, somewhat bitterly, her mother was the type to resort to a clichéd pep talk rather than engage with anyone on a meaningful level. Maybe that was an unfair judgment, but that was the way Olivia saw it.

And her grandmother . . . Olivia shook her head though no one was there to witness the dismissive gesture. She had never been particularly close to her grandmother. Lily was the favorite there. And that was fine. Really. If her grandmother wanted to play favorites with Lily, like her mother had done with David . . .

Olivia paced more quickly. She knew that some might argue that she had missed an opportunity for understanding and friendship with one or more of the women she had met during the exhausting years spent visiting fertility clinics. But for Olivia, that hadn't been an option. When it was all over, when the final negative verdict had been delivered, she had wanted nothing to do with any of the women she'd met. When it was all over, she'd given up on finding emotional health and friendship at support groups where other women struggling to get pregnant or to sustain their pregnancies shared their trials and tribulations.

And sometimes, their triumphs. The hard-won triumphs had been the most difficult for Olivia to bear. She knew that she should derive some hope for her own situation from the fact of another's success. She knew that as a decent person she should feel glad for another's achievement of happiness. But all she had ever felt was bitter and angry and jealous.

Olivia was facing the dresser. On top of it sat one of the notebooks she used for recording the contents of her grandmother's attic. The blue notebook was for clothing and other linens, like tablecloths or draperies. The red notebook was for furniture and appliances, of which there were disappointingly few. The green notebook was for toys—like the doll Becca had almost broken the other day!—and other, miscellaneous items.

Olivia abruptly stopped pacing and stared at the notebook. Why was the accumulation of past things, the accumulation of facts, and names, and dates so awfully important to her? How had they become so important?

It had started with a simple curiosity. What had her ancestors looked like? Did she inherit her great-grandmother's hair color or her great-uncle's interest in business? And then, imperceptibly, her interest had grown. She bought books on ancestor research. She contacted the headquarters of the Church of Jesus Christ of Latter-Day Saints in Utah for access to their vast stores of genealogical information. She joined chat rooms and spent hours each evening communicating online with other people who shared her interest in the past. She began to catalogue each and every bit of her family's possessions in order to create her own detailed archive.

She hadn't seen a movie in over a year. She hadn't been out with any of her friends for a lunch or a dinner in months.

Olivia sank onto the edge of the bed. If she could be totally honest with herself—and right at that moment it seemed as if she could be—she was tired of the control the search for things past had over her. For some time she had been feeling as if she was operating under a compulsion, something she simply could not command. What had once been a pleasurable pasttime was now—an addiction.

Olivia was startled by the thought. Could it be? Was this what it was like to be addicted to something, to need it and yet at the same time to be repulsed by it—rather, repulsed by the need for it?

James. The memory of James's face as he'd left their room earlier came to Olivia now and it saddened her deeply. He had looked so—miserable.

The awful fact was that she had been spending so much time avoiding a confrontation with her own deep unhappiness, largely by redirecting her energies into her research, that she'd become blind to the obvious unhappiness of her husband, the person who had vowed to stay by her side for better or worse, through sickness and in health. . . .

The person who now wanted to break that vow. Or, at least, to put that vow on hold. She couldn't even be mad at him. She had been, briefly, when he'd talked about a separation . . . but now . . . No. How could she be mad at someone for trying to help her—and for trying to save himself?

She knew there was no other woman in James's life. She also knew that he could hardly be blamed for finding love elsewhere if their marriage continued on in the cold and strained way it was going, if it continued on in the alienating way she'd been directing it.

Oh, what was wrong with her!

Olivia felt tears come to her eyes. She hadn't cried in what seemed like years. Now the tears came freely and though Olivia had never felt so desolate, she was aware on some deep level that the tears were those of relief as well as of pain.

She knew that she needed help. And she knew, finally, that she very much needed James, in whatever way she could have him—in whatever way he would have her.

Olivia looked around the room for her bag. It was on the floor by her side of the bed. She dug around in it until she found the small notebook she kept there. The thin, lined paper was nothing like the thick, beautiful paper on which James had written his Christmas letter to her, but it would have to do. On a clean page, Olivia wrote three simple words to her husband. She felt that her message was complete. And she hoped he thought so, too.

44

Alex had been right. His house was not as large or as pretty—at least on the outside—as her parents' house. There were similarities, of course, the houses having been built around the same time and, quite possibly, by some of the same people. Like the Rowans' house, Alex's had two stories, an attic, and four-over-four windows. From what Becca could tell, no additions had been added over time. A quick peek in a window allowed her to see that the ceilings were lower than those in her parents' home. Beyond that detail she couldn't tell much else. Sections of the exterior paint were peeling, and the small front porch, which might not have been original to the house, looked slightly lopsided. Still, Becca smiled to see a simple but elegant pine wreath on the house's front door. Maybe Alex was just very busy and not negligent about home repair.

Becca went around the house to the old barn. This, too, was smaller than her parents' barn, and the exterior was not as well kept. Becca knocked loudly on the weathered wooden door.

"Come in!" a voice boomed.

She pushed open the door just a bit—it was heavier than she had imagined it would be—and peered inside. "Are you busy?" she asked.

Alex was bent over a long wooden trestle table, but he looked up at her briefly. "I am busy but I can talk. Or listen. If you don't mind my working while I do it."

"No, of course not," she said. "Work is important."

Becca came all the way into the barn and closed the door behind her.

"Yes, it is," Alex was saying. "And so are deadlines. I'm afraid I've been dragging my feet with this commission. But I need the money and, more importantly, I made a promise so—here I am."

It was cold in Alex's studio. Colder than it should be, Becca thought, given the working woodstove and the fiberglass "batts" stapled to the walls. (She had learned a lot during the construction of her condo and the other condos in the building.) She shivered and wrapped her arms around herself.

"Sorry about the cold," he said, noting her discomfort. "I try to keep my heating costs as low as possible. Of course, I can't go without heat out here entirely. I'd never be able to hold a gouge, even with work gloves."

Alex held up one work-gloved hand, in which he held the gouge, as if to prove his point. Hs jeans were splattered with paint and messily tucked into partially laced work boots. A long red scarf was wound several times around his neck, the ends tucked into his heavy corduroy jacket to keep them out of the way of his work.

"I like your wreath," Becca said, suddenly unsure of what she had come here to say—if anything. "The one on the front door."

"Thanks. Free materials all around, you know. And yes, I know the house needs repainting. It's happening next spring."

Becca smiled. "And a new porch?"

"Oh, yeah. It's been rotting away since I bought the place three years ago. At least the plumbing is intact. Otherwise I'd have to call a plumber, and they can be pretty expensive."

"You're no good with a plunger?"

Alex just grinned.

Becca pointed to the trestle table on which sat a piece of wood (Becca didn't know which kind), which was screwed to the table, and a variety of tools (few of which she recognized). "What is it?" she asked. "I mean, what are you making?"

"It's going to be a bird. Rather, a representation of a bird, for a private client. It's a pay-the-bills kind of job, not something I'm particularly enjoying but . . ."

Yes, thought Becca. *I know all about pay-the-bills kinds of jobs.* And about the clients—some bearable, others not so bearable—who made them possible.

"Make yourself at home," Alex said. "I'll be able to be a better host once I finish this step. It's still early in the process. . . ."

Arms folded across her chest against the cold and damp of the studio, Becca strolled around the old barn. Against one wall stood a large wooden cabinet of no particular style; Becca thought it looked as if it had been cobbled together long ago, maybe by the former owner of the house. On its open shelves were several books—mostly spy novels, Becca noted; a stack of art-related magazines from years earlier; a can of paintbrushes of various sizes; a vase of pussy willows in fuzzy water that should have been changed some time ago; and an old transistor radio of the sort

Becca remembered her father having kept from his childhood.

Becca moved on, interested in her finds. In one corner of the studio, laid out on the floor, Becca counted five copper weather vanes, including one, fairly traditional in style, that depicted a running horse, and another more quirky one that depicted a Halloween-style witch, complete with beaked nose and high, pointy hat, soaring on her broom. It made Becca smile to think about who might choose such a weather vane as a year-round decoration, and as a symbol of her home.

An oil painting—at least, Becca thought the painting was done in oil—depicting what looked like the rocky Maine shore during a summer storm was propped on a wooden easel near the collection of weather vanes. Becca didn't know a lot about painting, but she thought that this one was rather good. She felt almost as if she were right there on the blasted shore, awed by the storm-tossed sea, her skin prickled with drops of salt water.

A wheelbarrow held a pile of what looked like giant wooden spools. Becca made a mental note to ask Alex what exactly they were or had been used for. On another table were displayed several chunks of wood of various types and sizes. From the roof hung a collection of old tools used in farming; Becca recognized the tools as such but had no idea what exactly they were used for. A collection of cast-iron horses and buggies stood in a row on a shelf close to the door through which she'd entered the old barn-turned-artist's-workspace.

Alex's studio was a hodgepodge of items, random but not without coherence—if that made any sense. And Becca couldn't help but note the vast difference

between Alex's personal space—his studio, yes, and
not his living quarters; she wondered what they would
be like—and her own. Alex's studio was so . . . personal. It was quirky and, she guessed, informative
about his personality, his likes and tastes and prefer-
ences. While her home . . . Well, her home was not.
She'd furnished her new, high-end condo on Wash-
ington Avenue entirely from a Pottery Barn catalogue. Everything, from the furniture to the framed
art on the walls, was preselected by the Pottery Barn
buyers. It could be said that yes, Becca had chosen
particular pieces from their inventory, but still . . .
There were no tokens of travel on an end table, no
knickknacks spotted at a flea market, no collections of
seashells or ceramic frogs or glass figurines. The only
items that betrayed Becca Rowan's presence in the
apartment and not the presence of some other
woman were several photographs of Rain. And, out of
a sense of family duty, a few photographs of the
twins, school pictures that Naomi had sent, thinking
that Becca would actually want them.

As for her office, well, that was even more nondescript, even more impersonal. To avoid questions
that might betray her own anxiety about exposure,
she had no photographs at all on her desk, not even
one of Rain. Her assistant, Mary, had brought her a
potted plant once, but it had died within a week.
Becca had neglected to water it.

And what did that say about me? Becca wondered
now. Nothing good, it seemed.

Becca walked over to the only item she hadn't yet
explored. There was a large corkboard on the far
wall, and tacked to it were a jumble of images—some
were obviously torn from magazines; some were post-
cards; some were photographs; a few were rough

sketches in charcoal—and quotations, the latter printed in a strong, vertical hand that Becca assumed was Alex's hand.

"What's all this?" Becca asked, gesturing to the display.

Alex glanced over his shoulder to where she stood. "Food for thought. Words and pictures to keep the mind alive and well. Inspiration, if I'm lucky. A way to kill time if I'm not."

Becca walked closer to the wall. Her eye was immediately caught by a phrase printed on a three-by-five index card. She proceeded to read aloud.

" 'We are by nature our own enemies . . . we seek events that unconsciously befit us, which consciously we fear. Richard Ellmann, *OSCAR WILDE*.' "

Alex seemed to have completed the immediate task that had required most of his attention. Now he put down his gouge and perched on a paint-spattered stool. "It's a wonderful biography," he said. "Have you read it?"

Becca shook her head. "No. So what he's saying, this Ellmann, is that a person's greatest strength is his greatest weakness."

Alex considered. "I'm not sure that's quite what he's saying, but yes, I think your observation is probably true for most people. Maybe all people. People who are super-organized might be missing out on the creative aspects of chaos. Someone who's always nurturing others might be emotionally starving inside."

The thought scared Becca because she suspected its truth. She liked things to be obvious and clear; she liked things to mean what they were supposed to mean and nothing else. The fact that one trait—generosity, for example—could mean something both positive and negative within the one person who owned the trait, well, that was disconcerting.

"I'm uncomfortable with paradox and uncertainty," she said abruptly.

Alex looked at her, as if wondering what had been going on in her head in the last few seconds. "As an artist," he said finally, "I dwell almost exclusively with paradox and uncertainty."

"Do you think there's any way to avoid yourself?" she said, not in response to Alex's statement, but struck by the quote tacked to the wall. "What I mean is, do you think it's inevitable that everyone betrays himself in the end? Is it inevitable that, for example, my generosity is going to be my downfall?" *That if I'm always and exclusively concerned with another person—my daughter—I'm going to live and die unfulfilled?* This last question Becca posed to herself.

"I think," Alex said with a smile, "that I'm going to have to give that question some consideration. It's a complex question with, no doubt, a complex answer."

Becca turned back to the board and read aloud another quote, this one also by this Richard Ellmann person. " 'To replace a morality of severity with one of sympathy.' "

"What are your thoughts about that?" Alex asked.

"I doubt that sympathy is always appropriate," Becca said quickly, turning to face him. "I mean, some people make their own unhappiness and I can't feel much sympathy for that." *Like my older sister,* Becca thought. *And like me?*

"That's where we're different," Alex replied. "I'm not claiming to be a saint, but I do urge sympathy at all times. Sometimes, I'm wrong, but I'd rather start from a place of kindness than one of judgment. Maybe that unhappy person isn't able to be otherwise. Maybe he simply can't be other than who and what he is. And for that, I can feel sympathy."

Becca looked closely at this man working on his pay-the-bills project. She found herself admiring his dedication, and his competency. And more than that, she found herself admiring his kindness. "I think," she said, after some time, "that you're a much better person than I am."

"Don't say that," he replied quickly. "You don't know me very well. Besides, I also don't believe in putting oneself down, even in a roundabout way. Which is not to say that a person shouldn't hold himself accountable to good behavior. But that's another topic."

Yes, she thought. One should hold oneself accountable to good behavior. Otherwise, there would be chaos all the time. No relationship would ever be safe. "Alex," she said, "do you ever regret something you did? Or something you didn't do?"

"No," he said firmly. "To both questions. I believe that regret is useless. More than that, I believe that it's poisonous. I just can't see anything constructive about it. Which is not to say that I don't try to learn from my mistakes. I do try to learn. I just try not to regret."

"Oh." Could regret really be avoided? Becca wondered.

Alex shifted on the stool, which was not the most comfortable perch he'd ever sat on. "Why did you ask?" he said. "Are you suffering regrets about something?"

"Maybe," she said. "But not about something I did or didn't do. I think I might be regretting something I plan to do. Rather, something I'd planned to do."

Alex raised an eyebrow at her. "You know that makes no sense. You can't regret the future."

"Intentions," Becca argued. "You can regret or feel bad about intentions. You can feel bad about having announced your intentions and maybe having hurt people by announcing them. You can feel bad about revealing thoughts and feelings you should have kept to yourself or conquered or . . . or maybe never had in the first place."

Alex folded his arms—damn, it was cold in that barn—and looked at Becca with concern.

"Becca? What are you trying to say?"

She laughed a bit and waved her hand dismissively. "Nothing. I'm—I'm just thinking out loud."

He eyed her carefully, not at all sure he believed her but sensing it would be stupid—at least, pointless—to push the issue. "Okay," he said.

Becca looked back to Alex's wall of inspiration.

" 'My life,' " she read, " 'cannot have been other than what it was, and what it is, and what it is becoming. Such is Fate.' Where did that one come from?" she asked. "I don't see an attribution."

Alex shrugged. "I guess I was lazy when I copied it out."

"A belief in Fate lets you off the hook for having screwed up." Becca believed that, or she thought she did. "You can't be responsible for an action because you were fated to take that action. You had no choice. It was all in the cards. It seems to me that believing in Fate is the coward's way of living."

"But that's if you're positing Fate as a force outside your self," Alex said. "If your self—your mind and heart and soul—is your 'fate,' then you are, indeed, responsible for your actions and choices. Right?"

Becca nodded. "Yes, I suppose that is right. But at the same time, if you are your own Fate, then you still wouldn't be exhibiting free will because you're not making choices. You're acting as you have to act because you're you."

Alex grimaced. "It's not easy stuff to wrap your

head around, that's for sure. But it does make for good thinking."

Alex suddenly turned back to the worktable and began to sketch something with a stub of a pencil on a piece of torn brown paper. Inspiration, Becca wondered? Or maybe it was something as mundane as a shopping list. Left to her own devices for the moment, Becca continued to think about their conversation.

Whatever it was—Fate, her own nature—that had directed or caused her to have unprotected sex at sixteen, she had done it. And she wondered now why had she—why did anyone—run to her ruin? Becca, for example, had known the risks of having sex without birth control. She hadn't been stupid when it came to accumulating facts. But when it came to judgment, to putting that store of facts to good use in daily life, well, there she had been lacking.

Since then, since the birth of her daughter, she had been perfecting her judgment. She had become proud of her rational self . . . and yet, only now, during this bitter cold week in December, was she coming to see that in wanting to tell Rain the truth in the way she had, she had been executing very poor judgment.

Why the slip in rationality, she wondered, and why such a massive one at that?

Becca looked hard at her parents' neighbor. "You've insinuated yourself into our lives, haven't you?" she said abruptly.

Alex put down his pencil and turned to her. "Have I?" he asked, with a grin. "I assure you I had no intention of insinuating. I find the word and the action it describes a bit too snakelike for me. A bit too reminiscent of Uriah Heep."

So he read Dickens, did he? "So," she asked, "what word would you prefer to use?"

"Let me think." Alex looked to the beamed ceiling as if inspiration was to be found there. "How about 'barge'?" he said finally. "I barged into their lives. It's so much more direct and honest. When someone barges in, you can easily see him coming."

"And you can run away. Or hide. Or both."

Alex looked at her closely. "But you didn't do either, did you? Run away or hide."

"No, I didn't," she admitted. "Which is not to say that I didn't try."

"How hard did you try?"

Becca gave this question some thought. "I guess not very," she finally said. "When I set my mind to a task, I usually succeed." She paused as a stray thought pushed its way to her tongue. "By the way," she said, "and I don't know why I just remembered this now, but Rain told me that you like her long nails."

Alex blushed; Becca could see it through the scruff of his unshaved cheeks. "Oh," he said. Did his voice sound a bit squeaky? "It's just that I think it's kind of, I don't know, exotic. Different. I spend a lot of time with artists, and long nails just get in the way of clay and paint and wires and tools."

"You should hear them on a keyboard!" Becca laughed. "Anyway, I think Rain might like to wear her nails long because of me. I'm her—I'm her favorite aunt."

"She's a good kid. And it's pretty clear she adores you." Alex came to join Becca by the inspiration board. "Really, Becca," he said, "your hands are—well, they're beautiful. Even covered in heavy winter gloves."

Becca had the ridiculous urge to hide her hands

behind her back. Instead, she just said, "Thanks." And then Alex took one of her gloved hands in his.

It felt like an important moment. It felt like a moment in which she might just be kissed.

And oh, how she wanted him to kiss her! It had been so very long since a man had touched her, and even then she hadn't responded with equal passion. But this was different. Becca knew that she would respond to Alex's heat easily and immediately.

But it wasn't so simple.

She was bothered by the fact of the secret she was keeping from Alex—by the secret she had vowed to keep from the world. And if you thought you were falling in love with someone, didn't you owe that person total honesty? Didn't you have a responsibility to be who you really were and not the character you pretended to be in the larger world?

She liked Alex. She respected him. She might even be coming to love him. What would he think of her if he knew the truth about what she had done sixteen years earlier? Would he willingly join the family conspiracy or would he reject Becca—and the Rowans—with disgust? Besides, how could she ask it of anyone, that he become part of a lie? It was the same old problem that she'd had since a boy in her freshman year of college had asked her out. But now . . .

Maybe, she thought, it would be better for her to remain alone and aloof. Better—and safer—for everyone. All this rushed through her head in the matter of a moment.

"I've got to go," she said then, pulling her hand from his and walking rapidly to the door of the barn. "Um, thanks for the talk. It was—fun."

Alex wouldn't have chosen the word "fun" to describe their conversation, but he wasn't about to argue. "Sure," he said, masking his keen disappointment. "Anytime. And be sure to get something hot to drink when you get home. You're turning blue."

And then Becca was gone and Alex was left alone with his board of quotes and images, his collection of cast-iron toys, and his stack of paperback spy novels. He felt more than a little frustrated. He'd been dying to kiss Becca Rowan. And he'd give anything to know what was really going on in her head!

45

Becca was sitting in the living room, an unopened book about birds native to New England on her lap. Rain was stretched out on the couch under a woolly plaid blanket. The twins were seated on the floor by the tree, poking through boxes and boxes of glass ornaments, silver tinsel, and gold garland.

The Christmas tree, a large, long-needled Scotch pine that Steve had cut down and hauled into the house with the help of Alex, stood naked still. Decorating the tree was usually a family affair, with the requisite amount of arguing about the amount of tinsel that should be used, but this year nobody seemed interested in the ritual. Not even Nora, who always had taken an almost childlike pleasure in the event, insisting she be the one to hang the three remaining ornaments she had gotten from her mother when she'd died—three delicate glass birds with wings of some shiny white material that stuck out from either side of the birds like slim, shimmering brushes.

Becca glanced over at Rain. Rain had taken a prescription pill for relief of the migraine and was feeling much better, but was not into doing anything more strenuous than flipping through another of her glossy fashion magazines. She seemed to have brought an endless supply of mindless "reading" materials and Becca couldn't help but wonder if she was doing enough real reading. If she were Rain's mother—

The thought and the way it had shaped itself called her up short. But there was no time for further contemplation as David came in from the dining room.

Malcolm held up a box of ornaments. "Isn't anybody going to help?" he asked his father.

"Why don't you guys decorate the tree all by yourselves this year?" David suggested. "I'll help with the high parts. And be careful with the glass ornaments, especially Great-Grandma's birds. They're old and very fragile."

"And if they break we could get cut from them, right?"

"Yes, Malcolm, you could. *If* you break them, which you're not going to do, right?"

Becca looked up at her brother. His mouth was set and his posture revealed how tense, how full of anxiety she thought he must be feeling. Yes, there was a dark pall over the Rowan house, and Becca was terribly unhappy at having been the cause. What had she done? What havoc had she wreaked? And why had she not guessed just how bad she would feel for being the cause of so much misery? Her ignorance about her own emotions appalled her. Being the cause of such unhappiness was very close to assuming a larger importance inside her than her desire to "claim" her daughter.

"I'll help with the tree," she said suddenly.

Michael shrugged and Malcolm said, "Okay." The

boys seemed unenthused, but why should they feel otherwise? She'd never made much of an effort with them. They had been little more to her than afterthoughts, really. What sort of message do you send to a child by almost always calling him by his brother's name?

David eyed her dubiously. "You don't have to help," he said.

Becca knew that what he meant was "I don't want you to help if you're going to use my children to curry favor with me." "I want to, David," she said steadily. She put the book she hadn't been reading on a side table and got up to join them.

With one last look of suspicion, David continued on upstairs. And Rain continued to be oblivious to everything but her magazine.

Becca and the boys had been working for almost a half hour—and not one ornament had been destroyed—when the front door opened. It was James, returned from wherever it was he had driven off to earlier.

"Hey, Uncle James!" Malcolm cried. At least, Becca thought it was Malcolm. "Want to help us decorate the tree?"

James caught Becca's mildly inquiring look and attempted a smile.

"We'd love your help," she said. "But if you've got something else you need to do—"

"No, no," he said after a moment. "There's nothing else."

His choice of words struck Becca's heart. The feeling that something had gone terribly wrong between Olivia and her husband, the sense that some line had been crossed, was stronger than ever.

But she wouldn't pry. James was a private man and besides, why would he want to open up to her, the person who had been wreaking havoc in the family for the past few days? There was no conversation between Becca and James as they decorated the tree other than requests for particular ornaments and a brief discussion about the judicious use of garland.

Dinner that evening, a collection of reheated leftovers, was a grim affair. Conversation was sporadic and dull. Becca thought that everyone, even the boys, seemed not his or her usual selves.

Olivia's eyes were swollen and red, but nobody mentioned this fact. Becca noted that her older sister hardly touched her food and said not a word. Beside her, James ate little but made small, pleasant talk with her grandmother. Whatever could be said about James, it could never be denied that he was a gentleman.

What was Alex doing for dinner? The thought startled Becca. Though she certainly didn't think he would enjoy the glum party the Rowans were making that Christmas Eve, she also didn't entirely like the thought of his being alone.

Since when had she started worrying about her parents' neighbor? Alex seemed the sort who could very well take care of himself. He had such strong opinions, such well-considered convictions. Still, that didn't mean he should be left to his own devices on a holiday. . . .

Becca took a sip of wine. She wondered what she really knew about Alex Mason. She'd had a few conversations with him, that was all, and yet . . . And yet during those few conversations she had, indeed, learned a lot about the man. She had learned that he loved his suffocating family. She had learned that he really listened when you spoke to him, and that he asked interesting, if sometimes difficult, questions. She had learned that his smile was really very nice and that his hair, though shaggy, was very nice, too. She had learned that he blushed when embarrassed.

"I'll clear the table."

Becca was pulled back to the moment by Naomi's voice and her family rising around her. One by one they seemed to drift into the living room, where the tree now stood completely decorated.

"The tree looks very nice, boys," Julie said, when the table had been cleared and she had joined the others in the living room.

Naomi, who'd come into the room with her, raised a critical eyebrow. "Though you might have been a little less wild with the tinsel."

"That was Aunt Becca's idea," Malcolm said. "I think it's cool. It looks like a rocket ship."

Michael made a face. "It does not!"

"Boys. Don't argue."

Julie patted her daughter's shoulder, and this time, Becca didn't flinch at the touch. "Well, whatever anyone thinks about the tinsel, thank you, Becca, for helping out."

"I always liked to decorate the Christmas tree when I was a kid," she said quietly. "I looked forward to it all year."

Steve smiled at his daughter. "Seeing you stringing the garland earlier," he said, "was like a glimpse into the past. So many memories came flooding forward."

Becca smiled back, grateful for her father's words. Then she turned and caught Nora looking at her intently. Her grandmother was wise and knew her loved ones well. Becca was sure she'd sensed a subtle shift in the relationship between Becca and her father. Well, she was right to sense that. There had been a shift.

"Uncle James helped with the tree, too," Malcolm was saying. "He put the angel on top. Me and Michael—"

"Michael and I," David corrected.

"Michael and I held the ladder so he wouldn't fall down."

James smiled. "The boys were very careful. They took good care of their old uncle."

Before long, Steve and Julie went off to take a nap before leaving for church later that night. Separately, Olivia and then James retired upstairs, and Nora settled in the kitchen with a cup of tea. Lily and Rain remained in the living room to watch holiday specials on television with the boys.

And Becca went to her room, exhausted and yet somehow almost at peace.

46

It was Cliff's special ringtone, that stupid old pop tune, interrupting the television show Lily was watching with Rain and the twins.

Well, Lily thought, it's now or never. She excused herself—not that the boys would notice her absence, what with a screen full of animated holiday monsters in front of them; Rain wouldn't miss her either as she was multitasking, flipping through *Teen Vogue* while watching the show—and went into the kitchen where she knew her grandmother would be.

"It's Cliff," she said, phone still ringing in her hand.

"Do you want to take the call?" Nora asked from her seat at the kitchen table.

"Yes. I do."

"Well, then, go into my room for some privacy."

"Thanks, Grandma."

Lily answered the call while slipping into her grandmother's room. She closed the door behind her and perched on the bed. Just being in the presence of her grandmother's world made her feel strong and supported.

"Finally," he said, with a laugh. "I was beginning to think you'd never talk to me again."

Lily said nothing. His laugh had told her that he assumed he'd finally won her back due to his electronic harassment.

"Are you having fun?" he asked.

Lily thought it a strange question, given the circumstances, but answered anyway. "I always enjoy being with my family," she said.

"Good. Good."

Maybe he was waiting for Lily to ask if he was having fun during the holiday. Well, she wasn't going to ask. She really didn't need to know. In fact, she suddenly realized that she had absolutely nothing to say to this person who had once meant so much to her.

"Look," Cliff said abruptly, "I want you to come back to school early so we can talk and, you know, patch things up."

Patch things up. How casual that sounded! Cliff really hadn't understood the pain he'd inflicted on her. You didn't just "patch things up" after an affair. You apologized profusely; you did penance of whatever sort was required; you promised never, ever to break your vow of fidelity again. None of which Cliff had really done.

"There's nothing to talk about anymore, Cliff," she said. "There's nothing to patch up."

"Oh, come on, Lily," he said with an impatient laugh, "don't be like that."

"Like what, Cliff?" Let him articulate his thoughts. She was learning to articulate hers.

"You know. Like, all distant. Look, I already got your gift. I'd really like to give it to you."

So, Cliff had bought her a Christmas gift. A list of his previous gifts ran through Lily's mind and she realized for the first time how lame and impersonal they were, like the necklace of cheap wooden beads that anyone who even vaguely knew her could tell was not her style, and the pink sweatshirt with the word "HOTTIE" written in silver glitter across the back. That was more than tasteless; that was rude. And all the time they'd been a couple, how she had struggled to find him just the right gift for every occasion! Like the time Cliff had mentioned he was interested in learning how to fly-fish. For his birthday that year, Lily had scraped together enough money for a special reel he wanted, which had then never been used. Cliff had decided that fly-fishing wasn't really his "thing." Would he decide next month that gambling was also not his "thing"? It didn't matter. Lily would return the RiskRunner as soon as she got back to Boston. The money would be far better spent on textbooks the following semester.

"I'm sure you can return it," she said. Or give it to another girl. It really, truly didn't matter. Not caring, Lily realized, felt liberating.

There was a long—and to Lily, a boring—silence.

"Do you still hate me?" he asked finally.

"No," Lily said, honestly. "I don't hate you. In fact, I forgive you."

Cliff sighed. "Then I don't understand. Why won't you come back to Boston early? We can spend New Year's Eve together, like we'd planned to do."

Well, Lily thought, *I'll never get off this phone if I don't tell him straight away what I've discovered this week. If he understands, fine. If not, that would be fine, too.*

"I won't come back," she said clearly, "because I can't come back. I can't—I won't—take a risk with someone who's not worth taking a risk for. Maybe someday I'll meet someone worth fighting for. But it's not you, Cliff. I learned that the hard way."

There was more silence from Cliff. "That's a little harsh," he said at last. Lily thought he sounded—subdued.

"I'm sorry. I didn't mean it to sound harsh. It's just the truth."

"Yeah. Well. So, I guess that's that."

And in that moment Lily felt wonderfully calm, removed, and relieved.

"Yes, Cliff," she said. "That's that. Good-bye. And Merry Christmas."

Lily pressed the "End" button without waiting for another word from her past.

47

"This feels like the worst day of my life, Liv."

James sat next to his wife on their bed, legs stretched in front of him. They were close to each other but not touching.

"I know," Olivia replied softly. "I mean, it feels that way to me, too. I can't seem to stop crying."

"I'm sorry." And James was sorry, for many things, some of which he knew he couldn't have changed or controlled even if he had tried.

Olivia sighed a clogged sigh. When she spoke, she kept her eyes on her hands in her lap. "I've done a lot of thinking today, James. And I know for sure that I don't want to live apart from you. Not even for a day. I can't. Please reconsider the idea of a separation. Please."

James looked down at his own hands and thought. It was so terribly hard, trying to balance his own emotional health against the emotional health of his wife—and of their marriage.

"Would you agree to go to counseling?" he asked finally. "Alone or together, or maybe both. We can figure that out when we get home. But, Liv, I need you to say yes to this request."

"I'm frightened," she said immediately. "But yes, I'll go to counseling or therapy or whatever seems best. The thought . . . the thought of losing you . . ." Olivia looked up at her husband. "James, I'm so sad inside. And I don't know why, not really. Sometimes . . . sometimes I think I understand, sometimes I think I can locate the source of all the pain. . . . But then, it all slips away and I'm left totally confused again. I don't know if that makes any sense. I'm sorry."

James smiled kindly. He wanted to reach out and touch his wife but was still afraid of rebuff. "I don't think you should be apologizing for feeling sad, Liv."

"Maybe not. James? Do you really think therapy will help me? Do you think it will help us?"

"It's certainly worth a try. We've built so much to-gether, as a team. We have a business, a home, and a family. And we are a family, Liv, even if it's just us two. It seems such a terrible shame to let some unidenti-fied pain tear it all down. It seems such a terrible waste."

Fresh tears coursed down Olivia's cheeks. This time she didn't even bother to wipe them away. Why bother when more were sure to come?

"There's a future ahead of us, Olivia," James said now. Maybe. He was an intelligent man. He was real-istic. He knew that in spite of their best intentions the marriage might not survive. But he also knew that he, for one, had enough courage—and enough love for the woman he'd pledged to care for until the end of his days—to fight for its survival.

"I still have my letter to you," he added. "Would you like to have it? You can read it whenever you're ready."

"Yes. And . . ." Olivia reached into the drawer of

the bedside table. "Here's mine to you. It's not very long and I'm sorry about the paper but . . . But it says the truth."

"Do you want me to read it now?"

"Oh, yes."

James did and tears came to his own eyes. "Thank you, Olivia," he said. Three simple words could mean everything, if they were spoken honestly. James believed that they were.

"Can I hold your hand?"

James's heart leapt. It was the first time in so long that his wife had wanted to touch him. His heart broke again to see her eyes so sad and swollen with tears. "Of course you can hold my hand," he said. "You're my wife. If you really want to be."

"I do."

Olivia moved to sit close to James and took one of his hands in both of hers.

"I'm glad, Olivia," James said. "That you still want to be my wife. I really am."

"Do you still want to go to church with the family tonight?" she asked.

"I do," James said. "Do you?"

"Yes. But I'm afraid I'll be a weepy mess. It's been a long time since I cried and now I just can't seem to stop." She laughed a little. "I've become the proverbial leaky faucet, James."

"Don't worry," he said, placing a gentle kiss on her forehead. "I'll bring a box of tissues."

Olivia smiled weakly. It was all she could manage, but she meant it.

48

All of the Rowans but Nora and Becca were adding final layers of warm clothes in preparation for the drive to the local church. Midnight mass, in Massachusetts or in Maine, had been a beloved family tradition for as long as anyone could remember. A not so beloved tradition was the bone-chilling air in Kently's tiny wood-framed building.

"The cars are warmed up," Julie announced from the front door. "So let's get going!"

The family filed out—all but David, who promised to join them in a moment. "Grandma!" he stage-whispered.

Nora, comfortable in her favorite chair, looked up from the book she'd been reading.

"What is it, David?" she asked.

Her grandson came to kneel at her side. "Grandma," he said, more softly now, "what do you think she's going to do? Becca, I mean."

Nora gave him a little smile. "I think she's going to do the right thing."

"The right thing as she sees it?"

"Yes," she said. "But remember, David, that's all any of us can do."

David shook his head. "I'm worried she's going to break her latest promise not to do or say anything until after the holiday. Until we can all deal with this situation without the . . . Without the added emotional pressures of Christmas."

"I think that maybe you underestimate your sister."

"Let's hope I do. Because I can't get the idea out of my head that she's going to ruin Christmas Day with a big, dramatic gesture."

"David," Nora said, with authority. "Go to church. Try to calm down. Try to be peaceful. Please."

"All right, Grandma," he said, getting to his feet. "But I'm not going to rest easy until I've gotten Rain out of this house. Though I know that won't solve anything. I just wish this whole—"

"David."

Without another word, he left the house, closing the front door behind him.

For the first time in days the house was blissfully quiet. The only sound Nora could discern, and it was a pleasant one, was the fire crackling in the grate. The lights were turned low; in fact, most of the illumination in the room came from the single candles in each of the front windows, and the few pillar candles on the low coffee table. Henry Le Mew was asleep under the tree. Hank was curled up on the couch; he'd jumped there the moment the door had closed behind the family. Nora let him be.

This was the peaceful scene Becca saw when she came into the living room. She had been in the den, wrapped in blankets, waiting for the family to leave so that she might be alone with her grandmother.

"You didn't go to church, I see," she noted. She sat in the armchair to the left of her grandmother, close enough to reach out and touch her arm.

Nora laughed. "I'm an old pagan."

"I've never seen you worship a tree."

"The Druids aren't my style. But I'm a pagan nonetheless, my dear."

Becca smiled. "A witch?"

"Also not my style. I prefer to keep my clothes on in the great outdoors. But what about you? Why didn't you join the family tonight?"

"I'm not much of a churchgoer," Becca admitted. What she didn't voice was what both women knew. The family would not have been happy to have Becca with them. They were at church to celebrate a birth that was supposed to be an indication of supreme love and forgiveness, when all Becca seemed intent upon was hate and blame.

"May I say something to you, Becca?" Nora asked quietly. "No lecturing or scolding. Frankly, you're too old for that, and so, come to think of it, am I."

Becca nodded. She trusted Nora. "Yes, Grandma."

Nora settled herself more comfortably in her chair before speaking. "I know you've always thought your father was the person most in favor of the adoption. But actually, I was the prime mover. I was the one who first suggested the plan, alone to David and Naomi, and when they agreed, to your parents. Your father did the legwork, so to speak, but he had to be convinced it was a good plan. And he insisted that unless you gave your full consent, we'd drop the entire scheme."

"I don't remember that," Becca said after a stunned moment. "I believe you, but I don't remember."

"I'm glad you believe me, because it's the truth. But I'm not surprised you don't remember much of what went on in those first weeks. You were so upset. It was so hard for you. We were all so worried." Nora paused. "And honestly, we're all terribly worried again now."

Becca took a calming breath. There were words she had never spoken aloud to anyone. But they were words long overdue to be heard.

"It's just that since . . . since I got pregnant I've felt like a failure. Let's be real, Grandma—I let everyone down. So ever since then, I've been trying to prove my worth to you and to Mom and Dad. To everyone in the family. I'm tired of being seen as the Rowan who made the big mistake."

Nora's surprise was not feigned. "I have to admit, Becca," she said, "that I'm shocked to hear you say such things. Every single one of us, especially your father, considers you a wonderfully successful person. And not the least because you made such a noble decision to secure your child's future when you were only a child yourself. Where on Earth did you get the idea that you had to prove yourself to anyone? The only person you need to prove your worth to is yourself. No one else."

Becca could no longer prevent her tears. She got up from her chair and knelt at her grandmother's side. Without a word she rested her head on her grandmother's lap. Gently, slowly, Nora smoothed her granddaughter's hair, hoping to comfort her.

"I'm so alone," Becca whispered, as if she were still afraid to admit it, as if someone—but who?—would use that information against her.

"No," Nora whispered back, "you're not. I know you feel that way, but it's not true."

They sat in silence for some time, until Nora spoke again.

"You don't need to suffer alone, Becca," she said. "You have us—me, your parents, your brother and sisters. You can share the burden of loneliness and whatever else it is you're feeling with us. But you can't share it with your daughter. You can't share it with your child. I know that for sure. I know that like I know the liver spots on the back of my hand."

Becca looked up and smiled. "Grandma, you're incorrigible."

"It's better than being a bore."

"Oh, yes." Becca wiped her tears away, got to her feet, and settled back in the chair next to her grandmother.

"You know," Nora said then, "there's someone else who cares for you, someone not a part of the family." *Yet*, she added silently. "And if my experienced eye can be relied upon, and I believe that it can, he cares for you quite a lot."

Of course, Becca acknowledged silently. Alex Mason. Neighbor, artist, and yes, a friend.

"I worry," she admitted then, "that once Alex—once any man—hears the truth, that I gave up my daughter, he might accuse me of being uncaring. And I worry that he might not want to get involved with a family that has such a conspiracy at its heart."

Nora sighed. "Well, worry is payment paid on a loan that might never come due."

"I don't understand."

"What I mean is, why are you worrying about something that might never come to pass? The habit of worrying is a terrible waste of precious time and energy."

"Yes. I suppose. Still . . ."

"Well," Nora said, forestalling her granddaughter's objections, "I certainly can't speak for the average man, but I do feel I can somewhat speak for Alex Mason. He's a good person, Becca. He's the least judgmental person I've met in a very long time. I don't think you need to fear his rejection, certainly not based on the fact that you made a very difficult and very wise choice for your infant daughter."

Becca sincerely hoped her grandmother was right. Still . . . "I've been so afraid," she said. "I'm still so afraid, of real intimacy. The risks are so high . . . I don't know if I have it in me to be in a serious relationship, Grandma."

"Well, pardon me for using yet another cliché, but I must say that you'll never know unless you try."

Becca laughed softly. "I know. You have to take a chance if you want to succeed. Showing up is half the battle. I've got plenty of clichés at hand, too."

"Intimacy is frightening," Nora said now, as if to herself. "That's true. But what's the alternative?"

The alternative, Becca thought, was the empty life she had been living for far too long. She looked fondly at her grandmother.

"Thanks for not—for not forcing me to talk before I was ready to talk," she said. "I mean, I do understand why Mom and Dad and David felt that they had to . . . Well, it felt as if they were attacking me or accosting me, but I know that's not what was really going on. Anyway, thank you, Grandma, for your patience."

"You're quite welcome, Becca." With a little grunt, Nora rose from her cherished armchair and straightened her skirt. "I'd best be off to bed," she said. "This old woman still needs a few hours' sleep."

Becca smiled. "Pleasant dreams," she said.

Nora patted her granddaughter's head. "Sleep tight and don't let the bedbugs bite."

But Becca was not ready for sleep, with or without bedbugs. Instead, she moved to her grandmother's favorite chair. She had never sat in it before; she'd thought that maybe it would be disrespectful. But now, it felt right. It felt welcoming. It felt like a perfect place for reflection.

The pregnancy had been an accident, one that had changed everything. It was something unplanned, unlooked for, unexpected, and yes, unwanted.

But it had happened and it had led to everything else that had happened afterward and it would continue to lead to—to cause? to influence?—everything that would happen in her future, whether she could detect a direct causal connection or not.

The pregnancy had been an accident. But now Becca wondered if you could properly call an event an accident when you were partly or wholly responsible for it happening—and therefore, partly or wholly responsible for its outcome.

She remembered the conversation with Alex earlier in his studio. They had touched on the themes of chance and Fate, on character as the origin of one's actions, and on the notion of inevitability.

Well, whatever the ultimate answer to the impossible questions they had raised, one thing was certain: Becca had given birth to a daughter. Nothing would change that fact, not even being called "aunt" by that child.

But what about another child, one who could openly call Becca "Mommy"? Up until that moment on Christmas Eve, in her parents' living room in Kently, Maine, Becca had felt that it would be unfair to Rain if she had another baby. She'd felt that having another baby would be in some way compounding the lie under which Rain had been forced to live. It didn't make logical sense. Becca knew that. It was something she felt more than something she could reasonably articulate. She simply had never been able to imagine having enough love for a second child when so much love was already devoted to the child born under a blanket of secrecy.

There it was again, Becca thought now. A failure of imagination. Well, maybe it was high time to open up her mind to the idea of a family. But she would take one monumental step at a time. . . .

The crunch of car tires on packed snow startled Becca out of her thoughts. The Rowan family was back from church. She wasn't ready to face any of them, not quite yet, so she hurried off to the den.

Once she was stretched out on the lumpy old couch under no fewer than four heavy blankets, Becca articulated her decision.

No. She would not break the agreement she had made with the family all those years ago, even before Rain's birth. She would not presumptively reveal herself as Rain's biological mother. She would wait until Rain's twenty-first birthday and then, as a family, the Rowans would decide whether or not the truth should be told.

It had been a terribly tough decision to make—to abandon the scheme that had possessed her for the last year—but in the past several days, she had come to realize the many selfish motives that had prompted her to want to break her promise to her family.

Simply put, she had matured. And if this was what it meant to be mature, to be an adult, then life was more painful—and possibly more rewarding—than she had ever imagined. She'd have to wait for the rewarding part, but that was okay.

It had taken a long time for her to get to this place of maturity. . . . And there was still a long road ahead. Becca knew she had to build the life she had been neglecting for far too long.

But first, there was Christmas to look forward to. For the first time in over a year, Becca sank easily into a deep and very peaceful sleep.

49

Christmas Day, December 25

By eight o'clock Christmas morning every member of the Rowan family but Becca had gathered around the tree for the Secret Santa exchange. Nora had knocked on the door of the den, and when she'd gotten no answer, and feeling a bit concerned, she had gone inside only to find her granddaughter in a deep sleep. Nora was loathe to wake her—she looked so peaceful—but the family was waiting anxiously.

Once woken, Becca had promised to join the others as quickly as was possible. Ten minutes later she took a seat in the living room. She knew that her family—well, David at least—probably expected her to ruin Christmas morning by breaking her promise and making a dramatic announcement. She wished she could ease their worries by a look or a signal, but she acknowledged to herself that she needed every moment she could get to gather the courage she knew it would take to give her gift to her daughter—who was to remain her niece as long as need be, even if that meant forever.

The proceedings began. The twins, young enough to be exempt from the exchange, were given their gifts first so that they would be occupied while the adults shared their own gifts. "Wait your turn" were words that fell on deaf ears when you were eight years old and it was Christmas morning. Together Michael and Malcolm tore open several boxes containing the robot building sets they'd been clamoring for since the first television ads had hit the airwaves in late October. David mumbled something about the stuff being a waste of plastic, but the boys were oblivious to their father's disapproval.

Among the adults, there was in place a long-standing order of gift-giving. It seemed to Becca to be based on little more than habit. First Nora gave her gift, then Steve gave his, and it went on from there. Becca was the one to give hers last.

Nora handed a rectangular package to Naomi, who carefully removed the ivy-printed paper without a tear. Inside was a beautiful wool cardigan Nora had knitted for her.

"It's my favorite shade of blue," Naomi exclaimed. "Thank you, Nora. I can't wait to wear it. I'll put it on as soon as I get out of my nightgown after breakfast."

Rain also approved. "The color is perfect with your eyes, Mom," she said. "And that beige scarf you have, the one Dad bought you, that will work really well with the sweater."

Naomi rolled her eyes. "My fashion consultant."

"I wish! If you let me, I could do a total makeover. You wouldn't even recognize yourself."

"Uh, thanks, I think. But I'm fine the way I am."

Steve was the next to give his gift. He'd drawn James in the Secret Santa exchange, and gave him a cookbook entitled *Around the Hearth*.

"You mentioned it the last time you were here,"

Steve said. "I hope you haven't bought it in the meantime."

"No, I haven't. And thanks very much." James looked to his wife. "I look forward to making Olivia something special when we get home."

Becca noted this exchange. Maybe something good had happened between her sister and brother-in-law last night. One could only hope.

"Merry Christmas, Becca," Julie said, interrupting her daughter's thoughts. "And I'm certain this is something you don't have."

She handed Becca a thin, white envelope. Puzzled, Becca opened it. She smiled. Her mother was just not going to give up on her mission to force her daughter to have a life. And maybe that was a good thing.

"What is it, Aunt Becca?" Rain asked.

"It's a subscription to a travel magazine. *The Happy Traveler.*"

"Are you going somewhere?"

"Let's hope so!" Julie said. "All work and no play—"

"I get the hint," Becca said, but nicely. "Thanks, Mom, really."

Becca caught her brother eyeing her after this exchange; he looked tense. She smiled what she intended to be an open, friendly smile. David frowned and looked away. Olivia was presenting him with a package. In his usual manner, David tore the wrapping off the gift and tossed it aside. There was no reusing wrapping paper once David had been at it.

"It's a book on genealogy," he announced.

Becca thought Olivia seemed suddenly embarrassed. "I'm sorry," she said. "It's probably not your sort of thing. I'll give you the receipt and you can exchange it."

David, as he'd been known to do, rose to the occasion. "You know what, Liv?" he said. "I'm going to read it. If studying the family's past is so important to you, I'd like to know more about it. Thanks."

James squeezed his wife's shoulder. "It's my turn," he said. "Merry Christmas, Julie."

Julie accepted an oddly shaped package from her son-in-law.

"What is it, Mom?" Lily asked.

"Well, let me get the paper off first and I'll tell you!"

It was a new leash and collar for Hank.

"I noticed the one he's wearing now isn't in the best of shape," James explained.

"And he knows how you hate to spend money until it's absolutely necessary!"

"David!" Julie cried in mock offense. "Are you saying I'm cheap?"

"Not at all, Mom. Just—exceptionally frugal."

"Well, anyway, thank you, James. This is a very thoughtful gift. Hank! Come here, boy!"

Ever the attentive companion, Hank bounded up from where he'd been curled on a braided rug and went to Julie.

"Now me," David announced. "I wrapped it myself."

Nora grinned. "Yes," she said, accepting her grandson's gift. "I can tell." Inside the lumpy package covered in garish purple paper were a few skeins of very good wool. Even Becca, who'd never held a knitting needle but who knew how to shop, recognized the quality.

"David," Nora said after a moment of emotion, "I know I should say 'you shouldn't have,' but the truth is I'm very glad you did. This is lovely. Thank you very much."

"And now . . ." Naomi handed Lily a neatly wrapped package. Inside was a slim, brown leather envelope for storing or carrying papers.

"I know it seems a bit—corporate," she said. "But you are going to law school next year so . . ."

"It's gorgeous," Lily cried. "And so soft!"

"My friend Sally and her husband are leather workers. See? Your initials are on the bottom there."

"This is so special, Naomi. I don't know what to say."

"Just say that you'll be the best, most honest and hardworking lawyer you can be."

Lily looked at her father and smiled. "Just like Dad."

"My turn." Rain hopped up and gave her grandfather a package wrapped in candy cane paper.

Becca felt a swell of pride as Rain planted a kiss on her grandfather's forehead.

"Merry Christmas, Grandpa. I hope you like it."

"If it's from you," he said, "of course I'll like it."

"What is it?" Julie asked when her husband unwrapped a square box.

"It's an add-on light diffuser for the built-in flash on my camera," Steve explained. "But, Rain, how did you know I wanted one?"

Rain grinned. "I overheard you talking to Alex when we were here at Thanksgiving. I hope you didn't buy it for yourself already!"

"No, no. But what were you doing eavesdropping, young lady?"

Rain laughed at her grandfather's mock-stern tone. "Have you heard how loud Alex talks? You can't help but overhear at least his part of a conversation even if you're two rooms away!"

Becca smiled to herself. Yes, Alex didn't exactly speak in a whisper. He was not a person who insinuated. He was a person who barged. It occurred to her that there seemed little to fear from someone so open.

It was Lily's turn to give her Secret Santa gift. She handed Olivia a small, simply wrapped box. Inside was a pin, oval in shape, set with a large blue stone Becca couldn't identify. From the bottom of the pin hung delicate metal fringe, and on its top was a small cluster of pearls.

"It's an antique," Lily explained, perhaps unnecessarily, as the peculiar style of the ornament announced its age. "I got it at one of the antique shops on Charles Street. I know it's not from our family, but, well, I thought you might like it anyway."

"I do like it, Lily," Olivia said. "Thank you." She turned to James and asked him to attach the pin to her sweater. Becca noticed—as did the others, she was sure—that Olivia looked at her husband's face with appreciation as he attached the pin. Yes, she thought, something good definitely had happened between them. For James's sake, she was glad. Okay, and for her sister's sake, too.

And then, finally, it was Becca's turn to give her gift. She figured that by then, everyone had concluded she'd drawn Rain in the Secret Santa. And she assumed that David still fully expected her to ruin this happy Christmas morning with a big announcement. The deep frown on his unshaven face told her as much.

Well, she was sorry to disappoint him.

"Merry Christmas, Rain," she said, leaning over to pass the girl a large rectangular package wrapped in heavy marbled paper. "Open the card first."

Becca could feel the tension radiating from her brother. His wife could, too, because she took his hand to comfort him.

" 'The merriest of Christmases,' " Rain read, " 'and

the happiest of years to come, Your Always Loving Aunt Becca.' Oh, I can't wait to see what it is!"

Rain tore at the wrapping in much the same way her father had torn at the wrapping on his present. Becca smiled to see the similarity in habit. In a moment, Rain was holding up a pair of leather boots in a style currently popular with teen fashionistas. Personally, Becca thought they were hideous.

"Oh, Aunt Becca, thank you! I absolutely love them! How did you know I was dying for a pair of BoHos?"

"Your mom mentioned it in passing about a month ago. I was going to wait until your birthday, but when I drew your name in the Secret Santa, well, I figured, why wait?"

Becca hoped her message had been received. She thought that it had. David's face looked downright slack with relief. She struggled not to cry. She knew that if she allowed one tear to come, many, many others would follow.

Naomi, however, allowed her tears to flow.

"Mom," Michael said, looking up from the plastic robot villain he was already assembling, "why are you crying?"

Naomi blew her nose loudly on a tissue Nora had passed her and managed a clogged laugh. "I'm just so happy," she said. "I'm sorry."

"Now, there's no reason to apologize for being happy!" Julie sent a beaming smile around the room, a smile that fully included Becca.

"Hear, hear!" her father added. "To happiness!"

50

Torn wrapping paper had been gathered for recycling and Julie had collected what paper she could reuse. Ribbons and bows were in a pile under the tree. David sat leafing through the book Olivia had given him. Around the living room others read the morning paper or enjoyed their gifts. The twins sat among what looked like thousands of plastic robot and robot transport parts. Hank was sprawled in plain view in the middle of the room. Henry Le Mew, always wary of groups, was lumped majestically under the tree, his back against the trunk. From there he could keep an eye on the action and, if need be, make a rapid retreat up into the tree's lower branches.

Nora turned to Lily, who was straightening an ornament on the tree that had gone awry, and beckoned her to follow.

"What is it, Grandma?" she asked when Nora had closed the door to her room behind her.

"I have another gift for you." Nora took a package loosely wrapped in tissue paper off her bed and handed it to her granddaughter. "I want you to have this, Lily. It's old, so handle it with care."

"What is it?" Lily asked, even as she unwrapped the present. And then: "Oh, Grandma! It's beautiful!"

"It's my wedding veil. In case you'd like to wear it on your own wedding day."

Lily kissed her grandmother's cheek. "Of course I want to wear it." She laughed. "Assuming I get married someday!"

"Oh, I think you will. But there's plenty of time, you know. Plenty of time to chose the right man."

"Like you chose Grandpa?" she said softly. She was coming to understand and wanted her grandmother to know that.

"Yes. Like we chose each other. Lily," Nora said, "you must forgive your grandfather. I did, long ago. I forgave him and I continued to love him. You must do the same."

Lily thought a moment before saying, "You know that old expression: To err is human, to forgive is divine. I used to think that meant that only God could forgive. But now I think I see that when we, when humans, forgive someone, that's acting like God. I mean, assuming there is one."

"Whether there is a God or not, to forgive is one of the most noble things we can do in this life."

"Thanks, Grandma." Lily carefully rewrapped the veil and smiled. "You'd better stick around long enough to see me wear this!"

Nora laughed. "I'll give it the old college try."

"Now, there's an expression I never understood!"

Nora turned toward the door. "We'd better get back to the family."

"Wait, Grandma," Lily said, "before we go. I've been thinking about Becca. Do you think she'll ever really be happy?"

Nora thought of Alex and of the possibilities a relationship with him might offer her granddaughter. She thought about her conversation with Becca the night before, how Becca had admitted to such great loneliness, how she had admitted to her repeated attempts to prove her worth to her family. And then she reviewed what Becca had done for the family that morning, how she had gotten her troubles in hand and done the right, self-sacrificing thing. She wondered about Becca's innate potential for happiness or, at least, for contentment.

"If she wants to be happy," she said finally, "she will be. Happiness doesn't fall into your lap. You have to want it and work for it."

Yes, Lily thought. *I'll have to work for happiness now that I'm starting over without Cliff.* It was both an inspiring and a frightening realization. "What if," she asked her grandmother, "you want happiness and work for it, really hard, but it never comes? What then?"

Nora laughed. "Oh, that's a question for which I'm not even going to attempt an answer. Now let's go."

51

Nora and Lily returned to the living room just in time to hear Steve asking for everybody's attention.

"Ah," David said, putting aside his book, "the big unveiling!"

Steve proceeded to hand out the finished copies of what he called "a creative family portrait." "I took some risks," he explained, "so be kind in your criticism. And I didn't have them framed because I figured everyone might want something very different."

David laughed. "Something to go with our décor? I think I'd call it Overworked-Underpaid-Kids-Underfoot Chic."

"And my style is Paint-Peeling-Torn-Carpet-Bad-Plumbing-Student-Apartment," Lily added. "But I'm thinking of redecorating soon."

"And no one would have the nerve to criticize a gift," Nora corrected. "Especially one created and given from the heart."

Steve smiled and Becca thought he looked embarrassed, but pleased. Even adult children seemed to need a parent's praise, she thought. She certainly did.

Naomi studied her copy. "Thanks for using the double-chin filter, Steve," she said. "I look ten years younger!"

"Don't mention it. I might have eliminated a few wrinkles from my own face."

Julie pretended horror. "Oh, Steve! How vain of you!" She peered more closely at her own copy of the portrait. "Hmm. But I do notice that I seem to have fewer gray hairs in this picture. . . . I think I like it!"

"It's wonderful how you worked Grandpa into this, Dad." Lily smiled at her grandmother. "He really is still a part of our family, isn't he?"

Further comments were forestalled as Rain and her brothers emerged from the kitchen with some fanfare.

"Look what we made!" Michael announced, holding forth a large platter on which sat a pile of muffins.

"All by ourselves!" Malcolm added.

"I handled the oven," Rain assured her mother.

Grandma Julie's famous cranberry muffins were passed around the room and though they were a little burnt, no one mentioned the obvious fact.

"They're fantastic, Michael," Becca said, wiping a crumb from the corner of her mouth. A little dry, she thought, but if she chewed carefully enough, she wouldn't embarrass the boys by choking.

"Thanks, Aunt Becca. Want another?"

Becca smiled. She'd gotten the boys straight and was inordinately proud of it. "Sure," she said, "why not." She'd never mix them up again. At least, she'd try hard not to.

"Oh, my gosh," Lily cried. "Look out the window, everybody!"

There was a general rush to the front windows to see a doe and her fawn just outside, nibbling on the seed Julie routinely left for the birds and animals each winter.

"You know they're just big rodents," Olivia said. "And the population really gets far too big for its own good. I don't know why Dad doesn't hunt, thin out the herd. They do make pretty good eating, you know."

James laughed. "I married Miss Sentimental!"

"Even if they are just big rodents," Lily said, "and I'm not saying they are—who cares? They're so pretty."

Olivia grimaced. "They're loaded with ticks," she said, but nobody seemed to have heard.

"And here comes Alex," Steve said.

Becca felt suddenly—happy. Yes, here came Alex, trudging through the snow, long red scarf wrapped around his neck, and carrying a few small packages. As he approached the house, the doe and her fawn darted off in the direction of the woods.

A moment later, Becca let him in.

"Merry Christmas to all!" he cried when she'd closed the door behind him.

"You know you scared away that doe and her fawn," Becca said, pretending to scold.

"I did?" Alex looked behind him, but the animals were long gone back into the woods. "Oh, well, they'll be back. Every wild animal around these parts knows that Julie's got the best cold-weather grub."

Becca eyed him with mock suspicion. "These parts? Grub? What, you're a cowboy now?"

"I reckon."

"If you call me 'little lady' I'll have to bop you in the nose," Becca warned.

"Yes, ma'am."

"Oh, God! Stop!"

"Sorry," Alex said with a laugh. "I'm done. You didn't know I was a comedian, did you?"

"For good reason," she shot back, taking the coat and scarf he was handing her. "You're not."

"Touché! Anyway, I come bearing gifts."

They were joined in the living room then by Becca's parents.

"First, a gift for Sir Henry Le Mew." Alex handed a small package wrapped in green cellophane to Steve.

"He's been knighted?" Steve inquired with a grin. "He'll be happy to hear that. He's been expecting a preferment."

"It's some fancy organic catnip one of my students grows. She says her cats are wild for it."

"Well, Henry does have discriminating taste. . . . Thanks, Alex."

Alex then handed the other package to Julie. "And this is for all of you," he said. "The Rowan family."

Julie unwrapped a small, carved sculpture in an abstract design. The wood was American walnut, Alex told them. Its sheen came from a coat of linseed oil.

"It represents friendship," he explained. "Well, at least to me it does. Something natural, and beautiful, and solid. Something to be respected."

"It's lovely," Julie said feelingly. "Steve, don't you think so? I'll put it on the mantel right now."

Steve reached to shake Alex's hand. "Thank you, Alex. You really needn't have gone to the trouble."

"No trouble at all. You guys have been wonderful

to me. What would an old bachelor like me do on Christmas without a family to take him in?"

"Old bachelor!" Julie was back from setting the sculpture on the mantel and swiped his arm with the dish towel she'd been carrying over her shoulder. "Now, come on, everyone. It's time to eat."

"Again?" Alex groaned. "Oh, well, if I have to I have to." And then, when Julie and Steve had preceded them to the dining room, he grinned at Becca. "You see what a good deal I have here?"

Becca grinned back. "What a good deal we all have here."

52

After brunch, Alex took Rain and the boys out for sledding. Naomi, claiming that she felt a food coma coming on, went upstairs to nap. Olivia and James, Lily and Nora, Steve and Julie were occupied elsewhere. So by default, Becca found herself sharing a private moment with her brother. They were in the living room, each stretched out in a comfortable chair, each in a classic, and unattractive, pose that would hopefully aid in digestion.

"So," David said, in his usual blunt way, "what made you change your mind? You have really changed your mind, haven't you?"

"A lot of things. And yes, I have really changed my mind."

"Thanks, Becca. I mean, I know it must have been hard for you. . . ."

"Yeah, it was," she admitted. "But it's okay now."

The two sat in easy silence for a bit. At least, the silence was easier than it had been for some time.

"Look," David said eventually, "I want to apologize. I know I can be a bit of a bully."

"A bit?" Becca laughed. "Try a big fat bully."

David looked down at his middle. "Do you think I've gained weight?" he asked worriedly. "I have been eating a lot of rich food lately. Maybe I shouldn't have had that third cranberry muffin just now."

"A big fat vain bully. No, David, you look just fine."

"You gave me quite a scare, Becca."

"About your weight?"

David tried to glare at her; he was a terrible actor, Becca thought.

"I know, I know," she said. "I'm sorry. Really."

"Maybe a little heads-up the next time you're going to freak out, okay? A phone call, an e-mail, a text message, something."

"Deal. But I don't think this particular 'freak-out,' as you so interestingly call it, is going to happen again. In fact, I can promise it won't."

David nodded. "Good. You know, I have to admit I didn't believe you'd come through like this. I really was expecting you to ruin Christmas morning for us all. Not to mention the rest of our lives."

Becca took that in; she'd guessed correctly. "I've never given you any reason to doubt me in the past, have I?" she asked. "I mean, I've always done right by you—and by Rain."

"That's true," her brother admitted. "So, I'm sorry I didn't believe in you this time, but you have to understand how—how frightening this has been. Seriously, Becca, I feel as if I've aged ten years in a few days."

Becca felt newly stricken with guilt. There was little doubt about it. The Rowan family had been injured and it would take some time for the injury to scar over. She could only hope it would heal entirely. "I think I do know how awful it's been for you," she said. "And I can't apologize enough, David. It's been awful for me, too . . . this past year. . . . But that didn't give me the right to . . ." Tears threatened again.

"Hey," David said quickly, "I didn't mean to make you feel bad. Let's just move on from here, okay? Let's—let's promise to talk more about stuff that bothers you. Let's not drift apart again. Bad things happen when you drift apart from the people you love—and from the people who love you."

Yes, Becca thought. She knew that now. "Remember the time when you helped me with that Halloween poster contest?" she asked, more than willing to change the topic to something less fraught.

David thought about it for a moment. "No," he said. "But remember the time when you played hooky to go into Boston and wait all day on line for tickets to some concert? Mom wanted to kill you, but I thought it showed guts. If Dad hadn't been in the neighborhood visiting a client and seen you, you probably would have gotten away with it."

"I have absolutely no memory of that," Becca said. She laughed. "Maybe for good reason. I'm assuming I was punished."

"Well, at least we've got the memories tucked away safely. They're not lost as long as one of us remembers." David groaned as he got to his feet. "Now if you'll excuse me, I think I need to find the Tums."

An hour later, Naomi came downstairs and declared herself recovered from the food coma. In fact, she announced, she was almost ready for another meal. Almost.

Becca, still sprawled in the living room, smiled ruefully. "My trainer is going to ask me if I stuck to a healthy diet this holiday. And I'm afraid I'm going to have to lie and say that I did."

"I can't imagine working with a trainer," Naomi admitted. "I don't even think our local Y has such a thing. But I want to talk about something more pleasant than weight maintenance."

Becca was only too happy to agree.

"Let's do something fun after the holidays," Naomi suggested. "Maybe I could come down to Boston and we could see a movie and do a little shopping or something. Just you and me."

"That sounds good," she said. She had no clear idea if she and Naomi could rekindle the closeness they once had shared all those years ago, but she was willing to give it a try. Any sort of friendship would be better than the decay of good feeling that had been happening over the past years.

"Maybe," she said then, "I could make lunch for us. I've never used my good dishes and I am actually pretty good in the kitchen. When I use it, which is next to never."

"It must be hard to make a meal at the end of a long workday," Naomi said, and her sympathy was real. "Tell you what. I'll bring you some of the pesto I made this summer from our basil crop. I've got a freezer full of it. And I'll bring you a container of beet pesto. I know it sounds odd, but it has the sweetest flavor. And the color is so bright! You simply feel happy eating it."

Becca was grateful for the offer. "You know those mugs you made for Mom, the ones with the teal glaze?" she said.

"Sure. What about them?"

"I was thinking I'd like to commission a set. The color is really beautiful."

Naomi smiled. "First of all, thank you. I did work hard to get just that color. And second of all, I'd be happy to make you a set at no cost."

"Naomi, in a business transaction, a person pays for a service."

"Yes," she said pointedly, "but this is not a business transaction. This is family."

"Oh," Becca said, feeling a wee bit chastened. "That's right." She would try not to forget that again.

Steve was in the front hall putting on his coat when Becca approached him.

"Going out to your studio?" she asked.

Steve nodded. "Just for a minute. I need one of my cameras. I want to try the add-on light diffuser Rain gave me. Though I do wish she hadn't spent the money on me. I'm sure there are things she wants for herself. . . ."

Like overpriced jeans, Becca thought, proud of her daughter for having acted unselfishly. Well, she thought, she had good parents in David and Naomi and they had taught her well. She reached for her own leather coat. "Can I walk with you, Dad?" she asked. "There's something I want to say."

Steve smiled. "Of course. But bundle up. Oh, and Henry will be joining us."

Becca looked down to find Sir Henry Le Mew sitting at her feet, waiting for someone to open the front door. She laughed. "I didn't see or hear him coming."

"He's very stealthy for such a big guy. It's one of his many talents."

Together father and daughter and feline headed out for the old converted barn. They walked in companionable silence. But once inside her father's studio, Becca spoke.

"Dad," she said, "will you forgive me?"

Steve looked up from the worktable on which his

camera and equipment were laid out. He seemed surprised. "For what?" he asked. "You've done nothing wrong. I've nothing to forgive."

"Yeah," she said, "you do. I didn't trust you. Somewhere along the line, I lost sight of something I must have once known—that you and Mom and Grandma, everyone, that you acted honorably. I lost sight of the fact that you really were trying to help me—and help Rain. Somewhere along the line I started to blame my family for the inadequacies of my own life. And that was wrong."

Steve hesitated before answering. "I don't know what to say, Becca," he said finally, "except that everyone questions past decisions. Everyone reassesses his past—her past—and wonders. Everyone feels regrets, for better or worse. Second-guessing isn't a sin. It isn't an offense against anything but peace of mind."

"Maybe. But humor me, Dad. Just say that you forgive me. Please."

Steve looked into his daughter's eyes—the Rowan eyes—and realized that she really did need his forgiveness before she could be happy. "All right, then," he said. "I forgive you for whatever it is—"

"No caveats or conditions."

Steve smiled. "You're tough, Becca. You'd have made a good lawyer. Fine. I forgive you."

"Good. I mean, thank you. And, look, I was thinking, next time you and Mom are coming to Boston, you should let me know. I'll be sure to be in town. Maybe I could go to the museum with you. I mean, if it's on a weekend."

Steve slung his camera case over his shoulder. "You do work too much, you know that. You get it from me, I suppose."

"I know. I'm thinking about cutting back a bit. Though I can't make any promises yet."

"I think you should consider getting a cat."

Becca glanced down at Sir Henry Le Mew. He looked up at her and yawned. Becca was fascinated by all the—corrugation—inside his mouth. It reminded her that while cats were all cute and fuzzy in appearance, they were predators at heart. She supposed it was a key part of their charm.

"Why?" she asked. "For companionship?"

"For companionship, yes, and for the lessons you can learn from living with a feline. Lessons like how to be still. And how to be patient. And how to find great pleasure in little things like food and sleep. Plus, it's very funny when they chase their own tails."

Becca smiled at the image she'd conjured of Sir Henry Le Mew scooting in a frenzied circle of whirling fur. "I'll think about it, Dad," she promised.

"Good," he said. "Just promise me you'll get a cat from a shelter. Well, I've got my camera, so . . ."

There was one more thing Becca wanted to say to her father. Rather, one more thing about which she wanted to ask his opinion. As the three made their way back home, she said, "Dad, I'm thinking of telling Alex about Rain. We've become—friendly. It feels somehow wrong to be hiding the truth from him. And he's so close to you and Mom and Grandma. Anyway, I want to know if you think it's a good idea."

Steve couldn't hide the smile of pleasure that came to his face. Secretly, he was as much of a matchmaker as his wife. He knew why Becca would want to tell Alex the truth about Rain's birth. And he couldn't think of a better son-in-law than Alex Mason. But maybe he was jumping the gun.

"I think," he said, "that's a fine idea."

* * *

Olivia waylaid her mother as she was coming out of the kitchen. *When,* Julie thought, *will I stop associating my daughter with acts of confrontation and violence?*

"Mom," Olivia said, "can we talk for a minute?"

"Of course," she said. Mentally, she braced for a scolding and then thought the presumption unfair. Olivia did seem different this morning, more—mellow.

"When you asked me the other day if everything was okay between James and me, well, I lied. Sort of. Everything wasn't okay—isn't okay—but I just didn't know it. Or I didn't want to know it."

Julie nodded in what she hoped was an encouraging way. "I'm truly sorry to hear that," she said.

"So James and I have decided to go to counseling. We—he, actually, confronted me. He's been very unhappy. I know I've been . . . sad, but I didn't even notice how miserable he was. How miserable I was making him."

"Oh, Liv," Julie said, reaching out to squeeze her daughter's arm. "I think going to counseling is a wonderful idea. I have great faith in you, and in James."

"Thanks," Olivia said, with a wobbly smile. "Look, Mom, I'm sorry for giving you a hard time about the salt cellar. Maybe this counseling will help my—mood."

"I'm sure it will," Julie said heartily. "But in the meantime maybe this will cheer you up. I did some searching through a stack of old papers and I found a journal I kept around the time I got that old gravy boat you were interested in the other night at dinner. Here." Julie reached into the pocket of her skirt and pulled out a folded piece of paper. "I wrote down what information I found. I thought you'd like to have it."

Olivia accepted the piece of paper and read it. "You were right. It first belonged to your mother's aunt Clara. Then she passed it on to your mother, and then it came to you. Thanks, Mom."

"You're quite welcome. Now I really should—"

But Olivia detained her mother. "Mom," she said, "one more thing. I was thinking, maybe David was right. Maybe it's a silly idea after all, giving this house a name like it's a fancy estate or something."

"Oh, no, Liv, I think it's a lovely idea! And I was thinking that maybe my flower idea isn't the way to go. How about simply—Rowan House."

Olivia smiled. "Okay. That sounds nice."

"Good," Julie said. "Now I must go and put more water in the tree stand. The last thing we want is the newly baptized Rowan House burning down."

Her mother scurried off just as Becca was walking by, on her way to the kitchen.

"Becca."

Becca jumped. She had seen her sister standing right there but still, her commanding tone had taken her by surprise. She wondered if Olivia's employees dreaded the weekly staff meetings; she'd say "good morning" and everyone would think they were being fired. But maybe James was the person who ran the meetings.

"I want to talk to you for a minute," Olivia went on. Her face showed the signs of a recent inner struggle. But Becca also thought she caught a glimpse of something like a sign of relief.

"Okay." Becca was wary; she felt she was right to be.

"All that stuff I said up in the attic the other day . . . I didn't mean it. Or maybe I did, at the time, but I was—upset. I'm sorry. I took it out on you. My anger—and frustrations."

"That's okay," Becca said. "Really. Forget it." *Not that I'll easily forget it,* she added silently. There had been an awful lot of violence behind her sister's words, and her own words hadn't exactly been kind. Maybe she should be apologizing, too. And what was that nonsense she had spewed about everyone living and dying alone? No person was an island. That fact had been established long ago by better minds than the one she possessed.

"James and I are going into therapy," her sister went on. "Things haven't been right between us for a while now."

This was indeed a surprise. "Oh," Becca said. "That's good. I mean, it's good that you guys are going to try to work things out."

"Yes." Olivia gestured toward the living room. "Well, I'd better get back in there. . . ."

"Yes . . ."

Her sister walked off.

Well, Becca thought, not everyone got a happy ending. And it seemed that she and Olivia were not likely to be all warm and fuzzy any time soon, if ever. But that was okay. As long as her sister and brother-in-law worked to salvage their relationship—and as long as she, Becca, started really living her life—things would be well.

Things would be well.

53

She had asked him to go for a walk. Alex had looked at her dubiously.

"Are you feeling okay?" he'd said. "You do know it's midafternoon. The sun is starting to go down. The air is going to get progressively colder. Maybe you should tuck a hot water bottle under your sweater."

"I'm okay," Becca had assured him. "I borrowed a pair of long underwear from my mother."

"But you're . . ."

"So they're a little short. And a little big around the waist. At least they're warm."

Of course, he'd agreed, and together Alex and Becca headed out. It was essential that their conversation be private. Besides, if they were walking, she didn't have to look directly at him and risk seeing condemnation or reproach in his bright blue eyes.

She wouldn't be telling him the whole truth. She wouldn't be telling him that she had planned on revealing the truth of her parentage to Rain against the wishes and better judgment of her family. Maybe someday she would be brave enough to tell him, but not now. Not yet, not until she could be really sure of their relationship. If there was to be a relationship after this one week in December.

They'd gone several yards in silence before Becca summoned the nerve to speak.

"Alex," she began, "there's something I want to tell you. I mean, if we're—if we're becoming friends, there's something I need to tell you."

"Okay," he said.

Becca glanced over at him. His expression was attentive. "But the thing is," she went on, "you have to promise to keep it a secret. Seriously, if you can't make that promise, then I can't tell you. I'll understand, really. Some people just aren't good at keeping secrets, even really important ones. And some people—well, some people just don't like the burden a secret imposes."

Alex didn't answer right away. He was too busy deciding to accept the responsibility of keeping Becca's secret. He didn't like to give his word lightly. "I promise, Becca," he said after a moment.

She took a deep breath and said the words she had never said to anyone before. "I'm Rain's birth mother. Not Naomi. Her father is—he's some guy I knew in high school. Some idiot. And I—we, the family—don't want Rain to know the truth. At least not yet. Maybe never. For her sake, of course."

Again, Alex didn't respond immediately. Becca walked along next to him, her head down, and waited. Her nerves jangled with anticipation.

"Okay," he said finally, evenly. "So . . . So David and Naomi adopted Rain when she was born?"

"Yes." And as succinctly as she could, leaving out her recent acrimonious feelings and the self-imposed isolation that had led to them, Becca told Alex the

story of Rain's adoption. There had always been details unknown to her, but she could give him the outline well enough.

When she was done, Alex touched her arm. She
stopped walking, as did he. She looked up at him
and was relieved to see in his eyes not condemnation
or judgment but—sympathy? And acceptance.

"That's quite a tale," he said. "Thank you for
telling me, Becca. It means a lot to me that you trust
me enough to share something so important to you
and your family. Now may I share something with
you?"

Becca felt her stomach drop. Did he have a criminal past he'd been hiding? A secret drug habit? A
mortal illness? Was he moving to Alaska for good?
What could he find in Alaska that he couldn't find in
Maine? "Okay," she said. "I guess."

"I knew that Rain was your daughter. Not by anything anyone said or did," he added hurriedly, seeing
her look of alarm. "But—I just knew."

Becca was stunned. At the same time she was inordinately pleased. "I don't understand," she said.
"What do you mean, you knew?"

Alex shrugged. "She has your eyes. Not David's,
not the other Rowans'. Yours. The way she looks at
people. It's subtle but it's there. It's hard to put into
words."

"But an aunt and a niece can look an awful lot
alike," Becca pointed out, not sure why she was arguing this happy news. "There's genetics, DNA, inherited family traits. How did you really know that Rain
is my daughter," she asked, "without a doubt?"

"Let's walk while we talk. Your skin is turning blue
again." They did. Alex went on. "It was a good guess.
Instinct. The way you look at her. I don't have the
words to explain."

"I think you're very articulate. For an artist, I mean."

Alex laughed. "Uh, thanks?"

"Sorry. I didn't mean it as an insult," she explained. "It's just that you always hear that most artists have trouble explaining their work or putting their thoughts in words. But hey, I can't draw a straight line. And besides, half the words that come out of my mouth lately seem to be the wrong ones. I think I infuriated everybody in my family this week. And maybe you, too," she added, tentatively.

"I did think your attitude about your father was a little harsh," Alex admitted. "But I didn't know the full story of your relationship, so I knew I had no right to judge."

"Yes, well, my attitude was a little harsh. A lot harsh, actually, and wrongly so."

"Things are better now?"

"Yes," she said. "They are. And thanks for knowing about Rain and me. That means a lot. It means more than I can say." *It means that I feel comforted,* she added silently. *And maybe someday I can tell you that.*

They walked on in silence for a few moments before Alex said, "I think you were very brave to do what you did at only sixteen."

Becca laughed. "I don't know about brave. I was an absolute wreck."

"Maybe you were a wreck, but that doesn't mean you weren't brave. Courage is being scared but doing something anyway. And I think you're very brave now. It must take a significant amount of courage every single day to accept the sacrifice you made— and the decision your family made for you."

"Sacrifice?" Becca frowned. "I don't know if I'd use that word. It sounds so grim, so medieval or Gothic."

"It doesn't have to be," Alex argued. "Sacrifice can be instructive. It can teach you a lot about yourself and about other people. It can engender sympathy, and it can foster empathy. It can even make people happy."

"No doubt you're right. But I'd like to come up with a better word, one that doesn't make me think of blood and ritual altars and, I don't know, suffering in dungeons and hanging in chains."

Alex smiled. "I'll work on it."

Becca thought for a moment before saying: "Anyway, don't you think that sacrifice has a lot to do with vanity? Don't you think it has a lot to do with feeling superior to others, with thinking that you're better than others or maybe even better than you yourself actually are? I don't think I'm better than I really am, Alex. I'm well aware of my faults."

"I suppose sacrifice can be self-serving," he admitted, "if you want it to be. But not in your case, Becca. You're not a whitewashed sepulcher, to borrow a turn of phrase from the New Testament. You don't parade your good deeds in public. You made and continue to make, every day, a sacrifice for the welfare of your child, and correct me if I'm wrong, but I don't see you crowing about it."

Becca flinched. How could she ever tell Alex how close she'd come to doing just that, to bragging about what she'd done for her child to that very child? How could she ever tell him how close she'd come to ruining everything she and her family had built?

"Becca?" Alex touched her arm, as if to call her back to the moment. "Are you okay?"

"Yes," she said, "fine."

"You looked pained for a moment. Something you

ate? Not that Nora and Julie aren't great cooks, but they have been stuffing us all for days now."

"No," she laughed, "I'm fine, really."

"Okay, then. Do you mind if I change the subject?"

"Please do!"

"Do you ever travel in February or March?" he asked. "Go someplace warm and sunny? Escape the dead of a New England winter? You know how depressing the long winters are up here."

"I can't take time off work." As Becca said the words she knew they were her usual, knee-jerk answer to every suggestion of relaxation. Not that she'd had many of those suggestions made to her.

"Why not?" Alex asked. "Why can't you take time off?"

"You know what?" she said. "I have no good answer for that except 'I can't.' And I know you won't accept that as a good answer, and it isn't one. My office can live without my physical presence for a few days. I know that. I'm here in Maine right now, aren't I? It's just that—"

"Just that what?"

"Just that I've rarely acted on that knowledge," she said. "Well, except for the time I had to spend two days in the hospital for some—well, some female-related thing—and I brought my computer and my Black-Berry with me. So I guess that doesn't count."

Alex laughed. "No, it doesn't. Unless you spent the time reading celebrity gossip Web sites like Lily does, or texting your friends."

"I'm afraid not." Becca paused. She felt suddenly embarrassed. "Alex, I don't have many friends. I don't have any friends, really."

"You've got me," he said. "And you've got your family. There's no reason, is there, why you can't call their love for you and yours for them a sort of friendship?"

"I guess not," she admitted after a moment. "Okay, so I have a few friends. And a few acquaintances from the office. About once every two months we go out for a drink after work." But drinks had never led to dinner or the movies or a shopping spree on a Saturday afternoon. Why?

Becca pushed those unhappy thoughts aside and changed the subject. "You can't commute every day between Portland and Kently. Or do you?" she asked.

"No. I have a small studio apartment in Portland for the days when I'm teaching. It's clean and the location is good—I've even got a view of Casco Bay—but it's nothing fancy. Which is fine because as soon as my classes are over for the week I head up here."

"Not a city boy, then?" she asked.

"Oh, I've got nothing against the city. Portland's a great town. It's just that I like having the option of a retreat. Up here, I can work and think undisturbed. And untempted. There's not a lot to spend your money on in Kently. This way I'm able to make my mortgage payments every month. On time, too."

So, not only was Alex kind and sympathetic and intuitive, he was also responsible. Becca liked what she was learning.

"Do you ever come down to Boston?" she asked then.

"Is that an invitation?"

Becca felt her cheeks flush and wondered just how awful she looked. Alex had said she was turning blue; now she was flushing. What was she, purple? "If you'd like it to be," she said boldly.

"Then I accept. Do you ever get up to Portland?"

"Is that an invitation?" she asked.

"Yes, it is. I've got a gallery show at the end of March. I've already given an invitation to your parents and they've promised to come. Maybe you could be persuaded to join them."

"That would be interesting. I've never been to a show of the work of someone I know."

"Then I'll put you on the guest list," he promised. "But I'm hoping you'll pay our fair city a visit before then. The sidewalks are pretty treacherous until about May, but there are other things to recommend Portland."

"I'll certainly try," Becca said honestly. "You know, Alex, this just occurred to me. The other day, when you asked me what I wanted to be when I grew up, I never asked you that same question. So, now I'm going to ask it. What did you want to be when you grew up?"

Alex grinned. "Am I supposed to be grown up now?"

"Just answer the question."

"A sherpa."

"What?" she laughed.

"I'm only kidding. Actually, since I can remember, I've always wanted to be just what I am—an artist. I don't even mind the teaching, mostly, because I'm still involved with art. I consider myself pretty lucky."

Becca thought about that. Had Fate granted Alex luck, a contented life, or had Alex made his own luck? She rather thought it was the latter.

"Here's a question I haven't asked you," he said now. "Why do you hate the winter so much? Is it purely a physical thing? Something against numb fingers, runny noses, and chapped skin?"

Well, Becca thought, there was certainly no reason to withhold from Alex this bit of information. Not after all that she had shared with him.

"I found out that I was pregnant in the middle of December," she said. "I guess ever since then, everything about cold and snow and ice just—just brings me back to that awful time. I was so scared. I was in an absolute panic about telling my parents." Becca paused. "You know, before that I loved the cold weather. And I especially loved Christmas. The whole season, from Thanksgiving on, felt so—romantic."

Alex shrugged. "Maybe it can feel that way again. I mean, why not?"

Why not, indeed, Becca thought. If she took the trouble to imagine a happier, more romantic life, then one might actually follow. She might will a better life into being.

"I've been missing my own life, Alex," she said now. "I'm already thirty-two and I've never taken a proper vacation."

"Here's the good news," he countered. "You're only thirty-two. With any luck, you've got at least another thirty-two years ahead of you to ski in Colorado—well, if you can get past your psychological hatred of the cold—or lay on a beach in Puerto Rico or roam the streets of—well, of Rome."

"I grind my teeth at night." Becca wondered what had made her tell Alex that. And then she said, "And I clench my jaw pretty much all the time."

"Do you have dental insurance?"

"Yes."

"Good," he said with a laugh, "because you're going to need it. Unless, of course, you work on some stress relief techniques."

"That's what my doctor told me. What do you suggest? Yoga? Meditation?"

"Those are good," he said. "Not that I have any experience of either. But I was thinking more along the lines of regular vacations. Even a mental health day here and there can be very restorative. And about being plugged in all the time . . ."

"What about it?" she asked.

"The other day you were declaring that anyone who's got half a brain should be always plugged in. You were declaring that people should always be available to whomever needs them."

Becca squirmed inside. "I declared?"

"Yeah. At the cocktail party. Remember, your grandmother made her famous cheese puffs?"

"Oh," she said, embarrassed. "Well, I think I might have had one too many Brandy Alexanders and not enough cheese puffs."

Alex didn't comment on Becca's alcohol-to-food ratio. "So, about being plugged in. Your stress level might just go down a bit if you weren't always going online or checking your phone for messages."

Becca thought of the fact that since arriving in Maine she hadn't received one electronic communication. "I know," she said. "I do know that."

Silently they walked on. And then Alex's voice in the still air startled her.

"Maybe this is obvious by now," he said, "but I don't like to assume, so . . . So I'd like you to know that I'm falling in love with you."

Becca's knees went weak. She'd always thought that was just an expression, but now she knew better. "Oh," she said. "I had no idea. So, thank you for telling me."

Alex shrugged. "Okay. Sure. I just thought you should know in case . . ."

"In case what?" Becca's voice sounded squeaky to her ears.

"Well, in case you might, you know, in case you might happen to be falling in love with me, too. I know it's only been a few days, but stranger things have happened. . . ."

Becca felt her cheeks flame. Again. "Oh," she said. "Yes. Well. I guess that does make it easier to say. I mean, I've never said that to anyone before."

"Said what?" Alex prompted, with a smile.

"Said, 'I'm falling in love with you.' So, I'm falling in love with you. Too."

"I am so very glad." Alex laughed. "I was feeling like a big idiot there for a minute. Whew."

Becca laughed, too. "Sorry. I guess I'm a little—slow—in the romance department. I guess I've got a lot to learn."

"That's okay. I think it might be nice to be without a big history of romantic disappointments. Maybe you're lucky, coming to love now and not before."

"Maybe."

Instinctively, they stopped walking and turned toward each other. Alex stepped closer and put his hands on Becca's upper arms. "So," he said, "now's when we kiss. In case you were wondering when that big moment was going to happen."

"Okay," she said. She was both eager and apprehensive. She felt like an innocent all over again. She wondered if they could be seen from the house. She wondered if anyone was watching them.

And then they drew together and Alex's lips were on hers and hers were on his. The kiss was intense and yet gentle. It was over too soon.

"My lips are a little bit frozen," she murmured, looking up into the penetrating blue eyes she had feared only days before. Now she found them terribly exciting. "Sorry."

"Like mine aren't?" Alex shook his head. "And never apologize for a kiss, Becca. A kiss is always a good thing."

His arms were still around her. Becca thought she would like them to always be around her.

"Alex?" she said. "You don't think I'm insufferable?"

"Not in the least. Well, maybe you're a little—tense. But artists enjoy a challenge."

"Good. Because I'm afraid you might be in for a mighty big challenge with me."

Alex laughed. "Do I look like I'm afraid?"

"Actually, you look kind of like a mountain man. When are you getting a haircut?"

"Next week, when I'm back in Portland. Anyway, as I was going to say, all of life is a challenge. The big question here is, are you up to it? Will you give me—us—a chance?"

"I'm going to try. Really."

"That's all anyone can ever ask for. A promise to try."

"Not all anyone can ask for," she corrected. "I have to ask for one more thing, and right now."

"Again with the haircut?"

"No. I'm going to ask—insist, actually—that we go back to the house. I'm freezing my butt off out here."

Alex laughed heartily. "I so don't want that to happen. It's a little skinny, but I'm rather fond of it. Let's go."

They began their way back to the house, arm in arm. Alex's last words had made Becca feel a bit nervous. It had been a long time since she'd been with a man. Now she knew for sure that it had been too long. She'd been depriving herself of so much joy and pleasure. But reclaiming that part of herself was scary.

"So," she said then, "before we commit to a long weekend in a warm climate someday, we'll spend lots of time talking and stuff, right? We'll spend lots of time getting to know each other."

"Absolutely," Alex said, nodding. "Lots of talking and stuff. And by 'stuff,' do you mean to include some—er, fooling around?"

Becca laughed. "You are blunt, aren't you!"

"What? I'm a guy. Sex is pretty much all that's on my mind at any given time. Well, that and art and the environment and politics and—"

"It's okay, Alex," she assured him. "I might be a bit rusty, but I'm not opposed to sex."

"Okay. That's good. You know," he added suddenly, "there might be things about me you'll hate."

"Like what?"

"How should I know what you'll hate about me? I once dated a woman who freaked out when I chose the boysenberry syrup instead of the maple syrup at IHOP. Apparently, syrup was a deal breaker. A nonnegotiable issue. Who would have thought?"

"I can assure you I'm not that fussy. Well, about syrup, anyway. I usually don't use any."

Alex pretended horror. "Now, that is just sick and wrong. How can you eat pancakes without syrup?"

"Syrup has a lot of empty calories," she said, repeating the words of her trainer. One should always be on guard against empty calories.

"Oh, please, don't tell me you're one of those weight-obsessed women! Someone's got to eat nachos with me, please, Becca. One of the best things about a serious relationship is the hanging out and eating part."

Becca wondered. Maybe she had been spending a bit too much time at the gym and counting calories. When *was* the last time she'd had nachos? "I've been known to eat a nacho or two," she said finally. Once upon a time. Suddenly, she had a craving for melted cheese. Lots and lots of melted cheese. Cheddar would do, but Havarti or Swiss or Jack cheese with jalapeño bits would be better.

Alex grinned. "Then I think we're going to be just fine." They walked on a bit before Alex added: "Oh, by the way, I like my nachos with chili."

"Veto. No chili. It gives me indigestion."

Alex roared with laughter. "How romantic! I'll be sure to carry a roll of Tums when we eat out. Okay, then, how about chili on the side?"

Becca pretended to think about this suggestion. "Well," she said finally, a grin that felt goofy spreading across her face, "okay. We have a deal."

54

In the late afternoon, Alex, feeling he'd come dangerously close to overstaying his welcome—and needing to put more time into his latest commission—headed back to his own home. Before leaving, he managed to steal a brief kiss with Becca, and yes, with unfrozen lips it was much better.

The warm feeling of Alex's lips on hers still alive, Becca went in search of Lily. She felt she owed her younger sister a gesture of friendship. It hadn't even occurred to her to offer Lily a ride to Maine for the holiday. Why? Because she had been immersed in her own self-pity, that's why.

She found Lily curled up on a chair in the living room, reading a novel.

"Hey," she said, sitting in the chair next to Lily's. "Am I interrupting?"

Lily smiled and closed the book. "Not at all."

Becca felt a bit awkward—she really wasn't sure what sort of answer she'd get—but she plunged on.

"So," she said. "Do you want to maybe have dinner when we're both back in Boston? I know you must be pretty busy with classes and law school applications and all but . . ."

Lily's answer was immediate and enthusiastic. "I'd love to, Becca. Thanks."

Becca smiled. "It'll be my treat. I know how tight a student's budget is. Is there some place you've wanted to try? Do you like sushi? There's a new place in the South End, just a few blocks from my place, that's supposed to be good. I haven't been there, but the *Globe* reviewer raved about it."

Lily smiled back. She really had quite a lovely, genuine smile, Becca noted. "Yeah, sure, that sounds like fun. I love sushi."

"Great. You have my number, right? Call me when you're settled in after the holidays and we'll make a date."

"That should be easy for me," Lily replied. "Now that Cliff and I are over . . . And I don't really have any close friends. . . ."

Becca smiled ruefully. "My social schedule isn't exactly full, either."

"It might be, now that Alex is—around."

Becca felt her cheeks grow warm. Did everybody know what was going on between her and her parents' neighbor? She got the odd feeling that they did and that they'd known even before she had. "Well," she said, "he teaches here in Maine. And I can't take much time off work."

"I'm sure you'll figure it out. Nothing stands in the way of real love."

Becca laughed. "Love!" she bluffed. "Who said anything about love? Lily, I hardly know the guy."

"Have you kissed yet?" her sister asked.

"That's personal!"

Lily looked intently at her sister. "Yes, I think you have. Well, that's a good sign. I don't think you should wait a long time for the first kiss. That's just my opinion, of course."

"Thanks for the nod of approval. Now, no more questions about my love life. At least until I'm really sure I've got one."

"Deal," Lily said. "But you will keep me posted about you and Alex, won't you? And about—well, about you?"

"Okay. But I can't promise there'll be anything fantastic to tell. My life has been pretty boring for the past ten years or so."

"Maybe that will change now," Lily suggested.

Becca laughed. "If Mom has her way, by this time next year I'll be cruising the Nile or climbing to the top of Notre Dame in Paris or swimming with the dolphins in—well, wherever it is you swim with dolphins."

"I could be persuaded to come with," Lily said quickly. And then, as if fearing she'd taken a step too far, she added: "I mean, assuming I could afford the trip and that Alex wasn't coming along. I wouldn't want to interfere."

Becca smiled. "I'm sure we can arrange a girls' weekend someplace fun. Maybe a spa?"

"That sounds great. I've always wanted to have one of those hot stone massages. Though it does sound kind of scary . . ."

"I've had them. They're not at all painful and you'll be addicted immediately. And by the way," Becca added, "I'm sorry about that Cliff guy. I should have said something before. Men can be idiots."

"That's okay," Lily said. "Women can be idiots, too."

Becca laughed. "And you're looking at one of the biggest idiots right now!"

"You? Look at me. I mean, I was totally blind to the

real Cliff Jones. Thinking back on our—relationship—I can't believe how much nonsense I put up with. Anyway, Grandma was a huge help. She . . . she opened my eyes to a lot of things."

Becca smiled. "She does that, doesn't she? I wonder if she was this smart back when she was my age or your age?"

"I don't know. But I'm glad she's smart now!"

Becca thought back to the previous night, when she and her grandmother had sat up while the rest of the family was at church. She felt she'd always remember that Christmas Eve as one of the most special moments of her life.

"Yeah," she said. "I'm glad, too."

55

It was late, about eleven o'clock on Christmas night. Becca was sprawled on the couch. She had been doing a lot of sprawling since morning. How many calories had she consumed that day—five thousand? Six thousand? Rain, next to her and wearing her new boots with her nightgown, seemed to be faring better, if her upright posture was any indication of easy digestion.

The two women had the living room to themselves. Everyone had gone off to bed. Becca felt too full to sleep. Rain, she suspected, was simply too psyched about her new boots.

"Something really weird went on here this week," Rain said then. "I don't know what it was, but I'm so glad it's over. Everyone was acting so uptight."

That was one word for it, Becca thought. Uptight. "Like I told you the other day," she said, "adults are an odd lot. And someday soon, you'll be one of us."

Rain made a face. "Lucky me. Well, maybe I'll be different. Maybe I won't be so odd. Maybe I'll be the first really normal adult!"

I hope so, Becca thought. *I hope you'll be happy and honest and fulfilled. I hope that you will find true and lasting love. I hope that you won't have one single regret. But I know that you probably will.*

"So," she asked, "are you still thinking of legally changing your name when you turn eighteen?"

Rain mused for a moment. "No," she said then, "I don't think so. It's kind of grown on me. It's actually kind of a pretty name. Rain Julia Rowan."

Becca smiled. "Well," she said, "I've always thought so."

"You know," Rain said suddenly, "whenever I'm mad at my mom I think how cool it would have been if you were my mom instead."

Becca felt light-headed. It cost her much to keep a tremble out of her voice. "I don't think I've ever seen you mad at your mother," she said. "Not really mad, anyway."

Rain rolled her eyes. "Oh, she can drive me pretty crazy. Like when she insists I be home by nine when everyone else can stay out until eleven? I mean, come on! It's very embarrassing."

Becca fought back the tears that threatened to spill down her cheeks. Glad of the low light in the room, she reached over and took Rain's hand in her own.

"Listen to me, Rain. Your mom is the one with all the hard work to do, you know. She's the bad cop to my good cop. It's easy being an aunt. I get to have all the fun." Somehow, she managed a smile. "Besides, I can be pretty unbearable on occasion."

Rain laughed. "Oh, I can't imagine that!"

"Trust me," Becca said, sitting back and letting go of her daughter's hand. "You have no idea. If—if I were your mother, there'd be times when you'd wish Naomi were instead."

"I guess," Rain admitted. "You're the best, Aunt Becca, really. Every girl should be as lucky as I am."

"Yeah. You are pretty lucky. Just don't let it go to your head."

Rain laughed again. "You sound like my father now!"

Yes. She did sound like David. Her brother. And Rain's father.

"It's the Rowan bossiness," she said lightly. "We've all inherited some of it."

56

Wednesday, December 27

It was the morning of December twenty-seventh. James and Olivia were out in front of the house, packing up the car for the trip home to Framingham, Massachusetts.

Becca was in the den, tidying her things in preparation for her own departure the next day, when she came across the card from her old friend Molly. She smiled. Only days ago Molly's desire to catch up with Becca had worried her. Now she didn't see Molly's desire for renewed communication as suspicious. She saw it as friendly.

Becca returned the card to her briefcase. Still, she didn't feel that she was ready to reach out to her old friend, not yet, anyway. But she was glad that Molly had made the gesture. It seemed like some sort of benevolent sign.

So much could happen in one week, Becca thought. So much could change in the blink of an eye. The course of a life could so easily be changed to a path unimagined. And sometimes, that path was smoother and wider than the bumpy, narrow path you had been trudging along in the first place.

Becca left the den and joined the others outside, gathered around James and Olivia's SUV. Alex, she saw, was striding toward the house to pay his farewells as well.

"It's been one heck of a few days," David said to her with a grin.

"A few days?" Becca laughed. "You mean we haven't been in this house screaming and yelling at each other for months?"

"It does feel that way, doesn't it?" Naomi added.

"I feel," David said, "like a prisoner being let out of jail after years of compulsive communal living—with hyenas."

"That's not how I'd put it," Naomi said now. "I feel it was as if we were all plants just about to bloom and someone decided to force the process by putting us into a hothouse. And then, within the space of a few days' time—combustion! Bloom! Everything hidden was finally thrust out in the open. It was chaos for a while and then it was calm and beautiful."

David grimaced. "Or something like that."

Naomi swatted her husband's arm. "I never claimed to be a poet. Anyway, I'm just happy it's over. Not the vacation part, but the explosion part."

"It was like being in a pressure cooker," Becca said, watching Alex drawing closer over the snow. The thought suddenly reminded her of how much she loved a rich and hearty stew, and her mind conjured an image of sitting by a roaring fire and sharing a bowl with a shaggy-haired man with piercing blue eyes and a sexy way about him. . . . Oh, my God, Becca thought. Was that just a winter fantasy?

Alex stomped up to the family just then. Becca

couldn't bother to hide the smile that came to her face at the nearness of him. When he reached her side he gave her hand a squeeze. A kiss in front of the other Rowans would have been premature. Becca knew that, but she was longing for him to grab her in a passionate embrace. She vowed to waylay him later. If she was going to try to change her life for the better, she was going to do it the way she did everything—with gusto.

"Oh, there goes Mr. Pollen," Nora said, squinting off into the distance. As he came closer to the house, the Rowans could see that he was dragging a makeshift sled on which sat a very large—thing. Nora wasn't entirely sure but she guessed the lumpy, bulgy, brown thing was composed of pinecones.

"What the hell is that?" David said, and Becca thought he sounded genuinely horrified.

"Language in front of the boys, David."

"Dad, that man looks like a serial killer."

"Michael!" Naomi whispered. "What a horrible thing to say about someone!"

Michael shrugged. "Christian says the janitor at school looks like a serial killer. That man with the sled looks kind of like the janitor."

"He does not," his brother protested. "Besides, you don't even know what a serial killer is. And if you don't know what a serial killer is, then how can you know what he looks like!"

"I do, too, know what a serial killer is!"

"Boys! Enough!" Naomi frowned. "I'm having a word with that Christian's mother. Selling Pop-Tarts to his classmates. Calling the school janitor a serial killer. I can imagine what else he's up to."

"Oh, boy," Lily said. She raised her hand to shade her eyes as she watched the neighbor's progress across the snowy field. "I so hope he doesn't have another—gift—for us."

But Mr. Pollen and his sled continued on.

"Oh, no," Alex said. "It looks like he's headed for my place. Can I stay here tonight?"

"No," Nora said. "If we can brave Mr. Pollen, so can you."

James and Olivia said their good-byes quickly. Becca thought they were probably, and understandably, eager to be alone, and eager to begin the difficult work on their marriage. As James pulled out of the driveway, Julie called after them.

"Everyone meet back here for Easter! We'll have a fresh ham and a carrot cake and we'll all go on an Easter egg hunt!"

James waved in response and the rest of the Rowan family watched as he and Olivia drove down the southbound road.

"I hope they'll be okay," Lily said.

I hope Olivia starts to color her hair, Becca added silently, and, she was aware, uncharitably.

"Yes," Julie said. "I hope so, too."

She and Steve turned back to the house, herding the twins along with them. Rain and Lily followed closed behind.

Nora looked at the slim silver watch on her left wrist. It had been a gift from her husband on their twentieth wedding anniversary and when she died, it would go to whichever granddaughter would cherish it most. "Well," she said, "it's getting close to lunchtime. I'd better go in and help Julie. Oh," she added, with a sly grin at both Alex and David, "and I think I've got one last cinnamon roll tucked away in the kitchen. In case someone needs a snack to tide him over."

Alex's hand shot up in the air. "Dibs!"

"No fair," David cried. "You live next door. You can get those rolls anytime."

Alex frowned. "Okay, okay, we'll split it."

Becca grinned. Naomi, too. They watched the guys go into the house, trotting after Nora like two puppies being led to the bowl of kibble.

"I think," Becca said, "that we're witnessing the start of a beautiful friendship."

Naomi laughed and linked her arm with her sister-in-law's. "The start of more than one beautiful friendship."

**Please turn the page
for a very special Q & A with
Holly Chamberlin.**

*You have been writing books for some years now. Were you always interested in writing?

Yes, I suppose I was, though I've always been more interested in reading the work of others. I still am. I read all the time. The owner of my local independent bookstore loves me. I visit him at least once a week and say, "Chris, what do you recommend?" Invariably, I leave with an armload of books. It would be cheaper to frequent the library, but I have a need to keep books with me.

*What sort of books do you like to read?

I read lots of fiction but also a fair amount of nonfiction, especially biographies and historical studies. I very much enjoy rereading favorite books, especially when I'm blocked with my own work. I don't understand the term 'used books'; it seems to imply that books that have been read once are somehow less valuable than books that haven't been read at all. Aren't books meant to be read and reread and read yet again? I don't really like borrowing books from friends, though, because then I can't write in them. It's the same problem with books from the library.

*Who are some of your favorite writers of fiction?

Peter Ackroyd is at the top of the list. I also love Patrick McGrath and Graham Swift, and have just discovered—thanks to Chris at the bookstore—a wonderful young writer from Maine, where I live, named Ron Currie, Jr.

*Describe as best you can your writing process.

For me, the entire process of writing a novel is incredibly painful! First comes the germ of an idea, and it can come from just about any place—a random bit of overheard conversation or a bit of poetry I happen upon, even a passing mood. Then, I start to write around the germ—thoughts, questions to myself—and hope that during this process a basic story will show itself. That completed, I face the difficult task of growing the story into a more detailed outline. Of course, as the chapters come about, the outline undergoes change for the better. I see many more possibilities than I did starting out. I am always surprised by the finished product.

*In *One Week in December* several characters debate the importance of family history. How important is your family's heritage to you?

Very important, actually. My father has spent years researching our ancestors and has compiled an impressive—and very detailed!—history of us all, dating back to the eighteenth century, in both Ireland and Germany. I find it moving to read the old documents—birth and death certificates, immigration papers—and to look at the old photographs he's unearthed. I feel that somehow these ancestors are being honored by our interest in their lives. Now, whether all of them deserve to be honored, we'll never know!

*Also in *One Week in December* you have several young characters acknowledge the wisdom of elders. Do you really believe that with age comes wisdom?

If you're lucky, yes, wisdom will come with age. And if you keep your eyes open. And it doesn't hurt to be sort of smart to begin with. Personally, I'm a bit less of an idiot every year, but I do know some older people who are still making the same mistakes they've made for years—and they don't show any signs of stopping!

*You write a lot about the relationships between parents and children, particularly those between mothers and daughters. Do you have children of your own?

No, but I do have a mother and she lives just down the block! I often receive e-mails and letters from readers who are mothers and who thank me for perfectly expressing their feelings about their children and about their own mothers. I am lucky to have a largely sympathetic and empathetic imagination and am very interested in the lives of other people. I'm a good listener.

*And cats do appear with some frequency in your work . . .

I am a cat lady. I am happy to admit to that.

*You also write often about forgiveness. Why is this one of your central concerns?

Because I firmly believe that one of the noblest things we can do in this too short life is to forgive. Real forgiveness isn't easy but it is worth every effort. Judge not lest you be judged. Of course, there are limits to this.

*You were born and raised in New York City. How did you wind up in Maine?

It's a simple answer—I fell in love. Isn't that how a lot of people wind up in places they never dreamed they would be? I hasten to say that I love Maine and since moving here in 2003 have met and become friends with some of the best people I've ever known. Plus, there's a lot of good local cheese.

*Cheese is important to you?

Yes. My husband is a fantastic cook and most of our friends are as food obsessed as we are. Living in Maine allows us access to fresh ingredients—from seafood to produce to meats—pretty much all year round.

*If you could be given a talent you don't possess, what would it be?

I would love to have the ability to paint. I love art and especially painting. It seems like magic to me, but that's because I can't draw a straight line.

ONE WEEK IN DECEMBER

Holly Chamberlin

ABOUT THIS GUIDE

The suggested questions are included to enhance
your group's reading of Holly Chamberlin's
One Week in December.

DISCUSSION QUESTIONS

1. Thinking about her husband's affair and about the human appetite for gossip and rumor, Nora posits that "No relationship was entirely private." Do you agree with her assessment?

2. From her vantage point of almost ninety years, Nora believes that "The young thought they were noble, but nobody untested can be noble. . . . To forgive in the wake of betrayal, that was nobility." Do you agree that nobility—wisdom, wise action, and selfless behavior—comes only (though not necessarily) with age?

3. In a similar vein, listening to her granddaughter Lily's condemnation of her grandfather's affair, Nora reflects on "the rigidity of the young." She believes that "the concept of compromise was one that came to a person only with the accumulation of experience." Do you agree?

4. Olivia argues that "objects have meaning beyond their physical presence or their usefulness or their monetary value." Her mother, Julie, argues against this notion and claims that too often objects seem to own people. Are both women right, to some extent? Discuss.

5. Becca states that you can't hold someone to her word if it was given under pressure. Discuss this in general (what does "pressure"

mean in various contexts?) and in terms of Becca's own situation as a pregnant sixteen-year-old. (For example, she claims to have been coerced into giving her baby to David and Naomi; David argues that she was counseled.)

6. Discuss Becca's shame and guilt over not having bonded immediately with her baby. How do societal expectations act unfairly on women at various stages of their lives?

7. Lily wonders if it's possible to live a perfectly honest and open life. "If guilt was possible, then why couldn't innocence be possible, too?" Later, she wonders: "Was everybody doomed to dissemble?" Is Lily simply naïve, or does her belief in the possibility of a life of honesty hold some merit?

8. Lily thinks about secrets and the various motives behind them. Do you believe that some secrets—perhaps of the sort found in this novel—should be kept and others broken? Why? In what circumstances?

9. Olivia declares: "Without our memories we're nothing." What does she mean by this? What might a person less obsessed with history understand by this statement?

10. Early on in the novel, Becca reminds herself: "Sentimentality was as dangerous as its trouble-making cohort, nostalgia." Do you agree with her wariness regarding these two emotional states?

11. Late in the novel, Lily tells her grandmother that she believes the Rowan family has been "defined by deception." Nora argues that the family has been "defined by love." With whom do you most agree? Can deception and love coexist?

12. Nora tells Lily that she must not "underestimate the appeal of domestic habit." What do you think of the value of domestic habit in a marriage or other long-term relationship? Do you think it is generally of more importance to a woman than a man, or do you think both sexes equally need and find comfort in domestic habit? Do you think the value of domestic habit increases or decreases over time?

13. When Olivia tells her husband that she was too busy to write his Christmas letter, he claims to be more hurt that she chose to ignore a cherished ritual than if she had simply forgotten to write the letter. Do you understand and agree with James's position?

14. In Alex's opinion, a person who allows a past sadness to continue to color his present displays a lack of imagination. Discuss what Alex means when he talks about emotional creativity and its relation to happiness.

15. Becca repeatedly says that she wants to "claim" or "reclaim" her daughter. At one point, Naomi argues against the choice of those terms. She finds them in some way demeaning of Rain's full status as an individual. Do you agree with Naomi's interpretation of Becca's word choice?

16. In your opinion, what is the most important stimulus behind Becca's seemingly abrupt decision to finally talk with her father and begin the healing process between them?

Romantic Suspense from
Lisa Jackson

More by Bestselling Author

Lori Foster

Available Wherever Books Are Sold!

Check out our website at www.kensingtonbooks.com